THE X PRESIDENT

THE X PRESIDENT

A Novel

PHILIP BARUTH

BANTAM BOOKS

THE X PRESIDENT
A Bantam Book / November 2003

Published by Bantam Dell
A division of Random House, Inc.
New York, New York

Cover design by Jorge Martínez

Book design by Lynn Newmark

Library of Congress Cataloging in Publication Data
Baruth, Philip E. (Philip Edward)
The X President : a novel / Philip Baruth.
p. cm.
ISBN 0-553-80294-1
1. Cigarette industry—Fiction. 2. Presidents—Fiction. I. Title.

PS3552.A7794X67 2003
813'.54—dc21 2003041893

Manufactured in the United States of America
Published simultaneously in Canada

RRH 10 9 8 7 6 5 4 3 2 1

To my wife, Annika, with whom all things are possible.

Min kärlek till dig är evig.

"Billy Pilgrim has come unstuck in time. . . . Billy is spastic in time, has no control over where he is going next, and the trips aren't necessarily fun. He is in a constant state of stage fright, he says, because he never knows what part of his life he is going to have to act in next."

—Kurt Vonnegut, Jr., *Slaughterhouse-Five*

THE
X PRESIDENT

PROLOGUE

LAWSUITS AND THE SAD, THREATENED CUCUMBER: WHAT YOU NEED TO KNOW ABOUT BC AND THE CIGARETTE WARS

Let me take a moment here, before I do anything else, to expose the two biggest lies I can think of offhand. The first is that BC himself started the Cigarette Wars, that he is not just politically or institutionally but somehow personally culpable. That is a lie, told by those who would like it to be so. The historical responsibility doesn't rest with him, or with his presidency, and it never has.

The second lie is a good deal older: that every story has a beginning, and a middle, and an end. This also is not true of BC. BC's story has only a highly elongated and elaborate middle, a middle that flattens out in the distance like low-desert highway, so that perspective alone seems to give it a start and a finish. It has that, and nothing else.

But of course there's no coherent or useful way to tell a story like that, no way to be true to it. And so a biographer has to do what a biographer has always had to do: pretend to a beginning, and then pretend with all her might to the very end.

It all began with two ideas, two ideas in the head of a man for whom ideas were like salted peanuts. And I can't help but think even now, even today, that it should have been okay. Neither idea was inherently dangerous, especially in the late 1990s: stop people from smoking cigarettes—the old-school butts, that is, useless filters, impurities off the charts—and expand what used to be the world's biggest, baddest military alliance, NATO (North Atlantic Treaty Organization). They were both classic BC, absolutely classic. Because both paid triple dividends. They were win, win, win, no downside, real kiss-my-ass initiatives.

Take pushing for the Anti-Tobacco Accord. You can see how elegant and balanced and true it must have seemed when the idea first broke the surface of BC's consciousness. Once he saw what he had in the focus groups, BC ordered the federal government to sue the major tobacco manufacturers for all of the money it had paid out over the years, for iron lungs and radiation treatments and portable oxygen tanks. The states had already launched their own suits, but their claims were bought up and bought off, one by one. But BC had no incentive to settle. The fight itself was a continual winner.

One, it allowed BC to go out on the stump and absolutely disembowel Republicans who wouldn't admit that smoking was addictive (I have period video of then-Senate Majority Leader Robert Dole making this claim on a morning talk show and just getting *reamed*) or that Big Tobacco was shining their shoes for them. Big Tobacco quickly became evil incarnate, and anyone taking their PAC money all of a sudden found that he couldn't wash the blood off his hands.

Two, it was *really good policy*—more people would live, less children would die, and there isn't any stat that plays better than even a handful of live children who would otherwise be corpses. Eleven thousand kids were getting hooked on cigarettes every day, or at least that was the figure that got bandied around.

And three, the ATA was like hitting the lottery for the government. Once the government's lawsuit looked like it was going all the way, the major tobacco producers started offering serious annual restitution, the kind of money that used to buy kings divorces from the Pope. All of a sudden BC and friends had an additional $175 billion to spend every fiscal year ($430 trillion in current numbers), and that kind of money creates its own new realities. More bridges and fat construction contracts and rapid rail for more cities around the country.

The same holds true for the 1999 expansion of NATO. In spite of the scare pieces you can find in the contemporary periodicals, it was a gift for BC, a windfall. It didn't take a lot of meetings. Hungary, Poland, and the

Czech Republic were pleading to join the alliance, had been for years at that point. The Soviet Union had atrophied into Russia, and Russia was lost in a fog of destitution and senility. It was a decision that could be felt in the blood. The Cold War was over; we won; but if we won we had to acquire something, and here were three former Soviet satellites we could have for the asking.

It wasn't liberating Paris, but it put some delicate perfume, some real hint of Prague spring in the air. It must have really hardened some of the old guys' silos over in the Pentagon. And it put the Republicans in the position of looking soft on Russia, like they didn't want to pull a few teeth from the mouth of the Bear. They debated it in the Senate, for something like an hour.

So when BC saw Big Tobacco and three little ex-Soviet republics lying around, he intuited the right decisions, given the information he had at the time. He didn't have any reason to regret them until he was an old, old man, when the Chinese supercrunched the NATO early-warning system and flattened Warsaw, then Budapest. Like I say, it should have been okay. It's just that the two initiatives collided somehow, combined and intensified each other somehow.

Big Tobacco squealed blue murder when Congress finally got serious about writing the Tobacco settlement, but all the while they had lobbyists mixing drinks in hotel rooms and Senate cloakrooms, and when the deal finally took shape it was tacitly understood that if North America was now off-limits to aggressive cigarette sales, Asia and Russia were the global boomtowns.

Profits had to stay high, especially with the government muscling and skimming like a silent Mafia partner. So the understanding was: *Go East.* There was even language—this was half of the third chapter of my doctoral dissertation; I can quote it verbatim for you—specifically authorizing the U.S. Commerce Department to *facilitate and speed acquisition of new and emerging non-U.S. markets*. It was reverse manifest destiny, with full-bore advertising and without a hint of conscience. The Big Three dusted off campaigns they hadn't had the gall to use for fifty years: men in white lab coats on TV promoting the health benefits of menthol, etc. Hundreds of millions, maybe billions, of Chinese and Belarussian and Kazakhstani citizens realized that while they had never actually seen Marlboro Country, they wanted desperately to Come Home to Flavor.

And of course their governments weren't stupid—they watched it happen, skimmed and took bribes where they could, until eventually their countries' own health problems mounted and they put their own sharp-eyed populists in office.

At that point, the Chinese, Russian, and Indian governments, along with a handful of less-imposing countries like Georgia and Latvia, brought suit against Big Tobacco in the World Court at the Hague, in 2016. And essentially these governments (not exactly the Eastern Affiliates, but close enough) together filed what amounted to a copy of the U.S. federal government's own nineteen-year-old brief—except the U.S. government was now cotarget of the suit with RJR, Philip Morris, Liggett, et al. It was the World, basically, suddenly, against Big U.S. Tobacco.

By that time BC was long out of the White House, running his own policy group and pet projects out of the Library down in Little Rock. I like to think if he'd still been around he would have smelled the nip of blood warning in the wind. I like to think he would have found a way out.

But it was an election year, 2016, and both the Republican and Reform parties had made UN-baiting and isolationism basic party planks. So the Justice Department lawyers and the Tobacco lawyers flew over to the Hague together, singing fight songs all the way, and got their Guccis handed to them.

This hybrid team of U.S. and Tobacco lawyers didn't just lose. They gave an entirely new and all-encompassing definition to the word *loss*.

Within a single year, the World Court awarded the largest settlement in the recorded history of the world, literally, an amount nearly equal to one-fifteenth of the GNP of the United States of America. That's one dollar out of every fifteen produced by every living soul in every one of the fifty states. The Security Council and the General Assembly both backed the verdict. Pope Pontus I called it God's judgment. Only England—the ancient and eternal home of the cigarette, the cigar, and the pipe—supported the U.S., and then only in a general slap at the regulation of tobacco itself.

There was a time when flouting a decision of the World Court would have meant nothing to Washington, a tongue-lashing in the Security Council. It would have been nothing more than the biggest kid on the block taking his ball and going home. The other kids would have grumbled, and then they would have showed up on the stoop the next morning, whining and looking for another game.

But in the years after NATO expansion, a couple of the other kids had put their heads together. Russia, in the face of a larger Western alliance, had been willing to settle some territorial claims and go to the Chinese as equals, even finally as something of a junior partner; China, for its part, saw a Sino-Russian alliance as the only way to break U.S. hegemony. And of course, the NATO muscle-flexing in Yugoslavia—including the bombing of the Chinese embassy in a raid over Belgrade in 1999—gave the nationalists in both countries plenty of ammo.

By the time China and Russia combined to bring suit against U.S. Tobacco, Russia had withdrawn from what until then had been laughably called "the international space station" (a U.S.-operated venture from the start) and thrown in with their new partners to orbit a "space station" of their own—that is to say, an orbiting military command-and-control. A Russian cosmonaut and a Chinese taikonaut appeared on CNN, weightless and joking, hanging a handmade sign together as their first act of housekeeping: *Thank you so much for not smoking.*

In 2018, the Chinese premier denounced the U.S. outright, accusing it of "acts of commercial warfare and flagrant, criminal disregard for the rule of law."

Now, if you look at the maps of the redrawn NATO alliance circa 1999, you'll see a peninsula of land surrounded on three sides by the three newly added partners—you can't miss it, it looks like a half-flaccid (or half-erect), slightly misshapen penis about to be caught in a vise. That sad, threatened little cucumber of land was Slovakia, and before long a Russian convoy trundled west carrying fifty theater-scale nuclear missiles for deployment there.

NATO and the Eastern Alliance clashed in Slovakia, then in Serbia, and then in Hungary in a three-stage war that was initially called World War III, but within five years there was fighting in Siberia and Mongolia and then half a dozen locations around the globe. Pretty soon it was too chaotic and interwoven to seem like one war. It would die down and then flare up again, both sides threatening nukes but grudgingly, brutally using conventional means, tanks and planes and attack helicopters and endless waves—two generations—of conscripted ground troops, and napalm again, after all those years and promises. They were wars without definition, wars like sirocco winds, blowing up suddenly, moving everywhere. Countries jumped in, pulled out, taking massive casualties with them.

They came to be called the Cigarette Wars, partly because a lot of our pilots took to painting the infamous big-nosed camel on the sides of their gunships and partly because the tobacco companies saw it, straightforwardly enough, as a marketing gambit. And if we'd won, I'm sure it would have all worked out for them just fine. Nothing sells like success.

We didn't win, of course. We lost in Asia and finally Eastern Europe, and it became clear that the Sino-Russian forces were regrouping and massing to take the wars to the mainland of the enemy, to New York and San Diego and eventually on into Washington, D.C. It was World War II all over again, with us as the Japanese, and that led the suddenly desperate men at the Pentagon and in the Situation Room at the White House to pursue Other Options a little more aggressively.

Such as me.

Sal Hayden
Georgetown
Washington, D.C.

The Year
2055

The First Part:

THE BRIDGE TO THE TWENTY-FIRST CENTURY

"Will you help *me build that bridge, will all of you help me build that bridge to the twenty-first century? Will* all *of you walk across with me?"*

—BC, campaigning in late summer 1996, Sommerville, Georgia

1

IN BC'S LIBRARY

The lights in the administrative wing of the Presidential Library in Little Rock were state-of-the-art in their day, designed to be as omniscient and as easy on electricity as possible. The Library's designers tried their best to make them a monument to BC's take on the environment, that the choice between profit and environmentalism is a false opposition. A brass plaque on the Visitors' Arch says so in plain English, for anyone to read. It also tells you that most of the orientations in the Library match the White House: West Wing, South Lawn, even a Rose Garden, though with an overblown backdrop of a certain lavender-and-white wisteria that BC's mother was said to love.

The lights are fed information from sensors embedded everywhere in the complex—walls, floors, ceilings, door handles. The building sees you, and it gives you only the lighting it feels you need, unless you trip wall switches manually (which BC does not do, and which is therefore not done). It isn't that the building's trying to be stingy. It just feels it knows better.

So no matter where you are in the West Wing, you sit in a pool of light exactly one office and one-half corridor long, with other corridors and archival caches and administrative offices at first darkly visible, then vanishing altogether in the high-tech gloaming. When someone nears your location in the building, they approach in their own moving corona of fluorescent light, corridors winking out behind them.

But the years have accumulated, and the system is past its prime, its wiring and memory and collective sentience degraded. Sometimes lights flicker on in an empty hall, tripped by the ghost memory of a twenty-five-year-old footfall. Without input, late at night, empty of administrators, the West Wing will very occasionally illuminate a whole floor of offices, slowly, one after another, brooding, as though in search of an item lost generations before and all but entirely forgotten. I know this because I've driven by at three in the morning and seen it happen, seen the building at its least imposing and most pathetic.

But the designers were big on windows, and during the day the lighting system is mostly beside the point. I prefer to work in the early morning, when the sun is waxing, and to leave by mid-afternoon. Those hours happen to coincide with BC's workday. He was once infamous as a night owl, working the Rolodex until the wee hours, laying down solitaire on his desk while he gabbed, but no more, not for years.

I can always hear him before I can smell him, and I can smell him long before I can see him. He always wears an extremely expensive Italian cologne, and the bite of citrus precedes him down the hall relentlessly, like a blind man's stick. In this, as in many things, he takes his cues from Ronald Reagan, an earlier ex-president who never let himself go to seed after leaving office, who despite advanced age and advanced Alzheimer's never stopped looking presidential. No photo opportunity, no matter how close to death, ever caught Reagan looking elderly.

And so BC too must clothe himself in Italian silk and splashy ties each and every day, wear ten-thousand-dollar black wing tips when deep inside himself he must crave sheepskin-lined slippers. Why couldn't he wear those dreamed-of slippers? I ask myself. Who would know, and who could begrudge him?

And how, for Christ's sake, could a sweater hurt? It's his due. It's his Library.

But the first token of BC each morning is the faint sound of magnets and metal snapping disconcertingly into place and then releasing, a noise without context at first, muffled but not drowned by his thin trouser legs. In the smooth marble hallway, the sound bounces everywhere.

Like most of the very, very old, BC uses a walker, but unlike most, his encases his weakened lower body and doesn't show. It is cutting-edge geriatrics, and it walks him. A padded titanium exoskeleton, custom-built, is locked to his mottled shins and thighs. These flat, slightly bendable, absolutely unbreakable shafts are sequenced with magnetic joints; a sensitive and solicitous computer pack nestled at his lower back constantly searches for the sturdiest pressures and angles. BC's knees can't fail him. His backbone is stiffened. The intelligent pack at the small of his back calculates which resistances increase his leverage and which subtract, and it feeds current to magnets or cuts it off accordingly. More than physics, it functions along comfortable political lines, and no device on earth could be more appropriate for a one-hundred-and-nine-year-old ex-president with tricky hips.

His body-walker is only one of several ways that BC has cheated age and gravity, outwitted decrepitude. About six years ago, a year before I came to Little Rock, rheumatoid arthritis was threatening his ability not only to dial phones and manipulate a keyboard but to shake hands—for him, the unthinkable. BC was roused violently into action. Thirty-five- and forty-year-old favors were called in. There was a video conference with the head of the FDA, the president of Johns Hopkins Medical School, and the CEOs of two global underwriters of medical technology.

With acceptable speed, a research team at the Mayo Clinic performed what was then only the fourth complete digital ceramic replacement, a procedure they haven't yet been able to patent or market. Small, weblike scars at each finger and thumb crease mark the spots where microsurgery removed entire joints and replaced them with smooth ball sockets made of treated dental ceramic, then nailed each construct together with doll-sized pins. Finally they infused the whole works with sea-green polymer gel—a lubricant and an antirejection agent all in one. The fingers work perfectly now, sleekly, and BC has adopted a habit of drumming them on tabletops. When he does it, I can't hear but I feel as though I can hear the ceramic shuffling and clicking like loosely stacked poker chips.

Like the rest of the very, very old, a group once known as the Baby Boomers, BC insists upon the very best care. He is the nation's poster boy for raging against the dying of the light.

He remains something of a spokesman for them, the hundreds of millions in the Southwest, the New South, and retirement villages in the Northeast. He is, after all, a two-term president who once made the preservation of the old Medicare and Social Security systems his middle name. The current administration, like the last five or six, works hard to be seen as good sons and daughters to BC. If they have cut subsidies to the Library over the years, they have regularly increased funding for his medical care and staff. When he's brought down by pneumonia or small cancers, the current Vice-President may drop in with soup and a photographer.

His quadriceps, hamstring, bicep, calf, and deltoid muscles have all been coaxed into hypertrophy with regular gene therapy. His genes have been isolated, sequenced, resequenced, sliced, diced, and julienned. The idea is to create stronger muscle bases, allowing the limbs and trunk to function more easily, with less strain. It does work; I've seen BC reposition his heavy oak desk with none of the trembling hands and knees you associate with the very aged. Between the body-walker and the gene work, he gets around. He's perfectly viable and does without a day nurse.

Still, the proteins produced by the injections are indiscriminate, and the long and short of it is that his geriatric technicians can make muscle tissue regenerate but they can't stop the process just like that.

So BC has the slightly comical Popeye arms and legs that have infiltrated the gene pool—artificially but literally—of every geriatric community in the country. He has the inflated forearms, the bulbous shoulders. He has a partial fan of back muscle that fills out his Dao/Armani shirt in a way that must be very satisfying when he catches a glimpse of himself in his tailor's cutaway mirror.

But in other ways he is old, and unable. He is stooped, with none of the tall, straight-carriaged swagger I see in the file photos. His hearing, always dicey even during his years in the White House, is very poor. Only an extremely quiet room and careful pitch can make a voice completely understandable to him. He tells me that my voice gets through, that he needs me for that. But I have a feeling it's just a little bit of blarney. He's spent an entire lifetime making people feel especially, particularly close to him.

His own voice is lost, along with teeth and hearing. It is dry now, the voice, powered only by determination and an indomitable larynx; the diaphragm hasn't worked for decades. Although he can occasionally rouse himself to indignation, for the most part he speaks like an old, old man in a nursing home, asking a passing orderly for a cup of water.

In my apartment, on a row of shelves over my work desk, I have an enormous collection of video and audio discs. Ninety percent of these are BC material. As his only authorized biographer, I have access to it all, the biggest cache of historical material ever recorded during a single presidency. To one side is a small subsection of discs with a little white label beneath, reading simply *Greatest Hits*.

These are BC's best: his anniversary address outside the Murrah Federal Building, his first and fifth State of the Union Addresses, the brief spots he did on his opposition to shutting down the government in 1995, his second inaugural speech on healing the breach, and the eulogies—for his friend dead by suicide, for his commerce secretary killed in a plane crash, for Richard Nixon, the evil shibboleth of BC's youth, for a pretty young woman ambassador killed abroad.

One of these funeral addresses is my favorite. It's a video of his eulogy for an assassinated Israeli prime minister, and it is devastatingly effective. BC's voice, with its soft, lower-middle-class, Hot-Springs-and-Hope Arkansas accent, moves out into his audience like a prayer and a promise. Once, when my old boyfriend Steve and I got high and watched it late at night with the lights way down, we both started to cry, out of nowhere. Not racking sobs or anything, but we did both cry.

Partly it was that Steve's brother had been killed in Azerbaijan the previous year, in the wreck of an Apache attack helicopter, and the memory of his funeral was still too fresh for us both. It was a closed casket, after all, body scorched beyond the reach of postmortem cosmetics. But partly the crying was in answer to the voice itself.

Because BC's was a voice that reached out and embraced you, comforted you. It knew where you hurt, you personally, for whatever reasons. It understood the depths of American sympathy, our ancient feelings of loneliness without a king, without a God, without real friends in a world always rightly suspicious of us. BC called this slain Israeli minister "friend" and said good-bye to him in Hebrew, and he preached to us about the forces of light and the forces of darkness, and about God's plans for both.

Steve and I blamed it on the pot the next morning and laughed about it, but the truth is that BC's voice was one-in-a-million. It could turn night into day, or at least into approaching dawn, and more than intelligent missiles and better early-warning equipment, a nation needs a leader who can move an entire people up and out of grief. It was a seductive voice, but it couldn't have been nearly as effective if BC didn't believe in the sound of it himself, if he didn't speak from his own undeniably scarred heart.

But that voice is gone now. When he walks past the door to my office most mornings, clicking softly beneath his clothes, his greeting doesn't carry far. If it weren't for the cologne, I might miss it altogether.

* * *

His mind, his clarity of thought, he's both kept and lost. In our interview sessions my first year in Little Rock, he could go on for several days about a given topic, health-care initiatives, say. He could speak about them for a long afternoon, then pick up the next morning more or less precisely where he left off. And that's still true today, that his mind can suddenly and unexpectedly focus like a laser.

"The Republicans screwed me royally on that one," he'll say, angry again, "wouldn't even allow a vote on cloture, not even a *vote*, but insisted on bringing it up in . . . I think it was the Omnibus Funding bill we made out of funding for State, Justice, Immigration, and Commerce—I'm pretty sure it was, but you check that. Those tight-assed bastards."

Other times, especially late in the afternoon, in the wash of sun from the tall windows in his office, he'll turn inward, unfocus. His mind will drift, and worry will crease his lightly spotted forehead. Sometimes the toe of his shoe will start to saw up and down, in a kind of unconscious physical counterpoint. When that happens I know he's back in the world of what he calls his "troubles," the scandals and missteps that dogged his presidency and that still eat at him now, nearly sixty years later. The interviews we did on those scandals—and he insisted that we spend long months on them—were clearly painful for him.

I had only recently met him at that time. He seemed to me then like the lone survivor of a horrible jetliner crash or movie-house fire, alive but traumatized and left wondering forever about his own culpability, whether and how much he was to blame for the blaze, whether and how much he'd trampled over others in his panic to escape. In our discussions, he would agonize about the lives destroyed, the promise wasted.

But his defenses, even now, are labyrinthine. He spent a long, gray March afternoon explaining several of his eleventh-hour pardons, an explanation tying together common, civil, and criminal law, the Department of Justice, the Israeli Mossad, and the Make-A-Wish Foundation. Almost more than the sex scandals, BC remains bitter about those scandals marking his departure from office, the stories about clemency for sale and filched gifts and vandalized offices in the West Wing. In his mind, his enemies bided their time until he was forced to decommission his spin army, to take off his personal armor, and then they struck mercilessly, news cycle after news cycle. BC's nationwide approval ratings and the invincible Dow Jones Industrial collapsed simultaneously, and like the stock market BC took a good long time to recover, to climb up out of national disgrace.

Not that anyone but BC cares anymore about land deals gone wrong or love affairs gone cold. A tempest in a D-cup, as my dissertation adviser used to call the events that led up to his impeachment. His wife and his daughter and his chocolate Labrador and all of his enemies are dead. Only scholars are interested anymore, and then mostly only to know what glancing effects the scandals had on BC's foreign-policy motivations. All anyone wants to know about him is how he figured in the making of the current conflicts. But that era of scandal is BC's own purgatory, and it still has the power to pull him out of a discussion of NATO expansion or the Oslo Peace Accords, to draw his eyes down and his refitted hands nervously to his lap.

"I'd have gotten Fast-Track Authority renewed," he'll maintain, using a shorthand he knows I know, eyes flicking up to mine before returning to the window, "but, you know, well, Sal, that was a very troubled time for me. For us. It was coming down thick at that point."

Still, he faces it with his own kind of courage. Richard Nixon had exhibits in his library that addressed Watergate, and so BC has insisted that the Library here mock up a Scandal Room. It is a small room, and hanging in it are the faces of several women, several prosecutors, several prominent political enemies. The women's faces are strange, like animate caricatures, certain features disturbingly out of proportion: a nose you can't look away from, lips like matching coral pillows. BC doesn't go there, although I know he okayed the original exhibit texts for it, as well as each successive revision.

I think it made him comfortable, at the time, to have it all represented in that one room of the building. It put four walls and one door around it, and he could know for sure exactly which room contained it all. If it was all in there, chances were better it wouldn't be anywhere else.

Very occasionally, a colleague in my area of specialization will know enough about late-twentieth-century politics to make a joke about BC recruiting me to write the authorized biography. "He may have lost his hearing, but he clearly hasn't lost his eye," a much older woman from Duke remarked sweetly to me a few years ago, looking at the hem of my skirt. I didn't even bother to set her straight.

But the fact of the matter is that BC thought I was a man when he flew me to Little Rock to sound me out about the project. For his generation, Sal is invariably a man's first name.

And he was honest about what he thought after we'd met: I was clearly capable, as he'd read my work and the one previous biography I'd written, but I was a fairly young, attractive woman and that would be awkward for him. It would give the wrong appearance. The way he said it I could tell that it had been standard operating procedure for him for more years than I'd been alive.

I told him that if I took the job I'd be in Little Rock not as an aide or an employee but to write a biography that would almost certainly be critical of him in spots. And that people didn't attribute sexual motivations to men in advance of one hundred years of age—they viewed them as asexual, great-grandfatherly.

But, I added, if he was especially worried about gossip, we could leave the door open when we talked. In fact, he could have Secret Service pull up a chair. In fact, we could have live audio/video from the time I entered the office to the time I left. Basically, I let him know that if he wanted to get all worried and kittenish about having a woman under fifty in his administrative wing, I wasn't going to play. He'd come to me, after all. He was the one who'd read *my* work. And he was older than any Galapagos tortoise in any zoo anywhere in the world.

When I got back to my apartment in Burlington the next day, there was an audio-only message for me. It was BC, offering me an office, clerical support, and an unconditional authorization for the biography. His accent and his wariness were magnified by the machinery. "I understand you may be critical in the book at times, Sal, I do. And you may not believe it, but I welcome that. I welcome it. Because I'm not after a put-up job. I want a good, solid, readable, truthful record of my life and my presidency."

There was a little pause in the message, as though he were unwrapping a lemon drop or buffing the toe of his shoe. "All I want is a chance to argue my case to history. And it looks like that'll be you, Sal. I couldn't ask for fairer." I heard the telltale ring of his hearing aid, the irritated sound it occasionally makes in its relentless search for intelligible frequencies.

"And I will leave that office door open, Sal," he put in, but not really as a joke. "Because if I learned anything in my life, it's that the attacks never stop. Not ever. I don't care if I live to be two hundred, if I so much as kiss a rabbit's foot for good luck, somebody somewhere's gonna want a picture of it. You start writing my biography, and you're gonna come to know that firsthand." A final soft snort. "And 'nother thing you'll find out is if I ain't around, they'll attack any book about me in a hot second. You want to steel yourself for that, Sal, when you're finished writing. Because that's a thing in this life that *will* happen."

No author understands this last truth better than BC himself. Like one of those early Mars landers—the kind that just went ahead and crashed into the Red Planet inside a cluster of Vectran airbags—BC's autobiography was designed to survive the initial critical impact. He knew no one would be kind, not in 2005, not with the book years behind schedule and his excesses still fresh in the minds of critics and book-buyers. So the idea was that when the impact was over, the airbags would peel back like flower petals, and something like a Rover would emerge—a positive version of BC that would eventually re-acquire and dominate the landscape. The language of the text had to be just so, BC felt, the various explanations superbly engineered.

And the book did crash, but of course there was nothing controlled about it. The autobiography was almost universally repudiated, and BC took it very badly, nursed a grudge, and vowed never to try to explain himself to anyone ever again.

He spent nearly the next five decades thinking about how to begin all over again, thinking about that glimmering contradiction in terms, the authorized biography.

2

WHAT BON VOYAGE REALLY MEANS

I don't know about you, but I think it's perfectly legitimate for a woman to ask the tough questions in life, like why if you're God you select the female breast as the most prevalent site for terminal cancer. The breast is the fuel tank for every developing child in the world. What kind of engineer designs faulty fuel tanks straight into the blueprint?

In the 1970s there was a certain model of gas-burner that was famous for bursting into flames if another car so much as nudged its fender—they called it the Pinto. I was reminded of this car when my aunt Mary died, still undergoing radiation therapy, during my sophomore year in college. One of her fuel tanks leaked death everywhere in her lymph system, and she was gone in three months. So that's one of the very hardest questions. Creator, there is a never-ending plague on the breast. What is Your point?

But it's one of those questions that just don't get answered, ever. You have to either accept the fact that God isn't always up front with His plans and move on, or go insane. Eventually I moved on. My life flowed slowly into the gap Mary left.

Now, every other week I take a five-day working weekend at my aunt's house in Vermont, which she left me when she died. When she told me about the change in her will, I asked her why she wasn't leaving it to my father, her little brother.

Mary was sitting in an Adirondack chair on her front porch, looking out over the passing university students and the svelte green whisper trams floating slowly, soundlessly up College Street. She took a sip of her tall bourbon and water, chewed some ice to stall for a second. My father was one of those topics on which we agreed but still approached with maximum caution. She'd made me cry once, as a girl, by saying something offhandedly cutting about him.

But this particular day she wasn't in a cautious mood. She was just two months from death, and you could see she knew it in the way she plucked a leaf from the vine next to her hand, stuck it with her thumbnail, once, twice. Chemotherapy had taken most of her hair, but she had her makeup on, bright red lipstick and mascara, a flat signal to Death that he could expect no help.

"Because I hold a grudge," she said finally, tartly. "That's why. I'm not ashamed to say it, even if he is your father, Sal, which I would note that no genetic test has ever definitively proven. Sometimes a grudge is all the relief you can get from some people.

"Your father is the kind to do something hurtful and then wait to be forgiven. He's my little baby brother, and nobody knows it better than me. And then he'll do it all over again. After a certain number of years, you have to face facts." She nodded her head slowly and fiercely, for her. "Years ago I did. Now, I don't have any illusions about you. You're due to forgive him at least once more in your life.

"But I'm going to take care of one thing. I'm writing it into my will that the house is all yours, free and clear, not even property taxes to worry about; I've got an escrow fund to pay those. But if the house is ever sold or transferred, the profits go to my church. Because you're a soft one, Sal. And if I can't stop Ronnie from breaking your heart, I can at least make sure he doesn't retire to my house to pat himself on the back about it."

She was right. My father came to town for her funeral, and for a week he was charming and thoughtful and full of plans for putting things right. We went out to dinner at the nicest places, him in a killer double-breasted blue suit and me in my black interview unitard. He'd offer me some wine and listen to me, really listen, nodding his head. He wanted to know how I was doing at the University of Vermont, was I still majoring in Media Sciences, did I have friends, good friends, to help me through the grief. Health and family were all that mattered, he said.

But he was visibly angry when the will was read, in a lawyer's office down on Battery Street, overlooking the lake. He told me his version of his relationship with Mary, later over dinner, but he never really looked at me while he complained.

And that was the beginning of his second long disappearance. He stayed two more days, but he was more distant every hour. Finally, he left me a voice mail while I was in class, saying good-bye, he'd be in touch about Christmas in the Bahamas. It was almost four years before I saw him again, for a surprise two-day ski visit, and then sixteen more long years after that with no word of any kind. I still have no address for him today.

So I wound up with an imposing indigo-blue two-story Victorian on College Street that's probably worth a mint and that I can never sell. Not that I'd want to sell; it's the one place in the world that holds even a sliver of the feeling of home. There's a pool table in the basement, an eight-foot slate, the same one my aunt used to teach me the game, with truly elegant champagne-colored tassels below the pockets. It's my emotional gyroscope, that table.

I can still go down there for an hour and shoot a couple of racks and smoke a marijuanette and after a while if I'm lucky I'll see my aunt setting up to make a shot, with a cigarette balanced in her painted lips, silver hair meticulously permed and combed, splayed out over the table, wool skirt hiked awkwardly, one toe brushing the floor to render the shot legal, and then *Shit!* taking the two ball into the nine ball and the nine downtown for the game.

Those are the kind of visions that can come together only in the rooms where the real bodies spent real time, rooms where chance silver hairs found their way into floorboards, and cigarette smoke filmed the diamonds of a chandelier. I'm not saying I worship my aunt's relics, but she was my idol and I loved her like a mother from the time I was nine years old, with the entire sweep of my heart, and I'll keep what pieces I'm allowed to keep.

When I moved to Little Rock to do BC's biography, I sublet the ground floor, keeping the upper floor for myself and making it clear that I expected to use the kitchen and the living room and the porch when I managed to get back. It's a bit of a pain, but I couldn't stomach the thought of Little Rock three hundred sixty-five days a year. To a lifelong Vermonter, the Arkansas humidity is like walking out of your air-conditioned apartment and being slowly immersed in warm latex. So the three days I get in Burlington are necessary, if only to give my sweat glands a rest. And the two travel days are not all that bad: I take quick-rail to Jacksonville, the

East Coast Bullet from Jacksonville to New York, and then the smaller Montreal Bullet to Burlington. It's a nine-hour trip, but I write and I read, and I like the bratwurst they serve at the kiosks on the ECB.

When I first told BC about the working schedule I planned to keep, he wasn't upset that I wanted the time away from Little Rock, he was worried about all the time in the train stations. "It's more than Mormons and New Moon people hanging around in those stations, Sal, there's the real bad element too. And not just the sex sickies. The political types too, with a grudge to settle. Don't take my word for it, you look in *The New York Times*."

That was all before the White House and the Pentagon announced the Domestic Defense Initiative last year. The DDI more or less mooted the whole issue. That's when the soldiers began to patrol airports and shopping malls and the train pool stations. Every Bullet now has a uniformed GI within two cars of your seat, guaranteed. At first it was unsettling, passing the young men with helmets and rifles, but pretty quickly that feeling mellowed into solid reassurance.

There'd been quite a few high-profile explosions in the past several years, at least a couple of them the work of American citizens sympathetic to the Eastern Alliance. They'd shout, *God is Great* or *Death to Satan, Death to his Cigarettes, and Death to his Evil,* there'd be one horrible silent second while the detonator introduced power to fuel, and then it was Marlboro Country for whoever happened to be within a three-car radius.

So when the men in camouflage khaki showed up on the ECB, I didn't have a problem with it, although some people did, Libertarians and pacifists. For me, it was fairly straightforward: armed escorts have got to be a serious piece of discouragement if you're all dressed up in a Semtex corset with nowhere to go.

And you'd think, since he'd been such a neurotic about safety in the beginning, that BC would have relaxed when the soldiers began to oversee the transit system. But he didn't. It put him into one of his brooding moods, remodeled fingers raveling and unraveling.

Luck only exists in theory for me, never in practice. I get the urge to go home a week earlier than usual, and up in my neck of Vermont, it turns out it's a countywide Bon Voyage Night.

All the small towns in Chittenden County have young people shipping out the following morning for processing and training. Even on the

Montreal Bullet, moving at well over four hundred miles an hour, you can see the bonfires in Vergennes, Jericho, Ferrisburg, Charlotte. If I had known it was Burlington's BV, I'd have postponed my trip for a week. It isn't the noise or the madness or the crowds. A slick pair of headphones takes care of that. It's the sense that they don't want to go, these kids in new uniforms. Or few of them want to go. You do see the odd group here or there, of gung-ho marines or airmen, enlistees not draftees, styling down Church Street with their new military hats cocked and Extra Fats dangling from the corners of their mouths like big white cheroots.

These are the same boys who will tip their hat to you at the ATM machine and ask politely if you're a med student, because they have this horrible lump down between their legs that's getting bigger and bigger and they can't figure out what to do about it. They're the kind that think of the Wars, and women, as action.

But for the most part, for all their celebrating, the inductees give off a silent wail of protest. Riding the glider tram into downtown Burlington is like wading into a Mardi Gras crowd, except for the lack of authentic gaiety, the whiff of desperate display to the new GIs and their families and friends milling on Church Street. Once it became clear that thirty percent of the local kids shipping out vertically would ultimately be shipped back in horizontally, once the Chinese took Hungary, the local BV became a place I wanted to avoid.

We round the corner to my street, the tram in electromagnetic whisper mode. I look up the darkened street, and look again. All the lights are on at my house.

All the lights. I stretch my neck out the window to make sure that it is, in fact, my house that is lit up like the World Soccer Dome.

As the glider floats up College, I can see bodies moving around in the living room, the back kitchen. When I step down at the corner of South Union, I suddenly see a salvo of bottle rockets go up from the backyard and detonate in the darkness above the tree line. Before I can look down again, a microrocket follows them skyward, its thrust converted by a clever set of filters and pipettes into an almost recognizable human scream. It sounds like a woman screaming in pain and rage, and it's an unmistakable wail. The scream is followed immediately by a serious flat *boom* that rattles the windows of every house in the neighborhood.

The Remnicks, the family that rents the bottom floor of the house, are clearly throwing a BV party. I was put-upon and irritated before. Now I'm officially rip-shit. Bottle rockets can set someone's garage on fire, but micros are Class C explosives, a misdemeanor to sell or use. And on top of that, they're only made in China, contraband war material. If there's one thing I don't need tonight, it's a trooper shooting video of my bedroom closet and my underwear drawer.

So I start walking toward the house, my house, like a landlady instead of an exhausted biographer. I've got my shoulders pushed back, my chin pushed out.

It can't be Lecia, I'm telling myself, and even as I'm telling myself I'm not believing myself. The Remnicks' daughter, Lecia, and I aren't quite friends, but we've played a little pool on the cellar table, and a few months back I took her downtown to Ake's for a game. She shoots fast and doesn't think for more than a token second about where the cueball's going to park.

So I'm lying to myself as I near the house, because this big-ass fiesta has little Lecia's style all over it.

At the steps, I can pick out the sweet odor of the commercial marijuana-tobacco mix, as well as the flatulent signature smell of Extra Fat. As I come through the screen door, I take a quick scan of the living room, as everyone in it takes a quick scan of me. It's obvious to all of us that we're of two different species.

What I see: they're all more or less under twenty-one, five or six are in uniform, and the rest are wearing army surplus and Apache jeans and Tomahawk jackets with all kinds of promotional badges pinned front and back. The girls I can see range from about fifteen to eighteen, and they've all got some version of the cutaway blouse, the bare skin from their neck to their belly buttons scented and powdered to match their eye shadow. Four or five have on what look like actual Camel Shaydz, sleek night-vision wraparounds that cost about a third of what I make in a year. They're all kids from the suburbs, rich, young, pumped up on testosterone and patriotism and sex.

I've hit the party at that tentative interval where enough beer has gone down, and enough rockets have gone up, to create the necessary end-of-the-world atmosphere, this allowing Moves to be Busted.

What they see: a small woman just old enough to be their mother, in black tights and black cotton T-shirt and black big-shoulders jacket, her eyes red and puffy from napping on the Bullet, her red hair flattened from same, and her white hand gripping a suitcase handle like it was a nightstick.

"Where's Lecia?" I say, just loudly enough to carry over the music. I see that a number of them are focused on my suitcase, for whatever reason, and I let it fall with a smack to the hardwood floor. "I'm looking for Lecia," I say again.

Somebody says she's in the kitchen, somebody says she's out back.

"How about the Remnicks? Lecia's parents?"

At the mention of parents, there is a polite wait for unpleasant consequences. When none are forthcoming, they all begin tentatively to resume their conversations, hoping the lack of attention will drive me away.

So I sweep into the kitchen and confront a similar group there, with the exception of some tube-and-tank equipment for doling out vaporized Powershots of schnapps and Stoly. Here the tank master, a jaded guy about twenty-five with an aviator mustache, doesn't even flinch, just keeps counting his bills and moving the next person up to the hose.

The young brunette at the nozzle gives me a doe-eyed stare. She's got her hand on the plunger, ready to drive her shot home. She looks fourteen, at best.

I put my hand on hers. "Where's Lecia?" I ask slowly.

"With Danno," the girl says before she thinks. I keep my hand on her hand. Then, like a prison snitch, she flicks her eyes to the ceiling.

I release her, and she hits the plunger immediately, pulling in the plume of alcohol, visibly relieved.

3

A THORNY WAY, AND DIFFICULT TO SAY FOR SURE

The second floor of the house is mine still, and I keep it locked when I leave for Little Rock. But the lock on the landing door is ancient, the kind that takes an ornate metal key, the kind you can trick with a bent bobby pin. I open it and come up the last half-flight of steps, my breath coming short and feeling for some reason like I'm breaking into someone else's apartment.

But it is mine, my antique political posters on the stairway walls, one of an old Soviet technocrat from days before the fall of the Berlin Wall, one from BC's first campaign, and my most valuable one, the rarest kind you could never replace, a red-white-and-blue banner for an infamously failed Democratic presidential nominee from Massachusetts named Michael Dukakis. My throw rug at the top of the stairs, and my books in the shelves along the hallway.

And two problems. The bedroom door at the end of the hall is shut. This tells me clearly enough that Lecia, or someone, is or has been in my room; I never leave *any* of the doors shut because I hate coming home and going through the wincing process of opening them all to check for stalkers.

But there is also the matter of the forty-six-ounce plastic cup on my kitchen table. There's an inch or so of Russian Mule left in it, tonic water mixed with equal parts 151 rum and peppermint schnapps and euro-proof Stolichnaya. No one over twenty-five drinks Mule. Consuming forty or so ounces of Mule would incapacitate a fifteen-year-old girl. Ergo, either Lecia is in my bed passed out, or she's in my bed with a drunk but no doubt highly operational young man. Since the door is closed, I have to believe the second option is far and away the most likely.

I walk halfway to the door, stand in the dim hallway. It's hot in the apartment because I closed the windows, and I start sweating all of a sudden. I think I can hear something from behind the door, but I can't be sure. I decide to take the indirect approach.

"Lecia?" I call, voice calm but loud. No answer. I take another step, my heart flailing in my chest for some reason. I'm not in trouble, I remind myself, I'm the grown-up. "Lecia!" I call again, louder still.

No answer. I can't be sure if the noise I hear is from my bedroom or the beat of the music from downstairs. I'm standing right in front of a framed photo of BC in 1993 on the White House lawn, overseeing a handshake between an Israeli prime minister and the onetime head of the Palestine Liberation Organization.

"Lecia!" I yell, giving it one last, slightly shrill try. Still nothing, except for faint creaks and bumps. So I open the door.

On my bed are two naked young people. A big beeswax candle on my dresser and the moonlight through the bedroom window make the whole scene much clearer than I'd prefer. Below is a male with fairly large feet and bony knees. His Marine uniform is folded a little fussily over my aunt Mary's bentwood rocker. His right hand is dangling beside the bed, holding a glowing Extra Fat, which is poised over an ashtray resting on the floor.

Above is the barely fifteen-year-old daughter of my downstairs tenants. Her single side-braid is easy to spot. She is running her hands over her pale, partially developed upper body. Both are wearing black ultralight headphones connected to a disc cache set up on my bedside table. Both are evidently moving to the same music; I can hear it escaping the headphones from across the room.

I don't have too many choices. I'm not waiting outside for them to finish, and I'm not walking over next to them and tapping one of them on the shoulder. Instead, I hit the light switch, and while they're scrambling like a couple of pale cockroaches, I toss Lecia the quilt that I keep folded on my cedar chest.

"I'm going out to the kitchen to make myself a cup of tea," I say. I've got a fairly good grip on my voice. It's definitely landlady. But my breathing and my pulse are seriously out of whack. "By the time the water boils, I want him out of my apartment. And I want you, Lecia, to go downstairs and get rid of the rest of your friends. All of them, right now. I'll be in my office when you're done."

The marine looks spooked; I don't know if he knows how old Lecia is, but he knows she's too young for comfort. I see him look for his boots, and that's all I need to know about the depth of this relationship.

"Now," I throw in before turning around, because since I'm the adult I can't throw anything else. And I'm still spitting mad. My hands have a little tremble.

The marine and Lecia leave the apartment together a few minutes later, saying nothing as they slide past my office door, and I hear the music downstairs abruptly switched off a few minutes after that. It takes another twenty minutes for Lecia to clear everyone out. Not everyone is in a mood to leave, it seems; I hear her raising her voice several times, screaming once, and slamming doors.

It helps to be in my office. I sit in my chair and power up my Wide-eye monitor, and while I wait for it to reach out to the various networks that drive it, I remind myself that I am an adult and a professor and a respected author and the authorized biographer of an actual ex-president.

I throw some video of BC up on the monitor, and I start slagging out some clips for the eventual ROM of the biography, marking, copying, and compiling them. It's a clip from one of BC's news conferences, some foreign dignitary by his side, and he's clearly working his way with extraordinary care through a question. He's got his hands out in front of him, as though to smooth things over, and I freeze it. The shot suddenly says something to me.

In the last several weeks, I've come to the point in my work where I feel I have the whole story, or what I think of as the whole story—BC is clearly content to revise his version of events unto death. But my interviews and fact-finding are done. The database is bursting. What I'm doing these days is deciding on the big themes, my take, my spin, the story I plan to tell through it all.

I've come home with the idea that maybe I can stitch the clips and photographs together and use them, in a kind of writer's reverse, to put together the narrative they support. That's the moment of truth in writing biography, when you begin consciously to use story to assign meaning to the otherwise random life of your subject. You tell your reader not only what happened, but why.

And at that point you cease to be a collector, an eye and an ear and a memory, and you move irrevocably into a position of judgment, of experience and mistake-making. Maybe it's the scene with Lecia, but it suddenly seems to me a loss of virginity.

It's also the movement to commitment. You can't disentangle once you've affixed a story to your subject. You remain married to that biographical decision, your name is forever linked to that version of that person. Consequences extend outward from there. History starts to roll over you and through you.

Part of the reason I've come home this particular weekend, I see now, is that the overarching themes I've felt coming together over the last months are not positive themes. The book I've been mentally writing is not the book BC has in mind. For all of the promise and all of the charisma and kismet of BC's life, what knits it all together is an undeniable weakness of resolve and failure of integrity, in any venue other than the strictly political. BC's greatest successes, like the Dayton Peace Agreement, were the direct result of a pressing need for reelection. Absent that pressure, he was a man adrift, unable to focus and direct his unconventional gifts. I know that in his mind, it's his *troubles,* the scandals, that he thinks will sink his place in history, but it's not. It's the man he could have been and never was. It's the way he could never bring himself to look greatness in the eye.

I've come home to be further from him in saying these things to myself for the first time. As hard as I've tried to avoid it, I've come to desire his approbation. Maybe that's why I have to keep reminding myself that I haven't done anything wrong tonight. I feel guilty, down deep, for the book I'll need to write. Because to BC, it'll be worse than some scorched lawn or beer spilled on the sofa, or the lingering stench of Extra Fat. It will hit him like a long sliver of glass in the heart.

I'm on my second cup of tea when Lecia comes to the door of my office. She's a fairly attractive young girl, with pretty fawn-colored hair that she despises and has dyed impenetrable raven black. This curtain of black she parts down the middle, over her snubbed nose. You'd have to drink a lot of Mule to see her as anything other than a child, in spite of the occasional streetwalker touches to her wardrobe.

At this point, she's wearing a T-shirt with the U.S. Marines logo on it, the neck of it deeply notched to reveal the upper band of her chest, and the long sleeves pushed up on tiny forearms. She's got her shoulders hunched in, and it's obvious she plans to cry quickly and try to get a promise of silence out of me before her parents get home, whenever they get home.

She leans against the doorjamb. "Sal, I am so, so sorry. I'm serious," she says, eyes wide, "*so* much." Then she waits for me to show my openers.

"How long have you been having sex?" I ask, turning away from the Wide-eye. Looking at her makes me a little sadder, because I can see that we won't wind up being friends. I had an idea, when I took her downtown that once for some pool and an illicit beer, that I could teach her the game, be like an aunt to her. More specifically, be like my aunt Mary to her, while she would, naturally, be me. Looking at her long color-copy nails, each a little image of Danno, I see she needs an upstairs aunt like she needs a disc-size hole in the head.

"Two years," she answers, with only a slight hesitation. She started when she was barely thirteen, then. We're both going to shoot for no-nonsense, it looks like.

"Your parents know?"

"Yup."

"And they're okay with that?"

"They're not going to legislate my morality, they said."

"They know you're making it with a marine?"

"Not yet. I'll wait a while before I tell them."

"How old is Danno?"

She smells a trap, but answers anyway. "Nineteen."

"And he's shipping out tomorrow?"

"Yup. To Georgia. Then probably to Mongolia, or Kazakhstan."

"And you think he's going to write you and keep this thing you have going while he's over there fighting? A nineteen-year-old marine who smokes while you have sex? Tell me one thing. Was that his music on the headphones or yours?"

She doesn't say anything. I feel a little bad about saying it; it was a cheap shot. Nobody wants to be called on the particulars of what they do for love. And for whatever reason, the anger and the outrage have all washed out of me. I'm having a hard time even pretending anger with her anymore. All I want is a solid nine hours of sleep and the certainty of no wake-up call.

"Look, Lecia, I'm not your parents. You three rent that lower floor from me, and you can do whatever the hell you want down there, as long as it's legal. And breaking into my apartment is not legal. I also think it's criminal that you're going to let some Mule-drinking stud get away with statutory rape because you're in love, but that's your parents' deal."

Lecia's got the look of someone who was in over her head and now feels sand under a toe. But she doesn't want to look relieved too soon. She knows I'm still going to yak at her for another few minutes, maybe change my mind.

"About fifteen minutes ago, I was ready to call the police, but for some reason," I glance back at the video on the Wide-eye, BC with his hands patting and calming the air, "I've lost the energy. I also had a bunch of things I was going to try to make you understand about this, but there's one really, really important one. So I'm just going to let it go at that. Here's what I'm going to do. Tomorrow I'm going to get a locksmith to come in and install a really cranking lock on my landing door, and I'm going to have him put double-jams on both the windows you can reach from your part of the house. And you're going to pay for it. You took my sense of security away, and you're going to have to pay to get it back."

Her eyes are wider now. She wasn't expecting any money to change hands. "And you won't tell my parents then?"

"Right. And I just want to tell you one more thing. Then you can go downstairs and start cleaning up after the animals. The point I want to make to you—and you won't learn it now, it takes a long time to learn—is that when you screw over other women, whether they're your best friends or not, to get some guy into bed, it's always a lot more expensive than you think it's gonna be. A lot more."

"That's it?"

"That's it."

Now she's had enough. She's got a tougher look, like she's taken my best shot. "So I can go and clean up and you won't tell."

"I'll put the locksmith's bill in your mailbox out front once he's gone. You pick it up tomorrow night. If it's paid by the time I leave Tuesday, then you've got nothing to worry about from upstairs."

"How much do you think the bill will be?"

"Expensive." I'm not worried about breaking her bank; she almost certainly had a split with the guy running the Powershot tank in the kitchen.

"Great." Now she's even flirting with a little sarcasm, making a show of dealing with my irrational behavior. "Whatever. Well, maybe when I'm cleaned up downstairs, we could shoot a game in the cellar." A bit of hesitation. "If you're up for it." This is insurance; I can tell by the way she says it, she's not really in the mood for nine ball.

"I don't think so. Long day traveling."

She nods. She gives my office a glance, the Wide-eye, the racks of books and video discs, the diplomas, the framed campaign posters, and the covers of my three books, then makes a quick clicking noise with her tongue, dismissing the entire room and the life it represents as weird but okay, if that's what turns me on. "Well, thanks, Sal. Sorry about the smoke, so much, and using your bed. Everything got crazy, with Danno shipping out." Lecia twiddles her fingers in the air at me. "Latermost," she says, and then she's gone, her sneakers making the stairboards creak. Then it's just me, and the Wide-eye.

I stroke the sound cue, and BC tells me, "I know we're all hoping for the best possible solution. But it's a thorny way through this, and it's difficult to say for sure. I want to find the way through as much as all of you do."

I hit the reset button and listen to a line again. Then again. And just like that, I have a working title.

A thorny way, and difficult to say for sure.

Like the very best of BC, it's true and nonspecific and vaguely biblical and entirely without a purchase for any after-the-fact prosecutor, or historian for that matter. It says almost nothing. But the spat with Lecia has put me in a low mood, and I'll be lying if I don't tell you that I listen to the whole exchange seven or eight more times, taking a kind of shameful comfort in the low, silky, meaningless growl of the voice.

4

EAST COAST BULLET

The big joke out in L.A. is that the West Coast Bullet was the beta version for the East Coast Bullet, which was finished a few years later. But I've ridden the WCB plenty of times, and it's safe and well-lighted and the seats are fairly comfortable. The ECB is a little sharper and sleeker, granted, and it has the interactive television monitors, instead of the command-mode monitors they deal with in San Diego.

But both are smooth, almost flawless ways to move from one place to another at speeds in excess of four hundred miles an hour. And they're both backed by a switch-and-control network that can think situationally, as well as by rote. The guide network knows, for instance, that there is such a thing as a "terrorist," and that such individuals occasionally cause one or more cars of a train to be converted without warning into flame and particles of twisted debris.

In this case, theoretically, the brain would immediately begin piloting the two remaining strands of train independently, including dousing fires and contacting law enforcement. Fifteen bombs, same result: thirty independently sentient micro-ECBs. It's the oldest and the newest technologies on the planet, centipedes and cybernetics, fired down a superconductive magnetic track, with cocktails and microbrews available at a cruel twenty-three dollars a pop.

This Monday evening I'm on the ECB somewhere between Delaware and Virginia, and I've opted for the Full Complement, as the seat-pocket menu calls it: kung pao turkey, spring roll, fried bananas in rum, and an undersize split of chardonnay.

The Full Complement is not cheap. In fact, it is extremely expensive, even as Bullet meals go, but I'm trying my best to celebrate. In addition to preventing two young people from reaching technical consummation in my otherwise virginal bed this past weekend, I've worked out the big bones of the biography, and in my briefcase is an annotated chronology of BC's life and political career. That timeline breaks up the events of the life itself with an extensive set of digressions, those places where I'll eventually go into something like an argument for how I interpret that segment, that piece of BC.

And better than that, I managed in a single jag between Sunday 1:00 P.M. and Monday 2:30 A.M. to draft an eight-page single-spaced memo to myself that looks like it could be the early, beating, infant heart of an introduction. It's got all of the right cadences and the kind of phrasing in spots that seems gifted rather than earned. In other words, I'm still on the tail end of a powerfully righteous writing high, and that high has mostly counteracted the guilt I was feeling Friday night. BC won't love this biography, I'm telling myself. In fact, he'll be livid over it. But he'll read it, and today I'm still positive that somewhere inside the shuttered part of himself he'll be nodding as he does.

So I'm turned just a bit in my seat, to see the hard copy of those eight pages I've got propped up against the empty little wine bottle on the left end of my tray table. The other three people in my row are also eating and reading, or eating and watching their monitors; it's somewhere near six o'clock, the time when the ECB begins to look like a veal-pen with visual diversions.

I glance at the guy sitting next to me. He's a beefy, red-faced businessman, with an affected little swirl of watery yellow hair turning gray at the edges. It's lemon-meringue-colored hair. When he sat down he gave me a sort of dutiful once-over while stowing his carry-on, and every twenty minutes or so he stretches, looks around the compartment, has a quick glance at my legs, then goes back to his book.

Now, he's methodically pushing salad and reconstituted fish patty into his mouth as he works through the Metro section of *The New York Times*.

Englishman relocated to Manhattan to manage a British securities division, wife back in Surrey and a mistress over in the Bronx, off for a bit of fun in Florida on the company dime, the kind of guy who still calls women "birds." It's a guess, but he's showing an untanned band of skin on his ring finger, so I'm not far off. Maybe the chica's in Malibu, and maybe he brought his wife to N.Y. with him. But he's a lurker, for certain.

A middle-aged man in a black Lycra bodysuit is making his way up the aisle, hands clasping seat tops as he goes. I don't register him fully, except to note that he seems a pleasant sort, sandy-blond hair, a smile hovering somewhere at the corners of his lips.

I'm reaching for my wine bottle. I'm wishing I was feeling cocky enough to blow another twenty-three dollars, because in addition to the small buzz I'm getting, I like being a woman alone on a speeding train with a wineglass in her hand.

There is another half inch or so left in the toy bottle, and the image of my hand nearing the neck is the last thing I remember distinctly before my head smashes into the seat in front of me, almost hard enough to black out my vision, before my body follows, crushed against the seat until I feel myself about to vomit. The lights are out. I'm being thrown through the dark. My tray table snaps up under the impact of my rib cage, shattering the plates and wineglass. Flying glass and silverware and paper and the arm of the man next to me strike my neck and face. I hear and feel the train itself struggle and grind against the track.

And then in a sickening reverse, the entire world moves instantly backward and my head and shoulder slam into the partially padded seat behind me.

Now food and luggage are sliding down from the seat on top of me, because I am lying facedown where my feet were a second before, my legs and torso on top of a man and at least part of a woman. My eyes are stuck open and I can't breathe, because I know that in a fraction of a second a man somewhere in this car will stand up and reveal that he is not overweight, not genuinely cold enough to need a jacket. He will begin to pass judgment at the top of his lungs, and the words won't matter. We'll all watch helplessly as his fingers fiddle with something, a button, a switch. I wait for the bomb to explode, without breathing.

Emergency illumination powers up, small lamps at regular intervals, falling like moonlight on the spilled contents of the car. On the floor to my left is a fork and an untouched dinner roll. Both are lying on a sheet or two of my introduction.

A fully formed thought finally inches its way across the Wide-eye of my mind: *Where in the hell are the other pages?* I think. Then: *What in the hell is taking him so long?* But a full four or five seconds pass, and I feel the two bodies stirring beneath me. There is a sharp pain in my side, a broken rib at least. I'm just about to reach up to the seat for leverage when the pneumatic doors at the end of the car suddenly swish open, and I hear shouting and the sound of heavy boots on the carpeted floor. A woman somewhere on the other side of the car screams, a plaintive wail.

"Down! *Down!* Heads *down*!" It's a pair of soldiers running down the aisle. They're shouting the same thing in a tight, practiced cadence. "Down! *Down!* Heads *down*! Now! Now! *Heads down!*"

I manage to twist my neck so that I can see them as they half-run, half-shuffle past. They both have infrared wraparounds, and the laser pointers on their rifles are searching everywhere, red bulls-eyes like angry crimson insects crawling over floor, ceiling, walls—then once directly, crazily into my eye—before scuttling off. God knows what the soldiers are looking for as they sweep their eyes over us and mumble into their cheek mikes. Is there a profile for the reactions of a conspirator wedged somewhere in a carload of debris and busted humans?

I glance over at the man and woman beyond the Englishman, and the four or five scattered bodies I can see across the aisle. Two of the women are crying. One of the men is holding his shirt up to his nose to stop a nosebleed. Blood stains his forearms as well. All of us look sufficiently traumatized. But what does a layman know about Bullet guerrillas? Maybe a bloody fake-nosebleed shirt is the first thing they tell you to pack in terrorist school. Maybe the soldiers aren't really soldiers, maybe the real soldiers are dead in the rearmost car, mouths taped shut, and these boys want everybody down and quiet for their own convenience. Not only is nothing what it seems, but nothing even really seems like anything, really.

The air-conditioning is down, of course, along with the lights, and the air in the car is starting to feel used, like breathing your own exhalations back in. Crunched into my little corner, I can smell my own new sweaty fear.

But the soldiers don't find it, whatever or whoever it is they're looking for, and they move quickly toward the far exit. "Stay *down*!" one of them yells back at us, a young voice, maybe early twenties. "Keep your heads *down*!" I hear the doors at the far end of the car come apart and snap together in a burst of air. Then our car is quiet again, waiting again.

The man I'm partially covering, the Englishman, suddenly shifts and pulls himself violently upward, to a sitting position. I sit up a little too, crammed into the corner between the train wall and the seats behind and in front of us, but I keep my head well down. In the pale light, I can see that the Englishman is bleeding from a deep gash on his temple; he notices it, brings his hand up, brings it away wet with blood. I look for something he can use as a compress, a towel or a travel pillow, but there's nothing near us. So I pick up the four or five pages of my manuscript that I can find, and I fold them in quarters. I nudge him. "Here," I whisper, "put some pressure on that cut."

He looks at me wildly, not seeming to grasp what I mean.

"Pressure," I repeat. "To stop the bleeding."

"How bad is it?" he asks, quickly probing the side of his head with his fingers. Sure enough, an English accent. "I can't see. Is it a bad one, very bad?"

Making sure he sees what I'm doing, I take the folded wad of paper and I press it against his temple, lightly at first, while he winces, and then more firmly.

"You take it," I tell him, and he puts his own hand to work holding the wad in place. "Just keep it pressed tight. They're going to have help here in a minute or two." He still has a look like a cow that's been struck by an eighteen-wheeler and thrown into a ditch. Big nostrils flaring, wild eyes, flushed face.

"I need first aid," he announces to me all of a sudden.

"I know you do. You'll get some soon."

"Was it a bomb?" he asks me, struggling to right his leg beneath the seat.

"I don't think so."

"How do you know? How do you know it wasn't a bomb?"

"I don't know. Maybe it was. I don't know."

"Did those soldiers say anything?"

"I didn't hear," I say.

"Have you a phone on you? In your bag? I've got to call."

"Just hang on. It's not the time to start reaching for small electrical gadgets."

His bloodshot eyes flip fully open. The thick nostril wings flare again. "Well, for Christ's sake! What the good fuck are we supposed *to do?*"

"I don't *know,*" I whisper at him fiercely. "Keep our heads down. Keep quiet. Let them search the train. I don't know any more than you do." I pull back toward the wall, trying not to make it obvious that I wish I weren't pinned down next to him. I feel like slapping him, a quick, crisp stroke across his self-centered face, and I feel guilty for not feeling guilty about it.

A woman starts to scream—*really* scream, out of control—and my insides clench up again, everything tense, but again no explosion, just the high-pitched screaming from somewhere not too far ahead of me in the car. Just as suddenly, the screaming is cut off, muffled, as though by a hand wrapped across the woman's mouth. I don't want to poke my head up above the seat, but I twist around and press my eye to the wall of the train, looking past the shoulder of the man in front of me. That way, I can see an open inch or two all the way to the end of the cabin, six or seven rows, in the pale light from the emergency fixtures.

And there is the man in the black bodysuit I saw walking down the aisle earlier, lying on the floor, crumpled against the bulkhead, neck twisted almost at right angles so that the head is nearly upright, looking back at me.

The eyes are in shadows, but there's no mistaking the death mask. For some reason, the hair looks almost combed. I jerk my head back. Again I feel the quick brush of vomit against the back of my throat, but I make myself breathe deep. I'm trying to breathe and feel lucky. I'm not expecting a bomb anymore. If we were all going to Marlboro Country, we'd be riding the range by now.

"What is it?" the Englishman whispers, touching my shoulder with a blood-smeared knuckle. "What was the yelling about? Who is it? Can you see?"

"A guy's dead up there. I think a guy's dead. I could see him at the front of the car, through the crack over here."

"Dead," he whispers. "Was it the bomber? A suicide? Do you think it's him? I hope to Christ it's him, the fucking Mongoloid." He squeezes his eyes shut and clenches his teeth, wincing in pain. "I hope he blew his prehistoric Mongoloid fucking brains out."

My stomach begins to unsettle again, and I close my own eyes. I just feel I need some *quiet*. "No. No, it's not him. It's just—" I try lowering my voice even more. "Keep it down. He's just a guy who's dead. From the impact."

But he doesn't get it. His voice is still ugly and too loud. "How do you know it's not him? Why do you keep saying it wasn't a bomb, when you don't have any idea if it was or if it wasn't?"

I open my eyes to look over at him, but he's pulled the wad of my manuscript away from his wound and is staring at it, transfixed by his own crimson blood. I can read a set of phrases at the curled bottom of a page: *of seemingly contradictory appetites, for Elvis and Oxford, for long, genuinely athletic jogs that ended with a McDonald's Quarter Pounder and fried apple pie.*

"Look," I tell him, "I don't think there is any him. If there was a him, if it was a bomber, we wouldn't be here. That guy wasn't a *him*, okay? He was a *guy*, just on his way to the bathroom or something."

He seems unconvinced. Then, like he's remembered something he'd forgotten, he looks down at my curled legs. Now I'm wishing I'd opted for pants, instead of a skirt and bare legs and walking clogs. Although it gives me the creeps, it's not like I can put them away anywhere. They're my legs.

"Sorry," he says, changing his tune, eyes back up on mine, "didn't mean anything." He arches his thick yellow eyebrows at the cut on his head. "It's just a hell of a situation we suddenly find ourselves in."

"No offense," I say, in such a way as to indicate that I've taken offense.

And then, just like that, the lights come on, and the air-conditioning, and the seat-back monitors. It all comes up in a smooth hum, and the train feels alive around us again. Heads, including mine, pop up above the seat backs. I assume I have the same look as everyone else: hunted and hurt, but willing to believe that lights and the whisper of cool air are good things.

The Bullet's soft female voice begins to make a brief statement, accompanied by the taped image of a woman in a captain's uniform on the seat-back screens. She's in a stage-set version of the Bullet's engine. She smiles and gives it to us as straight as she's capable of giving it, which is to say bent: "Good evening. U.S.-Rapid's East Coast Bullet has been delayed. We're sorry for the inconvenience. Please stay seated, and a representative will explain the situation shortly. Again, we're sorry for the inconvenience. We are aware that you have other travel options, and we value your customer loyalty."

It's so absurd, such full-scale corporate repression, that I begin to laugh, and as I look around the car other people are laughing. It's a highly nervous response, but it feels like someone opened a tiny release valve for the tension in the car. And the fact that someone at U.S.-Rap cued up the corporate apology video seems to argue that it's their snafu.

If that's the case, later on maybe I'll Websearch a really carnivorous lawyer. But right now I'm praying that someone was asleep at a switch, that this was all stupid human error. Relief is creeping into all the faces I can see. Even the man with the bloody shirt has pulled it away from his nose in order to laugh. He looks, all of a sudden, like a fairly happy guy at a picnic with ketchup smeared all over his face.

Finally, the soldiers move through the car again, more casually this time, guns slung again across their backs, telling everyone that there is no bomber. "This was not a terrorist-related incident," they say. "It was a massive power outage," they say. "Not terrorist-related. Power went out. No bomber. Loss of power."

But it doesn't take an Einstein to figure that the explanation's bullshit. It's not as though the designers didn't plan for the Bullet to function safely in lieu of power. It's supposed to flywheel down to normal speed and eventually stop. No smashing force, no locking up of brakes.

The Bullet limps into Roanoke, where U.S.-Rap has set up a triage situation in the station. We detrain and right there in the massive arch of the tunnel are clumps of soldiers, rifles ready, and doctors and paramedics with stretchers and IV equipment, and Red Cross volunteers holding blankets fresh from their plastic wrap, and twenty or thirty journalists feeding their respective satellites live, and family of passengers, crawling over us as we come out, calling, screaming, crying for their particular loved ones.

Nobody's there for me, of course, but I get a blanket and a cup of coffee, and before long I'm on a stretcher, and a doctor is tracing the broken rib with a thumb.

While I'm lying there, the Englishman comes by, unnecessary blanket around his shoulders, head done up in a new white bandage. They've cleaned the blood from his head; his yellow-gray hair's even been slicked back with water or hair gel. I have the quick sense that he thinks he looks pretty dashing, like an action hero at the tail of the last reel. He gives me a knowing little smile, then he kneels down.

For a second I half-expect him to propose. But it's almost that bad.

"Look, I don't know your name," the Lurker says, "and you don't know mine yet. But it looks like we'll be here in Roanoke through tomorrow, once they've checked us through. And don't take this the wrong way, but I haven't got anybody here, and I'd just as soon not be alone." He waits a second, then pushes on. "If you don't mind, I'd like to suggest we stay together. Same hotel or whatnot."

"I mind," I tell him.

The doctor working on me gives us both a glance, says nothing.

"Right," the Englishman says after a beat. "Just as you like."

After he's gone, I just watch the scene, the flashing red lights and professional people of all kinds trying to get at us, the survivors, and I'm struck by the overwhelming sense of *priority,* of entitlement. Survivors of a tragedy. We're extremely high-profile victims, and in another way we're God's chosen, because we're alive, we've passed through the veil on our way back here to the living.

And I'm lying on the stretcher, thinking to myself that in his day BC would have been all *over* this. This was the kind of thing he did best. Big-beat tragedy. Healing the breach. "I didn't know the man in black," he'd have said, to us and to the nation, and our power would have become his, and vice versa. His voice would have been solemn, but steady. "But I've known a lot of men like him. Good men who worked hard and played by the rules but who found themselves in the wrong place at the wrong time." In his prime, BC wouldn't have left until he'd hugged every single damn one of us and listened to each of our stories, told our way and at our own speed. And it would have helped. We'd have all felt better. That's a real fact about him. All the sources agree on that.

By the time I get to bed that night, in a Sheraton Poshtown in downtown Roanoke paid for by U.S.-Rap, the story of the Bullet failure is everywhere, and it's bigger than I knew: the West Coast Bullet apparently experienced the same "massive turbulence," as they're now delicately calling it. Same effect at exactly the same time, a country apart. Two people dead out there, outside of Berkeley. There is a capsule bio and a photo of our lone casualty on this coast, our man in black. He worked for Erikkson as an ergonomic engineer, designing more-comfortable headsets for the rest of us. The anchorman doesn't say so explicitly, but it's clear the man in black worked hard and played by the rules.

I move the coverage from the wall to the ceiling as my eyes start to close. The "power failure" story has already been picked apart by three or four of the major news-and-content outlets. None of the big outlets is brave enough yet to put another story in its place, but several are passing on a rumor being bandied about by some Unix-stringer out of Seattle called DarkShadow News: that it wasn't mechanical failure at all but a more sophisticated version of the supercrunching technology the Chinese used to open the Hungarian NATO defenses a few years back. They're toying with us, DarkShadow says, to create a month of panic before a massive invasion of the West Coast.

Finally, a Defense Department official comes on to bat the quirky story down, with an air of undisguised disgust, and it stays down, except for some minor rehashing, as the premier outlets shorten and recast it as a pithy morality tale of What Happens When the Little Newsfolk Overreach.

And so, by the time I fall asleep in a room-for-hire somewhere in Virginia, I'm about eighty-five percent sure that it's the God's honest truth.

The Second Part:

THE TAKING OF THE LIBRARY

"In the wake of the conflicts in Nevada, Montana, and most recently in South Carolina, I would like to reaffirm our commitment to rooting out the threat of violence wherever it lies. Security can no longer mean simply a door locked against foreign armies, for we are the second American generation to feel true conflict within our borders.

"During the campaign I swore to the American people that I would not rest until our security was once again a national matter of course. But this will require discipline such as we have rarely exercised at home, accustomed as we are to the openness of a democratic society.

"As a nation we must be committed to our Union above all, repelling any attempt to weaken or threaten or subdivide it. As a nation, therefore, we must occasionally accept the small inconveniences associated with social safety.

"And finally, sadly, as a nation we must steel ourselves to look within the hearts of those around us, those working beside us, those using the appearance of normalcy to hide the telltale signs of violence. This will not be easy; it will be, in fact, one of the hardest things we have ever had to do: sow suspicion in our hearts as the last rampart of our freedom."

—Elizabeth Dole, Inaugural Speech, January 4, 2016

5

SOMETHING IS BROKEN

It's three days later. My cracked rib is wrapped with a lo-flex Lycra bandage and only hurts when I eat too much, which I have only twenty minutes ago finished doing. I'm sitting at my little cherry desk in the West-Admin Wing of the Library, looking out my own small bank of windows, wondering why three fat military helicopters have settled like pregnant wasps onto the hot green stretch of the South Lawn.

Two smaller copters come shooting in and settle a second later, drones aggressively covering the rear. All of a sudden it's like an air show out my window. Even through the thick bullet-proof glass I can hear the dwindling scream of the engines and the stropping of the propeller blades.

Before I can call my friend Abu at the security desk, the copters disgorge.

I press my nose to the window. Little soldiers climb out and skitter over the lawn. Ten, fifteen, twenty-five of them. They come sweeping up the rise toward the Library, guns held at their chests, growing larger as I watch. The men are all wearing short-sleeved green shirts and green berets, something I've never seen except on television. Usually the soldiers that show up at the Library are in Marine dress blues, with the white mortarboard hats and the crisp white gloves—impressive escorts, not ground troops.

These Green Berets are in a formation of some kind, but they're dogtrotting up the rise. Clearly they're not expecting the assembled secretaries, bureaucrats, and archivists inside to prepare to repel boarders.

I've seen presidents and dignitaries set down on the lawn before, and they always come with armed escorts and personal flaks, but never this many, never. The Library is a secure government installation, after all, with its own Secret Service detail. Abu's people always work hand in glove with the visiting security people.

But this is different, even to my eye, four stories up. This is a small invasion force. In addition to the wave of Green Berets, I can see a follow-up team of marines ferrying what looks like a series of communications components up the lawn toward the South Entrance. A sixth copter hovers momentarily into sight, slowly circling the compound, watching, aiming, waiting, reconnoitering, whatever it wants to do, really.

No VIP emerges from the lead copter. Just the rear guard, a couple of nondescript men in civvies, and five last marines, walking at a leisurely pace, poking in bushes and the stand of wisteria, turning in circles on the grass, looking for resistance.

What do you do when your building is being occupied by the good guys?

I do what any self-respecting civilian would do: stick just my head out my office door into the hall.

It turns out there are two other heads out there already, a mid-fiftyish archivist named Douglas Deaver and an older woman at the far end of the hall I've met only once. I can't even remember what she does, or why she's never in the Library. I remember that her name begins with an H, but that's all.

But before we can do more than gape at one another, a life-size Green Beret moves into the hall, weapon held casually across his chest. "I'm going to have to ask you to stay in your offices for a few minutes, folks," he says, loudly but not rudely. "Please stay off the viewphones and in your offices until we come and clear you individually." It's a takeover with at least some of the civilities intact.

"What the heck is this?" H says to him as he approaches her door.

"Just stay inside your office for a minute, please."

"I want to know what the heck's going on," H insists. She opens her door and begins to come out into the hall, a small, gray-haired woman in tailored blue slacks and a white silk blouse. "Whose security detail is this?"

"Back in your office, please."

"Why weren't we told in advance?"

"This is a security lockdown situation. Do you understand that? That gives us plenty of authority to secure the building. Step back inside. Now."

Another Beret comes around the corner, weapon tipped up, as the first one carefully thrusts H back into her office, despite her protests, then closes the door.

Douglas Deaver and I pull our heads back into our individual offices, saying nothing, and softly close our doors. We might as well have grown up in twentieth-century Stalinist Russia, for all the time it takes us to learn the Rules.

About ten minutes later, there's a crisp knock at the door. Before I can say anything, the door opens and a pair of Berets come into the office. They're big men, both of them. Up close, I realize that either one of them could probably poke a forefinger directly through my rib cage and into my lung without a problem. Both of them have massive hands and forearms, more like earthmoving equipment than human limbs.

"Sorry about the inconvenience," one of them says smoothly. "The building's in a national security lockdown. We'll need to ask for your cooperation for a bit."

"Certainly," I say. It's carefully said, that word, and I'm proud of it.

Immediately, they begin to move around my office in the way big men always move in the presence of a very small woman—slowly, easily, unthreatened, and with a consciousness of their own strength insinuating itself like a static electric charge.

This is the second time in three days I've been hoping my own armed forces won't shoot me. Something's broken in America. Or maybe this is just the way it feels when you're on the side that seems to be losing. We're not used to it in this country, and maybe that's our real Achilles' heel.

I make myself straighten out: these two may not be honor guards, but they're definitely Ours. Friendlies. GI Joes. Much safer, when all is said and done, than the soccer players at your average high-school dance. They have a job to do, that's all. One of the men is holding a metal-detecting wand, his rifle slung over his shoulder. The second takes up an observer stance just inside the door.

"You're Sal Hayden," the one with the wand says, looking at a small card he's taken from his khakis.

"Right."

"You're the biographer."

It would have been hard for him to say anything more shocking. I can't believe that he recognizes my name, or knows my books, but it's harder to believe that I'm one of the names on the short list in his uniform pocket. I nod.

"Any weapons or explosives or other contraband to declare before we conduct a routine security search, either on your person or in this office?"

"Nope."

"Okay, then. Quick check," the wand handler says. He takes a step toward me, big black boots silent on the carpet. He's looking at my clothing, sleeveless blouse and a pair of brown cotton walking shorts. I can only assume he's checking for suspicious bulges.

I raise my arms, wincing from the pain in my ribs, and he passes the wand up and over me. As he passes it over my shoulders and then back down along my back, I feel it brush my butt and I crane my head around, but it seems to have been an accident. At least the Beret at the door has a straight face when I turn back.

The wand handler nods to his partner. "You take her down," he says. "I'll finish the lookie-checkie up here." He turns back to me. "You're good to go. The sergeant here will escort you to your meetings."

"What meetings?" I ask, looking up at one, then the other. They are each easily a foot taller than I am.

"You have a couple of meetings," the sergeant says matter-of-factly. He's looking at some switch on the side of his rifle. "That's not our duty split. We just bring you."

"Don't take this the wrong way or anything," I say, leaning against my desk and holding a hand up, as though to stop and put everything in perspective, "but do you guys have any identification on you?"

They look at each other again, and now they just go ahead and smile. Not nasty smiles, but definitely the smiles of men with guns and the authority to use them who are being asked if they have any identification.

And then suddenly I'm smiling nervously too. Isn't that what's supposed to happen when you're kidnapped, you start trying to be one of the gang? A name floats up from my undergraduate twentieth-century culture survey: *Symbionese Liberation Army*. But for the life of me, I can't remember the name of the debutante they made off with. And suddenly it seems like it matters a lot.

* * *

The sergeant seems to know where he's going. He escorts me through two or three corridor switchbacks, finally bringing us out to the Gallery, a large, graceful, domed space open to all six floors of the Library complex. Four stories below us, running in a sinuous pattern across the floor of the lobby, is a scaled-down model of Maryland's Wye River, recessed into the marble there. It's an elegant hybrid of sculpture and kinetic, interactive art.

Water tinted a delicate blue actually flows through the precisely etched channels and tributaries. Children can dip their hands, even trace underwater topography with their fingertips. A small scale model of a series of buildings rises up at one particular bend of the river—the Wye River Complex, where BC and several Middle Eastern leaders hammered out a follow-up to the Oslo Peace Accords over a brutal nine days in 1998. Children can peek in those little windows, while a recording tells them about the Wye River Accord, after which a snatch of BC's signing speech rolls softly through the hush. Every once in a great while, the real BC will get to feeling low and old and unloved, and he'll go down and shake hands with visitors at the water's edge. It's a damn nice thing to see.

It was a gift from the state of Israel, this unassuming indoor river, and it's the prettiest part of the Library, to me at least. To my knowledge, no one else anywhere has ever thought to pair a Jeffersonian rotunda above with a winding river below, but it's absolutely magical. Most days, sunlight filters over the scene from several spectacular angles. From my floor, the view down always has a bracing effect, like looking down on the spreading capillaries of the Mississippi from one of the space stations. The sergeant says nothing as we walk. Obviously conversation isn't his duty split.

We walk halfway around the open Gallery and enter the East Wing, then make our way past actual open stacks of books—a working library within the Library that BC began with the hundreds of thousands of books he was given while in office, both the thirteen years as governor and the eight as president, and to which he has added lavishly every year since. BC has always insisted that the Library be technologically cutting edge, and paperless for the most part, but he makes a big, fat, self-indulgent exception for books. When the Library opened, he issued library cards personally to one thousand Little Rock first-graders.

For a second I feel a twinge of sadness, because my first biography is shelved somewhere in this room, as are my two previous studies of twentieth-century politics and marketing, but the book I'm writing now—the most important book I'll ever write, maybe—will never wind up here. BC will read a copy, maybe even reread it, and he'll remember certain sections almost verbatim. But no copy will be shelved here. I know: of his nine biographies, only two are officially available from the Library's library. He doesn't like to preserve unflattering portraits.

As we walk along, I suddenly turn to the sergeant. It can't hurt to ask what I'm wondering. "Are your people working with Abu's people here? Our security?"

"No," he says.

"Is the President coming to visit? Is that what this is all about?"

"No," he says.

We pass the last public facility on this floor, a series of high-access terminals that allow the user to flit through endless film and tape clips. BC remains the most photographed, the most fully documented president in history. The Republicans ran something like fifty-eight separate investigations of his administration during his years in office; the Office of the Independent Counsel managed to match that total output on its own. BC's particular DNA structure can be modeled and viewed.

The news coverage generated by those investigations alone represents an exponential increase in data. He was a pretty man with a celebrity's hunger for the lens; everyone wanted to photograph him, but no more than he wanted to be photographed. All a way of saying that there is more of BC in the world's archives than he or anyone in history could have even imagined. By contrast, we have the equivalent of a few snapshots and a lone, pathetic home movie of JFK.

The tech people did some interesting things with all that documentation: much of the film has been perspectivally enhanced, three-sixtied, so you can interact with BC as he works a room at a White House coffee, and there you can buttonhole him about a range of issues, from the deficit to the Razorbacks. And just as he's been a stickler for representing the "troubles" in the physical library, BC has insisted that the cyber-library deal at least glancingly with them as well. Among other options, you can attend Judiciary Committee hearings and hear them shout along party lines for impeachment. You can sit on a little velvet couch in the Residence on the evening a strange young man crashed a plane into the White House.

But BC, as far as I know, rarely if ever visits the on-line version of his life. I can't say I blame him. There would have to be something vacant and queasy about meeting up with a previous version of yourself, one who couldn't begin to understand his own disastrously limited perspective.

It's clear to me now that we're headed to BC's private office. He has a more public working space in my wing that everyone on staff refers to as "the Oval," but back at the tail end of the East Wing he has a quieter, more personal study. I've never seen it. All of our dealings—release negotiations, interviews, chats, birthday parties—these have all taken place in the Oval, the public space. He wasn't kidding when he gave me the initial authorization to look into the archives; he was, and he remains today, scared to death of a scandal.

We finally reach a secure set of double doors. Ordinarily, these unmarked doors are locked but unguarded. Today, a marine stands outside the door as we approach. The sergeant says nothing, but gives the marine on guard duty a curt little nod. The guard nods back. He reaches into the pocket of his khakis, pulls out a key, and unlocks the double doors, then holds the right side open. Not a word from him the whole time.

But he looks at me as I go by, not lewdly, but with a certain skeptical curiosity, as though I were a bearded woman in a freak show he suspected of being a fake.

We go through the door held open for us, and we're in a small, featureless, carpeted hallway about thirty feet long. Actually, there is one feature: another marine standing guard at another, smaller door at the hallway's end.

We walk the thirty feet and stand in front of him. This marine is dressed in impeccable dress blues for some reason, trouser creases you could shave your legs with, polished brass buttons catching even the indirect light. His uniform jacket is starched and stiff. His mortarboard hat is overwhelming, jutting out over his face.

This one seems somehow to have been selected for this particular task. He's tall and straight, and his face looks like it was turned out of the same marble they used for the lobby floor. This one has no rifle like the others, only the long regulation sword in a scabbard by his side. He's got his white-gloved hands clasped behind his back. He looks at us. Even the sergeant seems a little disconcerted. He says simply, "Sal Hayden. She's the biographer."

The perfect dress marine looks down at me solemnly, seems to consider the implications, the concept of biographer itself.

There's a little pause, so I say, "Hi."

6

IN THE HIDEY-HOLE

The elegant marine knocks softly on the inner door. He waits silently for a moment, then knocks again, a bit more loudly. When there is no response, he opens the small door for me with one gloved hand and half-waves me in with the other. But as I'm about to enter the dim room, BC's voice suddenly comes up in a hoarse roar from somewhere inside. "You will stay the *fuck* out of my office, do you understand me," he's sputtering, trying to get it all out, "you candy-assed rat-fucking cocksucking *son of a bitch*! Just stay the *fuck out*!"

I freeze with my weight half shifted forward.

"The *fuck* out!" BC yells into the tight silence.

"Mr. President," the marine begins. His voice is respectful, at-attention.

I hear BC moving around somewhere in the office, desk chair complaining as he reaches for something. "You don't think I got a pistol in this desk, and a bullet with your shit-for-brains *whore-baby* name on it"—BC coughs once, then again, and his voice loses some of its force—"then you got less brains than I thought. You will stay the fuck out of this office! I mean it. The *fuck out*!"

So BC is locked down too. It never occurred to me that he wouldn't be at least part of the driving force behind all of this, somehow, in the loop if not directing it. The reassurance I felt when I realized we were headed here fades and disappears altogether. BC's voice, for all of its rage, sounds confused and off-base, threatened, even frightened.

The marine catches my eye and shakes his head softly, reassuringly. I take this to mean that BC does not have a pistol, and that as a result neither of us will be taking a bullet in our candy-asses. I realize that all of a sudden I'm looking to this strange marine for protection from BC, and in the next second I remember the elusive name: *Patty Hearst.*

"Sal Hayden is here to see you, sir," the marine says solicitously.

There's a pause, and then BC's voice repeats my name. "Sal?" he inquires, searchingly. "You out there, Sal?"

The marine looks at me, nods encouragement.

"Right here, Mr. President," I call in.

There's another longer pause. Beneath the marine's stiff white hat, his face is calculating as he listens, thoughtful and a little bit cunning. Then I get it: whoever is directing this lockdown knew that locking down an ex-president of the United States, especially one well past a hundred and conditioned by more than sixty years of privileged status, would be the most ticklish detail.

And so they've made his guard, his particular jailer, a dress marine of the sort that used to salute him as he sauntered out of Air Force One, one of the peacock honor guards he had in attendance when he could move the entire Sixth Fleet with a sharp flick of his thumb. One of his long-ago imperial guards.

"Shall I send her in, Mr. President?" the marine asks. "You asked to see her earlier." The pause goes on, and the marine gives another courteous nudge. "We brought her to you as quickly as we could, sir."

"Send her in," BC says suddenly. "And you stay the hell out there, yourself."

"Of course, Mr. President," the marine answers. He gives me a nod, and I walk past him into the dimly lit room. It's only then, with the door closing softly behind me, that I realize the dress marine never actually said a word to me. Talking to me doesn't seem to be anybody's duty split.

Abu told me not long after I came to Little Rock that BC calls this shuttered room his hidey-hole. He once had a basement space in the old Executive Office Building across from the White House that went by the same name; in the years before the White House, he had a bolt-hole in the Capitol Building in Little Rock, a close, windowless nook protected by state troopers and stocked with liquor and cigars and anything else that might sway a last-minute vote on chicken sewage or highway tariffs, a place to stroke egos and to plot revenge when egos failed to stay stroked. The room is here in the Library now because BC is here—the hidey-hole moves with him like a diving bell, wherever in political waters he wanders.

The hidey-hole is not exactly private. Over the years, it's seen a fairly broad cross-section of the country's rich and powerful. But if not private it has always been the killing field for publicity. Anything that happens here, even in front of witnesses, can never be told, or if told can never be proven. It looks a lot like you'd expect, or at least like you'd expect if you'd spent a third of your life studying the man's life and minor idiosyncrasies. No windows, no ingress for a lens of any kind. Long leather couches built for a tall man; deep but supportive reading chairs. At least one of these recliners is top-shelf geriatric design: it can bring the occupant slowly to an upright or sitting position, and in times of greater need, concealed wheels, onboard control system, and fingertip mouse allow it to double as an extremely fast and maneuverable wheelchair.

The chair, like BC's old presidential limousine, seems designed to thwart a sudden kidnapping attempt. But its place in the far corner couldn't say any more clearly that BC holds it in disdain.

Tall, thin bookshelf-refrigerator, stocked, I'm certain, with all of his various weaknesses—Dr. Pepper, Little Debbie cakes and Brazilian flan pies, and multiple tubs of mango ice cream. A stand-up bar. A single massive oak desk—the same desk, by the looks of it, that BC worked out of at Camp David during the boom-boom days of his presidency. On the coffee table a big bowl of Fritos corn chips, the snack of choice during the War Room days of the 1992 campaign. Fritos are no longer made in the U.S., having been discontinued about thirty years ago. These Fritos are flown in from Argentina, each and every corn chip.

And over all the walls, covering almost every inch like big square barnacles, are photographs, photographs of BC with Everyone. From where I'm standing as I come into the room I can see a pastiche of the late-twentieth-century elite: John F. Kennedy, Desmond Tutu, Helmut Kohl, Steven Spielberg, Mother Teresa, Barbra Streisand, Pope John Paul II, Tony Blair, Ronald Reagan, Margaret Thatcher, and for no apparent reason an obscure pop transvestite named Boy George. BC has his arm draped gamely around Boy, and in the wilting flash both look helplessly stoned. The hidey-hole is a kind of hunting lodge, but the trophies are all human and discreetly flush to the wall.

Beside the impressive oak desk sits a nice straight chair for visitors. BC is seated in that chair, his back to me, as though he's here in the hidey-hole visiting his normal self, currently invisible and seated in the big chair behind the desk. He has his head in his hands, shoulders slightly slumped. His silver hair—limited now to a low fringe running from temple, around the back of the head, to temple—looks unkempt, even wild, for the first time I can remember.

He seems to sense the unreality of the moment, and he gives a hoarse little laugh and pulls a silk handkerchief from his jacket pocket, blows his large nose, and speaks. His voice is thick with mucus and bitterness.

"Invasion of the cocksuckers," he says distinctly, back still to me, thrusting the flimsy handkerchief angrily back into the pocket. There's a long, pregnant pause. "Goddamn rejects from Bridge over the River Cocksucker," he adds. "Just come whistling in here and take over the goddamn building."

"Mr. President," I say, because I have absolutely no idea what to say to that. It's the first time I've ever heard BC swear. He's always been the courtly Southern Baptist around me, and now he's clearly well into a kind of modified Tourette's response to the events of the afternoon. "What's going on?"

His voice is hesitant. "What's that, Sal?"

Even though he can't see it, I gesture a little wildly with my hands, to everything around me. "What's—you know—what's *happening* here today? The soldiers and all the choppers. Marines, Green Berets. A guy with a gun just walked me over here."

He doesn't turn in his chair, but he addresses me after a second: "It's that fuckin' Domestic Defense Initiative. Their position is that the Library is a semipublic installation and they can damn well militarize it if they damn well see fit. I told you when that thing passed it was trouble. You didn't believe me. But I knew it then. Goddamn military authority, it's like kudzu. That's what's kept the U.S. the strongest democracy in the world for so long, is *civilian* control.

"That's what I told the Joint Chiefs when I met 'em in 1992. I said, 'Now, look, gentlemen. You may not like me, and you may even think I dodged the draft—which I *did not do*—but, goddammit, the Constitution makes me your boss from this day forward and I'm going to demand your respect for my office. I'll try every single day to earn that respect too, but I insist you show it to the office.' And now we got the God-blessed DDI, and any tin general can show up and tell me not to leave my own goddamn office and not to speak on my own goddamn phone."

I wait for more, but nothing more comes. "But why are they here in the first place? Is there some kind of security threat or bomb threat or something? Why us? I mean, we're a library."

Again, BC muses for a minute. He shuffles his shiny shoes over the floor aimlessly, back and forth. He's not tracking. "You ever read *Gulliver's Travels,* Sal? Jonathan Swift? I know it isn't your area, but you ever pick that up?"

He hasn't invited me any farther into the room, so I stand there in the gloom. The room is incredibly quiet. I have to suspect it's elaborately soundproofed. "Sure, of course. I read it in graduate school, at one point." I wait, then say, "I didn't know it was going to be on the test."

No laugh. BC goes on almost as though he hasn't heard me, his soft accent slightly warped by the quietness of his voice: "It's a real good book. Lot about life there. Lot of wisdom. I been thinking about it today in particular."

Another long pause, before I realize I've missed my cue again. I'm about to ask him what his point is when he gets to it.

"At one moment," BC says, "Gulliver gets to one place or another—I can't remember now which of the islands or societies it is where he finds them—but he finds this place where there's a race of people called the *Struldbruggs*. And they're just like everybody else there except they never die, see, these Struldbruggs, they're immortal. First thing he finds that out, Gulliver gets all excited, he thinks he's found the Fountain of Youth or something. But as he gets a good look at these very old, old, *old* people, he finds out the truth is these people never die but they keep aging all the while. All the while, every day. They're hideous to look at, all shriveled up and frail and spotted and stinking. But they never die."

He runs a hand slowly over the hairless dome of his head. He fingers a spot absently, tentatively, a holdover from his balding period, when he had hair to inventory. He goes on, his voice no longer bitter, just lost. "And Gulliver finds that nobody envies them. They're pitied, and avoided by all the normal people. Struldbrugg becomes a kind of a swear word."

As though remembering his manners, he twists a bit in his chair and cranes his neck so he can see me. I'm struck, as I occasionally am, by the absolute vastness of his nose. It was always bulbous, the only thing saving his face from true glamour and rendering him ultimately acceptable to the masses. But the nose never stops growing, cradle to grave, and now BC's is vast enough to throw its own small gravitational field, the Irish potato nose given time and space in an otherwise shrinking face to reach its fattest flower. "You want something to drink, Sal?"

I shake my head. "No, I'm fine."

"There's soda or beer or wine, scotch, whatever floats your boat. You hungry? There's ice cream. I got some good Swiss chocolates in the fridge. Oh, and I got some empanadas. You can nuke those. Take a minute."

"No thank you, Mr. President."

He motions me over to the desk, with a weary air. "Well, then, come on over and sit down. We got some things to talk over."

I come over to the desk area, expecting him to haul himself out of the small visitor's chair and walk around behind the desk. He doesn't move. His eyes look a little rheumy today, and they're fixed on a spot somewhere near the baseboard behind the desk. Without looking up, he indicates his normal chair behind the desk with his finger. "Go ahead and have a seat there. Try it on for size."

He chuckles slightly, almost in spite of himself, at my hesitation. I can tell it's a little drama he's run through thousands of times before and never fails to enjoy, allowing visitors and supplicants and children, the powerless, to assume the throne. I sit down behind the desk, settle into the chair.

"How's that strike you?" he asks, head up now, a little real eagerness in his face. He so clearly wants me to love it, this tired old man who no longer has access to elections to tell him what he needs to know about himself.

"Not too shabby," I say, patting the arms, trying my best to look like I'm really relishing the opportunity. "This is a nice room to get away from it all."

"Bet it is," BC says, absently stroking the arms of his own chair.

We sit quietly for a moment, and then he rubs his eyes and begins. "First thing is, I want to ask you how far you are with the biography, what you got."

I consider reusing the line about not knowing there was going to be a test, but then I don't. He didn't get it the first time around. "What have I got finished, you mean, or what have I got that I'm working with?"

"Working with. Finished. Raw materials. Everything."

"Well, I was going over that this past weekend. The database is finished."

His eyebrows shoot up. "Finished?"

"Yup. I've got all the interviews done. I've boxed out what of the Library archive documents I need and don't need. I'm sure I don't need to tell you this, but there's a landfill worth of stuff I had to pick through. The don't-need boxes are already going back to storage today. I've got an outline."

I hesitate in telling him about the draft introduction, but he's clearly still waiting for something and the urge to seem like an efficient worker gets the better of me. Even though I'm my own boss, I care what he thinks. "And I wrote a first draft of the introduction this last time I was home. So if you look at it that way, I'm done with the preliminary stuff, and I'm starting on the finished stuff." I even exaggerate a little. "I'm maybe twenty pages into it, at this point," I finish.

"That's better than I expected. That's fantastic news, Sal." He gives me a smile that's almost sunny. "I know you writers are temperamental and all, and I certainly wouldn't want to throw a jinx on the project, but I'd be honored, really honored, if I could take a peek at those pages."

"My draft?"

"I know it'd be in a rough form, but you been here painting my picture now for over four years. That's a president's term in office. My administration stopped three different conflicts around the world in the first four years, and that ain't countin' what we did in Ireland. And I'm dying to sneak a look."

He smiles again, and—call it charisma or whatever you want—I start to tell him I'll think about it.

He sees the little hesitation, and he pushes a little, puts a hand on his chest. "I'm a *snoop*. Guilty as charged. And nobody knows that curiosity killed the cat better than this old man." He smiles again. "But I'd get such a kick out of it."

Since I came to Little Rock, BC has done his best to make nice, which makes sense; he feels that my biography will be the final word, the definitive work, and he wants it to recast him in a more flattering light. He's convinced that any biographer given total access to everything—even things not one hundred percent declassified five decades later—can't help but write a more flattering story. So there's always been that low-level campaign. But this is the first time he's ever wanted something specific from me, wanted it enough to wheedle and charm. And he's really good at it. He's still grinning guiltily.

But I don't have to think about it, and I say what I have to before it can go any further. "I'm sorry, Mr. President. I couldn't possibly do that. Not at this stage. Of course, the idea is for you to have a look at an entire early draft. We've always agreed on that. But I couldn't show you this stuff. It would affect the later stuff."

"Won't say one single word. Just hand it back and go about my business until you got the draft together. Absolute word of honor."

And then, instinctively, I know which button to push. "It just—I don't know. It almost feels unethical, somehow. I don't think it would be, but it almost feels that way. Letting the subject work into the process."

My aunt Mary used to hit her tomcat with a squirt bottle when he got near her plants, and the tom wouldn't run when he was hit—he'd draw himself up, slick his ears back, give her a struck look, and walk stiffly away. That's the way BC takes my answer, as though he's affronted at my bad manners but too polite and saddened ultimately to test them again. He sits straight up and way, way back in his chair, laces his fingers over his small belly.

"I understand you, Sal. And I'm sorry to have suggested something that seems wrong to you. I'm feeling old today. I've been sitting here thinking that I could be gone long before you're done. And I value your work, that's why you're here in the Library. I value it highly. And I just wanted to get a glimpse at what I look like through your eyes, through the lens of your talent, your craft. That's all."

Now I despise myself. "You don't have to apologize. It's just—you know, it's just a little early. But there's no need for anybody to say they're sorry."

"Too late." The ghost of a little boy's smile. "I just finished doing it."

"Well, then, I can't accept it, because it's unnecessary."

"Well, I won't retract it, because it's important to me that you know I've appreciated everything you've done here. Really appreciated it, Sal."

I'm putting together another little bit of repartee when I realize BC is speaking in the past tense. He must see the perplexity flit across my face, because all of a sudden he just answers everything at once.

I'm watching his mouth while he says it. He has deeply embedded wrinkles extending downward from either corner of his mouth, and it's like watching the oversimple movement of a ventriloquist's dummy. "The army wants you, Sal. They brought the paperwork this morning for me to have a look at; I don't know why they gave me that much consideration in the matter—I'm not a parent or anything—but they did.

"Sorry to drop it out there like that, but there's really no way to lead into it softly. It's a travesty, and I've been raging mad about it all day. I don't completely understand it myself, at this point, but they've come here to sign you up. They want some help from me too, I guess. Seems like I'm not completely irrelevant just yet. But they want to draft you into the war effort. Not the army, really, but the National Security Council. That's their purpose here.

"Now, why that had to involve a goddamn siege of my library, I don't know. But that NSC mind-set is squirrelly. I remember when I started working with that group, they were always talking about *totalizing the situation*. Whatever it is, they want a ring around it, and a ring around the ring, and a goddamn ring around that."

I can't speak.

BC keeps talking. I can tell a weight's been lifted from him now. He's more engaged, less burdened. He lifts both his legs, stretching, and I hear the body-walker shifting and clicking beneath his clothes, accounting for his desire. The organizational chip realizes BC wants to stretch the legs, and it begins to help, mid-stretch; the legs suddenly rise up surely into place, flexing, and then reverse.

"My sense is the war's going a lot worse than we knew. A lot worse. And they got full conscription authority now, all branches of the military and Justice too. Full. No age restrictions, no 4F even. They can chopper paraplegics out to Kazakhstan if they want. They can take anybody they want. I put in a call to my lawyer—and I'm sure they monitored that damn call, even though this system here's supposed to be knit-crypted—but Warren says they got the right."

I still can't speak.

"I bet you're wondering why you. That was my question exactly. Now, don't ask me why, but they say they need someone with your historical background, and someone with knowledge of NATO expansion, stuff like that. My guess is they got some propaganda project in mind, some kind of revisionist history work. I don't know. But we got a meeting with them in about an hour."

He fixes me now with his gaze. He wants me to know that he understands the gravity of my situation, that I have his attention. "I asked before about the biography database. Where is all that now; is that here?"

I feel like I'm recovering from being punched in the stomach. I can take in only little sips of air. "Everything's in my office."

"That's good. I was worried you might have half up in Vermont, and then we'd probably lose it to the NSC people. No doubt they been up there by now, knowing those ass-bitin' NSC groupers." The profanity just pours out of him, with not a particle of his normal chivalry impeding it. It's the only thing he has anymore, the only power left anywhere in the world to him. "But I'll be goddamned if those pricks walk away with that project. As of today, I'm going to have Abu seal your office, and reclassify it with the level-nine stuff. No access to anyone ever, without my express written permission."

He glances at his telemonitor, as though there's a call he wants to make immediately, then thinks better of it. He looks back to me. "If it's all right with you, Sal, I'll go ahead and have your Wide-eye's data cache moved right into the bomb-proof. That's two stories below ground. Nothing can get to it there, water, shock. You could hit this building with a bomb twice as big as Timothy McVeigh used and it'd clear out most of the interior of the Library, but you'd still have the bomb-proof. You could just rebuild the Library right around it."

He's clearly thought through in minute detail what he wants to happen to my work. He'd never admit it, but the book is the priority right now.

BC picks up my thought, catches himself. He nods slowly and compresses his lips in the worried, determined expression I've seen in a thousand speeches and news clips. In the old days, it conveyed the sense that he understood the dangers and the ramifications and, even recognizing those dangers, he was assuming the mantle of responsibility. But now, without the bulk of his hair, and with his facial structure more or less fallen in, the expression becomes one of petulant stubbornness. Now it's almost a Popeye look, minus spinach.

"Now, I don't want you to worry. It's not like you don't have friends. I'm old, and I may not have my own teeth anymore, but they're going to find out that I'm not helpless. Once we find out exactly what they got in mind, I'm going to make my number-one mission in life getting you permanently assigned to the Library. They can draft you, they got that right, but I know more than a few people with four stars, and if I have anything to say about it, we'll get you transferred here in a month or two, and you can spend your hitch finishing the book. How's that sound?"

And then he does something that he's never done before. He leans around the desk, and he takes my hand, and he holds it in his. His hands are large but bony, and they look oversized on his long, thin wrists. They're big, cold, old-man hands. The reworked joints allow the fingers to coil smoothly over mine. He squeezes the hand ever so slightly, and I imagine the zombie muscle groups coaxed genetically back to life in his back and arms.

"Sure," I say, and that's all I say. Because it's all too absurd to be believed, and there must be some error. A platoon of soldiers come to Little Rock to draft me into service. I'm thirty-nine. I have two cracked ribs. I'm an *academic*. There is nothing I can do that any nineteen-year-old with a gun or a computer or a dispersion helicopter can't do better, lots better.

But there's something else, something worse. There's a strange, undeniably paranoid feeling moving through the room and over me like the first wet fingers of a fog bank, a feeling that all of BC's old friends and allies and political advisers experienced at one point or another. The records and the interviews describe it happening in remarkably similar ways again and again and again, like a mummy's curse. I had thought, what with BC being one hundred and nine years old and with his hands completely off all the levers of power, the curse was long broken. But here it is again, and it's somehow found me, a biographer. A nothing.

And the curse is this: BC's acts are his, but his consequences are yours.

He doesn't know how to tell you, but his enemies are desperate and if they can't get to him they'll take whatever and whoever's close to him. He can't speak or meet with you anymore, but he wants you to know that a special prosecutor will be in touch with you and that you'll be fine as long as you keep the faith. He fondles an intern in the White House, and suddenly you're losing your job as Speaker of the House. He takes two terms, and the voters repudiate you, his loyal, his principled and long-suffering vice-president. You're going to spend several years in a medium-security federal prison, part of that time in leg shackles, and while BC can't explicitly indicate his desire to issue you a pardon should he be granted a second term, he will not explicitly indicate that he doesn't plan to do so, leaving a kind of undernourished hope to languish out there in the media. He has needed you, but suddenly events dictate that he need you no more.

He promises with all of his heart that it won't be for long, but he's staying right where he is, and you're going away somewhere not very nice at all.

7

EVEN A GRASSHOPPER

I'm in the White House Map Room, standing next to a table of bagels and finger sandwiches and a small mound of tan things that look suspiciously like apple fritters. It's 1995. On the other side of me a table holds several tureens of brewed coffee; additionally, a small man in a white coat stands beside a cappuccino maker. He is the official *baristo* of this White House coffee.

I'd love to pump him for some inside information—staff are always the shock troops of history—but his buttonhole is empty, indicating that he's noninteractive. All of the interactive avatars wear flowers, boutonnieres for the men, corsages for the women. It's a pleasant form of coding that the techies worked out, making the event much more colorful and human than it must have seemed to the original attendees, all of whom are dead now, I would imagine, except BC.

I'm here because I've got forty minutes to kill before my next meeting with people whose identities no one is allowed to share with me, and for those forty minutes I'm not allowed to leave my office in the Library. A guy with a beret, hairy thumbs, and a gun is standing in the corridor to make sure I understand these things.

And, although I've written about them and heard BC gab in interviews about them and how unfairly they were eventually characterized by the press, I've never been to a Coffee.

The way it works is this: if I stand absolutely still, I get something close to a living documentary. The old White House Communications Agency, the people BC counted on to archive his presidency, dutifully produced tapes of these coffees, and they're medium-quality, workmanlike, almost impenetrably dull for the average viewer. The three-sixtied footage moves past and around me, people mingle, and I see and hear pretty much what Congressional investigators saw when they eventually subpoenaed and watched the old-school videotapes, with missing parts of walls and ceiling and feet added by the techies.

But if I move, things get increasingly fictional. Movement triggers an infinitude of potential scripts. Once I stop moving, the simulation reverts to showing me more or less straight footage—who was actually here, where they actually moved, what they actually said. This is every kid's favorite part of the Library tour. They'll spend hours in the log-in booths, chatting up late-twentieth-century tycoons and climbers, goofing on the humorless avatars.

I can talk to anyone with a flower, and they'll answer me. We can converse all day if I like. They won't approach me, though. The simulation puts the power almost entirely in the viewer's hands, probably another reason I've chosen to kill my time here. Since BC told me what he told me, I've been fighting a kind of helpless flailing anger, with my life for always taking the shortcut to chaos, with the soldiers who are suddenly telling me what to do, and with BC himself for somehow being at the heart of it all. I can't prove it, but I can feel it.

So I'm in the Map Room waiting for BC, like all the rest. I look around the Map Room. It's a very well-heeled crowd, very. Crisp blue Italian suits for the men, bright red and pink Year of the Woman outfits for the women. Top-shelf dental work. Most of these people ponied up between twenty-five and one hundred thousand dollars to the Democratic National Committee either before or after the event, though never during, a distinction utterly without a difference. The coffees were shameless money shucks, but BC has managed to convince himself over the long years that they were friendly gatherings or policy gabfests. He okayed these simulations because he was deeply convinced that anyone who actually attended one would see their essential innocence.

He's stone wrong. These prosperous people, even as amalgamated pixels flowing across a wraparound screen, still manage to reek of *quid pro quo*.

Suddenly BC enters the room, like a lion taking the veldt. He comes in with a clear swagger, chin out, a big man with a big ego moving into a roomful of people who want him enough to pay twice a professor's yearly salary to spend half an hour sipping coffee with him. All eyes in the room turn his way. The two men next to me, who have been talking football, drop all pretense of interest in each other and stand silently, facing BC, waiting their turn.

I don't have to wait. I walk straight forward, not bothering to excuse myself. The various avatars in my way see me coming at the last second, and each goes out of focus, clearing a path. BC is talking with a small but portly man who looks like he made his million bucks as a New Southern Baptist minister. As I near, the volume of their discussion increases: they're talking about school uniforms, clearly one of the world's more pressing topics. But this is in the run-up to the 1996 elections, and BC is scoring big with microconservative proposals like school uniforms and ratings for television shows.

I tap the preacher on the shoulder and he turns, eyebrows up. "Beat it, pulpit boy," I mumble to my screen.

The televangelist hesitates, then smiles. "Of course," he finishes, giving BC a final nod before gliding away. Of all possible responses, it's probably the most subtly cutting, and I can't help but feel that even this avatar, this set of variations on a real image, has kicked my butt today. If there's one rule for this simulation, it's that the characters stay unfailingly on message. They keep their tempers.

I face BC. He's taller than I expected somehow. In 1995, he's imposing. He waits for me to speak.

"Mr. President," I say. "I'm Sal Really Pissed-Off Hayden."

BC takes my hand, fixes me with his gaze. He's affable, charming, clearly in his element—easygoing conversation that segues briefly and occasionally into speculative policy discussion. "I used to play golf with a guy named Jimmy Hayden down in Little Rock," he remarks. Probably there are sound links to most any name a viewer could come up with, but the techies have remained faithful to BC's infamous ability to build kinship quickly. "I used to lose to him too."

"Yes, he's my uncle," I reply. "He used to come over on Saturdays and slap my brother and me around. Then sometimes we'd all play a round or two of Don't Tell Mommy. You know, good clean fun."

BC nods, smiles. "He was a great golfer, I'll tell you that. He was the only man I ever knew—Jim was—who took a mulligan on every hole and claimed that was all in the rules. He was a wonderful man."

"Actually, what I wanted to talk to you about was this quarter of a million dollars I have here in my pocket, Mr. President. I admire your agenda. I want to give it to the Democratic National Committee so that we can get this country back on the right track."

A cloud passes over BC's face—perplexity, not anger. "This event's strictly social, kind of an issues-fest. I'm just here to pick some people's brains. But the DNC'd love to have your donation. Why don't you contact them next week sometime?"

"I have the money right here." I reach my hand into my pocket. "Let me hand it to you—quick!—so nobody sees."

"I'm sorry, Sal Really Pissed-Off Hayden. We got financing laws that forbid that. I'm sorry, but the guidelines are pretty strict. Have you had any of the lox over there? It's from a little deli over in Georgetown I used to go to as an undergrad." BC has pulled away from me slightly. An aide is now hovering near us, clearly listening.

"If I give the money to the DNC next week, can I still get some action on my issue of choice at some future time? I mean, like a *quid pro quo*?"

Then BC's face shifts. He narrows an eyebrow, compresses his lips, and begins to lecture. I have the sense immediately that, of all the scenarios, I've triggered the one that the much-older BC probably oversaw most carefully. It's got his rhythms and his outrage. "You know, as I've said, these gatherings are strictly designed to facilitate discussion and interaction between real people. People of all different walks of life. Some people who've done well in life, but not all. It's hard, as president, to stay close to people's concerns. So some of my staff members came up with the idea of coffee socials—actually, they took the idea from the Kennedy administration.

"And I'll tell you flat out I thought it was a great idea. We picked this room in the White House, the Map Room, for the feel of history. That's a 1945 FDR map over there on the wall. That was part of the D-Day Invasion that brought democracy to Europe. We thought it would let real people feel closer somehow to their history, and their country, and their president. And so that's what this is. We talk over anything on people's minds. Now, do some of these people agree with my agenda and want to help out later? You bet. Is there somethin' wrong with that? Not at all. Not at all. That's how democracy works. The careful exchange of ideas, thoughtful exchange, friendly exchange. And when people make up their minds about whose ideas they like best, whose vision, they sometimes want to help out the effort. And that's free speech, that donation. Supreme Court said that."

He salutes me briefly with his coffee mug. "Now, it's been nice to meet you, Sal Really Pissed-Off Hayden, but I better start doing a better job of mingling."

He begins to turn away, and I reach out to put a hand on his shoulder. I try to grab it hard, but the simulation will only let me touch it briefly, as a social prompt. BC turns back, once more cheerful, affable.

"One more question. Why is it everything always happens to everyone else?"

"Beg pardon?"

"Why is it you never seem to get punished, but everybody around you drops like flies?" I hear my voice, not much more than a whisper, getting ready to break. "Why is getting close to you a curse, even fifty years after it could make any possible difference? Why is that?"

BC gazes at me, and for a weird second it's as though it's not a Wide-eye simulation I'm staring into but a telemonitor, as though I'm actually talking to a real, live, forty-nine-year-old BC, as though he's thinking hard about my question. Really thinking, in 1995. I know it's really only the basket-shuffle of millions of potential responses, but it manages to look a lot like thought.

"There's a line in Ecclesiastes that I like a lot," he says finally. "It talks about a time in one's life when even a grasshopper is a burden."

He pats my shoulder. "I think about that sometimes," he says, "and it gives me comfort."

He turns away, moving on to the next paying guest, and I stand stone still. I become, effectively speaking, invisible. I can see the attendees, but no one can see me. Imperceptibly, the simulation returns to documentary mode, period images moving in the ways they actually moved, performing purchase-without-contract, no one paying me the slightest attention, because, let's face it, I wasn't there.

8

FINGERNAIL PHILOSOPHY

The Beret directs me into an unmarked and windowless room two floors down from the hidey-hole, then closes the door quickly and quietly behind me. And there's my father, Ron J. Hayden, sitting at a pathetic little conference table.

He looks older, a lot. His salt-and-pepper hair is now pretty much just salt. He's got a cup of coffee in front of him and an empty candy-bar wrapper.

He looks horrible. Partly it's the fluorescent lighting and partly it's that he looks horrible. Not only that, but something tells me he knows he looks horrible. His eyes admit it when he looks up at me.

His hair seems unwashed, combed but stringy, and his tan suit jacket clearly doesn't fit. I can't ever remember seeing him in clothing not specifically tailored to his shape. Not only doesn't the jacket fit, it doesn't match his navy trousers. No tie, just a white shirt open at the collar. Scuffed black boots. He looks like he's been dressed by a Goodwill volunteer who didn't have all day.

His face is out of whack too. Normally presentable, comfortably fleshed and attractively dimpled, a natural deal-closing face, it's now a little gaunt and the flesh beneath his eyes has just given up. A web of tiny broken vessels has spread over his nose and cheeks. He looks up at me again. His eyes are a filmy, watery pink, and I see he's right on the verge of crying. He grins without showing his teeth, keeping his composure.

"Sal," he says, standing on his side of the table and then awkwardly coming around toward the door.

"Dad," I hear myself answer, and he hugs me and, although I hate myself for it almost immediately, I have the quick thrill of relief that he's here, that he's come to put a stop to this lunacy. Even as I feel my heart lift with gratitude, I'm rehearsing a quick speech about how I didn't need the help, how I've gotten along and could've continued to get along just fine. But I can tell it's a speech that won't get delivered. It's been almost sixteen years, but if he was ever going to show up, ever get involved, ever in his life going to kick a little ass on my behalf, now is a capital time. We hug, and I wince a little at the pressure on my ribs.

He looks me over and appears pleased. "Sal Mineo," he says wonderingly, a nickname he hasn't used since I was twelve. Up this close I can see that the sleek black eyebrows he always raises in my memory are really only memories. Like the rest of his hair, the brows are now mostly dull white, and untended.

"What are you doing here?" I ask him. And then, like a true idiot, I say it again. "I mean, what are you *doing* here? They told me I had a *meeting*. Some meeting." A smile leaps onto my face, in spite of everything. "Where'd you get this coat? You look like a beat detective."

He looks down and touches the lapel, wider than any lapel he's ever worn in his life, just gives it a poke with his finger. It might as well be hanging on a rack in Hackensack for all the connection to it he displays. "Where'd I get the coat? Where'd I get my ulcer, Sal? Where'd they put my old body, the one that didn't used to hurt? What'd they do with those weird-looking green unitards you and your girlfriends used to wear when you were twelve, thirteen? Your little space suits."

He points to the candy-bar wrapper. It's a Critical Mass bar, which also doesn't seem quite right. My father, as I knew him, was never the caramel-and-creatine-muscle-enhancer type. "I brought you lunch but you were late, so I ate your half. Peanut and all." He pokes a finger into my side, grinning.

Inside of three minutes, it's old times again: he's ducked my questions, maybe the most innocent questions possible, and he's putting up a smoke screen of jokes that I'm obligated to laugh at, lest his own emotional clumsiness strike him too painfully. Our roles are inverted, me parenting him, him little-boying me, in the way that he's always insisted upon and absolutely refused to acknowledge.

And I realize I just can't do it, the ability to give that open-endedly is not in me anymore. So just like that, I act my age.

"Let's sit down, Dad," I say, drawing out one of the pastel-colored plastic shells from the table. He does likewise. He adjusts his pant legs at the knees with pinched fingers before crossing his legs, the ancient, fussy, clothes-horse gestures.

I resist the urge to lean toward him, to take his arm.

"Look, I'm glad to see you—really, it's a nice, nice surprise—but tell me up front what you're doing here. I just . . . I'm hoping you're here for something *good,* good news of some kind or other. Because it's been a bad day so far, you know? A bad, bad day. I'm trying hard to convey the extent of the badness. So far it's been almost inexpressibly bad. Do you understand what I mean by that?"

He nods silently.

"So I'm hoping, I guess, that this is good news, seeing you. I don't mean that as an insult, I'm *always* glad to see you, but, you know, Dad, what the hell are you doing here? You've been gone for a very long time. I mean, you've been gone almost as long as it takes for a newborn to reach National Service eligibility.

"That's almost sixteen years, Dad. And something tells me that you showing up here, at the Library where I work, in Arkansas, today of all days, might be a good thing, might very well even be an *excellent* thing, and I'm absolutely ready to hear that and believe that, but something also tells me, in a nagging kind of pessimistic way, that it just as easily might be a bad thing. Does that make sense, the way I'm torn between the idea that this means things are going to suddenly get better or suddenly nosedive and get worse superfast, Dad?"

He nods again. He seems relieved to have everything comfortably in the context of explanations demanded. Clearly he didn't want to say what he has to say on his own initiative.

He clears his throat. "I understand what you . . . what you're saying, Sal. I just wanted to come down here and and tell you, to come and say—" He struggles for a second, and I think he's looking for suitably indirect words, but then tears well up in his eyes, big, unavoidable, crystalline tears. "Wanted to say thank you, Sal," he gets out. And then he begins to sob, face hidden in his small hands, shoulders shaking just perceptibly.

I can't believe it. I've seen him cry once before, after my mother died, when he'd been drinking and read a set of letters my mom had collected over the years from a girlfriend of hers in Pennsylvania. He cried up in his bedroom, but I could hear him clearly enough down in the den. I was watching a rerun of Liddy Dole giving a speech of some kind—not a State of the Union or an inaugural but something long and highly ritualized—and her stiff words and the sounds from my parents' room mixed in a way that made it hard for me to hear video of her from then on.

That night, I wanted to run up and knock on the door and throw it open and tell him that whatever the letters said it wasn't true, and even if it was true, it was past and dead and it was just the two of us now living, so life had made its own rough determinations, and we should just accept them and move on. I wanted desperately to comfort him, and I remember feeling positive that if I could, if I could take away that one new pain from his heart, we'd both move into one of the later, final stages of grief I'd read about.

Of course, we didn't, and he finally disappeared, and I went on to become the woman with, according to several mental-health professionals, the Free World's most multitiered and impacted set of externally projected absences, or what BC would quaintly call abandonment issues. Still, that night I wanted more than anything to comfort him and to whisper in his ear, *Nothing matters.*

But now it's different. Now it's the strangest thing: I sit and watch him crying. Part of me is listening to the hum of the air-conditioning. My father, arrived out of nowhere, is sitting here in my life just like a normal person, tears rolling down the palms he has pressed close to hide his face, and although a part of me registers sadness, understands the weight of this minor collapse, I don't cry myself and I don't hug him. In fact, I have presence of mind enough to notice that a few of the tears are standing, unabsorbed, on his jacket sleeve. Ipso facto, the jacket is synthetic; ipso facto, my father must have gotten himself into some kind of very bad trouble.

It's like I'm one of the guys I used to date in high school and graduate school, the ones who could end a six-month relationship by observing me crying, offering me boxes of tissues. I look at him, and there's an intuited obligation and a general connection, a fistful of fairly vivid memories, but there's no way for his crying to produce tears in me.

Still, I pat his shoulder, leave my hand there. He reaches up quickly and holds my hand, and we sit like that for a second. I squeeze his hand. He squeezes back, just as though we were sharing, empathizing deeply.

Finally, he takes a handkerchief out of his jacket pocket, and it's the only thing so far that seems right—it's silk, a peacock's burst of rich color, and I can see his initials, RJH, monogrammed at the corner in royal blue. He swipes at his eyes and his nose with it, clears his throat very loudly, sitting up straight in his chair.

He looks into my eyes, and I can tell he feels the way I always felt in graduate school, looking at the dry eyes and unflushed faces of my very-soon-to-be-ex-boyfriends. I can tell he's suddenly vastly uncomfortable with me, with his own unrequited tears, and I am a little too, but I'm also amazed and relieved. I'll worry about turning into a heartless alien later. For now, it's clear enough that over the years I've undergone some kind of emotional root canal, and I'm just glad to be sitting here in almost no pain.

"For what, Dad?" I ask, when I feel he's mostly got his game face back. "Thank me for what?"

"Well, it's kind of a long story, kid. I was hoping I wouldn't ever have to tell it to you."

My stomach starts to turn. "How bad is it?"

"It's bad. But it's a bad luck story, really, more than anything. But it gets really good at the end. It's just, well, it's embarrassing. No father wants to tell his daughter this kind of story. You want to be able to—well, what the hell."

"Just tell me."

"You have no patience, Sal. This is tough."

I look at him. He's still handsome, in spite of being poorly turned out today. It's amazing to me, to sit and hear him talk about patience. It's really amazing to me. He uses the word as though he understands the meaning. Ronnie, my aunt Mary always called my father. He's Ronald on his birth certificate—my grandpa Jerry was one of the original mutant Reagan Democrats—but he's made a point all his life of insisting on Ron. Drawing himself up to say his piece, whatever piece he's come here to say, though, he's Ronnie. He's my aunt's bad-seed little brother.

"You know I've been working down in the islands now for a long time, Sal. I started a little import-export business down there right about the time I saw you last. And I nursed it along, got myself in good with the right people, made sure that everything was on the up-and-up. I was a fanatic about that, I'm telling you. Taxes *paid,* permits *valid.* I'd run some other businesses earlier on kind of"—he reaches into his pocket and pulls out a pack of Eastwoods, puts one of the long cigarillos into the corner of his mouth, fires it—"well, anyway, within the spirit and not the letter of the law. I don't make any real excuses. A young man pushes his way in the world and doesn't buy insurance, because he trusts his luck. And I was lucky then, had good luck, and I think as a provider I always did all right by you. Your education was not cheap, Sal.

"Not a guilt trip, nothing like that, just the fact. The University of Vermont should name a swimming pool or a dorm after me, or something. I worked hard at putting that out there for you, and now you're set and so that seems to have all worked out. That was the plan, and that plan was *executed.*" He winks at me, pokes my shoulder with his finger again.

"But seven, eight years ago, I took on a partner. Didn't want a partner, necessarily, but sometimes business conditions are such, *social* conditions are such, that you find yourself taking on a partner. Especially out in the islands, Sal. When the Brits and the Americans and the French pulled back in the Caribbean, other people, other *countries* started to establish an interest. All of a sudden you've got extra licenses to buy, and then sales routes to protect, etc. It's like the way the world was isn't the way the world is now, and the islands were where everything started to do some slipping. All of a sudden there were new rules. Rule one: you needed a partner."

He needs to ash his Eastwood but most of the conference rooms are off-limits for smoking, so no ashtrays. Originally the entire Library was off-limits, given BC's place in history as an antismoking advocate. But as the Wars stretched on, attitudes changed, to put it mildly, and a completely smoke-free environment became tantamount to Collaboration. But common spaces here are still mostly off-limits, and that's a situation with which my father is clearly uncomfortable. He strikes his own compromise. With elaborate care, he ashes the cigarillo on the candy-bar wrapper.

"So I won't make a simple story complex," he goes on conversationally. "You have a partner, and when the partner brings in extra money, you split it down the middle. When the partner goes bad, goes criminal, you take fifty percent of the rap. You can cry all you want, but you're going to take fifty percent of the rap."

My father, my aunt's little brother Ronnie, has come to the point, the thing he wants to say. He raises his eyebrows and gives me a serious look. "So three years ago, I'm arrested for trafficking in contraband from hostile nations. It was actually the government itself that brought the charges, the ATF. They had video of six or seven kinds of sensitive technology coming over our doorstep, going out in our trucks from our warehouse.

"Now, I told the Alcohol, Tobacco and Firearms people, Look, you got the wrong partner in this operation. I was nowhere in any of this video, nowhere. I have *orthodox* interests, and I have never touched any drugs or weapons or refugees or black-tech. Clearing Extra Fats into Brazil is a very lucrative and honest sideline. Why take the business into the illegitimate?"

He's looking down at the carpet now. He's narrowed it down to this, rhetorical questions and all. His face looks slightly queasy, resigned but queasy. "But they're not hearing any of that. I think, seriously, Sal, I think they all know how much influence the U.S. has lost down there. They know that it's a different management down there now; the Eastern Affiliates have their fingers in pretty solidly.

"And I think it pisses them off, knowing they can't do a thing about it. So who can they do something about? Small-time Americans, the little guys."

He looks around the room, quickly, lowers his voice. "Story of every losing fucking army ever fielded. In the end, they turn on their own people." He takes a drag on the Eastwood, seems to be assessing how that last remark is sitting with me. I realize he's as in the dark as I am after sixteen years. I could be a double agent for Uzbekistan for all he knows. And our own government has been gingerly promoting the idea of informing on family as patriotism for years.

"In any event, ATF says, testify against your partner and we'll keep it to seven years minus time served. And so I do. In video, nobody testifies against anybody, like you have a huge moral choice to make. You don't. So I testified. I went to jail, sentence was six years, four months. Probation possible after five."

He stops, gives me a quick smile, eyes pleading for a laugh. "You okay, Mineo? I know it's not the greatest news in the world to hear your dad's been in jail, but we're almost to the good part. Give me two minutes more."

I can tell he's waiting for a sign that I'll live, even though my pristine image of him has been shattered. He'd hate to know that I'd already guessed some of this, years before, and knew some more of it when I saw his new jacket refuse teardrops. But like my aunt Mary once said, I'm a softie. So I give him what he's after. "I'm okay, Dad," I tell him quietly. "I never took you for a choirboy, even in the old days. You used to say to me that my teachers had their opinion of me, but you'd always have your own, no matter how I did in school."

And then I give him the laugh he wants to go with it. But I can't hold it for very long. "So the ATF's got their opinion of you"—I lock eyes with him—"and I'll always have my own."

He takes only the half of my meaning he's comfortable with. He chuckles to himself, smooths his hair once more, and moves ahead with it. He can finish now.

"So you find yourself in prison, outside of Charlottesville, Virginia, at the Albemarle County Correctional, after all's said and done, and you try to make it work, good behavior, etc. You're focused on not getting demerits," he says, as though this is always the case when good people are unfairly imprisoned, standard human practice. "You're worried about the partner on the outside having connections to people on the inside, but it turns out that's strictly Hollywood.

"There's no real organization to deal with, but there's enough unpleasant people still, some unstable people obviously. There's a kind of daily routine you have to go through. Threats, shakedowns. Every now and then somebody has to be a hard guy, prove they can push an older guy around. Big deal. Time heals all wounds."

His eyes tighten again, at the corners, but I can tell he'll die now before he lets his emotions loose again. "And then a couple months back the ATF guy, the lead prosecutor, comes to see me with a couple of military people. Not soldiers but young lawyer types, one step up from the wire-in-the-ear kind of guys. And they tell me that my little girl"—he points to me, gives a proud little grin—"my Sal Mineo is up for a fat job at the Pentagon or somewhere. And they want me to cooperate in a security check, background check. And once that's done, they want to let me go. Wipe the slate clean. They say they can't see justice being served by my doing the last three years of the sentence. And I said to myself, the hell with justice. Serve me the hell out of here."

He tilts his head back and lets a long, satisfied stream of smoke geyser up from his mouth. In spite of the air-conditioning, the room is now a little murky with smoke. This is the effect of hanging around with my father.

"So I do a couple of interviews with them. They bring some records and personal effects for me to identify. I give them a list of people who we used to live near, people you used to go around with. Did you ever do drugs? No. Did you ever travel in Russia or the East? No. Ever a member of a Libertarian caucus or cell? No. They want to know about your aunt Mary, your mom. Pretty simple.

"And then yesterday they tell me, number one, you got the job." He beams and looks somehow proud of his own role—in addition to thanking me, he seems clearly to feel he deserves thanks for his own part in it all. "And number two, I'm invited to leave the prison and take a ride. Your daughter's mustering out in Arkansas—Little Rock, they said—you've got time for a quick good-bye if we chopper you in. I said, what's in Arkansas, is she doing time on a chain gang?"

He lays another half inch of ash in his makeshift, candy-wrapper ashtray, then puts a hand up. "I didn't mean that, Sal, that was prison humor. Then they told me about the presidential library and the book you're writing and all of that. And I was quite impressed. They said, let's go, we got a kit bag packed outside for you.

"After my expedited review hearing next week, my record's clean. They're gonna pull the felony conviction, wipe it. They said after next Thursday I could get a job as a bank teller if I wanted."

Now the Critical Mass bar makes sense. It's probably the creatine candy of choice with the ATF and the Berets. They thought my father could use the help.

He's done with his story. I can tell his conscience is squeaky clean, because he's come down here and told me his shameful secret. He has no idea that I'm not up for a big job at the Pentagon, that instead I'm fighting all of a sudden to stay in civilian life. He has no idea that I might find it a betrayal, his giving up everything he knows about my early life, my haunts, my friends.

I can't hate him, though. He really seems to believe that he's pushed me forward in the world, through sheer force of will, and that he deserves his quick release from prison by being properly grateful for it. He's confessed, and I'm obligated to forgive, by all the most ancient codes. Biographers are cursed with endless unbidden mental connections to their subjects, and suddenly I can see BC at a Rose Garden event following his impeachment, and I can hear him say, slowly and feelingly, "I think anyone who asks for forgiveness has to be willing to give it." But, of course, that was the purest bullshit. BC wasn't remotely willing or able to do it, and neither am I, not completely and not now, not in the most important ways.

My father is now snuffing his finished cigarillo on the bottom of his boot.

"Dad," I say, to get his attention.

"Yeah, Sal."

"When they came to you for this background information, did you tell them we hadn't seen each other in over fifteen years?"

He puts the dead butt in the candy wrapper, folds his hands on the table. "Yeah, I did. Told them everything. Anything that would help." He's pretending not to see where I'm going.

I wait a second. He's fidgeting almost imperceptibly, mostly just his eyes.

"Well, what did you tell them? How did you explain that?"

"Jesus, Sal. How does anyone explain something like that?"

"I'm not asking how anyone explains something like that. Or how someone other than you explains it, or even hypothetically how you, yourself, might explain it under other circumstances. I asked you a straight question. How did you explain it to *those* people? What was your real answer when you were asked that real question? That's what I'm asking you to tell me."

He straightens a little. "I didn't give a good answer, if that's—"

"Dad, listen to me." I lean forward now, and I hold his shoulder with my hand. I look him in the eye. I feel like my looking at him is holding him to earth, like a captive genie. "I want this answer, now. Just this one. I listened to your whole story and didn't interrupt you once, or make it tough for you. But this one question I want answered. I didn't ask you whether you thought your answer to the ATF people was good or bad or indifferent. I asked you what it *was*."

So then my dad, Ronald J. Hayden, formerly of Albemarle County, formerly of the Bahamas, formerly of New Jersey and Vermont and six or so other states, failed minor-league catcher, importer/exporter, salesman, smuggler, widower, father of one, cheater at Monopoly if you ever let him run the bank, says, "I told them that I was a defective human being." He meets my gaze. "I told them my marriage got bitched up, and my wife died, and then my sister died, and I went running around the world and I left my little girl in the States on her own because I didn't know what the hell to do with myself. Everything was wrong. I was without a mind."

It's not at all what I expected.

He pauses and then, reliably enough, doesn't quit while he's ahead. "I told them I thought about it the last two years and it seemed to me like when you smash your fingernail and it goes black and dead-blue, and then when your new nail comes in, the good pushes out the bad, little by little. I used to be a smashed purple fingernail, when you were a kid, and after."

He's almost smiling now, genuinely happy with the way things are going. "But I'm not anymore, not today. I grew back healthy. That's what I told them. That's the analogy I go with now."

Charming. I look at him in an entirely different light. My father: brand-new fingernail. I can tell this is his new religion, and why shouldn't it be? Smashed fingernails happen by accident. They're never anyone's fault.

But the first part of his answer was something, anyway. It was worth hearing him out. And I realize that whoever's behind the lockdown of the Library clearly expected as much. Whoever it is clearly wants me to know that my father was in jail and is now almost out of jail, but not quite. What he needs continues to be an issue, if not the issue, as much as I told myself it wouldn't be when I saw him sitting at this pathetic conference table with his empty candy wrapper.

He smiles at me, and I guess he deserves some of his relief. It's hard to begrudge him that. "How was that answer, professor?" he asks.

There's no way I can tell him about what's really going on, not yet. So I give as much of a smile as I can. "It's not so much what the answer was, Dad. It's more that there was an answer, of one sort or another. You know what I mean?"

He nods, wisely. "I know what you mean." He looks at his watch. "I wish we had more time, I'd do better. But there'll be plenty of time now, once things are settled out."

I look at his watch, then at him. "You have to go back now?"

"Nope. You do." And sure enough, just as he says it, there's a polite rap on the door, very much as though someone was listening to the entire conversation but waited for some kind of natural pause before interrupting.

"*What?*" I yell at the door.

"Sal," my father says, automatically reproachful.

I whip around to face him. "*What?*" I whisper.

"They're just coming to get you for your meeting. You have a meeting. They told me that earlier, we'd only have about forty-five minutes."

"They told *you?*"

"Yeah, earlier on."

"Time for us to move out, Ms. Hayden," the voice beyond the door puts in.

My father, newly returned, stands up and there's nothing much for me to do but stand up as well. If I'm not going to tell him about the situation, I can't very well protest what seems to be a normal meeting. So I stand. He hugs me, less awkwardly now, with more self-assurance, and then he quickly lets me go. He shows me his dimple, then his killer smile. He holds up his index finger before my face, nail out. I look at the nail. It's nicotine-stained, almost camel-colored.

"Don't forget," he says, and winks.

9

LOAVES & FISHES

When BC built the Library, he was still a relatively young man: mid-fifties in a world where people were just beginning to live comfortably into their nineties, the youngest two-term ex-president in the nation's history, except for Teddy Roosevelt. His disappointment at being forced to leave the White House was palpable.

Here was a man who had fitted himself since puberty for an intricate and laborious political climb designed to culminate in the presidency; instead, he reached the pinnacle a full twenty years ahead of schedule, unbelievably, on his first try. The Presidential Library in Little Rock was his understandably desperate attempt to fashion an Afterlife quickly, with the pressure on.

As with his wardrobe and his small Scandal Room, BC's life after the White House was patterned almost self-consciously after that of another ex-president, Jimmy Carter, although BC would never publicly admit this. But it couldn't be clearer that Carter's diplomatic think tank in Atlanta fanned BC's desire to make his own presidential library a stop on the international conflict-mediation circuit, if not an alternate national capitol. But, predictably, he wanted to go Carter one better. Although he's never come right out and admitted it to me, it's clear from my interviews and the correspondence I've sifted that for years BC secretly cherished the idea of becoming Secretary General of the United Nations someday, once his immediate international enemies had fallen from power and a properly respectful young Democratic president had inherited the White House.

In those days, the UN seemed poised to become a de facto world government. Anybody who knows anything about BC knows that one last campaign to lead a nascent world government would have been, for him, a final rapturous delight. He would have made it his mission in life to win over all the doubters, the isolationist Republicans in the U.S. and the anti-hegemony chorus in the Third World.

But it never came together. The one Democrat to take the White House in the decade following BC's terms was cast from BC's own steadfast centrist mold—he associated mostly, in public, with Republicans. And the UN became the victim of its own success. The more powerful it grew, the more successful it became at peacekeeping and deal-making, the less support it drew from its most powerful members. If the rhetoric surrounding world government had always seemed soothing—full of world communities, global villages, and families of nations—the actual prospect of it proved terrifying. The UN was systematically and deliberately crippled.

Dues went unpaid, Security Council votes deadlocked again and again, ad nauseam, until the organization became a thin shadow of its former self, a jilted Cassandra railing at aggressors and prophesying punishment but clearly powerless in its own right.

For all of those reasons, BC was forced to incorporate the heart of his UN dreams into the Library itself. And he made a pretty good job of it. Funded partially by the government of Kuwait, the Settlement Room occupies almost the whole of the sixth floor, and it is a breathtaking space. Its walls are made up entirely of carefully polarized glass, providing a rolling view of the river and of downtown Little Rock. From those windows, you can see the entire seventeen-acre campus of the Library, reclaimed from what was once a slag heap of weeds and decrepit riverfront warehouses. Polished, mobile teak panels divide the vast open space of the room into individual meeting spaces, big and small, formal and informal, like a ludicrously well-appointed Soho loft. Woven into the ceiling and the walls is a latticework of fiber-optic video leads; it's possible for BC to relive a day's session and see who in the room is signaling whom, making the next day's pitch that much more effective.

This is the room where BC planned to continue meeting with world leaders, where he planned to hammer out treaties and smooth over ancient hatreds. But that, too, failed to come to pass. Little Rock, for all the boom-and-bust it had seen during and following BC's eight years in the White House, was still Little Rock, and it turned out that world leaders preferred something a little more cosmopolitan and a little less swampy in the summer.

This is not to say that BC has not made use of the Settlement Room. He has. Over the years, he's mediated a high-profile world soccer strike, he's hosted World Trade Organization talks between the European Union and the U.S. over banana tariffs. He's tried, and he's had some genuine successes, but above all the Settlement Room stands as a monument to BC's too-early retirement. He, more than anyone else inside these glass walls, has been forced to settle.

I am currently seated at the massive and reassuring yet undeniably chic conference table in the very center of the room. Although there is a nice assortment of sparkling waters and muffins on a silver tray in the exact center of the table, no one else is here.

I was told by the Beret who double-timed me here that I am precisely on time. This, if true, can only mean that in spite of everyone's talk about how crucial I am to the chaos sprouting from every direction today, none of the other participants has the slightest qualms about keeping me waiting.

Potentially, the delay is to give me time to simmer down, to allow them to debrief the Berets I've been assigned. I resolve to die before simmering down.

I wait another five minutes or so before getting into the muffins. I pour myself a tall glass of French water and continue waiting.

To kill time, I play a round of Loaves & Fishes. It's a mental game with very few rules: I try to list as many flaps and controversies from the BC years as I can think of, excluding the obvious as unsportsmanlike and focusing instead on the more bizarre, recondite incidents, with bonus points for recalling actual assertions, quotes, news-cycle spins and counterspins. I invented it once about ten years ago during an endless wait to see my gynecologist, and it's served me well over the years. Because it seems, somehow, almost mystically, never to be a zero-sum game. There are always more imbroglios to remember and list and dissect—the half-brother who surfaced just after BC became president-elect, the off-color joke BC made about a five-thousand-year-old mummy ("That's one good-looking mummy"), which in turn led a White House spokesman to make what he thought was a private off-color joke of his own ("Well, it's gotta be better than the mummy he *has* been sleeping with"), etc., and so on. Hence the name of the game.

Today, for some reason, I settle mentally on a curiously little-remarked affair late in BC's second term: the revelation that one of the federal grand jurors in the Whitewater proceedings had been wearing a Star Trek Federation uniform every day to the Little Rock courthouse. Like most BC-related oddities, it allows you the brief conviction that your own life is normal.

After another five minutes, I hear a quick, muffled burst of profanity from the antechamber. It is, predictably enough at this point, BC.

The door to the Settlement Room opens, and he shuffles and clicks his way inside, turning almost immediately to call over his shoulder, "That's as far as *you* come, dickless. You just read a magazine or something, but I don't want you inside this conference room, you get me?" He faces front and moves slowly toward the table, and I can see that he's already fallen halfway into the illusion that he's still giving the orders. He's got a grim but satisfied look on his face. Whoever assigned him the dress marine is someone who knows something about BC.

He spots me then and gives a little start. "Well, Sal," he says. Then he sees that the table is otherwise empty. And he cranes his head back around to look at the door.

I can't resist a dig. "The important people aren't here yet."

He doesn't rise to the bait. "I can sure see that," he answers glumly, continuing his slow journey across the big open room to the conference table. Once he's in range, he has to make a quick decision: head of the table, or one of the less imposing chairs near the middle, the common-participant chairs I chose without thinking about it. In a sign that most of the fight has gone out of him, he hesitates and then sighs and pulls up the chair next to me.

Or maybe, I tell myself, it's a show of solidarity. Either way, he lets himself carefully down into the next chair, the body-walker beneath his slacks holding him, holding him, and then bringing him softly in for a landing. And then he offers me a dig back, out of nowhere. "How was your daddy?" he asks, giving me a sidelong look.

"Newly released from prison," I say, startling even myself. All of the protocols BC and I have built up over the last handful of years have disintegrated. He can swear himself blue in the face, and I can voice the smart-ass remarks I've muted as a matter of course. "Did they tell you he was here?"

"They did."

I pick up the last corner of my muffin, pop it in my mouth. "Well, thanks for telling me."

He pushes his lips together, contrite but resolute. "They asked me to stay out of that, and I—frankly, I thought that'd be better. I didn't have any idea what you and your father had between you."

I let it go. As breaches of trust go, today at least, it's nothing. "We haven't seen each other in almost sixteen years," I explain. "This is only the second time since my aunt Mary died."

"What'd she die of?"

"Cancer. Breast cancer. Her fuel tanks leaked."

"Sixteen years. Lot of time," he remarks.

"Yeah," I say. "Not time enough to call or write or visit. But time enough for him to go bankrupt once or twice, and get busted by the feds for trafficking with hostiles. But it's okay now. He told me he feels like a new fingernail. So that's good. Imagine my relief."

BC gives a dour little chuckle. He's got his eyes on his hands, turning them over slowly, examining the calluses, the prints, the scars. He brings his head up finally and gives me a look. "He's hurt you, and I'm sure he knows that, and God knows that, but you want to think seriously about forgiveness, Sal."

I look over at him to see if he's serious or if he's just having fun playing preacher. But he means it; his eyes are fixed on the table, his head's nodding slowly. And then he goes on: "My own father—my biological father—died before I was born. I know you know all this, but think about it. Sedan flipped over in a ditch, but it didn't kill him. He made it out of the wreck. He survived. But he was injured somehow, I guess, not thinking clearly, and in the dark he stumbled into another shallow little ditch of rainwater and drowned, just months before I was born.

"So that's how close I came to meeting my own daddy—he survived a high-speed crash, but he was weakened and he stumbled and drowned a horrible death. Almost like God saved him, gave him one more chance, and then changed his mind at the last second. I used to get mad enough to cry when I thought about it like that, as a kid. I used to curse the Lord for not knowing His own mind."

It's all come spooling out of him, without warning, and like it or not, as angry as I am at everyone, he's got a point of sorts. He goes on, just a bit more. "So I had a little string of father figures instead of a father. And it ain't ever the same thing. It *ain't*. So I'd think about that. At least you got the raw material of the father you always wanted. Some of us start and end with the substitutes."

He's got a point, but he's still on my shit list, and I'd rather be shipped out to Mongolia in a Ford Pinto than admit it to him. I'm quiet for a second. "I'll think about it," I say finally.

BC gives a soft little snort, then reaches for the snack tray. But before he can connect with the banana-nut muffin he's targeted, the conference-room door is opened by a completely new Beret. As he swings the door open, the Beret's face remains utterly expressionless—any sign of personality would clearly be taken as a sign of disrespect to the higher-ups about to enter the room—and he flattens himself out along the door itself, as much like a vertical doormat as possible.

And through the door walk six people, three in uniform, three in civvies. Two of the three in uniform are apparently bodyguard/honor-guard types, and as the door closes they take up positions on either side of it. They have their weapons holstered. I have just time to notice that each takes a set of headphones from a side pocket and slips them on, before one of the men in civilian clothes walks up to my chair.

He's a small man, about forty-five years old, in a dark jacket without lapels. His hair gives every indication of being pill-farmed. It's thin and brown and straight at the fringes, and dark and thick and curly across the central expanse. Oddly two-toned, like dog fur: Yorkshire terrier at the edges, and cocker spaniel in the center. In BC's day, he would have been almost entirely bald and probably would have provoked fewer puzzled looks on the street. There is no mistaking that he's a lawyer. He's carrying a set of folders as though they were a brace of pistols.

He sets the top folder down on the table beside me and fixes me briefly with a kindly, almost shy smile. "Hello, Ms. Hayden," he says. "I'm Pat Evans. You might have a look at this while we get settled in." He draws a finger down the sleek brown cover of the file. Another quick smile. Then he goes to find a spot at the front of the table, not the head of the table, but two careful seats away.

I don't open the file.

My time is better spent figuring out the other three people in the room, and additionally I've decided to be as balky as possible without actually locking myself in a bathroom. Over the last fifteen or so minutes, I've resolved not to do anything or say anything that indicates my assent to what is happening in the Library today or to anything they may have planned for me tomorrow. This will mean acting impolitely, even rudely. I focus on an image of my aunt Mary. I see her mouth shape the words: *Because I hold a grudge.*

I study the remaining three. Although it's not immediately clear to me which branch of the Armed Forces she represents, the woman who has taken the chair at the head of the table is in khaki uniform pants and blouse. The outsize uniform hat rests casually on the table. She is relatively short, very stocky, with a cropped head of mostly silver hair. She is what we used to call monobosomatic in college—her chest projects like a single, carefully horizontal shelf beneath her chin, with no suggestion of duality therein. Across this shelf she wears an impressive and indecipherable array of medals. She has brought a small, extremely elegant pop-up computer link with her. The sleek navy-blue unit is now plugged in to the tabletop before her, and she has commenced noodling with it.

On either side of her sits a man in civilian clothing.

To her left, a man in his late forties in a dark blue suit. Very high forehead, the rest of the hair cut H. R. Bob Haldeman-close. His thin strip tie is a retiring mix of blue and red. It's the power broker's camouflage; he could slip into any board meeting, governor's conference, or trustee dinner anywhere in the country and immediately be lost from sight. A company man, but not soft. He doesn't need the shoulder pads in his coat.

To her right, slouched in his chair, a surprisingly youngish man with pointy features and small cat's eyes over a crisp white oxford shirt. Twenty-six or -seven or -eight at most. He's got straight, dark brown hair, cowlicky and boyish, not so much combed as thrust across his forehead and over the opposite brow. He's wearing chinos, white socks, loafers. His small eyes and the upward slant of his eyebrows give him a vaguely angry look that doesn't seem to coincide with his actual mood.

Occasionally he doodles—not on a smartpad, but on a regular, old-school legal pad. He wears no coat, no tie, no military uniform, but has managed to hit the cold minimum in terms of formality. First approximation: the prep-school wiseass who refuses to grow up but makes it stick because he's intelligent and pedigreed and destined to come into money someday, if the old man doesn't unexpectedly cut his financial balls off.

He sees me looking and, with his hand still resting on the conference table, gives me a little three-finger twiddle-wave. And then, with a flick of a sidelong glance at the woman in uniform, he holds up the piece of paper he's been doodling on. There are some curlicues and flowers and geometric shapes sketched at the margins, but in the center it says clearly:

THE ECONOMY, STUPID!

As quickly as the paper came up, it goes down, and his attention goes back to the blank corner of the room. But now he has a deeper, slyer, more secretive grin, a dimple showing in one cheek like he's pulled off an absolutely sensational joke he's been planning for months.

It's the slogan from BC's first national campaign, in 1992.

Carefully fostered legend has it that a very similar piece of paper was taped up on the wall of his consultants' War Room in Little Rock. It was the Vision and the Message both in one, rendered down finally to three combative words, campaign poetry that made haiku seem flabby and nerveless and long-winded. The fact that this joker knows these three words says something. The fact that he knows the correct slogan—instead of the four-word version the media got wrong but made famous—says something more.

Other than those two things, I have absolutely no fucking idea what in the world it means.

10

TAKING A MEETING ISN'T SO DIFFERENT FROM TAKING A BEATING

After another blank five minutes, in which we all wait for someone else in the room to stop waiting, the meeting begins without beginning. With the stocky woman in uniform tapping carefully on her pop-up and taking no official notice, Pat Evans leans forward and stage-whispers across the table to me. "Did you have a chance to glance at those documents at all?" He pokes his fingertip in the direction of the folder still sitting beside me.

I lean forward slightly too, congressional-hearings posture. "No, I haven't, Mr. Evans."

"Well," he wrinkles his face, nodding urgently, "that'd be a good idea. I think"—he glances at the colonel beside him—"I think that's what we're waiting on. That really should be the first order of business." He gives two strong, final nods. It's classic good-cop stuff. If I'll follow him into the minefield, he'll show me just where to put my feet.

I shake my head. No doubt they have the fiber optics in the walls online, and I'd like the involuntary nature of the discussion to be clear from the outset. "I absolutely and categorically do not agree. Obviously our opinions about the order of business differ by a good margin. As far as I'm concerned, *my* first order of business is downstairs, in my office. It's sitting down there, without me, because I've been herded up here, at gunpoint, to deal with your first order of business."

Evans is not easily shocked. He nods again, sympathetically. He wants me to know he hears me. "That no doubt seemed frightening, Ms. Hayden—"

"You put it exceedingly well."

"But I assure you, your order of business and ours are the same at this point."

"Now you're using sloppy, or at least self-interested, language again, Mr. Evans. When you refer to *my* order of business, you signify that that order of business belongs to me, that it is *mine*. That should I find, in fact, that it *doesn't* dovetail with yours, I am free to act as though there *weren't* men with guns on both sides of the door."

"Ms. Hayden, what you say makes good sense, in any normal situation. But we are not in a normal situation, believe me."

"Have I committed a crime?"

"Not that we're aware of."

"Not that you're aware of?"

"That's correct."

"You checked? You poked around?" I know they have from my father, but it seems like a good time to up the indignation quotient.

Evans folds his hands. "I'm not going to get into specifics, but we've checked your suitability for *very* high-end security clearance. No bones about it, that's a very, very, very thorough check—that involves background and foreground, to the end of building a really *solid* subject portfolio."

"You said foreground?"

"Past and present. Your record and your current situation."

BC leans in, keeping both Evans and me in his glance. His tone is earnest. "I told you, Sal, that they'd come to me for some information, and I gave them what I thought they had a real right to. That I've told you myself." Already he's not on my side, but in the middle, the center, ready to bring the sides dramatically together. A new disgust raises its head in me, but I don't let it show. He's still all I've got left.

I can feel my temper build as heat across my neck and face. I know myself well enough to know that I have to keep a firm grip or I'm liable to start shouting, and at that point the argument's always over. I try to keep it icy, disdainful. "You take a lot on yourselves," I say, looking at the woman with the medals.

Evans doesn't see any need to disagree. "Actually, you're right. At a moment like this, we do. And without apologies. We're in an extraordinary situation."

"Then what constitutes this extraordinary situation?"

"That's part of the reason we're all here. We can't tell you everything, but we plan to fill in a lot of the picture. That's why the high-end security clearance. That's why the area-wide lockdown and so forth."

"But I didn't ask for a security clearance! Do you understand that? Ordinarily, people *ask*, and are investigated, and then cleared or not cleared, right? Do I have that right, Mr. Evans? I mean, is the Bill of Rights still in play here?"

The decorated woman leans forward and fixes me with a look. She's not impressed with my wordplay. She lets the look stretch out a little, until it takes on the force of spoken language. It's at once withering and bored, the look you give a punk kid puking up his Mule in the street at his older brother's BV, sympathy overcome finally by contempt.

She's deliberately blunt, deliberately unsympathetic. It's strange, because her voice is low and pleasant, almost musical. "Most of this extraordinary situation, as you call it, is quite honestly none of your business. At least the specifics of it."

I look at her for a minute, digesting. "Who the hell are you?" I ask.

"I'm Colonel Margaret Turner. This is my unit here today. And I'd suggest you watch your language, Ms. Hayden." She gives BC a disapproving glance, the great-grandfather who failed to bring me up right.

"Well, respectfully, Colonel Turner," I begin, "I disagree with you. I think it's very much my business to know who and what are depriving me of my most basic civil liberties."

"Sal," BC says, hand on my arm. Invoking civil liberties is standard operating procedure for Libertarians, and it probably isn't a very smart rhetorical move, but I move my arm out from under his hand just the same. To keep up the pretense of mediating, he takes her to task too. "Colonel, I don't know who's going to be well served by saying things like 'that's none of your business.' That's the kind of thing nobody takes well."

Nobody says anything to that; it's too feeble to require response. It's the kind of Sunday-school remark that people make when their own lives and land aren't at stake, and I find myself wondering how often and for how many hours Yasser Arafat and Ehud Barak had to listen to interruptions like it when the Oslo process was fraying.

"Unless there's been some sort of nationwide junta," I continue, letting the word do its work, drawing myself up in my seat, "while I was at lunch today, I not only have a right to specifics, I have a right to make a call. I have a right to be *read* my rights. And I have a right to my *own* lawyer with his *own* understanding of the law and his *own* head of pill-farmed, cocker-spaniel hair."

And there it is, I've crossed the line. The cat-eyed man sucks in his breath, brows lifted briefly in delight. Pat Evans's face flushes, but he and the colonel exchange a certain look of measured satisfaction: I've ceased to be reasonable, I've turned to personal ridicule, focused attack. I can now be dealt with less gingerly, more like the spoiled civilian they expected all along.

And maybe I am. I don't want my life disrupted, I don't want to sacrifice, not at my age, not for the reasons underlying the Wars. I don't want to lose myself and my life in some kind of mad collective effort to fend off the collective efforts of the rest of the world to secure payment of a legal judgment. I've always been disdainful of the handful of peaceniks protesting the Wars, their tambourines and their silent marches snaking through downtown Little Rock, filmed from the sky all the while. But now I feel realization gnawing at me, and even that, on this day, is no real satisfaction, because it's taken a direct threat to my own life to prize open my indifference.

Be that as it may, if all of this winds up with me strapped into the rear compartment of a Hornet VTOL taking fire over the outskirts of Beijing, no one is ever going to be able to say that I cooperated, even partially.

But the colonel isn't going to be flustered. "We have followed the procedures for identifying ourselves. We've been very careful of that." She points to the folder, eyes on the table. "If you choose to forgo a reading of those documents, that's your own lookout. But we have identified ourselves in good faith."

I open my mouth, but nothing comes out. It was bound to happen sooner or later. I turn to look at BC, incredulously. Finally I manage, "Look, I have no idea who or what you are. How can you say—"

"We're a special detachment of the National Security Council. We have ties to the Marines and the Army, but we're on permanent lease-loan to the NSC."

"Speak English, for Christ's sake."

The colonel gives me a look for half a second. And then she says, "Basically we're a task force put together out of several branches of the military and the intelligence wing of the National Security Council. The idea is to create a flexible team with the skills to do a given job, regardless of where in the government or armed forces or civilian population they come from." She looks at the cat-eyed man beside her, appraising him. He feels the glance and looks back, smiles a sleepy smile. "We find who and what we need based on the individual TSO."

"TSO," I repeat.

"Task and situation operations. We need different people at different stages. Nine times out of ten we find what we need within the armed forces, but when we can't we're forced to ask indispensable civilians to serve in various capacities."

"Different stages." I'm picking up phrases and looking at them like they're seashells, like I'll find something helpful.

"Wars have stages. First there's one stage, then another. Maybe another, maybe another after that. Until it's over. This one isn't over. We need things now that we haven't needed before. Conceivably, we won't need them later. No way to guarantee, but conceivably."

"You make it all sound so hip and ad lib."

She's got one eye on me and one on the elegant pop-up, at least half-heartedly monitoring something, somewhere. "A war is very much like a child. You bring a war *up*, you adapt to it as much as it adapts to you. You don't count the costs."

"It's your baby."

"That's right. It's your baby, and you'd rather be put in the ground than live to see your side go down first."

"Which stage is this, then? Adolescence?"

The sarcasm goes wide. She shakes her head. "Not adolescence."

"Well," I say, glancing at BC, who's got his eyes down on his hands, "I have no intention of leaving civilian life. I should tell you that up front. So consider the question asked and answered. In the negative. The extreme negative."

"You've left civilian life, Ms. Hayden," the colonel says bluntly. She's looking me right in the eyes now. She pulls down on the sides of her uniform blouse, readjusting something inside. "The minute you took that folder beside you there. You've been under military jurisdiction for the last ten minutes. Technically, you've been in the Marines and under lease-loan to the NSC, just like me. You're subject now to the uniform military code of conduct, wartime provisions in force."

"I never opened it. And I won't."

"It doesn't matter, Ms. Hayden." Pat Evans leans forward, doing his best not to seem to rub it in. He's got a pained look on his face: he sympathizes with my ignorance, in spite of my having called him a cocker spaniel. "It's the same principle as a subpoena. It's a matter of being served, of accepting the document before witnesses."

"That's not how the draft works."

"This isn't the draft, Ms. Hayden," Evans says mildly. "This is called a wartime compulsory activation. And if it makes it any easier, I can tell you we didn't make it up. This was created for the Manhattan Project, in World War Two, to make sure that we had the scientific minds on-line when we needed them. Some of those men had scruples about the project, turned down some of the most generous work terms in history. So the government activated them. The collective safety of the country *momentarily* superseded their individual civil rights. Momentarily, not permanently, I should stress. And World War Two came out the way it did."

"It's true, Sal," BC whispers to me. "They did it during the Manhattan Project. Bush and Colin Powell did it once or twice during Desert Storm, brought up some contractors who'd helped design parts of Baghdad. And I know the Dole administration did it covertly with some folks out in Montana, through the ATF, when it looked like the Freemen movement had legs."

I can't believe this. I turn to the colonel. My language is failing me. I can't find words. "I'm not a nuclear physicist," I say. "I've never fired a gun in my life. I know nothing about Mongolia, or Russia, or China."

I'm begging now, another stage.

She nods. "But we need what you know."

"I don't know *shit,*" I blurt out. Even to me it sounds pathetic and desperate. "Tell me what I know that could be worth—that could possibly help?"

There's a moment of silence, as though the people at the end of the table are figuring which way to go in a game of rummy.

"What do I know?" I ask again.

Cat-Eyes suddenly sits up straight and looks me right in the eye and asks, "Who signed the NATO expansion treaty in Independence, besides Albright?"

"What, you mean which countries?"

"Which people."

I can't help but laugh a second in frustration. "Geremek, Poland; Kavan, Czech Republic; and Martonyi for Hungary."

BC listens, but his face has a sour, dyspeptic look. "And we signed that damn treaty at Truman's library as a measure of respect to him. But you think anybody after me would ever do me the same courtesy, sign something here? Never."

Cat-Eyes waits, politely, for BC to wind down, then he asks a follow-up. "Just out of curiosity, what was Geremek's first name? You remember?"

"Bronislaw," I answer. I turn to BC for some kind of recognition, any kind of recognition, that these people are insane. They're proposing to overturn my life for the answers to trivia questions, answers anyone with a dictionary could give them. "Big deal. You could find that faster on your pop-up than it took you to ask me. What else could I possibly know?"

There is an almost polite silence, and finally BC leans in to my ear. His voice is an apologetic old man's voice, but somewhere down deep—faint but audible—he's proud. "Me, Sal," he says. "You're the living expert on me."

"That's partially right. We need your help with a project," the colonel continues smoothly. "We're interested in drafting some material on NATO expansion, the geopolitics of the 1990s. And of course how the tobacco dispute in Washington figured into that."

"And my role in that, as I understand it," BC amends. "My role as president. Those were two of the centerpieces of my administration."

"Very true, sir. Your role in a very primary way."

"We might as well call it what it is and call it a revisionist history," Cat-Eyes suggests, almost sweetly.

11

HOLD-HOLD-HOLD-HOLD-WIN

It's twenty minutes later, and BC is right in the middle of another trademark bit of mediation. He's just stopped the discussion to ask each of us to take one of the smartpads he had a flunky stack at the other end of the table, and write down a list of our nonnegotiable (he calls them "redline") items on one side of the page. Negotiable items go on the other side. But we're also to star any of the items we find ourselves hesitating over, a clever little bit. The pads are networked, and the idea is that we can keep constant and graphic track of one another's feelings, even when we don't feel like talking. I know from experience that BC adores these things. Like his leverage-savvy body-walker, smartpad technology takes an already obsessive part of BC's psyche to new and desperate lengths.

He's just gotten this suggestion out and begun the process of earnestly inventorying all the faces at the table, one by one, when the colonel cuts in, brusquely. "Mr. President, I'm afraid we'll have to ask you to leave, at this point. It's a matter of security clearance, and I'm sure you can understand the need for that. Thanks for your help to now. I'll stop by when we're finished and brief you if that's all right. We'll take it from here."

BC puts a big anxious hand out in the air, lets it turn there for a second. "But, Colonel, it was my understanding that this—"

"We'll take it from here," she repeats with unmistakable firmness, then turns in her chair and gives a raised eyebrow to the guard at the door, who in turn opens the door and gives a raised eyebrow to BC's personal peacock marine in the waiting room.

The peacock marine comes in and waits expectantly.

There is a long moment in which everyone looks at BC.

A sound, like a thousand-year-old cricket grating its legs together, leaves his throat. "Now, just a damn minute," he begins, by way of warning.

"Thank you again, sir," the colonel prompts.

Then BC explodes.

Even for those of us expecting it—me, maybe the colonel, maybe the lawyer with the folders full of contingencies—it exceeds mental preparation. It is the sort of tantrum that an adviser of his once referred to simply as "the wave," an elemental force of frustration and profanity that does in fact roll through the conference room like something vast and tidal, breaking on the teak dividers, buffeting the glass walls. It is something none of us will ever see again: a one-hundred-and-nine-year-old man with rebuilt hands and hips and eyes and muscle tissue regressing in an instant back to the Armageddon of the terrible twos.

BC is not, for those minutes, human. Small white flecks of his saliva dot the table in a wide, curving radius four or five feet from his seat. He's literally pouring himself out in livid anguish.

When he's near finished, his face red and wild, his knuckly old hands grasping desperately at the table and the back of his chair, moisture if not actual tears leaking from both eyes, I see him not as an old man who's been told to leave the room but as a man obsessed with his own place in history, Narcissus dragged forcibly from the stream.

At the height of his power, his enemies turned his failings and sexual sins into dinner-table conversation not only in America and Europe but throughout the Third World. All of a sudden he had a deep inner wound that literally anyone anywhere in the world could salt. Now they've hinted that, for whatever reason, somehow history will be reworked, done up in a different ribbon.

And he can't play.

Finally, he leaves the room. There's a moment of silence, like the seductively gentle aftermath of a squall, and it dawns on me: my security clearance is now higher than his.

* * *

Somehow, forty more minutes have gone by—forty minutes in which nothing has come any clearer—before Cat-Eyes leans forward and touches the colonel's sleeve and says, "Look, everybody in this room is on a need-to-know basis except for the two arm-breakers in the back, and they've got their headsets turned up so they can't hear a damn thing anyway. Let's just say what we've got to say."

He swings away from the colonel to look at me. "For all the talk about checking you out, Pat managed not to tell you straight out that you *got* the clearance. The security people didn't want to give it to you, but they had no choice. So yes, you're drafted, and no, there's not a damn thing you can do about it, except choose to get shipped off to prison for refusing, but you do have some rights. And one of those is to know what you're cleared to know, which is as much as I know, which isn't much, believe me, but it's enough to cut a pretty wide path through the acronym manure that everybody's been spreading for the last hour or so."

The colonel and the other man look on with various expressions of distaste, but neither jumps in to stop him. It's not so much that they want to listen to him, I don't think, as that they don't want to listen to any more from me.

"Okay," he says, leaning back in his chair, pursing his narrow lips, "you asked before what stage we were at in these wars. No, it isn't adolescence, although I thought that was a pretty funny comment. The stage we're at"—he stops and nods, looking around the room—"is called *losing*."

The statement just hangs out there in front of us, disembodied and unavoidable, like the first stray scent of something dead. No one wants to react, follow up on it, touch it. It's strange: the words are so close to my father's words. How many people in the country are saying this, whispering this?

The colonel purses her lips momentarily. "Let's keep something straight. This detail may run informally, but don't for a second start thinking that there's not military discipline underneath it all. Because you'll find that out in a *hot* second."

"You've about got her halfway to a cell in Leavenworth," Cat-Eyes says. "We don't have time to win her over inch by inch by inch. Tell her what's at stake. Tell her we're on our way to losing the farm over there in Asia." Again it strikes me how young he is. Almost half their age and he's hijacking the meeting.

I can't resist. "I don't retract anything I said earlier. I don't plan to cooperate with you in any way. But I'd like to know if what he says is true."

The colonel snaps the pop-up shut, fully engaged now. She leans forward on her forearms and brings her fleshy face out over the table, pugnacious but otherwise unreadable. "Losing and winning are elementary-school concepts when you're looking at a conflict like this," she says after a moment, carefully. Her glance flicks over to me, flicks back to the lanky young man. "It's like trying to use chocolate coins to explain hedge-fund management."

"I'm a little boy at heart. Indulge me." He sounds like he's enjoying this, like it's an argument he's been trying to start forever and now he's not only got it started, he's got an audience.

"It's not that simple," she starts out flatly. "There isn't *winning*, in the sense of winning. Soldiers die, parts of armies die. Territory changes hands. But that's not really what it's about."

"What is it about, then? For the sake of argument."

"It's *endurance*, on a national scale. It's physical resources, population curves." She grinds a plump finger into the tabletop. "Food and weapons production. Metallurgy. Single-molecule silicon platforms. This is evolution. Look at us, look at them, for God's sake."

"I've looked," Cat-Eyes shoots back. "That's my point. That's exactly the point I'm trying to make."

"It's deep, perennial attack patterns. We're a seasonal force in the Balkans, over the entire Caucasus region, and most of Mongolia at this point. Our gunships move in on the spring winds. They move down from the mountains with the snowpack and into the fields, lay down expeditionary forces. We come with the heat, we're out with the harvest. People crouch down in the fields and see our formations heading south. This will be a thirty-five-year war by the time we're through with it. You need to respect that. It's hold-hold-hold-hold-win."

"Agree completely," the other civilian beside her puts in tartly.

Cat-Eyes continues, ignoring the unified front beside him. "As I was saying, Sal, the stage of this war that we're in right now is called *losing your ass*." He leans back and laces his hands behind his head. "I defy anyone to look over any of the intelligence reports I looked at and come to any other conclusion, even with all the deletions and eyes-only parts given the most optimistic slant possible. We're losing in Southern Russia, and we've lost in most of Mongolia.

"James"—he leans around the colonel and addresses the other civilian—"am I laying it on too thick, or isn't it a fact that the United States of America is looking at broad-based retreat from *both* Thousand-Mile Fronts?"

The other man answers mildly, "I don't, personally, think this is really the time or place to air this question."

"Disagree completely," Cat-Eyes says, straight-faced. Then he smiles at his own joke. He knows he's being a brat, and he's enjoying rushing things along, but even I can tell from the reactions of the other two that he's a lot closer to the mark than they are. He smooths his mass of brown hair up onto his forehead, out of his eyes. "Correct me if I'm wrong about the pull-backs."

"You pick the worst moment to raise this. Worst possible moment."

"Air the question, James. Air it."

The other man turns his torso in his seat, leans an arm on the back of his chair. This has the effect of broadening his chest, and sure enough, he begins a round of mine's-bigger-than-yours. "Colonel Turner said winning and losing were elementary-school terms, and she's right. You read a set of briefing books—blacked-out briefing books—and all of a sudden you're General MacArthur. But if you want to know what I think, I think you're doomsaying. You've got no military training, and you misinterpret what you see."

"So that's the heart of the matter. I've got no military training. Well, that's why I need remedial education."

James conspicuously doesn't rise to the bait. He waves a hand, like you'd clear a tiny shaving mirror. "The situation is bad right now. But the EA is stretched way too thin, over a lot more open territory than they'd like. Most of the larger clusters of ground troops are unfriendlies. For our A-20s and Apaches it's pick and push."

Cat-Eyes turns briefly to me and gives a fragmentary eye-roll that only I can see. "The EA would be interested to know that the more planes they shoot down, the worse things look for them. Imagine their dismay when they realize."

"Look, the Eastern Alliance has got *twelve*-year-olds soldiering in Kazakhstan; they can hardly lift their AK-57s. They're looking at losing their entire fallback generation. After that, the land's population-fallow."

"You don't think, just for the sake of argument, that the Chinese could repopulate those defenses almost indefinitely?"

Before I realize it, I'm saying, "It wouldn't be the first time. Take a look at Vietnam, Cambodia. Last century."

After a beat, James nods politely in my direction, but you can tell he thinks the comment comes straight from the peanut gallery. He crosses his arms over his chest. He's said his piece. He gives the colonel a solidarity look, then finishes, "It might take two years, or five, but the facts on the ground will turn around. And then armchair generals like you will be marching in Memorial Day parades."

Cat-Eyes turns back to me, actually addresses me. "Okay, let's say that we're *not* hemorrhaging over in Asia. Ask them about the U.S.-mainland invasion."

He says it, and the colonel and James and Pat Evans go stone-faced.

"Me?" I ask.

"Yeah, you. Ask them about the new Thousand-Mile Front. The one here."

I hesitate. He's kidding. He's riffing, trying to get their goats, or mine, who knows. But he can't be serious. I expect the colonel to give it the big laugh, but she doesn't. Instead, she whispers to Evans and, with a parting look at me, he collects his folders and prepares to leave the room. But before he does so, he gives me a pleasant look and runs a hand casually through his hair. Then he's gone.

And for some reason, that's the scariest thing of all. For as much as I disliked the guy, at least he stood in some hazy, ethics-free way for the Law. Now I'm in a room with spooks.

12

MAY BE HAZARDOUS TO YOUR HEALTH

Turner gets up from her chair, smooths her blouse, and walks back to the guard behind her. She motions for him to turn off his headset and then tells him to take his partner and wait outside. They close the door behind them, and she comes back over to the table.

She's a short woman, maybe five feet one, and I wonder what kind of special hell life in the military must have been for her until she made serious rank, how many times she had to really tough it out. She's too short and squat to beat down; it's like gravity has already condensed her to the limits of possibility, the industrial diamond of womankind.

She walks over by the windows, looks out toward River Market off in the distance, then sweeps her gaze over the low-rise buildings and the withering Arkansas sun, which is rendered almost charming by the air-conditioning and the polarized glass. "Let's put up some facts, before we go any further. That kind of speculation is worse than astrology." She holds up her thumb, and strangely, for a second, she looks like a short, stout, female Ronald Reagan.

"There have been some unsettling developments overseas recently. I'll try to make this as quick and simple and untechnical as I can. One, the Yellow Sea fleet has been maneuvering farther and farther out into international waters. Two, Algerian Western Sahara has also become a major naval staging ground. We hit it a few times last year, but they've ringed it out pretty nicely with air-defense clusters. And three," the colonel goes on, "we're not sure but we think we've lost track of two out of seven of China's D-class submarines. We thought they'd shallow-docked at least one in the Solomon Islands and brought the other into the Northern Pacific, but now the patterns the Navy cat-and-mouse people had seem not to have been patterns, and they're starting from scratch."

Cat-Eyes elaborates. "She means starting from scratch to go through all the oceans in the world looking for them."

Turner pointedly ignores him. "There are a few schools of thought," she says speculatively, walking back over from the windows. "One is that these things mean nothing, that it's all about putting up a more robust defense presence offshore. Another is that they're thinking about some kind of symbolic strike on the American mainland as a means of bringing the Wars home to the civilian population, try to stir up some kind of antiwar sentiment.

"That way they could use the different sea and air groups as decoys. Move the Yellow Sea fleet out, out, out so we pull resources that way, and then have the subs run for daylight and try to take out Seattle, or San Diego." She makes it sound like rugby somehow, all strategy, no blood.

"And finally," she says, a smile creeping out, dimples drilling into her jowls, "the pessimists think that they're going to coordinate all the elements into two vast, Hollywood-style armadas coming full-speed into both coasts." She comes back to the table and takes her seat, chuckling a little at her own humor. Then, abruptly leaning forward, she plucks a muffin from the silver tray, and rather than cutting it or even removing the paper band, she simply begins pulling at its insides with her fingers and pushing them into her mouth. "As you might have guessed, this is George's pet theory." She gives a sarcastic little wave to Cat-Eyes, who doesn't look like a George, but who is, apparently.

"Tell her the other thing," Cat-Eyes/George prompts.

"We've overbriefed already."

"Correct me if I'm wrong, Ms. Hayden," George rolls on, focusing on me now, "but would you go along with what we're asking of you—assuming it's legal and that it would help—if you knew the war was already here on the mainland? If it wasn't a foreign war for fucking smokes, as the bumper sticker says, but a domestic war for basic security?"

I don't answer right away, and he turns to the colonel and says, "Tell her or I'm gonna tell her. You want her on board one hundred percent as of today, you said."

James pulls back into his seat with barely concealed belligerence. He runs both hands over his half-bald, half-cropped head, seems about to burst out with something, and then pulls back into decorum. The colonel suddenly says, "I understand you were on the East Coast Bullet train that locked up last week and resulted in a death. You had a small injury yourself, rib fracture."

I realize I haven't thought about my injury or the flex bandage over it in hours. Immediately it begins to throb. "Right," I say. Then it hits me. "What, did you have somebody following me up and back to Vermont?"

She looks at James, the other civilian, and he says evenly, "Yes. It's been an ongoing surveillance, no secret about it now. Mostly for your safety."

The Englishman with the leg fetish. Again I get a burst of anger that almost as quickly dissipates, in lieu of any target. All I can think of to say is this: "Yeah, well, he's a goddamn lecher."

James nods, jots something on a pad—*Ease off on the lechers,* maybe.

"About five minutes before those trains, the ECB and the WCB, went offline and locked up—before anyone had any context to work from—the Pentagon began to receive an odd transmission on the microwave frequency from one of our command-and-control satellites. We're not sure where the foreign transmission originated, or how it could have been beamed into a highly secure, knit-crypted line. In fact, it wasn't just highly secure, but our most secure. And probably it was picked for that reason. But the transmission was in English. A taunt, we expect."

Another beat. I'm the one to break first. "So what was it, anyway?"

"It was very flip. It said, *The surgeon general has determined that train travel may be hazardous to your health.*" Turner throws up her hands, as though to say, *You know these wacky EA types.*

I don't say anything because I'm remembering the darkened car and the rain of people and silverware off the seat backs, and then the sickening reverse, every person and object breaking gravity a second time to fly away in a new direction.

"It's a play on the old health warnings they had on cigarette packs," James explains after a second.

I look at him. I feel like getting up from my chair and going to the whiteboard and giving a crisp, ninety-minute lecture on the microhistory of the warning's evolution, how cigarette makers spent millions lobbying for the word *may* over the word *are,* the political infighting between the Justice Department and Congress, health advocates and Big Tobacco. How weeks were spent defeating a clause the manufacturers claimed they couldn't live without: *in rare circumstances*.

But it's hardly worth it. So after a second, I say, "Really?"

"Then several minutes later, someone—we're assuming a team of Chinese Webclippers, or hired diversionaries—supercrunched both rail-control networks. Accessed the trains and brought all the component intelligences off-line, car by car, nearly simultaneously. Then activated all the air brakes in a distortion pattern, all the cars braking and releasing at cross-purposes."

"That's not supposed to be possible," I argue. I notice that I'm passing my thumb back and forth across the section of my blouse that covers the bandage on my ribs, and I take my hand away.

Cat-Eyes laces his fingers across his lean frame, leans way back in his chair. "It's not supposed to be. Apparently they didn't even bother to find a back door, just went ahead and overwhelmed the security on one of the side doors. Just massive computing power."

Just then there is a mild announcement tone from the speakers built into the conference table, and a young man's deep voice says, "Colonel, sorry to disturb you. The former president is demanding to speak to you, or to Ms. Hayden. He's very . . . he's extremely upset. I conveyed your orders, but he won't hear it. He's threatening to harm himself physically. Sorry again to interrupt."

The colonel doesn't look up, but she answers immediately, much more sharply than I would have expected. "You have your orders, Sergeant. Carry them out. Don't disturb us again. The former president has a highly developed instinct for self-preservation. Pass that along to those assigned to him."

She goes back to wiping her short fingers with a napkin. She's got her eyes down still, focused somewhere inside herself. She's nodding, her fleshy double chin opening and closing like a second mouth. "We were very lucky to lose just three men. The Bullet technology actually performed a lot better than we had any right to expect. It proved a lot more resistant to those cross-stresses than the designers apparently expected. And needless to say, we've had a chance to go in and make at least a quick dirty fix on the data portals they used to enter the system.

"It was a good thing, in a way, in that we're now more secure domestically than we were. They tipped their hand, and we're much tighter across the board in terms of the security concerns than we were a month ago. That's all to the good."

George doesn't say a word, he doesn't refute the colonel's spin on the Bullet incident. He doesn't push anymore or jar the meeting along. He doesn't smile or ham it up. He just looks at me: an intent, overdetermined look that I can't quite read. But it's more persuasive than anything anyone has said or done all day. *We're dying,* the look says, *and no one will admit that they see us dying.*

Everything that George is saying speaks to my own feelings about where the Wars seem to be headed. It makes sense of the way that soldiers are a part of domestic life now, so much so that I don't even register them on the street, patrolling the occasional corner.

And I feel a small, unexpected part of me begin to want to help.

Almost immediately, though, this part is overwhelmed by another complete set of considerations. I'm moving, not for the first time today, toward trusting someone because he seems to be the least of a number of evils. It's still good cop/bad cop, when it gets right down to it, and I have no way of knowing that I can trust George any more than I can trust the people at the table he seems to be opposing. But I have to admit that I've crossed over some kind of line.

And so I hear myself begin to speak, and I realize only halfway through that I've finally become my subject, because what I say is pitch-perfect BC: "Look, I'm not relinquishing my right to fight this activation you've gone to so much trouble to trump up—and I'm not in any way indicating any desire to go along with anything you lay out—in fact, I'm as certain as ever that I don't want any part of any operation outside normal constitutional auspices—but what is it exactly that you want me to do?"

13

I-NARRATIVE IN BOYS NATION

James opens his briefcase and takes what looks like an eight-by-ten glossy from it. He stares at it for a second, then slides it across the table to me. It flips over halfway to me, and I have to get up and reach out and turn it over. My heart stutters for a second when I realize that this could very easily be surveillance footage.

For some reason, I'm convinced that it will be a grainy shot of my last sexual encounter, a long ten months ago, with a diplomatic attaché from Norway who had a month's worth of business at the Library and a more than ordinarily effective line of Scandinavian bullshit. A week after my first surrender, he announced the presence of a plump wife in Oslo, though assuring me that she was more a "Northern European" wife than anything—that is, while she would prevent him from developing anything lasting or meaningful with me, her existence didn't necessarily have to preclude more sex. I was cooking dinner for him, stirring homemade spaghetti sauce if you can believe it, when he calmly laid all of this out.

And I handled it not well. In so many loud words, I told him to leave my apartment while his manhood was still attaché. I now prepare myself to find out that he, like the British lecher on the Bullet, was only doing his job.

But I needn't have worried. Today is far, far too surreal a day for the picture to be what I expect. Instead, I flip it over, and a quick laugh slips from my throat—it's not the last picture I'd have expected, but close, and it's not something new and shocking at all. It's an old photo, roughly ninety years old, one I know in my sleep.

It's Washington, D.C., 1963. Wednesday the twenty-fourth of July, to be more specific, a sweltering summer day. A gathering in the Rose Garden of young men come to the capital to meet with then-President John F. Kennedy. The young men are members of an American Legion spin-off called Boys Nation, and each wears a white polo shirt with the Legion insignia emblazoned like a lawman's star on the left breast. They've been in the capital for a week, each a pretend senator to a mock senate formed to debate the issues of the day, race relations and education and welfare. Each is a young hustler, each is a budding policy wonk, but no one is out-hustling or outwonking sixteen-year-old BC.

In the foreground, a young BC is shaking Kennedy's hand. His face is working with tremendous excitement, awe: meeting Kennedy was the whole reason BC had joined Boys Nation in the first place. There is accomplishment in his face as well. Most of the facts suggest that BC was first in line for a handshake because he sprinted up the lawn to the site near the Portico and then savagely guarded his spot like a forward who'd just pulled down a rebound.

Both Kennedy and BC have the brush cuts, tended sideburns, and conservative clothing that distinguish the early from the late sixties. BC is three-quarters full-face, while Kennedy is caught mostly from behind, profile recognizable but face effectively hidden. Given that Kennedy's life would end in a fine mist of blood and brain only four months later, this aspect of the picture has always struck me as fitting, thematically speaking.

BC is obviously caught in the middle of stammering out something bordering on a confession of love to his hero. His eyes are locked on Kennedy's, and his head inclines slightly forward, reverentially. Kennedy's thumb hooks over the young BC's hand like a paper clip. I read this to mean that the handshake was deliberately firm on both sides, maybe BC—a hulking kid, six-foot-three—trying to show his grip, and Kennedy surprised but giving back pound for pound.

It's a photograph I've spent more than a few hours looking over, because it played such an outsize role in BC's later life. It was reprinted in his senior high-school yearbook, and when you asked BC to sign your yearbook he signed it there and more or less only there.

When he ran for president in 1992, an unknown nationally, his campaign released the picture at precisely the right moment and it made its own indisputable statement of legitimacy: this was when the torch was passed, it seemed to say, this was when BC was anointed. It became the political equivalent of pulling Excalibur from the stone.

"Have you ever seen this photograph before?" James asks, his voice suddenly without affect, cop-neutral.

I lift my eyes from the photo, which looks suspiciously like the original print. Possibly they retrieved it from the archives downstairs before the meeting, although that would have required BC's personal okay.

I push the photo back to him. "I reprinted it in my first book. I've seen it before. Yes. Many, many times."

He looks down at his notes, then back up, smiles with no teeth. "We knew that, of course," he tells me.

"Well, then, why did you ask?"

"Don't even ask why he asked," George cuts in, rolling his eyes. "You're wasting your time if you try to find out how James's mind works. What he's *trying* to find out is if you've studied the picture carefully in the past."

"Yes. I'd venture to say that after BC, I know this photograph better than anyone within a five-hundred-mile radius of this room, maybe even a thousand-mile radius. In fact, if you turn off the lights and put on some soft music, and then give me an hour with a piece of paper and a set of pastel crayons, I'm pretty certain I can turn out an exact replica for you, operating by touch alone. I wrote half a chapter on this thing. I am familiar with the photograph, okay?"

"I understand you," James answers quickly, an eye on Colonel Turner. "What I'd like to know is if you've ever looked carefully at the hats of the American Legion members in the background. Think carefully."

There are in fact two older Legionnaires in the background, chaperons for the boys most likely, and I'm about to give another smart-ass answer when I realize that for all the time I've spent poring over the photo, I've never actually zeroed in on that particular detail. But after my last shot I'm not going to come right out and say so.

"Well, I've seen the hats, obviously," I hedge. "They're American Legion hats. Insignias, quasi-military. Silly-looking. Hatlike."

Colonel Turner crooks her fingers impatiently for the print, and James hands it over. She opens her pop-up, strokes a series of keys, waits a second, and then presses the photo to its reading surface. An intense white light swells at the edges.

"I'll throw it up on the wall for you," she says.

A small green ready-light fires up in the wall behind me. Immediately thereafter, a large square of teakwood grain ceases to be teakwood grain, resolving itself instead into the largest version of the BC/Kennedy shot I've ever seen. The colonel's pop-up is correcting and deepening light and shadow as a matter of course, so that it ceases to be a creased print and becomes as professional and compelling as a movie still.

At this size, I'm struck even more powerfully by the way in which BC seems to be *sharing* the foreground with JFK; matched in height, good looks, and ambient psychic force, they seem like two celebrities exchanging greetings rather than a boy in a miracle meeting with his president. Clearly, most of this sense comes with the historical hindsight of the observer, but not all. The young BC always managed to look extraordinarily on a par with his unquestioned political superiors, whether it was Jimmy Carter or Arkansas Senator William Fulbright.

I look at the chaperons: two of them, one to either side of JFK. Older, shorter, doughier Arkansas guys. I've never really noticed this before, but the one to the left has his eyes nearly shut, whether from sun or a photographer's flash or an inadvertent blink remains unclear. The other man is reduced by JFK's head and shoulder to a fragment of a face and an eye. And a hat. Actually his hat is more visible than the other chaperon's, and I focus in on it. Beneath the American Legion insignia, it appears to read, *St. Matthews,* but it's too indistinct to be certain.

"One second, I'll parse it," the colonel says, glancing down at her small touch pad. She strokes at it once, twice, and an oversize jeweler's lens appears in the corner of the wall screen. It's an exquisite avatar, lovingly done by some faceless military code-drone somewhere: heavy, smooth, finger-worn Turkish-leather cup surrounding a burnished crystal lens. The lens moves smoothly over the second chaperon's Legion hat. In the lens's eye, the American Legion insignia jumps into focus. The lens grows larger until the image inside it dominates the screen. I'm looking at the insignia, AMERICAN above and LEGION below, and thinking about the odd iconography of male social clubs, this one a star inside a circle inside an odd geometric shape that looks suspiciously like a grinding wheel.

Then, startlingly, like a purloined letter, I see that there actually is a purloined letter: the word AMERICAN in the insignia has been mistakenly spelled AMERCAN, probably the way the Arkansas Legionnaire wearing it usually pronounced it anyway. The mistake is so obvious it's invisible.

"We're missing a letter," I say, quickly, like someone's going to beat me to the punch, and I may as well be back in a graduate seminar, trying to impress people with my acuity.

George nods, looking at the screen. "Do you have any clear sense of whether that word was misspelled whenever you've looked at it before?"

I think about it for a second, then shake my head. "Couldn't say."

James rubs it in, another good thing to know about someone. He's a lot more sarcastic than he's allowing himself to seem in this meeting. "So you won't be needing the mood music, then," he puts in with a straight face. "We won't need to rush out for the pastel crayons."

"I guess not." All of a sudden I'm exhausted and starved and worn through. I don't have a watch, but suddenly my body knows that we've been in here for hours, and it's time for dinner, for some small shred of normalcy. "So the word is misspelled. So some late-1950s felt-hatmaker in Arkansas somewhere isn't going to win the National Spelling Bee. Look, I'm not trying to be negative or anything"—I turn in my chair, looking at each in turn, projecting reasonableness—"because if you've got something huge and earth-shattering to say about this then I'm all ears. But, I mean, so what?"

"It wasn't misspelled last week," James says carefully.

"What wasn't?"

"The word AMERICAN on this hat, in this particular photo."

I look back at the magnified image. "You mean in this print."

"No, I mean in any version of this photo. And in the original. It was spelled correctly until last Monday. We made sure. We documented that. And then"—James looks at the colonel, who's lost in her pop-up again, and then back to me—"we rewrote it. The photo now reflects the change. We were looking to you for outside confirmation, but it isn't really necessary."

I have no idea what he's talking about. But he goes on.

"Put it this way. We have a way of contacting previous National Security working groups. We asked the NSC chiefs of that particular administration"—he points to Kennedy—"for a favor, so to speak, as a way of demonstrating the validity of the connection. Communication is via the NSC's on-site database, which, fortunately for us, was up and running in 1959."

I'm still trying to get it.

The colonel lifts her head. "The technology for this kind of correspondence has been available for years, but there's been a hold on it. For obvious reasons."

"Obviously," I mutter.

"We wouldn't be using it now except that the NSC has gotten hold of it under the Pentagon's first-strike guidelines. At least one of the Joint Chiefs is buying the theory that the EA are looking to strike U.S. soil, and he's leveraged that into a go-ahead for several prohibited technologies. We have authorization directly from the Commander-in-Chief for targeted usage of this technology, this retroactive coding technology, with the instruction that we're to keep any potential contact or changes in the historical facts on the ground to an absolute minimum."

I feel like discussion has moved on to some book I've never read, that everyone's using a term I've never heard defined. "Technology to do what? To code what retroactively?" I blurt out. "Can we please, for thirty seconds, talk in direct sentences? I'm a biographer. I have no idea what you're talking about."

George squints at the Rose Garden of 1963, makes a phone with his thumb and pinky, puts it to his ear. "Technology to talk to those guys back there," he says. "Write to them. Get code to them, code they can read."

"And you wrote to them and had them misspell a word on a hat?"

Everyone nods, no one finds it amusing. "That's right, more or less," James says, nodding. There's a faint whiff of braggadocio to his response. He stares at the photo, and I can see that my own boast about knowing the photograph better than anyone within a thousand miles was clearly an empty one. Probably they've all studied it in more detail than I have. Probably they've had a team or teams of people studying it for weeks now. These people know BC.

And then I have a hunch. I turn to George, who returns my gaze placidly.

"George isn't your real name, is it?"

He doesn't crack a smile. "For now it is."

"And what's your last name, for now?" I can't let it alone. I have to see if I'm right about their code names.

Now he cracks a smile. "Stephanopoulos."

I look at James, who seems about to share his operation name as well. "Don't bother," I tell him. "I have a glimmering of an idea."

He shrugs, then goes back to where he left off. "This Boys Nation chaperon here," he explains, "is not one of the Arkansas contingent. He's a 1963 NSC operative. What we did was ask the NSC of that time period to mock up an insignia according to our specifications and then have this man place himself at the head of the line for the pictures taken that day. Fairly simple for them to pull off. But a fairly dramatic result for us, with minimum potential historical disruption. And, really, they owed us some confirmation. We had their day codes, of course, to identify ourselves. It was kind of lopsided up to that point."

At least one thing has fully penetrated. "You changed the actual hat," I say, enunciating carefully. "There was an original hat in 1963. Now that hat is"—I make a stretching motion with my hands—"a changed hat."

"Essentially. We caused the hat to be changed. And the man wearing the hat. It's probably hard for you to remember what the photo looked like before we effected the change, but in the original it was a different man entirely wearing the hat. You have to take our word on that."

I look at the colonel, who has been drifting in and out of the conversation, but now she's paying strict attention. I motion to the print she has resting on the tabletop beside her, and she slides it over. I feel a powerful need to hold it.

I take it in my hand and this time I'm convinced it's the original print, the one BC bought from the Boys Nation photographer in mid-1963. It has a quaint, old-fashioned look, with its thin white borders and its haphazard lighting and focus. It feels heavy, much heavier than an image you might print out today. It's an object in its own right.

And now, if I believe them, it's a different photo, measurably different, because several of the objects in it are measurably different.

They might be lying. I'm more than willing to believe that the military is capable of a complex four-hour lie with visual aids. But it doesn't feel that way.

It feels true. Now BC's unlimited fury makes a whole new world of sense to me. This is more and larger than new propaganda, some new textual version of old histories. This is changing everything, potentially changing everything that was. It couldn't be clearer to me that the Wars are essentially lost, if they're even playing in a limited way with an idea like this. The Manhattan Project must have seemed like the same sort of half-admission, a horrific goal that made sense only when measured against the white space of obliteration.

The historical facts on the ground, James called them. BC's youth, his world, his achievements, his successes and scandals, and the rest of the entire evolving world through him and his actions in it. Now the lockdown of the Library makes sense. He must be just raging down there in the hidey-hole, like a lion tricked into an unbelievably deep pit, bellowing and kicking over chairs and striking the walls with his frail fists.

If what they're telling me is true, then this isn't just hell for him, but hell built to his own precise ironic specifications. Because, along with what was, they're also talking about changing what *is*, changing in fact what the definition of is *is*.

14

BC UNCHAINED

We're leaving, suddenly. I've been allowed to spend fifteen minutes in my office, packing my leather satchel. I have not been allowed to speak to anyone, to say good-bye to anyone. I am carrying the satchel, walking down the corridor to the Library's formal rear entrance onto the South Lawn. I am surrounded by six Berets, with their weapons unholstered, and we're moving faster than a walk. George and James trail behind. The colonel is nowhere in sight.

The only thing anyone will say, when I ask where we're going, is Virginia.

I have not said in any way that I want to go anywhere with these people or help them accomplish whatever it is they plan to accomplish, and they haven't asked.

We come out into the Rose Garden, and I have the brief sense of déjà vu that hits me whenever I use this exit, which isn't often. More or less reserved for BC and the occasional formal Library event, the Rose Garden and the South Lawn beyond it have been designed to look nearly exactly like their counterparts in Washington. From the rear, the Library could be the White House.

Moving out into that deliberate mock-up, I always feel for a second as though I've blundered somehow into the endless video I've watched of BC signing bills and politicking in the original version, video of him signing the Family and Medical Leave Act, his first solid legislative win, and video of two busloads of Democrats joining him for a strange pep rally immediately following his formal impeachment, video of endless press conferences and policy rollouts.

The air is still very hot and pulsing with humidity, even now, a half hour to sunset. My blouse and my shorts are sticking to me, and the moisture in the air exaggerates the sense of mulishness and lingering anger I feel. I'm hustling along with these men because of their size and their guns, but I don't want to be here. Still, if I haven't heard enough to make me feel obligated exactly, I've heard enough to intrigue me, to tweak my curiosity. I'm walking fast, the way you walk when you're ahead of a gun. I have the distinct sense that everyone locked-down in the building is watching me.

We move quickly down from the Portico, out of the Garden, and down the long, winding asphalt path toward the stretch of lawn where the Berets have parked their flock of fat helicopters. It's a fairly long walk, and I have time to appreciate the way these machines have been designed to intimidate, to suggest the stinging insect. They squat beside a stand of sweet gum trees, seeming to doze.

Then, halfway down the path, the heavy, four-bladed rotors on each of the machines begin turning at nearly the same moment, moving lazily into action.

We're approaching the center chopper, the largest and clearly the flying command center. It is a massive big-bellied machine, larger than a city glide tram, with expansive tinted windows and three separate transoms let down to the clipped lawn. Two thin nozzles poke from the tremendous nose of the craft, whittled-down Vulcan cannons, which look like nothing so much as black tusks.

George moves up from behind and breaks into the circle of Berets. He takes my arm, and he's just beginning to steer me to the center transom when there is a shout behind us, followed by another, and the soldiers surrounding me snap their heads around.

George whirls, dropping my arm.

The ground slopes slightly upward to the Library, and when I turn I have to shade my eyes for an instant from the sun setting over the river.

And then I make out what's happening: a man in white shirtsleeves riding in a brown leather armchair has cleared the Portico, and, as I watch, he jumps the small marble lip of the Library's rear patio and brings his chair down onto the head of the path, the back end of the chair fishtailing slightly from the accelerated turn.

It is BC. He's in his camouflaged wheelchair with the onboard mouse, the one he never, ever uses, the one designed to level the playing field in the event of an attempted assassination. But he is in it now, and once his tires touch level asphalt, he is *moving*.

Three Berets and the peacock marine come slamming out onto the Portico after him, running at the full tilt of men trained to sprint until they drop. They've underestimated him, that much is clear, let him nurse his grudge there in his leather armchair until he called feebly for them to open the door of the hidey-hole and then bowled them over with the chair's muscle-car engine.

As I watch, his dicey voice is trumpeting, louder than I've ever heard it.

"SAL! WAIT, SAL!" he bellows, and then again: "SAL!"

His chair can outpace a gazelle, and he opens up a big lead on the soldiers, but the curves of the path sap his speed. He's unfamiliar with the fingertip mouse, and there's a jerky quality to his steering. Still, he has them beat until they break from the path altogether and plot individual intercept courses, fanning out over the grass.

"Get her in the cabin!" James yells over the growing scream of the engines and the wash of the blades. "Now, do it now!"

"SAL!" I hear BC yell again, and as Berets on either side of me put their hands on my arms, I jerk away out of pure survival instinct and start back up the path. I only make it a step or two, but it's long enough to see one of the most amazing things I've ever seen.

As the Berets close in on him, ready to take hold of his chair at the final turn before the straightaway leading down to the choppers, BC leaps from the contoured seat, off the asphalt and onto the grass. And he runs.

It isn't the sprint of a young man, but he is running, arms knifing through the humid evening, thighs pumping, hairless head bobbing, and his mouth gasping desperately for air. He's digging it out, headed straight for this chopper. The ten-thousand-dollar wing tips flash in the light.

I've known for a long time that his muscles have been selectively strengthened and his joints successively replaced, but this is not within the range of his abilities. He is one century and nine years old. He can walk slowly and unassisted, but he cannot run, not for the last twenty-five years at least. This is utterly at odds with technology and measurable force. This is magic, this is rage and adrenaline and limitless desire unleashed, this is a mother lifting an entire Buick off the twisted body of her six-year-old.

And again, he's caught them utterly off guard. They catch hold of the chair as he jettisons it, and they seem for a second unable to believe that it's empty.

"SAL!" he yells, not as loudly or as drawn out, but more a single staccato exhalation. He's desperate to tell me something, but he's too far away to risk it, too far away to shout it. But he manages one phrase, for all of that: "STOP, WAIT!"

And listening to him call out, I freeze, forgetting to run.

"SAL! STOP!"

The Berets have my arms again, and now they're pulling me around toward the chopper, where George stands at the top of the transom, motioning frantically to me or the guards or both. They bring me to the steps, and the roar of the propellers is overpowering. The wind picks at my blouse, presses my eyes into their sockets. I relent and step up one, two steps, until the Berets are forced to let me go and move onto the transom behind me. And I take that chance to turn one more time.

I turn in time to see two of them finally overtake and blindside BC, double-teaming him and knocking him sprawling to the grass. There is nothing subtle about it; his arms and legs and head strike the turf in a whirl. It's a full tackle with all their weight behind it, more than enough to break one or more of his light bones. But there's no mistaking: their orders are to prevent him from reaching me, and again I have the dizzying sense that he and I have reversed roles.

"Stop it, for Christ's sake!" I scream. "You're hurting him! Goddammit, you're hurting him!"

Then I'm pressed into the cabin, cool, dark, air-conditioned, and wrestled into a large, soft, padded seat. James and George strap themselves into seats far in front of me, and behind me are soldiers, how many I don't know.

In another moment we lift off, and I see the other ships rise up with us into the sunset sky. Our lead helicopter executes a powerful bank, nearly rolling on its side, and I see the lights of the Library suddenly wink on below me, in sequence, floor after floor, the building having decided that twilight has come.

[illegible]

[illegible]

[illegible]

[illegible]

[illegible]

[illegible]

[illegible]

[illegible]

[illegible]

[illegible]

The Third Part:

WORSE THAN WORST-CASE SCENARIO

"On the way over here this afternoon, my wife and I passed a group of kids, group of students, who were visiting the White House. And I saw one young boy in that group—kind of a husky kid—who reminded me a lot of myself, when I was young and I came, as many of you know, to the White House to meet John F. Kennedy. And I thought, what's the real lesson in all this for this boy? What's the thing I'd wish him to take away from the things happening now over in the Congress? And I think it's got to be forgiveness. Forgiveness and a profound sense that people can learn from their mistakes and become better people, better husbands, better parents and fathers, better presidents and lawmakers, better servants of the Lord [applause]. So I said so to that boy. I walked up to him in the line there and I shook his hand and I said, 'Can you remember something for me?' And he said, 'Yes, sir.' And I said, 'Well, remember that a mistake is never too deep in the grain to change, to be put right somehow. And remember that forgiveness is the mark of grace.' And this big kid looks up at me [smiles] and he says, 'Okay, I will.'"

—BC, addressing a National Prayer Breakfast in the week preceding the United States Senate's vote on two Articles of Impeachment, 1999

15

LOW-OBSERVABLE TRAJECTORY

Somewhere over Kentucky, I'm guessing, someone's fingertip touches my arm. I'm very startled but there's no flinch. My body apparently doesn't see the point.

When I was seventeen, before the vice and consumption taxes on cars and gas became lark-prohibitive, my aunt Mary and I drove her old '06 Nissan Maxima to New York City from Burlington, which was absolutely certifiable because it was dusk when we left and our stated purpose was to find a nice restaurant somewhere in the city and have pie and coffee. Then the plan was to drive the seven hours back home, all of this at a cost roughly equal to a week in a fairly swank hotel.

This was in the days when Mary knew she was very sick, and I knew she was very sick, but when it still seemed possible that her illness might pass, or break suddenly like a five-year fever. It was a time when a road trip to New York City seemed like saying a rosary.

We talked and laughed and switched in and out of the driver's seat until somewhere around New Haven, when Mary fell asleep in the comforting grip of the car's contoured leather seats. I decided to let her sleep, decided to solo, and I drove on for another hour and a half or so, fighting sleep, feeling myself nod and unable to prevent it, biting my lip, taking off my shoes, trying anything but unable to stay fully awake and feeling the car always seeking the shoulder. It was a horrible, waking nightmare, and it ended only with Mary suddenly putting her hand on my shoulder, shaking it until my eyes focused.

Now, sitting in this hushed, surging helicopter, I don't react at first to the fingertip on my arm, because the feeling is the same. I'm rushing forward, encased somehow in threat, but unable to keep my energy focused, and I feel myself slipping into apathy. I turn slowly in the gloom and see that attached to the fingertip is yet another dark-haired Beret, this one clutching a small silver case. He nods hello, sits down in the seat across the aisle, and swings it around to face me.

He's noticeably younger and smaller than the rest, though well-built, and keener. His fingers are thin, dextrous. The eyes are small but relentless, the rodent eyes of a guy you could low-altitude-drop directly into a Shanghai trash Dumpster, if you needed to for some reason. The helicopter is lit only by small green emergency lights set like a string of emeralds into the carpeted floor, so his face has an extraterrestrial tinge. This puts a little English on even the most straightforward gestures.

He places his thumbs on the latches of the titanium case, rests his fingers on the top, and then hesitates, doesn't open it.

"Sorry to disturb you, ma'am. We have to seat a unit for you," he whispers, and there's a hint of apology in his voice.

"Seat a what?" I whisper back.

"An Open Info unit. That's an IV/IG rig. Intravenous, intraglandular. That's your military ID, ma'am."

Now I get it. "You're talking about a tapeworm."

He nods slowly, cracking the case open. He gives me the little rodent eyes, the way they do when you get up in the middle of the night and open the closet door. "That's what they call it in the movies, tapeworm. But it's actually an infraction to call them anything other than an OI unit. You can actually get written up." He glances a few rows up, toward the people with rank. "And these don't do a thing to your appetite, and they're safe, and microscopic in size, and you can opt to have it removed when your hitch is up." He's made these jokes before, this pitch before, calming down the horse before he hits it in the flank with a needle.

"You're telling me some people opt to leave them in?"

"Lots do, yeah. Lots. Some don't mind it, or they're afraid of retraction, which is deliberately low-impact outpatient surgery, but still there's the fear. Some feel like they'd be out of the family without it. They like going into their VA hospital or their PX and being in the system. Coming up valid, you know."

"Having everybody know your name."

Another one with no nose for irony. He nods soberly. "It's actually a lot of trouble communicating who you are all the time, what your story is, history, medical. You get used to people just knowing while you're in the service."

He's putting on latex gloves as he speaks, careful not to snap them in the regimented quiet, and drawing out a slim syringe. He taps the needle once, then holds it over a laser eye above the case's truncated keyboard. After a pause, while the light seeks a purchase, a short series of tones issues from the case, almost but not quite a snatch of melody. He sees me looking. "OI's suspended in saline solution. The notes tell you it's in there, and on-line."

"Can they use this thing to track you?"

He doesn't look up. "Certain conditions. Don't usually. Definitely don't once you're decommissioned. Against the law."

"Is it true that this thing can analyze your blood for chemical makeup and tell if you've been doing retro-drugs or something?"

"Certain conditions."

"Where's this thing wind up?"

"Lymph node." He taps the inside of his pectoral. "Ninety-eight-point-five percent of the time."

"What about the other one-point-five?"

"That would be what we call fecal matter. Then for a day or two the system isn't aware that it's tracking waste product. It gets comical sometimes."

"I bet. Are you a doctor?"

"Don't I wish," he whispers slowly, rasping his fingers and thumb in the money sign, eyes checking whatever data has come up on the inside of the case's lid. "I do wetware mostly. Body mechanic." He pauses a second, thinking about himself, looks up at me over the top of the case. "Let's say you have a subcutaneous system of some sort, pacemaker or adrenaline-relay, or embedded chip maybe with a hair-wire electrode port. That's a sensitive marriage. Somebody has to be in charge of the interface. Creating it, tweaking it. It's not applied particle physics, but it's not tossing pizzas either. I'm gonna need to ask you to take off your sweater."

I watch the needle enter the vein, and I watch him slowly empty the saline solution into me. Swimming somewhere in that vial-size sea is an etched grain of silicon-iodine alloy, trailing a microscopic fiber-optic hair. Already it's moving through my bloodstream to the lymph node under my arm, where it will take up residence, drawing a minuscule amount of energy from the reactions in the gland itself. I've seen these things in hundreds of army movies, the boot-camp montage, the buzz cut and the drill instructor and the tapeworm.

And then you're a GI, general issue. I look down at my arm. Already the arm is prepared to confess to the first scanner I pass everything the worm knows about me, which is everything the NSC knows about me, which, I can only assume, is everything about me there is to know.

He swabs my biceps with alcohol, quickly sprays skinfix on the wound. Body mechanic is right. His latex fingertips brush the spot. "Didn't hurt much if any at all, am I right or wrong?"

I take my punctured arm back. "It hurt my pride," I tell him, and I put my sweater back on, then turn back to face the window, the shutter of which is held down with a series of small black screws.

A few minutes later, a small orange light begins to pulse at the corner of my vision. It's telling me that there is a pull-down pop-up set into the seat back in front of me.

I let it pulse, eyes on the window. As far as I'm concerned, I've been summoned and signaled enough for one day. I've had five hours of meetings, and I think I'd prefer to finish this little ride in silence.

During this interval, I'm guessing, whoever is sending the message sends another to the enforcers in the back of the chopper. That electronic order, I'm guessing, elicits a crisp electronic yessir in response, because after only a minute a Beret walks up the aisle to my seat and taps my shoulder, tells me politely that I have a message. It's all typically extravagant high-tech posturing; whoever's sending me the original message could have scribbled a note with a crayon, crumpled it up, and tossed me the ball for far less time and money and trouble.

I nod at the Beret and go on looking out the window, in a manner I mean to seem contemplative. The Beret stands in the aisle, quietly psyching me out, until I relent and reach around to push the corner latch on the pull-down.

The pull-down isn't like any I've experienced flying commercial. It's not scratched or stained, and there's the reassuring heaviness of quality materials, tungsten and gold and platinum instead of the standard plastic and tin and chewing gum. This pull-down is what generals and global CEOs use to ramp up productivity on long flights to Australia and Greenland and other parts of the world where English is still spoken with a smile. It lets down slowly, under exquisitely controlled hydraulic force, and the pinpoint laser finds my retina, adjusts for my posture and my angle of vision.

Before I read the message, I stop, glance up at the Beret, who's standing at parade rest. "Look," I tell him, "I get really nauseous when I read while flying, and I know you guys have to keep your shoes really shiny, so maybe you want to find your seat again, you know what I mean?"

He looks startled but fades into the darkened rear of the chopper.

I turn to the screen. The navy-blue header with the NSC logo notifies me that THIS IS A SECURE INTRA-UNIT LINE/POINT-TO-POINT DISCUSSION MODE/"ENTER" KEY DISPERSES PREVIOUS MESSAGE/ZERO RETENTION/TO SAVE INITIATE ARCHIVE SEQUENCE, and then the header politely vanishes. Below it is a little message:

origin: Stephanopoulos, G., Col. (Seat 1C)
cc: Carville, J., Col. (Seat 1B)

Sal,

Okay, so we rewrote the hat. Now let's talk about rewriting the Anti-Tobacco Accord, hypothetically. Let's say the anti-tobacco legislation never includes the rider about targeting foreign markets, etc. Let's say we could get 1999 BC to hang tough on that (maybe he could score political points by saying that children in Belarus are as precious as children in Baltimore, etc.). That way there's deniability when the suit against American Tobacco hits World Court. What's your thoughts?

George Stephanopoulos
James Carville

I read it twice, and then I just sit there looking at it. It's like everything else today, a focused little earthquake. If I assume that they aren't merely pulling my chain, and they are capable of getting code to previous administrations, sending ones and zeroes down the information root system to previous memories, then the idea seems pretty straightforward in terms of shutting down the Wars: they're talking about trying to reverse-engineer a win for U.S. Tobacco in the original world civil suit of 2016, staging a kind of evidentiary commando raid in time. And I'm more than willing to pretend to assume this, for a while, because it's a lot more fun to think about than what's probably really going on.

Still, I'm tempted to ignore the note out of sheer mulishness, but it's such a ludicrous idea that I can't help myself. It's a relief to be writing, to feel my fingers on the keyboard:

> You make it sound as though 1999 BC was in some kind of position to force the Republican-controlled Congress to meet demands. My hat's off to your vintage drug connection. He's apparently dealing you some really rugged and authentic crack cocaine. Look, the Republicans loathed BC. I can't even communicate their hatred. It had all the subtlety of a group of high-school jocks out for a gay-bashing. And that's no joke: it wasn't happenstance that "gays in the military" became the first flap of the BC presidency. They questioned his manhood constantly. They repeated the same confrontational strategies again and again, when polls and policy argued for conciliation, because they had this strange prison-yard response to BC's politics and his brand of charisma. The Republican majority support the Anti-Tobacco Accord simply to clear the political issue away, but they support it *only* with provisions Big Tobacco can support. Otherwise, they'll keep taking tobacco PAC money and try to ride out the issue under the old rules of engagement. Kill that rider, the Accord is dead.

I send the message, and my screen reverts to a screen-saver image of the Washington Monument in moonlight. I can't deny now that I'm interested, roped in. This is a game, like Loaves & Fishes, but better, because even though this kind of reverse-engineering is almost certainly impossible and ultimately some kind of war-game role-playing to get me to take a revisionist propaganda project seriously, I have to admit to myself that it's like a board game God invented just for Sal.

The helicopter lurches suddenly, surges away from whatever needed to be surged away from out in the blackness, then levels back off. Maybe it was a pocket of bad turbulence, but probably not. This is the first time I've ever flown in a federal aircraft, but I know that they take isolated small-weapons fire on a fairly routine basis. No doubt we're over the Carolinas now, certain parts of which trigger combat pay for federal pilots.

The screen saver switches to another image, this one a blast from the distant past: a daylight photo of the Murrah Federal Building following the attack by Timothy McVeigh in 1995. It's an image that always stuns me, the entire vast structure laid open, like a head with its face blown away to reveal only blood and hollowed-out skull bone. Below the image is the death count, 168, which must have seemed inconceivably high before the Billings and Taos bombings.

It's hard to believe that no one at the time recognized Oklahoma City as the Fort Sumter of a long, smoldering, fitful civil war, especially given the radical New Federalist bent to the concurrent Republican Revolution—shutting down the government repeatedly, even the go-ahead for states to produce individualized currency—this last, of course, at almost the same moment that Europe was moving collectively to the euro. But, then again, probably no one at Fort Sumter saw it as Fort Sumter, because it wasn't Fort Sumter yet.

I look at the devastated hulk of the Murrah again. I have only a split second—not nearly enough time to figure out why the NSC is using this horrifying scene as a screen saver—before the image fades and another image begins to form, this one from more than thirty years ago. It's a picture of President Liddy Dole in a bomber jacket, silver hair swept up in the infamous Carolina Deb 'Do, christening the first of the advanced Deep Threat nuclear subs, the USS *Goldwater*. Liddy looks determined to show the EA she's not about to be pushed around. In its own way, it's a scarier image than the bombed-out federal building it replaced.

16

THERE'S A REASON THEY CALL IT A COMPLEX

We come down in a muggy rain, lighting finally on a vast black circle of tarmac beside a brightly lit complex of offices and endless hangars and windowless bunkers. Waiting for us on the ground are more Berets, as well as a smattering of the less-elite, your more standard army guys. At the front of this tiny army sit six golf carts without canopies, painted flat stealth black.

Carville, who has produced a black London Fog by this point, walks up to the golf carts, wing tips clacking, receives a salute from the soldiers, and then gets in the driver's seat of the second one. George walks over next and climbs in the little backseat. He's still in just his white shirt, hair matting down with rainwater. It's only another second before men come up and hand over two long, dark, preopened umbrellas.

The Berets behind me nudge me forward until I realize I'm taking the passenger seat. I'm handed my own open umbrella. The peacock marine in his dress blues and two Berets get into what can only be the forward-recon cart ahead of us. Then all manner of soldiers and guards climb into the remaining four carts.

Six keys turn simultaneously. We lurch forward, one by one. The four rear carts fan and advance so that within seconds we are a squadron of low-observable golf carts. Somewhere inside the complex, you have to believe, they are closely monitoring our arrival, downloading our worms and analyzing blood filtering through the clearinghouse of the lymph, training the Doppler on the advancing munchkin screams of these battery-powered engines.

We have gone through a maze of security cameras and desks and verbal challenges, negotiating miles of corridors and connecting office suites. This is a very, very large complex. Almost infinitely complex, as complexes go.

Now we are sitting and waiting for our dinner.

Carville has some sort of eight-hundred-pound-gorilla clout, because before we'd threaded our way halfway through the empty cafeteria, a guy in a chef's hat came hustling out and led us to the back of the hall. A small leather-padded door led into the officers' mess, which seats about eight and is entirely carpeted, padded, tapestried, and gilt-trophied, snug as hell, like the inside of a baronet's coach. Carville ordered steaks and crab cakes, which seemed to be the specialty of the house, all around. Another showy perk: the soldiers in the big mess eat farm fish five nights a week, with hamburger or turkey the occasional luxury.

It's well past midnight when the steaks and duchess potatoes are served. I'm expecting a charred slab, as no one asked me how I like my meat, but I cut into mine to find it cooked within an eyelash of perfect: medium, not medium rare.

They know, apparently, how I like my meat.

We eat in almost total silence for about twenty minutes, everybody just shoveling it down. I'm famished; worry has consumed all my energy today. Finally, George pats his stomach, gives Carville and then me the sleepy grin. He pulls out a pack of generic cigarettes, shakes it my way. It says only *Smokes*.

"I don't smoke," I tell him, and before I realize it I'm giving one of the queasy little apologies that nonsmokers find themselves giving in certain situations, especially over the last four or five years. "No offense. I just could never draw the line, myself. If I smoke one, I'm up to three packs a day in a week."

"None taken," George says easily, lighting up with a pack of matches from the table's ashtray.

Carville surprises me by pulling a thick cigar with a thin prismatic band from his jacket pocket, a real five-hundred-dollar Fidel. He takes a neat little bite off the business end and turns his neck and spits it carefully on the Persian rug at our feet, a move that is so far outside his personality profile that it had to have been scripted several weeks in advance, then practiced before a mirror with newspaper laid down carefully on the floor. No doubt it's meant to suggest a kind of macho, just-us-chickens atmosphere in which we can all drop our mutual suspicions and get Behind the Program.

"Sal," Carville begins, letting out a white whorl of smoke, "George and I thought, even though it's late, we thought we could have a kind of private conversation here about what general directions this project eventually takes."

"Really," I say.

"Yeah, really," Carville says. "If you're game."

I glance over at George, who gives me a grin and a slow nod of his head that somehow total up to irony. His eyes are a little too wide and innocent. His expressions say one thing to Carville, another thing seen from my angle.

Bear with this guy, I read him to be saying, *take it for what it's worth, which won't be much but may, conceivably, be something.*

So far George seems more likable than Carville, but the cumulative effect of all of his attempts to make me feel as though he's sharing secrets with me is that I feel like he's been instructed to make me feel as though he's sharing secrets with me. But it's late, and I'm full. So I lean back, cross my arms, and nod.

"Fair enough," Carville begins magnanimously. He settles back in his seat, frowns at his cigar, then throws his arm out along his chair back. "Have you ever thought about how time works, Sal? Temporality, flow of events, duration?"

"You could say that. I'm a historian. We occasionally give it some thought."

"But what I'm asking is if you've thought about it as a"—again, he gazes off into the middle distance over his cigar ember—"more as a physical medium."

"If you mean have I studied gravitational physics or relativity or any of that, then no. If you mean have I ever wondered if déjà vu was accidentally bumping back three seconds in time for some reason, then yes."

"That's very amusing. You have a lively sense of humor."

"That's why people come to my office and wrestle me onto helicopters."

"You have what they call an irrepressible sense of humor, in fact," Carville observes. He smiles to himself, indulgently, and looks mid-fortyish. The lighting couldn't be better for his particular scalp-to-hair ratio. There's no glare off the impressive half-dome arching up over his slightly narrow brown eyes. Instead, it brings out the ruddy tennis-club flush to his skin. I have the quick sense that he does well with the ladies; there's a confirmed confidence in his manner and posture that probably works wonders with the occasional flight attendant or staff secretary.

I give him a deliberately bland look, like he's the after-dinner video. "Look, Carville, it's hard for me to take any of this seriously because you don't seem to take me seriously. You think I *believe* you when you say that you have the ability to change historical facts by sending secret messages to weird little army guys from the past. And I don't. Here's what I believe."

And as I frame it in my mind, the idea takes firmer shape. It's got the military's paranoid sensibility and the right corresponding whiff of imperialism.

"I believe you have some kind of huge disinformation campaign in mind, something where you go back and try to rewrite the entire history leading up to the Wars. Maybe you want to get the World Court to try the 2016 case again. Or maybe, somehow, I have no idea how, you plan to try to insert this into libraries and data complexes until people accept it as truth, some version where the U.S. has no complicity in beginning this whole stupid military nightmare."

"And we need you why again?" Carville asks, gnawing absently, teething almost, on his cigar. He manages to do all of this without getting the end shiny wet or even moist. There's a weird precision to it.

"Who knows why you need me. I still have no real idea," I admit. "Maybe you need me to make it all internally consistent, to vet it out for you. To make sure that judges and historians and experts and academics will swallow it."

"It's interesting to hear this response from you," says Carville, running a hand meditatively over his scalp. He puts the cigar down in the toy-size porcelain ashtray. "Really, it is. Because the working group that put together our PAS, or Pre-Action Summary, they came across this problem again and again. People don't believe, no matter how much evidence you give them, that history can be altered. We showed you photographic evidence, and so you jump to the assumption that the evidence is corrupt."

Carville waves this problem away with a hand and hits the cigar again, smoke bleeding from the sides of his mouth. "Put aside your skepticism for the moment. Stipulate that you wouldn't believe a piece of evidence if it bit you in the ass. Let me continue. Act as if what I'm saying is true. This fact-finding committee surveyed all the information on temporality out there and did a lot of work of their own. And they basically came up with three ways of looking at the problem."

He gives me a look, checking if I'm listening. Minimally satisfied, he continues. "The first theory is that the past can't be altered, period, because one could only move into the past if one had already been there the first time around. So we build a time machine now and go back and try to stop the Wright Brothers from flying their plane at Kitty Hawk. This theory says we're doomed to fail because we didn't succeed in the past as we know it. On the other hand, if we go back and tell them how to fix their design so it'll actually work, then that would necessarily be because that's *always* been how they acquired the knowledge. It's like predestination. You take my meaning?"

Before I can answer, George blurts out, "Jesus Christ, Carville, she's not a third-grader. I know predestination has a lot of syllables, but I think she gets it."

"I do understand English," I say.

"Calm down. You two are very touchy. You're like a couple of hecklers, Jesus Christ. I'm trying to put this all together. In any event, the committee thinks that this theory, the predestination idea, is wrong. So our orders are a direct reflection of that belief."

"Why?" I ask immediately.

"Don't ask. Not important. They do, and so the rules stem from the other two possibilities. Both assume that history *can* be changed, but they differ in terms of degree. The chaos model, which comes out of a hodgepodge of late-twentieth-century physics and philosophy, says that the smallest change in the past, like stepping out of your time machine and stepping on a beetle, produces total and devastating revision of the future. This change is indiscriminate. Looking at it this way, trying to create targeted alterations in historical facts would be like trying to dig a well behind your house with high-yield plutonium warheads. The committee doesn't hold with this theory either, and our orders reflect that.

"Instead, this group feels that history, temporality, the *flow* of it, physical medium or space-time fabric or whatever you like, is probably more like a river. You can walk across it and then get out and there won't be any apparent change in the river. You can take a small rock out or put one in, and again no apparent change. But if you put a big enough obstacle in the water, all of a sudden you have obvious new dynamics, ripples, white water, or, with a big enough object, you have a dam and the upstream area entirely floods out."

"So under this last assumption, you can make little changes and not have to pay any kind of real price for it," I offer. "The opposite of predestination. Like using your own free will in a world without a divine power."

"Right. Precisely. That's the committee's basic take. Some small changes might lead to big, systemic changes, but that would be the exception to the rule. And hopefully, with enough foresight, you could really minimize that risk way the hell down. That way, doing nothing would be a bigger risk than carefully doing something. That's where you come in. You're part of the foresight."

Somehow, this description calls Reagan's inaugural to mind, and I decide it's time to wow the yokels. "Reminds me," I start, "of this line from President Reagan's inaugural, beginning of 1981. He had this thing about individual action as opposed to fate, and—"

" 'I do not believe in a fate that will fall on us no matter what we do. I do believe in a fate that will fall on us if we do nothing.' "

This comes from George. He's got it word perfect. He even gives a faint imitation of Reagan's leading-man rasp. I was just going to do a paraphrase.

"Yeah, that's it," I say, trying not to look like my punchline's been grabbed.

"George has a pretty good memory," Carville tells me, squinting his eye at George, father evaluating idiot savant son.

I look over at George, but he's still collapsed down in his chair, letting Carville and me spar. He's turning back his oxford-cloth shirtsleeves, looking like he's making ready to go somewhere.

I turn back to Carville. "Sorry to be a pain about this, but why exactly do they believe this theory is true and the others aren't? I know you say it doesn't matter, but I can't help but think that it does. Why select this last theory?"

Carville picks up the Fidel again, revolves the cigar between his thumb and forefinger. He doesn't answer right away. Finally George speaks up. He's finished rolling up his sleeves, and he leans forward and enters the conversation in such a way that I realize he's been opting out to this point because he finds it impossibly boring.

"They selected *that* theory because if you really need for some strange reason to alter a historical sequence, and you believe either of the first two theories, you're substantially screwed," he says, putting a pretty fine point on it.

George leaves not long afterward, saying he's going to scare up some transportation. Apparently my sleeping quarters aren't walking distance, because he says he'll drive me. I can only assume that means he needs to go requisition one of the little stealth carts. When the paneled, leather-padded door shuts noiselessly behind him, Carville turns to me.

"You like George, huh," he says encouragingly. The cropped hair at his temples, although he hasn't lost it yet, is thinning noticeably.

"Why do you say that?"

"Am I wrong?"

"I'm just curious why you say it."

He shrugs modestly, like this sort of penetration is an ability he's just been burdened with his whole life. "Because he's your kind of guy. Class clown. He also has a hard time with people telling him what to do. He also has that kind of cocky academic view of the world. You're natural allies. You two are the kind who open your eyes in church while everybody else is praying, and then you see each other and realize you're the only two in the room with your eyes open."

"Actually, maybe we're the kind who don't go to church and worry about whether our eyes are open or closed."

"That's just my point. Tell me I'm wrong. Tell me he's not your type."

The best thing I can do is change the subject, because I can begin to feel anger pulsing, like a dull headache. "You said George is an academic too? He looks a little apple-cheeked for a professor."

Carville looks over at George's place, then leans forward to get a better look at the pile of tiny napkin and beer-label balls George has assembled nervously beside his plate. The various piles look like a miniature Stonehenge made by tiny insane people. "Actually, he's not your run-of-the-mill academic. We get a lot of people from graduate programs who are disillusioned with the low pay or who want a little more adventure or whatever. But every once in a while we go and recruit specific individuals, when we get a tip from a faculty contact somewhere. We like to know when somebody with special skills is coming up. In George's case, somebody had their eye on him in high school, eleventh grade."

Carville makes a sour face, then adds, "It was a *charter* school, the kind they used to call experimental, for whiz kids. In Massachusetts." He raises his eyebrows significantly. "George is what we call a sponge, in the trade. Always been the kind who could ace a test without studying, natural eidetic memory, which, if you supplement that with memory enhancers, can be pretty amazing. And he can usually intuit basic principles from fragmentary sets of facts. So if you only have a limited time and you need somebody to become expert in a given area, he's the kind of guy you use. He was supposed to be our you."

"I guess that explains the Reagan quote."

Carville runs a hand over his dome, slicks it through the thicker crew-cut hair at the back of his head. "Don't try to go toe-to-toe with him on retention. You'll just wind up feeling like an ignoramus."

I make myself smile. "Thanks for the tip."

Carville gives a grudging nod, shows the points of his canines. "Anyway, we gave him most of a year and a half to swot up on what he needed to know. And he took a pretty good cut at it over the last eighteen months. Absorbed a hell of a lot of material—unbelievable amount, really—but problem is, he can't simulate a career of judgment. Partly our fault too, we didn't know exactly the shape of the research to feed him. And problem is, he's fucking headstrong, he's fucking impulsive. He's not a bad guy. I like the guy, in fact. He's just a bad guy to command.

"So about six months ago, we started preparing for the possibility that he wouldn't be able to do your job, and that the backup software packet we designed might not be able to do your job, and that the two of them together might not be able to do your job. That we might actually need to go recruit you. Yourself."

He picks up his little snifter, toasts me, then takes a healthy sip. After a thoughtful second, he leans over with a fork and airlifts the uneaten portion of George's steak onto his own plate. I watch him silently. He cuts the steak entirely into bite-size pieces, twelve of them, before beginning to eat.

As he does so, he makes a noise back in his throat like an F-20 commencing a napalm run. "Incoming," he jokes in a whispered shout, and begins to swallow the chunks down one after another.

17

PROPERTIES

We are munchkin-screaming down a long, wide corridor, George and I. There's an odd museum smell to the air, air-conditioning and disinfectant and slipshod mummification. The floor is heavy speckled tile, streaked with the occasional tire mark, obviously built for stealth-cart traffic rather than feet, and the only thing to look at as we blow past are massive doors, one every fifty or a hundred feet, with little identification panels centered in each but unreadable on the fly.

The lighting is indirect, but halogen-vivid. It comes from nowhere and illuminates every angle of everything. I feel like a document being relentlessly photocopied. I can say for sure only that we are supposed to be headed to a portion of the complex called Properties.

George is hunched over the steering wheel, checking a lighted display glowing in its center. The display looks intricate and baffling, a series of seemingly three-dimensional and overlapping readouts, baffling even with the help of a small moving dot of violet laser light that clearly represents our cart.

George looks up and says something. His boyish shock of hair is lifting in the little cart wind.

"*What?*" I yell.

"We'll stop in *a second,*" he yells back, and whips the cart around a corner. "You really are quartered in East Bumfuck, without a doubt," he comments, once we've shot the length of another corridor, and then another. Finally, he slows the cart, trolling along, until I hear a noise, a steady and rhythmical pounding. He stops the cart beside a door that reads PROPERTIES—PHYSICAL PLANT #2. The noise level of the machinery inside is insistent but significantly lower than the cart's munchkin scream. He motions for me to get off the cart.

I look again at the door, then step down. "I'm quartered in the physical plant?"

George says nothing, just smooths his hair over and walks nonchalantly about fifteen yards from the cart. I follow him until we're both standing in the middle of the brightly, almost violently lit hallway. Then he turns and answers in a low voice. For the first time I realize that he's more than a full head taller than I am. "Not the physical plant," he says. "You're quartered around a couple of corners. I just thought we could talk for thirty seconds or so off the record." He points to the cart, puts a finger to his lips.

"What, you don't mike the hallways?" I say.

His eyes narrow a little at the word *you,* but he nods. "We do, randomly. And camera randomly. But not the stretches outside the various physical plants. Too much chum in the audio. This is actually the preferred spot for agents who want to nip a spliff while on the clock." He seems to think of something suddenly. "You don't happen to get high, do you?"

Obviously he's not talking about the mj's you can buy in the corner store, but in any event it's a question I can do without right now.

"Read my file," I say.

George gives a that's-cool-whatever nod. "Beside the point anyway. I just wanted a chance to tell you something. It's pretty basic but it's hard to see from where you're sitting. It's that you're getting hung up on the iffiness of all the stuff you're being told. You're getting paralyzed by what seems improbable to you, and that's taking up all your energy."

I'm staring blankly at him, and he realizes I'm not getting it, whatever it is. He shakes his head and tries again, voice more urgent. "And James was encouraging you with all that talk about, see this as a *game,* act *as if* it were true. He's leaving you the mental wiggle room to deny the reality of what's happening to you, and he's doing that because he needs you cooperative and you're more cooperative if you're in the dark about the actuality of what's happening to you."

Looking around, he says, "Well, not being one to waste an opportunity,

I think I'll indulge just a little bit." He reaches absently into his oxford shirt pocket and pulls out his generic cigarette pack, unfolds the top of the box. His fingers find a kink in the foil, and he draws out a concealed joint, nearly as thick as a cigarette, but elaborately hand-rolled, clearly contraband from the islands. There is some squiggly writing on the side. I lean in and squint and read it: *No woman no cry*.

"It's an old Bob Marley and the Wailers tune," George says, and then quotes it. *"I remember when we used to sit in the government yard in Trenchtown. And then Georgie would make the fire lights."* He shrugs. "Apropos, I guess."

"People ever get hacked off at you because of your memory?"

He thinks about it, holding the joint and the lighter. "All the time. My relationships tend not to last so long."

"Well, it has to be pretty daunting to get into a he-said-she-said argument with you. It would just be he-said-she-said-then-he-corrected-her all the time."

"Actually, that's not such a big problem. My girlfriends eventually just start accusing me of lying all the time when I tell them what they actually said and did. Either that or they start saying that I'm *unconsciously* skewing the record. You know. Which allows them to bring it back pretty quickly to he-said-she-said."

I think about it, then nod. "Well, yeah," I say, "they'd have to. To survive."

"Sure," he agrees, like somebody who doesn't hold a grudge.

I watch him fire up the joint. "Won't that register somehow on your lymph node? Can't they just hit playback on your worm?"

"You've been watching too much video." He shakes his head stiffly, holding the smoke. "Plus, you may have noticed, our unit has quite a lot of flexibility. Quite a lot. We're not regular army"—he lets the smoke jet slowly from his nostrils—"by any stretch of the imagination. We're the cavalry, Sal. By definition, if we're on the job, they need us too much to worry if we salute or if we smoke the occasional bone."

I look around suddenly. "Where are the guards? This is the first time all day there haven't been big guys with big guns."

"I waved them off. Technically, I'm guarding you. Plus we're moving through lockdown modules down here. Without me, you can't move from one module to another, you'd just be locked in a big box." He raises his hands, clearing himself of blame. "Don't look at me. That's from on high. I argued against it, but you're an AWOL risk. Even though you're a newly commissioned major."

So I'm a major. Better than a private, in any event. "But as you were saying."

"What?" He's completely forgotten where he left the conversation. Evidently his memory gifts are long-term.

"About James playing with my mind."

He nods, rubs an eye touched by the smoke. "But as I was saying, James has got you chasing your own tail with this what-if kind of mental game. I've read the operational summary sheets. The core technology's been available since the end of the twentieth century. So everything we talk about in terms of possible alterations is actually on the table. Not as propaganda, not as revisionist histories for libraries, but as things that are going to be done or attempted. By real fucking people. By fucking *us*. By our little unit."

George's eyes are wide now, and although it's ridiculous, I believe him, or I believe he believes absolutely in what he's saying. There's an unfeigned sense of enormity to his words. He stands silently, waiting for my response. I figure he's smoking the joint partially because he wants to and partially to show me as quickly as possible that he's not the Man, which about matches my reasons for taking it out of his hand finally.

I take a cautious toke, hold it. Almost immediately, it feels like someone has clapped the side of my head with a sheepskin-lined mitt.

"So fine, it's not a game," I say, holding the hit. "We're actually going to create some kind of strategic alteration instructions and pass them back to the weird little army men in the past." I exhale the rest of the smoke, and it comes out as sarcasm.

George shakes his head, eyes closed, as though he's in a tape loop he can't get out of. "You're not *listening,*" he says slowly, tapping me on the shoulder with his index finger. "*We're* going to make these changes. Us. *We're* the messages that are going to be transmitted back to the weird little army men in the past. We're the data, Sal. We are the data."

There's an interval where the two of us just stand there, in institutional corridor space, listening to the moaning of the physical plant.

Out of habit, I've taken another, deeper toke as I listen, and now the sheepskin-lined mitts are clapped to both sides of my head. I forget to pass the stubby joint back, and it sits smoking uselessly between my fingers until George suddenly plucks it out and shakes his head and says, "Wow, you are cut *off,* Major."

* * *

At the door to my quarters, George says, "You're all set up in there—bathroom, refrigerator, clothes, soap, toothbrush, midnight snacks, everything but windows. I come back for you at oh-eight-hundred. There's a field briefing book on your bed, but I don't recommend getting into that right now. Hit the sack. If you really need something, you can call through to me or James or the complex dispatcher."

I step down from the squat black cart, but before I can say anything in return, George speaks up again. "Look, Sal, one more thing. When you get in your room and you see what's there, try to see it as a favor, which in a very real way it is, instead of a violation. You'll sleep a lot better."

Lovely, I think.

He gives me a concerned look, fawn-brown eyes intent on mine, thin lips drawn down to a single straight line, then turns in the wide hallway, heads back the way we came. I watch him grow smaller, his tall frame hunched over the map in the wheel, the cart obediently munchkin-screaming into the distance. When he's gone, I feel instantly lonely, defenseless. I'm already counting on him. I'm counting on a twenty-seven-year-old sponge.

I turn back to the large double door, which reads: PROPERTIES, SOUTH—HAYDEN, T. SALSWICK. ACCESS CONTROLLED.

Just lovely.

I pause for a long second, feeling as though I can hear a wind whistling somewhere in these halls, although when I cock my head I can't, thinking about all the many, many ways a person can construe the word *violation*.

I open the door, and I walk into what would be an absolutely featureless institutional dormitory room, a prison cell, or undergraduate housing, if a handful of my possessions weren't scattered about in a vain effort to make it seem like home. My feet come to rest on my own antique Persian throw rug, and I stand there, hearing myself breathing. Softly, the door swings closed behind me.

On the high, sterile white walls are a few of my posters. There's a slogan for the young BC—*Putting People First!* There's the desperate poster Dukakis designed to fight the impression that he favored burning the flag—*Dukakis, President* against a stylized version of Old Glory.

I come through the entryway, stopping beside a little kitchenette. My copper Revereware tea kettle sits forlornly on a burner. I look around for a few minutes, taking it in, letting my stomach settle. In the institutional bathroom, whoever did the choosing selected my bathmat and my toothbrush and a little dish of potpourri I keep on the back of my toilet at home.

The tiny bunk is made up with my sheets and the comforter I threw Lecia when I broke up her tryst with Danno. All I can think of is some guy with a wire in his ear removing and handling and cataloging and transporting and reassembling and touching my stuff. Without permission, without any real authority except brute strength. The fact that they've only moved a handful of my things doesn't make it any better.

A word struggles up in my mind, a strange made-up word that I wasn't even aware I still carried around with me: *Unabomber*. It was the name that law enforcement gave to a mail-bomber in the 1980s and 90s, and it was an ironic thing to call him, because he specialized in sending packages through the U.S. mail that would eventually cause whole people and buildings to become fragments of people and buildings. He was a hermit, pathologically afraid of modern society.

And maybe as a particular form of poetic justice, when they finally caught him, tracked him to his Montana cabin and located and disassembled all of his pathetic little booby traps, they took his entire cabin and everything in it into custody. They put it on a truck and mapped and tagged everything inside it, read and published his diary, and entered it into the record against him. They shaved his beard and stripped away every molecule of privacy or concealment. And in so doing, they inadvertently elevated another martyr for the various Western militias that would eventually join under the name Freemen.

Unabomber. I hate them for putting me in a position where I feel like I have something, anything, in common with a mass-murdering twitch like that.

But there's nothing to do with my anger. I look around the room again and see something I missed: centered on the brilliantly colored quilt is a dull brown folder with a tie-down cover. It's not my folder. It must be the one George mentioned.

Printed in thin letters on the cover are three letters, meaningless and perversely childlike: *yBC*.

18

TIGHTEST, SHARPEST, HOTTEST

@1
yBC

This field brief consists of relevant and summary documents drawn from lengthier numbered and classified documents. All pages remain eyes-only. All pages remain level "@1" access required. All pages contain standard place-in-sequence numbers at upper left-hand corner. These place-in-sequence numbers are *no longer accurate.* CHECK PAGE NUMBERS ONLY AGAINST TALLY LIST BELOW AND HAND-LETTERED TALLIES IN UPPER RIGHT-HAND CORNER—DO NOT CHECK PAGE NUMBERS AGAINST INDIVIDUAL PLACE-IN-SEQUENCE NUMBERS. IF THIS BRIEF CONTAINS MORE OR FEWER PAGES THAN INDICATED BY THE TALLY BELOW, RETURN BRIEF IMMEDIATELY TO DISPATCH OFFICER. IT IS A CAPITAL OFFENSE TO DUPLICATE, SCAN, ELECTRONICALLY SENSE OR IMAGE THESE DOCUMENTS. EYES-ONLY. DO NOT DESTROY. YOU REMAIN RESPONSIBLE FOR THE SAFE RETURN OF THESE PHYSICAL DOCUMENTS.

Folder contains ___9___ pages:

1) Cover page (page including this tally)
2–4) Summary of task options (yBC), international focus, with final

recommendations and % [excerpt, Group Storyboard, pp. 274–276 of 918 pages]

5–7) Summary of task options (yBC), domestic focus, with final recommendations and % [excerpt, Group Storyboard, pp. 512–514 of 918 pages]

8) Go-To Directive, task options final version, plus summary, minus draft legal finding [excerpt, Directive issued by NSC/POTUS, p. 19 of 21 pages]

9) Authorization Directive, fr. Chairman, Joint Chiefs, countersignatories NSC/POTUS, re: prohibit-but-preserve technology, Maopi Reservation Complex [summary excerpt, directive issued NSC/POTUS, p. 5 of 6 pages]

<u>COUNT PAGES</u>—REPORT MISSING, ALTERED, OR IMAGED PAGES ASAP

This is page ___274___ of ___918___ pages
Group Storyboard: Task yBC / NSC/@1

SECTION XXXII
Summary of Task and Final Recommendations

On October 6, 2052, Group Storyboard (GS) was created by NSC. Personally charged by the Vice-President, October 17, 2052, NSC Towers, Vienna VA. Two subgroups, one international and one domestic, created *ditto*. [International Focus summary follows; see Section LX below for Domestic Focus.]

GS—drawing on statisticians, probability specialists, academics, military historians, geopolitical theorists, law enforcement, and others—was assigned a particular problem in an emerging discipline GS has itself since labeled "contingency budding." The problem (described in detail above, see sections I–IV) assumes both the ability and the need to bring about minor or major alterations in what GS came to call "historical facts on the ground." (For a detailed treatment of philosophical disputes, see Section XXIV, ii.)

Whether such changes are possible in actuality, and whether such changes, if possible, would constitute "objective" changes in a single linear historical sequence, rather than ruptures in multiple sequences or mere "localized" psychological effects within an observer or observers, GS was unable to say with any unanimity.

GS work proceeded on the twin (hypothetical) assumptions that 1) facts on the ground could be changed, and 2) for all practical purposes, "altered" facts on the ground would be indistinguishable from "prealtered" facts on the ground. Such change, in GS terminology, would be both *clean* and *total*.

Given the potentially all-encompassing nature of such change, GS placed a premium on solutions that produced the fewest budded contingencies while accomplishing the task at hand. GS came to use the metaphor of nano-directed laser surgery for this attempt: as with NDL surgery, GS attempted to map and affect the smallest "probability area" possible, without reaching a point of diminishing returns. These twin qualities were described as *tight* on the one hand and *sharp* on the other. Finally, GS sought the highest probability of success among solutions—that is, a *hot* solution, with a probability index above 50%. The best solution was considered that which was *tightest, sharpest,* and *hottest*.

<u>COUNT PAGES</u>—REPORT MISSING, ALTERED, OR IMAGED PAGES ASAP

This is page ___275___ of ___918___ pages
Group Storyboard: Task yBC / NSC/@1

GS located the international confluence between NATO expansion (1999) and the signing of the Anti-Tobacco Accord (ATA, 1998) as the most suitable first focus, and GS accepted unanimously NSC's original premise, that the President in office at the time (BC) would present both the tightest and sharpest second focus.

GS presents below final recommendations, ranged in ascending order (i–iv). Probability figures are provisional and represent chances of producing desired *clean* and *total* change.

SECTION XXXIII
GS RECOMMENDATIONS (INTERNATIONAL)

i. Attempt to restore contact with 1995 NSC. As described above (Section XIX), contact was made w/1995 NSC on September 11, 2052, but even with access to all 1995 day and SAR codes, present-day NSC was unable to convince 1995 NSC of benign intent. After suggesting Russian or Chinese origins for present-day NSC's coded communication, 1995 NSC terminated connection. GS was created as a result of this stalemate. GS suggests continued attempts to reach 1995 NSC, perhaps using information from BC to provide proof-positive authentication.

Drawbacks: 1) Continued unwelcome transmissions could exacerbate a decline in U.S./Chinese relations during this period.

Probability: ___13.6%___

ii. Placing Operative(s) in Proximity to 1995 BC. For much of the last year, this solution was favored by GS. Again assuming present-day NSC's ability to do so, the solution seemed initially to top out all three basic evaluatory categories. By limiting contact to 1995 BC, tightest and sharpest possible focus would be created. Such contact would be a straightforward matter of offering a suitable sum to the 1995 Democratic National Committee, which advertised varying amounts of White House interaction for corresponding sums. Operative(s) could communicate directly with 1995 BC at the moment of greatest potential for change.

Originally, GS assumed that this solution would be *hot* as well, based on the assumption that BC could be made to see implications of inadvertently overlapping international policies.

COUNT PAGES—REPORT MISSING, ALTERED, OR IMAGED PAGES ASAP

This is page ___276___ of ___918___ pages
Group Storyboard: Task yBC / NSC/@1

Originally scored 74% probability. Military historians have recently pressed GS into a stark reevaluation, pointing to 1995 BC's documented tendency to subordinate most other factors to electability. Even an initial agreement on 1995 BC's part to strike NATO expansion or ATA, if such were secured, would be thus provisional and radically dependent upon the "field-sample polling" then in use. GS assumed finally that BC could rationalize a need to continue with NATO and ATA, perhaps by denying the validity of operative(s) in lieu of absolute proof.

Probability: ___38.9%___

iii. Place Operative(s) in Proximity to 1995 BC / Coerce Cooperation. This solution follows the same basic parameters but coerces cooperation using information obtained in the years following BC's departure from office. While the most potentially effective material—the details of a sexual liaison that led to impeachment proceedings in 1998—unfortunately occurs too late historically for GS purposes, several other scandals that surfaced in the aftermath of BC's departure from office could be brought to bear. Drawback: as above, historians assert that such coercion would prove secondary to questions of electability.

Probability: ___46%___

iv. Utilize a Younger BC (yBC). GS initially storyboarded the idea of securing cooperation of BC at an interval previous to 1995. An advantage was radically decreased or absent security. But it was determined that this option, too, contained the flawed assumption of the two previous solutions, namely that BC at any age would surrender future electability in the face of anything other than absolute proof of operative(s) authenticity.

GS eventually proofed the related idea of *utilizing a yBC in conjunction with solution ii above*. There were distinct advantages: 1) yBC would most probably constitute absolute proof of present-day NSC authenticity, and 2) yBC, while in effect a separate individual, would in actuality occupy a continuum with 1995 BC, preserving the tightest focus available in solutions ii and iii. GS suggests making yBC the operative placed in proximity to 1995 BC.

Probability: ___50.3%___

<u>COUNT PAGES</u>—REPORT MISSING, ALTERED, OR IMAGED PAGES ASAP

This is page ___512___ of ___918___ pages
Group Storyboard: Task yBC / NSC/@1

SECTION LX
Summary of Task and Final Recommendations (Domestic)

GS, in its original charge of 10/17/2052, was also asked to consider the feasibility of limited changes in "facts on the ground"—a "microscopic packet of alterations," to use the Vice-President's phrase—with the stated aim of rendering the Allied Freemen Resistance weakened or inoperative. For purposes of the charge, GS was to consider the loosely confederated Freemen, Army of God, and Libertarian movements a single, geographically diverse phenomenon.

GS, in plenary session, initially attempted to storyboard solutions that would solve GS international and domestic problems simultaneously. Such a "magic-bullet" solution proved unattainable. All solutions proofed unacceptably loose and/or cold. Prolonged attempts to storyboard solutions to the domestic problem alone were also largely unsuccessful. All solutions proofed unacceptably cold, in addition to various degrees of looseness and/or bluntness.

In general, GS came to perceive individual changes, even linked changes, in historical facts on the ground as insufficient to suppress a broad-based, violent, and "homegrown" resistance to federal authority. The confluence of ideologies—religious, political, and racial—represented by the Allied Freeman Resistance resisted efforts to mock up credibly focused elimination scenarios.

In its last phase, however, GS Domestic proofed the NSC-preferred solution. This option, recommended to GS by Colonel A. Levy of NSC on 2/10/2054, involved "culling" the so-called "Founding Fathers" recognized in the evolving mythologies of the various interrelated resistance movements: David Koresh (Branch Davidians, "The Prophet"), Timothy McVeigh (Christian Identity, "The Patriot"), and Mark and Susan Dickinson (CyBurners, "Adam and Eve"). NSC believed that by culling these figures at a point preceding their most destructive periods, Allied Freemen Resistance could be "cut back," if not eliminated. This solution initially seemed the most workable of any GS considered.

The NSC scenario concentrated heavily on the Dickinsons, creators of both the "FedX" software and the shielded user network that disabled federal installations and ancillary law enforcement on the twentieth anniversary of the attack on the Federal Building, Oklahoma City OK, abetting destruction of Taos NM, Billings MT, and Reno NV federal

<u>COUNT PAGES</u>—REPORT MISSING, ALTERED, OR IMAGED PAGES ASAP

This is page ___513___ of ___918___ pages
Group Storyboard: Task yBC / NSC/@1

buildings. "Preinterdiction" of this software—still operative and encrypted, though technically dormant, at the writing of this report—would theoretically deny AFR the "communal brain" (Colonel Levy's phrase) that has allowed the Western and Southern fringes to coalesce around a single command structure over the last several decades.

GS was unable to reach unanimity concerning "Founding Fathers." While the majority proofed the strategy unfavorable, multiply unfavorable in most cases, a significant minority found the solution workable. As throughout, GS here reports majority findings, with minority dissent factored into success probability figures.

GS presents below a single final recommendation (i). Probability figures are provisional and represent chances of producing desired *clean* and *total* change.

SECTION LXI
GS Recommendation (Domestic)

i. Cull only "The Patriot." In general, the "Founding Fathers" strategy GS found ineffective in bringing about desired solution. The majority reasoning held that the various anarchic and/or New Federalist impulses at work in the late twentieth century were larger and more tenacious than any one individual or set of individuals.

David Koresh, in this view, achieves prominence for his historical positioning vis-à-vis the federal government rather than for any concrete action or actions. Culling Koresh, GS believes, would lead to a similar mythology attaching to a currently uncelebrated figure. In the analogy to NDL surgery, mapping and deleting a cancerous node would arguably lead only to the displacement of cancerous cells to and contamination of another proximate node. Solutions invariably proof cold.

Additionally, alterations carried out against Koresh and/or the Dickinsons would involve alterations multiplied many times over, in that these three individuals were by definition group leaders and catalysts of group action. Alterations carried out against Mark and Susan Dickinson, in particular, would involve a "dense mesh" of changes at the cybernetic level too far-reaching to estimate effectively.

With these assumptions agreed to, GS proofed the idea of culling Timothy McVeigh alone, who operated more or less independently and provided specific tactical and symbolic aid to the burgeoning AFR.

COUNT PAGES—REPORT MISSING, ALTERED, OR IMAGED PAGES ASAP

This is page ___514___ of ___918___ pages
Group Storyboard: Task yBC / NSC/@1

This solution carries several notable advantages: 1) McVeigh provides the tactical and symbolic model for the Dickinsons twenty years later, and while elimination of McVeigh would not necessarily prevent the eventual release of FedX, such might arguably be the case; 2) McVeigh operated with only the limited aid of one or two others, functioning in essence as a "cell of one"—changes carried out against McVeigh thus proof sufficiently tight in all scenarios; 3) McVeigh's model for the OK bombing—the underground tract *The Turner Diaries*—would be denied subsequent notoriety; and 4) no changes of any kind produce results even less optimistic than numbers reached herein.

In sum, this option proofs favorable as much for its lack of serious drawbacks as for any subsequent efficacy it may demonstrate. It can also be storyboarded quite fluidly into recommendations put forward by GS International, given the relative proximity of the geographical and historical points of contact. GS suggests annotating International Go-To Scenario with the culling of McVeigh.

Probability: ___24%___

ii. A Note on the Elimination Point(s) for Timothy J. McVeigh. As with GS International, more-detailed logistics are provided in rough form in following sections LXXX–C. However, GS wishes to stress here that elimination should, as a rule of thumb, *always occur in closest proximity to target moment of desired historical change.*

In this case, several previous intervals in McVeigh's history might otherwise prove attractive: first, his aborted attempt to join the Green Berets, in particular survival training, during which potential Berets spend 24 hours in isolation on rough terrain; and second, his duty during the Iraq/Persian Gulf War of 1990–1991. [McVeigh met then-President

Bush and General Norman Schwarzkopf during this interval, which points up the necessity of allowing the subject's "life-trajectory" to continue unabated for as long as possible.] Of these, the second scenario would seem the more workable initially. Given the presence in the war zone of depleted uranium, nerve and mustard gas in trace amounts, active biological elements, pyridostigmine bromide, and other

<u>COUNT PAGES</u>—REPORT MISSING, ALTERED, OR IMAGED PAGES ASAP

19

RELATIVELY COMFORTING EUPHEMISMS

NATVAC Point-to-Point Transmission, Audio Transcript Only. (Video portion on demand, Complex Archive.) Call initiated at 0246 hours, 21 July 2055, Major T. S. Hayden, Properties South, via Complex Operator. Connect to Colonel G. Stephanopoulos, Tripoli Wing, engaged 0247 hours.

Total elapsed time of call, 28 minutes, 34 seconds.

....

Complex Operator: Your party is on the line, major.

Hayden: Mr. Stephanopoulos? Hello. Good morning. You look like a real wreck. What, were you sleeping?

Stephanopoulos: [Pause] I don't know if I'd call it sleeping. What time is it?

Hayden: It's about a quarter to three. Your hair looks like you've got it up in a pompadour. Like 1950s style.

Stephanopoulos: Sal, what's going on? Is everything okay down there?

Hayden: Jesus Christ, George! What do you mean is everything okay? [Pause] I'm sitting here in a prison cell with just enough of my personal possessions to make it clear that someone went through all of my stuff. I mean, they brought my comforter. That's very nice. But it suggests that they probably went through my sock drawer too. Do you understand that?

Stephanopoulos: Calm down, Sal. I told you earlier, in a way it's a favor to you. Calm down. In a way, I said. Can you honestly say you're sorry to have some of your things around you, even if it meant somebody had to rustle them up?

Hayden: I've just gone through my briefing book too. I'm missing pages. I thought you should know.

Stephanopoulos: I know that already.

Hayden: Well, it says about five times on every single page that I'm supposed to report missing pages immediately. So I figured I'd better call and get you out of bed immediately and report my missing pages. [Pause] George? I don't want to get in trouble for not reporting my pages.

Stephanopoulos: You'd report them to James, anyway; he's your CO. But don't bother, he's the one who took the ones that are missing, the go-to directives and the other, the technical summary.

Hayden: The Maopi Reservation thing. The technology thing.

Stephanopoulos: They call it a prohibit-but-preserve technology that they have out there. James didn't feel that you were need-to-know for that and the actual final go-to's.

Hayden: What's a go-to?

Stephanopoulos: You got some summaries there from a group called GS.

Hayden: Right. Storyboard something Group. Or Group Storyboard, rather.

Stephanopoulos: Right. And at the end of those summaries are the working group's suggestions for actual action. Some of those suggestions the President and the Joint Chiefs authorize. Some they don't. And then some they just make up on their own, totally ignoring the experts.

Hayden: More power to them.

Stephanopoulos: Literally.

Hayden: Yeah.

Stephanopoulos: In any event, whatever the top rung decides finally to authorize, that's put down on paper as a go-to, as in fucking go to it, right now. In this case, it's called a black op go-to, meaning it's classified, even from people who normally get to read classified stuff. Like members of Congress, for example.

Hayden: So frigging military.

Stephanopoulos: What do you expect? That's how it's done. Oh, and the go-to usually has the legal authorization appended too. You don't have that in your brief either.

Hayden: [Pause] So I get to see the summaries and the suggestions but not the actual orders for what's going to happen? And not the legal justification? I just continue taking Carville's word for it.

Stephanopoulos: James says you're not need-to-know.

Hayden: [Pause] Well, as far as I'm concerned, James Carville, or whoever the hell he is in real life, can kiss my—

Stephanopoulos: Sal—

Hayden: —narrow little white biographer's butt.

Stephanopoulos: You know this is a monitored line.

Hayden: [Pause] It is?

Stephanopoulos: They all are. SOP. Unless you have authorization for a knit-crypted one. [Pause] I mean, it's okay. Nobody really cares what you say, as long as you don't start talking about treason or, for example, use of contraband substances or anything like that. See what I mean?

Hayden: Right. Sure.

Stephanopoulos: Besides, you have to stay consistent. I mean, are you pissed off because of being brought into this thing in the first place, or are you pissed off because you're actually not being brought in far enough and told everything? Because you can't read the go-to's?

Hayden: Both. Everything. I'm pissed off at everything. Besides, who'd ever pick a code name for themselves like James Carville? Did you ever read up on that guy, the Ragin' Cajun? He was a total asshole, a real atavism.

Stephanopoulos: Actually, I have, yeah.

Hayden: Oh, right. You would have.

Stephanopoulos: You're tired is what you are. And you need time to let it all shake out. Christ, I'm still unable to believe I'm in the military, and I've been here for almost five years now.

Hayden: Yeah, but you got scouted and recruited, like a star quarterback. Not kidnapped, like some of us.

Stephanopoulos: [Pause] Who told you I got scouted?

Hayden: Carville.

Stephanopoulos: Really? He said *scouted*? He used that word?

Hayden: He said somebody had their eye on you since eleventh grade. In your experimental charter school.

Stephanopoulos: [Unintelligible]

Hayden: What?

Stephanopoulos: Nothing. If that's true, which who knows with James, then that's news to me. I thought my first contact with NSC was when I was a junior in college.

Hayden: Maybe they were watching you for a while.

Stephanopoulos: Maybe they were.

Hayden: Doesn't feel real pleasant, does it?

Stephanopoulos: Never has.

Hayden: [Pause] And I have to tell you immediately that those summaries have some strange ideas in them. Some really strange and stupid ideas. Even if you forget for a second about this idea of a yBC—such a cute phrase—and you just consider the idea of McVeigh, you're into really dicey territory. I mean that could really put a rock in the stream, if you want to use Carville's quaint little metaphor.

Stephanopoulos: That's a suggestion by the working group. That's all. But if you want to rough out some ideas about why it's crap, I'm all ears.

[Portion of Conversation Deleted. This Constitutes a Legal Deletion, Authorization @1. It is Unnecessary to Report This Deletion.

Deletion length, 7 minutes, 18 seconds.]

Hayden: [Pause] This is so stupid—

Stephanopoulos: It isn't. You want it to be. You want it to turn out to be stupid and silly and a hoax. But it isn't. Did you look in your closet and your dresser yet?

Hayden: What?

Stephanopoulos: Did you check your clothes?

Hayden: Don't tell me somebody's been going through my panties or something gross like that.

Stephanopoulos: Go look. Really. I'll hold.

[Phone is placed on table. Assorted background noises. *Elapsed time of pause, 1 minute, 36 seconds.*]

Hayden: Where the hell are my clothes?

Stephanopoulos: They're in your basement in Burlington. In packing boxes. Fully watertight. I made sure of that.

Hayden: Why? Whose stupid idea was that?

Stephanopoulos: Oh, now you're mad because they *didn't* bring some of your possessions to Virginia.

Hayden: This stuff in the closet is all vintage.

Stephanopoulos: Exactly. Well, not quite. It's all new. Just vintage styles and fabrics. Even the tags. They were researched, and recreated too, sewn in for effect.

Hayden: [Pause] Am I supposed to wear this stuff? It's all 1960s polyester and synthetics.

Stephanopoulos: Some of it's cotton. But most of it's polyester. A lot of it's Dacron. That was DuPont's big product. You'll like it. It's supposed to be cool, brisk, and ever-crisp. And you got some Avril rayon in there too.

Hayden: I'm not wearing this stuff.

Stephanopoulos: Suit yourself. But that's your uniform dress, that's all you're issued. So unless you want to wear what you got on every day from now on, you're gonna have to dig into the retro stuff. It's part of the go-to, explicitly.

Hayden: I'm not wearing it. [Pause] They can go-to hell.

Stephanopoulos: Suit yourself. And, look, get some sleep.

Hayden: I'm missing pages.

Stephanopoulos: I know. Sleep well. I'll see you at eight o'clock.

Hayden: And I'll wear the clothes I've got on for the foreseeable future. I can wash them in the sink. Nobody's forcing me into a frock.

Stephanopoulos: So wash them in the sink. That's fine for the next few days.

Hayden: I'm still pissed off, George. But you seem like a nice enough guy.

Stephanopoulos: Thank you.

Hayden: I just have this feeling that you're probably not quite as nice a guy as you seem. That you're probably military first and a nice guy second.

Stephanopoulos: Who knows what I am first.

Hayden: You do.

Stephanopoulos: You'd be surprised.

Hayden: [Pause] One straight question, George. Just show me the respect of giving me an absolutely straight answer. What are the chances that anything you guys are expecting me, or us, to do might wind up with me dying?

Stephanopoulos: Dying?

Hayden: Ceasing to live.

Stephanopoulos: You want numbers?

Hayden: No. [Pause] Truthful but relatively comforting euphemisms.

Stephanopoulos: Okay. You're racking up combat pay on a continuous basis, the way you would on the front lines, Chechnya or Azerbaijan. Right now, talking on the phone. And the Army only comes up off combat pay if there is what they call a sharply escalated risk of injury or death. In this case, they're paying that out because they have absolutely no idea what the risks are.

Hayden: [Unintelligible]

Stephanopoulos: Sal?

Hayden: I said somebody needs to work with you on the comforting part.

Stephanopoulos: Sorry. I thought you wanted a straight shot.

Hayden: I did. Well . . . in any event. I'm tired. Sorry to get you up.

Stephanopoulos: No you're not.

Hayden: Not in the least. Right.

Stephanopoulos: See you in a few hours. We've got briefings tomorrow morning, and then we're running contingency scenarios.

Hayden: Okay.

[Call Terminated by Major T. S. Hayden, 0315 hours.]

....

NATVAC Point-to-Point Transmission, Audio Transcript Only. (Video portion on demand, Complex Archive.) Call initiated at 0317 hours, 21 July 2055, Major T. S. Hayden, Properties South, via Complex Operator. Connect to Colonel J. Carville, Tripoli Wing, engaged 0317 hours.

Total elapsed time of call, 14 minutes, 20 seconds.

....

Carville: Jesus H. *Christ,* Sal.

Hayden: I need to talk to you.

Carville: Jesus. [Pause] Don't ever call me in the middle of the night again. That's one of the reasons I have George. Call George when you get the urge.

Hayden: I called George. I want some answers to some simple questions he can't answer.

Carville: [Pause] If I can give them to you, you can have them. If I can't, you can't. And then you can apologize in the morning for waking me up.

Hayden: First, this technology that my briefing book mentions.

Carville: It's a prohibit-but-preserve technology. Out at the Indian reservation.

Hayden: Prohibit-but-preserve.

Carville: PBPT. In this case, the Maopi PBPT. Prohibit-but-preserve means that the technology was ruled out not only in the private sector but for government use too. Complete freeze on use and development. But the government retains the technology and maintains the right to authorize it in certain circumstances.

Hayden: Okay, the Maopi PPTB, then—

Carville: PBPT.

Hayden: What?

Carville: PBPT.

Hayden: PPBT.

Carville: Jesus Christ. No. What are you, dyslexic? [Slowly] Listen to me. It's PBPT.

Hayden: I don't care about the acronym! Look, it's after three o'clock in the—

Carville: What are you telling me for? You called me and woke me up. Don't tell *me* what time of night it is, because I'm the one of us who knows.

Hayden: [Pause] Is this machine—

Carville: It's not a machine. It's a technology.

Hayden: What does it do? Simply put.

Carville: Look, I can't tell you much about it. I'm sorry. I told you before that it allows us to communicate with previous NSC groups. One of these groups, which we're calling NSC 1963, was willing to concede that we had a kind of working authority over them—they didn't like it but they couldn't see their way around it—and so they agreed to do a couple of things for us. One of those things is that they were able to communicate to us some very, very precise data about where they're located, where some other things are located. I mean precise like astronomically precise, not just global positioning.

Hayden: Okay.

Carville: So we now know their address, so to speak, which enables us very accurately to send them stuff. Initially it was particles of light we sent. That's the second part of the technology.

Hayden: How do you send them stuff?

Carville: [Exhalation, unintelligible] I can't tell you that kind of thing. Come on, Sal. Get real.

Hayden: What do you mean, come on, Sal? I'm not asking for blueprints. I'd just like to understand what we're talking about.

Carville: Put it this way. Suppose you went to Dr. Oppenheimer before the tests for the atomic bomb, and you said, Look, uh, Rob, I'd like to know how the atom bomb works, you know? I'd just feel *better* somehow if I could know.

Hayden: So you're Oppenheimer in this scenario.

Carville: You're not a scientist, Sal, and you're not a commanding officer. I'm a commanding officer. You're a civilian recently turned GI with a courtesy rank of major. You're not need-to-know, and you're not gonna know. That's reality.

Hayden: [Unintelligible] crap. [Pause] But here's my real question. I'm beginning to understand that it's not just about sending messages, or instructions, or advice or something back to, you know, to earlier army guys, but moving things, maybe people—people like me in particular, say—back to the earlier army guys. It sounds ludicrous to me, but I am getting the sense that you people seem to feel this is a real possibility. I'm really most concerned about that.

Carville: That's yet to be decided. Right now it's just a possibility. Not even the most likely possibility.

Hayden: A possible movement of things back to earlier army guys.

Carville: That's correct.

Hayden: And this possible, unlikely movement could include people, which could include me.

Carville: I'll just say that to this point it has never included people. Hasn't been done. Just things. But theoretically there's nothing to prevent people from being among the things sent.

Hayden: Who in that case? You, me, George?

Carville: I can't say who it might include, Sal. Let's just say that anything like that is a worst-case scenario. Worse than worst-case. We're working around the clock on easier ways to accomplish our goal, which is to bring the Wars to a positive conclusion, hopefully in a way that leaves us more secure at home as well.

Hayden: You know, when you say things like that I always wonder if you think you're saying something that means something, or if you know you're not.

Carville: That's for me to know, Salswick.

Hayden: Don't call me Salswick.

Carville: What about Sal Mineo?

Hayden: [Pause] You slimy *bastard*. You were listening to my conversation with my father the other day.

Carville: [Laughter]

Hayden: You conscienceless prick.

Carville: Calm down. It was a joke. It was my job to listen to it. The guy is a federal prisoner, after all, and I was there to watch out for you, make sure you stayed a usable asset.

Hayden: [Pause] So you're not ruling out the possibility that this technology is possibly going to result in us or me being in a hell of a lot of danger, then?

Carville: One hundred percent conjecture. I don't know.

Hayden: Don't give me that. Do not give me that.

Carville: It's only a possible use of a PBPT, at this point.

Hayden: [Pause] Possible PBPT.

Carville: Right.

Hayden: Worse than worst-case.

Carville: You got it. Events are very fluid at the moment, unbelievably fluid. Everything we're doing is based on contingencies. In the meantime, all we want from you is some considered advice on refining some of the suggestions you saw put forward in your brief. That's all.

Hayden: You've been such a great deal of help with this. Really.

Carville: Oh, now. You embarrass me.

Hayden. No, really. You're so straightforward and unguarded. Thank you.

Carville: Don't thank me, Sal. I'm just fortunate to have a job that lets me be who I am. Get some rest. Don't call me again.

[Call Terminated by Colonel J. Carville, 0331 hours.]

20

VIRGINIA, FOR THE DURATION

I wake in a scale-up series of realizations. That it's pitch-black, and I'm sleeping in a makeshift apartment deep in a warehouse in Virginia. That I'm awake because someone is standing outside my apartment hammering on the door. That it's 4:32 A.M. according to my bedside clock, and that I've had only about one hour of sleep, since I was up until well past three trying my best to wring answers out of people who've made a career out of obfuscation.

The pounding goes on.

I'm disoriented but awake enough to find a robe in the closet and pull it on, because I know George well enough to answer the door in a robe but not in my UVM Catamount underwear. I yell to him to hold his horses.

But when I pull open the door, it's a Beret.

A woman. A female Beret.

She's in the same khaki pants, black T-shirt, shiny black boots, and green beret combo as the men who've been herding me around, but on her it doesn't look like a John Wayne retrospective. On her it looks perversely stylish, gritty but together. Her hair is blue-black, pulled tight into an almost invisible knot behind her head. The robe they've given me has a chain of daisies around the neck. I feel, by comparison, like I'm my mom.

"Sorry to get you up, Major Hayden," she says. Her voice manages to carry in the wide-open corridor.

"I am also sorry."

"Colonel Carville sent me for you. I'm supposed to get you packed and ready to move out immediately."

Maybe because of the daisies, or because it's late, or because it's just the way I am most of the time anyway, I get a little snotty. "You people have really odd manners. Number one, I have no idea who you are. Number two, whoever you are, you're not touching my things. Forget it. That's not happening again. And number three, I would have appreciated a call rather than someone pounding on my door in the middle of the night."

Unlike the other Berets, she's not standing straight. She's got her weight out on one leg, hands in her pockets. She looks pretty relaxed. Beside her on the floor is a plain brown leather flight bag. Although she's no runway model—for one thing, her arms and back crowd the T-shirt in a way that suggests judicious, long-term steroid use—she has the height and the shoulders, the cheekbones and the big starburst eyes of a woman sportscaster, or a celebrity jock, a beach volleyballer.

"You took your phone off-line," she says. "Carville called for a while. Then he sent me. He said to disregard any displays of attitude. His words, not mine."

It's true, of course. I unlinked the phone when I went to bed, in a vain show of independence. I should have realized he had more than just one way to make himself heard.

"He did."

"Yep. There's been a fairly drastic rescheduling. There've been some unexpected events in the field, and so we're all headed out tonight. Carville will fill you in once we meet up with them at the airfield."

"Well, I'm not going. I'm sure it can wait until seven or eight, and if he has a problem with that, tell him we can talk it over at seven or eight."

She shakes her head, looking down at the ground, showing me the neat putting-green crown of her beret. "Nope. I have to get you packed, and I have to bring you and your suitcase. I've got backup waiting for me to beep if I need help with either one. I'm sorry, but that's the way it is. Fairly drastic rescheduling." She's looking me in the eye now, looking down at me to look in my eye.

"This is insane. I want to talk to Carville."

"You can't. He's got more to pack than you do, believe me."

Without realizing it, in the space of a single day I've gotten used to the weird caste system that drives the military, and I'm irritated with her answers. The other Berets, even with their arm-twisting, always treated me like a superior officer. "Who the hell are you?" I demand, but even as I say it, I hear myself and I sound like an insecure suburban housewife who wants more respect from the maid.

She's patient with me. "I'm Virginia. I'm part of your go-to unit."

"Virginia what? And what's your rank?"

"Just Virginia, for the duration. And I'm officially rankless, for the duration." She flicks a finger toward my kitchen. "I have orders to come in and get you packed," she says, repeating herself almost apologetically, "and I have orders that it can't take more than about half an hour. Since we're going to be working together, I'd rather have you just invite me in. And I'm only Virginia at this point. Nothing personal. That's just what I'm supposed to say."

They just named her after the state we're in, another sign of the lack of imagination that seems to permeate this group. "At least tell me what's happened that's so earth-shattering we have to leave immediately."

"That will happen directly when we board the aircraft at the field."

I have the distinct sense that the door won't lock on her, that it will recognize and let her in even if I close it, and she's big enough to push by me if she has to, anyway. I stand aside finally, and she picks up the flight bag and walks in, someone else almost a foot taller than me. BC was right: military authority is like kudzu. Not resisting hard enough at the beginning means I go on not resisting hard enough forever after. It's nothing new—people picking up the pieces after a military coup have been finding this out for centuries.

Virginia holds up the bag. It looks oddly retro, nineteen-fiftyish. "This is how much space you've got to fill. If you want, I can do it for you, or you can lay out stuff and I can put it in, or you can do it all yourself."

"Since you don't know where my stuff is, I guess I'll go ahead and pack my own bag."

She tosses the bag on the floor between us, shrugs, then sits down at the featureless kitchen table. "Actually, I was in charge of final disposition in here once the property movers left. I was supposed to give it all a homier feeling. Woman's touch."

She crosses her legs, jiggles her big black combat boot, looks around. "It was George's idea to have me go through it before you arrived, just to put it back the way a woman would have had it in the first place. I thought that was thoughtful of him." She pulls a pack of cigarettes from her khakis. "Mind if I smoke?"

I shake my head, looking down at the empty leather bag in front of me. I hear the scrape of a lighter, and in a second the first drifting tendrils of smoke reach my nose. A silence stretches out as I try to put my thoughts together.

Virginia gazes toward the bedroom. "One thing was, I did your sheets," she offers after a minute.

I pick up the bag. "Yeah," I say, because what do you say to that? "Well, thanks." I look into the bag. It's empty and utterly featureless, except for a small tag that reads *Barnaby's, New York. A World of Flight.*

She nods modestly, watching me inspect the bag, glancing at her thin strap of a watch. She takes another easy drag, blows the smoke out in a nice fat little donut. "Not a problem. You'd do mine, if the situations were reversed."

That gets me moving. "I don't think the situations could be reversed, really," I say, moving slowly toward my closet. It comes out every bit as catty as I thought it would.

There's silence behind me. Then she says, "You're probably right," and I can tell that what she means is not that she could never be me, but that I could never be her. A little chill settles down in the room.

When I reach for my blouse and my walking shorts, the only two articles of clothing in my possession not supplied for me, Virginia clears her throat. "Sorry, I should have made clear. Only NSC-cleared wardrobe, NSC-cleared shoes. Anything here when you arrived, but nothing you brought from Little Rock."

I turn around slowly. "How could it possibly—"

"And you have to leave your jewelry here. And reading glasses, if you wear any. Contacts are approved, if you wear any."

"You are shitting me."

"Actually, it's no shit. It's in the go-to."

"I wasn't *given* a go-to. It was missing from my briefing book."

She nods matter-of-factly. She knows this already. "That was in the go-to too," she says, not rubbing it in but not sidestepping the point either.

"And you were need-to-know."

"I was need-to-know."

"And Carville and George."

"Need-to-know. Both."

"Well, you know what? You're wrong." I'm trying and finding it impossible to imagine myself wearing any of the things in this closet. "I do need to know, it's just that nobody wants to own up to it."

Virginia's voice comes up behind me. She's trying to be helpful. "You've got a couple of nice-looking dresses in there. A shirtwaist dress and a two-piece wrap job. Both pretty summery, pretty classic. Feel less like you're going to a costume party." She's trying to hurry me without ticking me off again. "Just an option."

I turn around to look at her. She's flipping through a little book of campaign gaffes I keep on the table at home to look at while I eat, quotes from as far back as Eugene McCarthy's crack about being brainwashed in Vietnam. I must have read it through seven hundred times. I consider telling her that that's my book but don't.

I turn back to the closet. There's a collared long-sleeved blouse that catches my eye, wide blue and white stripes, what they used to call broadcloth. It has a tag dangling from the arm, faded but well-preserved, museum-quality. The tag reads:

Brilliant as a Riviera sun.
Here's a blouse that won't let you forget
a summer on the Cote d'Azur.
Will a blouse as fashionable as this keep its exciting new shape—
even after it's been machine-washed and had little ironing?
With Avril rayon it has to.

I try to tell myself that it isn't really like giving in and wearing a uniform. The blouse is something I might have chosen for myself, this argument runs, at a slightly outré secondhand store in Montreal, if I only had thirty dollars or less and was forbidden to select natural fibers.

As I'm whittling my sixties retro wardrobe down to the size of a fat springer spaniel, I'm watching her out of the corner of my eye. It's not that I don't like her so much as that I get the sense that it won't ever matter if I like her. She's in my life the way she's in my apartment the way my apartment is in Virginia.

Her mouth is big—not big, but plus-size, with the straight jaw jutting below. She doesn't talk much but when she talks, the open mouth looks almost lazy, like forming normal words isn't an adequate challenge, like it'd be more at home cracking jokes on a sitcom or holding nails while she threw up a wall frame. When she smiles, the overlarge set of teeth suddenly match the overlarge eyes and it becomes apparent that there were other paths besides the military she could have taken, if she'd been content to hold that look indefinitely. Beauty—real beauty, the kind to which cameras attach themselves—was probably an option at some point, but not one she pursued.

The muscled arms make their own statement. She's got them crossed over her chest, and it's not hard to see that they're her badge of admission into a club she must have worked long and hard to enter. She's leading with them now because she doesn't know how big a threat I plan on being and because I've been giving her a lot of lip. They're big arms that could collapse a trachea or hoist a large man over a wall, and she's no doubt spent years envisioning them, building them, tending them. She's spent more hours with machines, isolating and encouraging muscles, than most people spend at church or with their kids. And now she's a Beret, at twenty-six or twenty-seven. Like Colonel Turner, she must have had her share of people wanting to see her tank when the pressure was on. But she didn't.

That's the look she gives me, when she catches me looking at her looking at my book of gaffes. It's an unembarrassed look, unembarrassed for having picked up the book uninvited, unembarrassed for everything. It says, *I didn't tank.*

Virginia's bag is waiting for us in the cart. It's another new-looking relic: powder blue Naugahyde, with a small frill of the fake leather running the length of it. It looks like the kind of bag sorority girls and cheerleaders took on the road with them in the sixties, stuffed full of hair curlers and tennis shoes and nail polish, Gidget gear. It really couldn't look less like Virginia's bag.

She sees me giving it the once over. "I had the choice between this one and yours. I figured you'd like the flight bag better."

"Thanks," I say, and mean it.

On the way to the airfield, a moment with BC keeps returning to my mind. It was St. Patrick's Day last year, and I had an interview hour scheduled with him. When I walked into his office, he was on the phone with Noddie Ahern, the president of the Unified Irish Republic, remembering the days when he was greeted by ecstatic crowds in Dublin, when he first promised to stand with those who stood for peace.

He turned around and saw me at the door that day, and there were tears swimming in his eyes. With a helpless little laugh, he brushed them away, and then spent the entire hour reminding me that the Good Friday Agreement, the first faint footfall on the road to reunification, happened on his watch and with his dogged encouragement. It was a nice hour, the kind of sweet moment in an otherwise businesslike relationship that creates its own disproportionate nostalgia.

I have no idea why it comes to me now, tunneling back upward, corridor by corridor, with this woman Beret beside me, but it does. As we reach the ground floor, two stealth carts fall silently into place about twenty yards behind us, each carrying a pair of standard-issue army men.

Virginia makes no signal to them, and they make none to her or to me.

Finally, a hangar door slides back and we are outside, rolling over blacktop in darkness broken only by wells of institutional lamplight. It's a good hour before sunrise. The July heat is swirling over the ground even now, accumulating slowly like gas fumes, waiting for the spark of sunrise.

It's while we're clearing the final checkpoint that I make the connection. The memory of St. Patrick's Day rolls through my mind again, but this time I see the rest of it: BC finishing his spiel on the Good Friday Agreement and turning to a picture of his mother that he kept on the stretch of wall nearest his desk. He told me, "I always said, if I won the Nobel peace prize I was going to use it to start a foundation in her name. Never did happen."

BC chewed his lip for a second, going over the colossal unfairness of it once more in his mind, but finally whipped around and gave me his sly, old man's smile. "That was gonna be my tribute to her. She would have just loved that, my mother. Sometimes—just in fun, you know, when we were alone—she used to call me her little Elvis. And that was gonna be my Graceland for her, if I'd won. A Graceland with a mission, with some class."

The Virginia Fund for Peace in Europe, he would have called it, if the Nobel committee hadn't sniffed him and passed him over six years running.

It should have been obvious, in this unit with its own Stephanopoulos and its own Carville, that a Virginia would be more than just a reference to Virginia. For some reason, it puts the small hairs on the back of my neck up.

I look at the side of her face in the weak light before sunup. She turns the big eyes on me, blinking, nocturnal, lemurlike.

"What?" she finally asks over the noise of the cart.

We're heading directly onto the airfield now, and I have a rushed impression of an aerial strike force laid out there, ten or fifteen aircraft, bombers, gunships, more night creatures, all huddled together in the thinning dark.

"You know, BC's mother was named Virginia," I remark.

"So I understand," Virginia says. Her big left arm snaps up, acknowledging a salute from a groundsman, then snaps down. It's quick as a karate strike, and when it's done she's seems altogether unaware of having completed it. It took BC a year in office to firm up his salute. But I can only imagine Virginia took to it right off.

We cut around a fueling truck servicing one of the helicopters that brought me here from Little Rock, then we straighten back out and head for the busy end of the field. I can hear shouting now, see men running with fuel hoses and weapons.

I pause and then go on. "He idolized her, you know. When she died, he was just utterly and completely devastated," I add, unsure myself what I'm getting at.

Virginia's got her eyes on the field coordinator, who is waving us toward the central gunship with a glowing orange baton. She doesn't seem to feel the need to respond. She doesn't meet my eyes.

Then, without any prompting, she suddenly offers, "I'm not supposed to tell you, but we're heading to Las Vegas, just outside Vegas. If it makes you feel any better to know. I'd appreciate if you didn't let on that I told you."

I close my eyes, tight, and I whisper, "Jesus Christ," under my breath. My heart's going again, beginning to surge.

Las Vegas is about as deep in the Allied Freemen's militarized zone as it is possible to get, with the exception of the Bozeman-Billings-Boise area, what the AFR calls Three Beez. Three Beez is as close to an effective breakaway republic as the continental U.S. has ever come, but south-central Nevada has been a guerrilla flash point for nearly as long.

Las Vegas is precisely where you don't want to be flying in a federal military convoy, because they are routinely shot down, and because every once in a while the AFR sends a video feed to the news media showing their little covey of captured pilots, chained together in a cave somewhere outside Pocatello or Rock Springs or Gillette, yellow-purple bruises on their faces and FEDMAN branded on the small of their backs.

The Lord knows I don't want to go to Las Vegas. But the thought that Virginia is wearing BC's mother's name won't leave me even so, and I find myself coming back to it once more. "He cared very, very deeply about her," I finish lamely.

Virginia's unfazed. "So I understand," she says again.

Carville is sitting in his own stealth cart on the tarmac, next to a ferocious-looking little green jet. The jet's engines are cockeyed, vertical rather than horizontal. Carts scream by in the neon glow of the field lights, hands whip by way of salute, carts scream away. At least as far as I can tell on our approach, Colonel Carville salutes no one. He only acknowledges salutes.

I think of Reagan's cowboy in the NSC, a rogue colonel named Oliver North. He, too, was supposed to have built a covert world within a world where being a colonel somehow trumped generals and vice-presidents. But the comparison with North goes nowhere—Carville gives off the nostalgic smell of Nixon-era heavies. He has that beetle-browed, Nixon-Now humorlessness, the air of a guy choosing mentally between two or three sets of balls to break.

As we roll up, for instance, he's jiggling one black wing tip, looking like he's just brushed his teeth with methamphetamine paste.

"Forget commissary breakfast," he says immediately. "And forget the complaints about skipping commissary breakfast." He gathers me in next with his glance. "Good morning, Sal. We had a leisurely breakfast planned, followed by a morning of briefings, followed by three or four days of contingency scenarios and planning exercises." He spins a finger in the air. "But I got word this morning that we're in an accelerated framework now. So I've got oranges and protein bars for both of you, and for George when he hauls his ass over here."

I step out of our cart. Virginia jumps down from her side, swings her bag out of the rear. The tarmac smells like warm, dead, wet worms.

"I was thinking," I venture, "that it might be nice to sit down with the legal counsel on the base and go over some of the violations of the Constitution involved with searching my house and confiscating my property."

Carville narrows his eyes slightly, but shows me his canines. I see now that something's got him angry, almost livid underneath the professional mask. "Unfortunately, we won't have time for that today, Sal. Accelerated framework."

This is my experience after nineteen hours in the military. Things mean things, sometimes aggressively mean things, but no one will ever specify exactly what.

"What does accelerated framework mean?" I ask him.

"It means chop freaking chop."

21

THIRD WAY TO VEGAS

There are currently three general ways to get to Las Vegas. The first, preferred by adventurous Hollywood billionaires and their friends, involves driving your own convoy of bullet-proofed vintage Land Cruisers or Cadillac Eldorados out through Barstow and into the desert. The old interstate highway system is still in service, although the Allied Freemen Resistance long ago mined and dynamited all the various rail lines running in and out of the desert. So if you can afford the consumption taxes and the gasoline, and you have pull with the AFR or the Mafia or both, then you drive, the old-fashioned way. You pay as much in bribes, probably, as you wind up losing at the blackjack tables, but everyone who sees you on the street knows you've got Serious Heft.

If you're somewhere in the middle tax brackets, you book a gambler's flight into Vegas from LAX or John Wayne in Orange County. Gambler aircraft are marked on their sides and their bellies with huge fluorescent dice, and they fly relatively slow and close to the ground, open to visual and radar inspection from the ground. They ferry most of the marks into Vegas, Nevada's less than seemly Red Cross. Freemen hidden in rock crevices with Stinger and PIN missiles see the glowing dice, and they hang fire.

The third way to get to Las Vegas is to fly toward it from the East in a big clumsy formation of twelve federal attack aircraft. Of the three ways, it is inarguably the best if your intention is to secure government death benefits for your family.

This morning, I'm taking the third way to Vegas. Specifically, I'm aboard a snub-nosed jet with four pivoting engines that allow it vertical takeoff, which it accomplished with spooky effectiveness in Virginia, and vertical landing outside Las Vegas, which remains a somewhat academic question.

I'm told that we are at the center of a flight group including several B9 stealth bombers as well as third-generation Nighthawk stealth fighters. We're all flying at 40,000 feet, out of reach of the AFR's antiquated radar systems. I am told as well that once we cross from Colorado into Utah airspace, the bombers and fighter jets will peel off and commence a series of diversionary strikes on installations in the Black Rock Desert of Northern Nevada. Our jump jet—only low-observable, not genuinely stealthy—will then descend dramatically and complete the trip to the Maopi Reservation east of Vegas without further escort.

I have asked what I think is a pretty good question, namely: why are we traveling with a heavily armed escort and then splitting off from that escort and descending when we reach really hazardous terrain? This seems, to call it what it is, boneheaded. The answer I have been given is that in the best of all possible worlds we would not do this.

"And we are no longer in the best of all possible worlds, Sal," Carville says testily, "because the Eastern Allies, specifically the Chinese Navy, it turns out, have put together the capacity to supercrunch our Navy's real-time battlefield communications. And that is supposed to be physically impossible."

He is seated across from me, both belted and chin-strapped into his plush leather seat. Stephanopoulos is strapped, chest and chin, to a seat beside him.

Virginia and I are in facing seats. We are all four wearing featureless green combat helmets and flak vests handed us by the copilot as we boarded. For some reason, my flak vest smells like ham. I picture the last soldier who wore it, calmly eating a ham grinder as he moved closer to wherever the action happened to be then, and I wonder if my terror is misplaced. Maybe the AFR have better PR than antiaircraft coverage. Maybe their reputation is just built on the deep myth of the Marlboro Man, without any tactical substance.

But I can't make the damp palms and the constant impulse to flee go away. The quadruple roar of the engines easily penetrates the heavily padded walls, and I have to raise my voice to be heard.

"Which means what?" I yell.

Carville looks at me for a second, and there's a real swelling of disgust there. For the first time, I get the sense that he's not simply irritated with my constant resistance but offended by it. "Which means, Sal, that they can penetrate, jam, alter, or otherwise co-opt our communications. That's what it means."

"Our AWACS routers are no good," George explains, leaning toward me. "Worse than no good. The Chinese can feed bad tracking data directly through the AWACS's big board, and we crash into our own aircraft. They don't have to fire a single shot."

"Shut the *fuck* up, Stephanopoulos," Carville yells at George, then turns back to me. The events of the last few hours have put him in a foul mood. His voice drops back down into a monotone. "So in the last seven hours they have sunk one of our aircraft carriers, the USS *Reagan*, and crippled another one, the USS *Vigilance*. Not transports or recon vessels. Aircraft carriers. One sunk—motherfucking *sunk*—and one limping to port half full of water. So far they estimate thirteen hundred swabbies under the water. That's *one* thousand and *three* hundred. And the Chinese did this with totally conventional Shenyang fighter jets. Nothing we haven't seen and handled a million times. Except this time our guys are suddenly flying blind, or passing each other false firing and target data.

"This is the kind of shit that *we* can do if we go to war against *Albania* or, you know, *Chad*. We can overmaster their communications, get them to run their defense in coordination with our offense. But this attack was done to us. And we can't be sure it's not going to happen again. The tech people say they've locked access down again, but you can't go into battle thinking *maybe* your communications are secure. So we've got squadrons right now on the water and in the air using goddamn *semaphore* to talk to each other, right now, today."

He gives me the hard look again, then goes on. "Another reason it's not the best of all possible worlds. Yesterday they pinpointed and took out the USS *Goldwater*, a nuclear sub that we had shadowing Iranian and Saudi maneuvers in the Indian Ocean. Two hundred thirty-five more swabbies under the water. There was an attempt to recover the missiles from the sub, which was successful. There was another attempt to keep word of the incident under wraps, which was fairly successful. We didn't tell you about it because nobody told anybody.

"But you don't lose two carriers and keep it under wraps, especially when the EA makes footage of the attacks available to all the major cable networks." He smiles without showing his teeth, then stops. "So the truth is you're probably the last person in the country to find out that things are not looking good for the home team." He glances at George, who seems to know better than to say I told you so, then adds truculently, "That things are looking like *shit* for the home team, okay?"

"Take it easy," George says, eyes narrowing, "nobody's happy about it."

Beneath their open flak vests, Carville and Stephanopoulos are both in suits, one charcoal and the other soft brown, but there's something off about the cut or the fabric. Their ties are very thin, matched by skinny lapels. The trousers have skinny legs. I look at George, who underneath his helmet has got his brown hair smoothed over and—for the first time since I've known him—parted.

Then I've got it: he looks like a lanky, cat-eyed Kennedy. The suits are early-sixties vintage, like my own outfit. Nobody's mentioned it, but we're moving slowly but surely toward a Camelot dress code. Virginia's the only odd man out, at this point.

Carville's looking down at the wall beside him, where the window would be if you could have a window in a low-observable aircraft. His lips are turned down, meditative. "Those people down there are going crazy right now. Probably buying out the grocery stores, packing guns under their pillows. It's gotta be an absolute nuthouse. People freak when they start thinking about reality. Can't handle it, most of them."

Something about his Olympian musings hacks me off, and I let fly.

"Well, maybe if you guys told the *truth* for a change, instead of doling out hopeful fiction all the time, you might have people who were ready to face bad news with some kind of real heart. You've been telling everyone for two decades that we were slowly winning these damn wars, that these gains were being made.

"Now they're turning on their TVs and learning that it's all been a lie for years. That's like a husband who's been having an affair and lying to his wife about it for twenty years, saying that she can't handle reality when she freaks out. Come on, Carville. It's the military's disinformation that debilitates people, weakens their resolve. Own up to it, for God's sake."

I catch Virginia looking at me with raised eyebrows, not necessarily displeased, just surprised at the voltage. George watches Carville with an amused look, clearly hoping he'll fire back, but Carville takes the rebuke without saying a single word. He goes on gazing through the wall of the airplane at his own conception of the people below us.

We ride in silence for a minute. While designed for VIPs, this is still a combat jet, and our cluster of four facing seats occupies nearly the whole of the interior compartment. Two pilots are behind a door in the nose; two gunners occupy the rear. It's cramped, and the jet pulls enough gravity every several minutes to drive me against the webbing of my harness. I've got a steel stomach for motion, but this aircraft brings nausea surging up every ten minutes or so. The cold-cut smell from the flak vest doesn't help.

It's not hot in the jet, but I'm sweating. At any minute I expect an explosion to rip off a wing or tear through the floor beneath me. This plane will land in hostile territory in an hour or two. There will be no time for me to learn how to be useful, how to protect myself, how to keep from getting other people killed.

Virginia takes a Critical Mass bar from her thigh pocket and rips it open. I find myself wondering idly if she's the one who slipped a bar to my father. She nods to George and Carville and not, it seems, to me. "How long do you think the Freemen and the EA have had their heads together?"

Carville shakes his head, makes a disgusted face like he's opened a particularly rank clam. "There's no collusion between the Freemen and the EA. The AFR is a bunch of psychotic patriots. The only thing they hate worse than the Fedman is Russia, or China. Intelligence shows nothing like that. Believe me."

"You guys in Intelligence don't read your history," Virginia murmurs, eyes closed, chewing, head back on the headrest. "The Thirteen Colonies weren't too hot on France either. That didn't stop them cutting a deal to get through the Revolutionary War."

"Not to mention the *mujahideen* cutting a deal with the U.S. to drive Russia out of Afghanistan in the 1980s," George says.

"Even if there isn't any direct collusion," I can't help but add, "the Freemen have satellite receivers too. They get the news. If they were looking for a moment to launch an offensive—an American Tet—it seems like a perfect opportunity."

Carville looks out the window, brooding. Recent events have shaken the bluff self-confidence he had during my first meeting with him at the

Library in Little Rock. But he's still unconvinced, or wants to be, more likely. He turns back, sticks a spread hand out in front of him to push the point home.

"Look, the fucking Freemen Resistance knows that if the EA ever *does* manage to invade the U.S., they're coming in from the Pacific side and they're coming right through the militarized zone, and Three Beez and all the rest is gonna be smoking ruins. So do I think they'll hit us concurrently? No. In fact, I wouldn't be at all surprised if we get some kind of offer of a temporary cease-fire if the fighting with the EA really does get close to U.S. soil."

He ignores a snort of laughter from George's direction, goes on. "Maybe you think that's overly optimistic, but I've read these wackos' profiles. America always comes first with them. Always."

"That's the point," Virginia says, tongue distending her cheeks as she works the last of the chocolate and creatine from her teeth. She smacks her lips. "To them, the federal government isn't America. It's an unlawful occupation."

"Whatever," Carville says.

"Carville," I say. Then I say it louder, startling him out of his reverie. No one's said a word for half an hour, nothing but the wailing of the engines. His eyes focus. "Let's talk about the possible PBPT," I say.

George slits his eyes for an instant at me, then closes them again.

Carville slowly laces his hands over his chest. "What about it?"

"Last night you said worse than worst-case scenario. That's a direct quote. You said the situation was pretty fluid, and you were working on ways that we wouldn't have to use whatever it is that you can't tell me about."

"And every particle of that was true, Sal."

"I'm not saying it wasn't. I'm just, you know, curious about now. We seem to be flying toward the Maopi reservation at a little under Mach three. So I was wondering if it was more likely than worse-than-worst-case now."

He purses his lips, eyes down on the knees of his sixties trousers. "I think that's accurate," he says carefully. "We're in a totally different scenario now, as I explained earlier. With one of our aircraft carriers slowly becoming a coral reef somewhere, it's looking more likely all the time that Maopi will be used in some fashion. Bet your ass."

"It is."

"Right. You're not off the mark on that at all. The question up in the air still is how that technology gets used. It's still probable that any use involves just a transfer of information, directives really, from us to them." He shakes his head and shrugs. "Nothing more dramatic than a phone call, essentially. So until you hear otherwise, you're still in an advisory capacity. Keep on doing what you're doing."

"What I'm doing is doubting that you're telling me the truth."

"If and when the decision is made to go ahead with Maopi, and if and when you're directed to take a more active role, you'll be briefed on what to expect."

George slits his eyes at me again, then his nostrils flare a little and he rolls his head over to face Carville. Carville backs away, slightly but noticeably.

"She's just looking for some reassurance, James," George says. "Nothing crazy, nothing intricate. She just wants to hear you say flat out that she'll have some warning if she's gonna be involved in anything experimental, or dangerous. Isn't that right, Sal?"

"That's right."

"Well, then," George finishes. He gives a thin-lipped smile, his narrow eyes narrowing even farther. "That's all she wants, James. To be consulted. To get some warning, you know. Nothing strange."

Carville fixes George with a look, and I can suddenly see Carville driving a black sedan all the way out to Stephanopoulos's experimental high school when George was sixteen. The sedan pulls up to the edge of a cinder track, and in the middle distance George and some other kids are mixing it up on the soccer field. I imagine Carville standing by a chain-metal fence in a long raincoat, watching, looking for playmaking skills, checking stamina.

Then I imagine him wandering into the experimental school building, to question George's teachers, maybe to sneak a quick look in George's doorless experimental locker.

This all comes to mind because there's ownership in the look he's giving Stephanopoulos, investment, proprietary interest. He's looking at George like George is a skyscraper he's got two-thirds financed and built, and this skyscraper only just now has begun to seem like it might be out of true.

"Well, let me reassure you, Sal, that that's the case," Carville says courteously.

George pats his shoulder. "Well done, James. Bull by the horns."

I'm about to ask about the clothing we find ourselves in when there is a sound like muffled fireworks somewhere outside and below the jet. I don't need anyone to tell me it's antiaircraft fire clawing for us, and no one does.

A claxon sounds suddenly from the front and rear compartments. The pilot's voice barks from speakers set in the compartment's ceiling: "Splitting off from air escort, five seconds. Four seconds. Brace for descent and evasive action."

There is another short instant of relative peace, and then the plane veers and dives at three or four times the angle allowed a commercial jet. The scream of the engines rises as we accelerate into the already steep dive.

I know it's Utah, because my iffy nausea suddenly seizes up, my stomach contracts, and I feel my head come forward convulsively, but I manage to lock my jaws shut at the last second. It's no good, though, and just before I let go I feel something soft slammed into place over my mouth, and I grab on to it for dear life and empty my stomach. I hold the thing in place against my mouth until the spasms subside. I close the soft material over what little I had in my stomach, wipe my mouth. I can feel sweat beaded on my forehead and temples.

I look down. It's Virginia's beret.

I sputter out that I'm sorry, holding it a little away from me, just like it was a hatful of puke.

"Toss it as far toward that corner as you can without loosening your straps." She motions toward the far wall, still only five or six feet from us. After a second's hesitation, I do, and the bundle lands damply against the bulkhead. George and Carville are politely looking the other way. If the jet ever makes it back to base, someone will come across a green beret filled with vomit and my ham-tainted flak vest, and they'll get a pretty accurate sense of what my life is currently like.

"I ruined your hat," I say.

"I can't take it where we're going anyway." She's got her eyes closed again, and her body is slumped against the side of the jet. I can tell this isn't her first combat mission. She's not sweating, like me, or trying to keep her own spirits up with cockeyed optimism, like Carville. She's saving herself, getting ready. I make a mental note to stay behind her, because whatever else may happen, whatever counterattack we draw or don't, Virginia will not tank.

When the pilot warns us that we have five minutes before deceleration, Carville leans forward and puts his hand on my knee.

"You okay?" he asks, shouting over the engine scream.

"Don't touch my knee," I shout back, tossing his hand away.

He holds both hands up, palms out, torso straining against the flight harness. "Fine. You're okay. Look, we're gonna land in a minute, and I want to tell you what to expect, okay?" Partly because he's having to shout, and partly because he can't help it, he sounds like he's explaining hopscotch to a four-year-old. "We're going to land for only a few seconds. When we do, the pilot's going to pop our *harnesses* and the *evac-hatch* at the same time, okay? We leave as fast as we can. Don't forget your *bag* in the rack by the door. George and I are first, you and Virginia are bringing up the rear. You got that?" When I don't answer immediately, he raises his voice even further. *"You got that, Sal?"*

"Okay, I got it, I got it," I yell back.

"Good. Okay, once you're outside the jet, fucking *move away* from it! Follow George and me away from the jet, because the pilot's going to slap the engine sequence the second we're clear, and there's going to be a hell of a lot of *thrust* hitting the ground from the tilt engines, okay?"

"*Okay.* Got it. Okay."

"There'll be a truck or a *car* or something waiting there for us. That'll be our rendezvous. They're going to be signaling with a night light. Okay?"

I make the OK sign with my fingers, because I can't bear to say it again.

22

BRIGHT, SHINING LIE

It happens pretty much the way I was told, except for a few interesting differences. Our forward descent slows gradually, and then very forcefully, and then we're doing what jets characteristically don't ever do: we're hanging in the air, engines screaming, drowning out all competing sound.

And we hang there. I can tell we haven't touched down, because the plane can't really hover, and there are all sorts of minor corrections, giving a slow rolling feel like you get if you stand up in a rowboat. Except this is a rowboat projecting about three hundred decibels in all directions.

I had it in my mind that this would be a split-second operation. Now we're hanging over the landscape, fairly close to the ground, I can tell, and deliberately going nowhere. A huge stationary target.

A stealth-black piñata silhouetted against the stars.

"Jesus Christ!" I blurt out. "Land! Land for Christ's sake!"

I look over at Carville. He's got his eyes closed. Sweat is now standing on his broad forehead, and that's another level of frightening. For the little time I've known him, Carville has seemed immune to fear—to any emotion, really, but certainly to fear. He now looks as frightened as I am, which tells me that I don't know everything there is to be frightened about. His fists are clenched and his lips are moving, and at first I think it's a prayer. Then I lip-read it.

He's saying over and over again, "Son of a bitch, son of a bitch, son of a bitch, son of a bitch."

George is straining against his harness, palms white against the dark nylon. The cat-eyes are shut tight.

We hang for another minute, and I can't help but think we're waiting to get hit with a missile, asking for it, and maybe this is all an elaborate suicide mission. Maybe we're supposed to draw fire from Freemen batteries in the hills, so that higher air cover can wipe them out for good.

Suddenly we fall, the plane's engines somehow useless. Now it's like standing in a rowboat and having the water level suddenly drop by six feet.

And there's another sensation, a strange queasy feeling that I can't bring myself to guess at. It fades quickly, and I let it go. I don't pursue it.

Then the jet bucks sharply back and forth, engines pushing at the earth again.

But we come back to rough stability almost immediately. Tiny static-electric charges suddenly jump where my hair meets the seat back, like living things, stinging my neck. And then I feel the plane's legs very, very tentatively touch earth. Whoever is piloting this thing obviously knows how to handle the fastball.

The hatch in the plane's side shoots up, and cool desert air surges into the fouled compartment. All of a sudden I can smell sage and smoke from a fire somewhere, faint in the air but unmistakable.

My harness springs open at the same instant, and Virginia and George and Carville are already rolling out of their seats toward the hatch. I struggle up, wobbly on my legs, and only when I see Virginia snatch her Gidget overnighter from the rack do I remember to grab my flight bag.

I jump to the ground, and it's farther than I thought—five feet instead of three—and then I'm down on the sand in the darkness, all bearings gone. I come up with sand in my mouth, in my eyes. Somebody grabs me and pulls me to my feet. It's Virginia; I can tell because she lifts me with only one arm, and I think even Carville would need two. It dawns on me as she moves away in the dark that none of us are wearing night-sight gear, which seems criminally stupid.

I stumble forward, but I'm not moving fast enough, because George dodges back to me and grabs my wrist, pulls me forward into the light wind still being kicked up by the engines. There's a small glowing green triangle on the back of his vest. Ahead I can make out Carville's vest, bobbing crazily.

Suddenly, way off to the left, I see a red baton flash once, then twice in the darkness, and as George and I clear the minimum blast radius, the plane explodes into sound behind me.

I turn and watch, transfixed, as its legs vanish and it rises up on four columns of turbulent air, each shot through with a crazy spray of orange sparks. Almost no flame escapes the engine pods, which are supposed to have a minimal heat signature, but the air feels on fire as it washes over me.

The jet quickly reaches a predetermined altitude far overhead, and the engines pivot. There is a crescendo of noise. The darkened shape streaks upward and is instantly lost. There are stars out in only half the sky, indicating that we've been set down in the cool shadow of a mesa. I have absolutely no orientation except up or down. I could be in Yugoslavia or South Dakota for all I really know.

I turn back to the others. George's triangle is about twenty yards ahead of me, stopped, waiting. James's triangle is moving forward somewhere ahead of him, somewhere near where the baton flashed. I feel a hand on my shoulder, and I start violently. It's Virginia. I exhale.

"Try to pay attention," she whispers, moving by me.

We walk forward slowly until we reach George, who's standing beside what looks like the beginning of a climbing ridge of rock, the first toe at the foot of the mesa. George puts out an arm to stop us.

Beyond us, Carville's emerald triangle bobs, then slows to a walk in the open sand beyond the low ridge of rock. Then it stops. He seems to have reached whoever's signaling us. There is a pause, long enough for Carville and the signalers to sort out who's in charge of whom.

Another second and the baton flashes crimson again, waving us on.

As the three of us approach, we clear one sharp angle of the mesa and walk out into comparatively bright moonlight. It's quiet except for the sound of our shoes and boots grinding over sagebrush and low cactus and hard sand. The mesa juts up, towering, rough-cut, under the hung moon.

I can see now that James is standing beside two tall men in dark suits. The two men are standing next to two automobiles, not sun-sourced but actual gas-burners. The moonlight is a bit murky, but I can easily make out the shapes of these automobiles, and I tell myself that there are plenty of explanations for these shapes. Because these are not the Land Rovers and Daimler-Lincolns that millionaires ordinarily race in the desert. These are antiques, real antiques. But new.

They're oversize, with huge shiny grilles that look like mouths full of chrome-plated teeth. Even in the moonlight the chrome gleams. At the other end, these cars have long, surprisingly graceful projections rising up over the taillights.

I tell myself that these projections are not fins, but I know in the deep part of me that finds it impossible to lie to the other parts of me that they are, in fact, fins.

I look at the two men standing talking softly with Carville. They, too, are wearing dark suits with skinny lapels and ties and straight-legged trousers. But unlike the suits George and Carville are wearing, theirs seem pressed but not new. They wear their suits like they belong in them. It's a small thing, but their jackets have no padding at all, and the shoulders of the men have this odd little authenticating slump. Both are sporting super-short crew cuts, giving them the jug-eared, burr-headed look I remember from reruns of 1960s cop shows. No one has told me, but I know what I'm looking at. Or when I'm looking at.

Now I pull out the sensation I didn't want to think about before, the sensation I felt when the plane dropped suddenly in the air. When I was first dating Steve, we spent a lot of time windsurfing on Lake Champlain, and we used to do a stunt where we'd manage to ride our boards close enough to link hands. We could only stay linked for a few seconds or so before one of us would need to tack to stay upright, and there would come that inevitable moment when the pressure on my hand, and then my fingers, would overcome my resistance, and we'd separate.

The sensation I felt on the plane was like that, except I felt suddenly pulled apart from me, separated from myself. Slowly, inexorably.

That's the best I can describe it. It wasn't a feeling you want to examine very much. There was something stomach-turning about it. But now I realize what it was. George was right: we are the data.

George is now standing quietly beside me, and I yank roughly on his sleeve. He turns from trying to catch the rise and fall of Carville's words.

"What kind of cars are those?" I demand, watching the whites of his eyes.

He doesn't look happy with the question, but he doesn't dodge. He knows I know. "Those are two 1959 Ford Fairlane 500 Skyliners." George pauses and then continues in a softer whisper. "Cruise-O-Matic transmission. Power steering, windows, seats. Retractable hard-top. Built-in tissue dispenser." He sees that I'm not mollified, goes on. "Select-Aire conditioner. Sky-blue body with white accents. Engine is an impressively robust 352 V-8."

I just look at him for a second. As much as I've come to like him, I feel like slapping him. But I say, "And they're new. Aren't they? They're brand-new."

"Actually," he tries to joke, "they're four years old. At this particular point."

Virginia is watching me intently, her bag tossed down in the sand, hands free. This is one of the moments she'd have prepped to handle: when it finally dawns on old Sal that she's been temporally deported.

I ignore her. My voice gets away from me, and it's loud in the mesa silence, loud without really carrying. "You *lied* to me, George. You promised me some kind of warning. I was supposed to be given a chance to decide."

George has his voice down low, in a fierce whisper. "I didn't lie, Sal. And neither did Virginia. So don't lay this on us."

I start toward Carville, and Virginia starts toward me. George steps between us. "Let her go," he says to Virginia. "She hasn't got any sharp objects on her."

Carville and the two men are standing close together, a little suit clique. There's something overly casual about the three of them, like members of rival high-school football teams who've met by accident at the local Burger King—everyone trying to look laid-back and unafraid of getting their ass kicked.

Carville has his back to me, but the other two suits see me coming and widen their eyes when I don't stop politely outside the circle but come up beside Carville and grab his arm and spin him around.

He's taken aback but he manages, barely, to keep his composure. He shoots a look out into the dark, where Virginia was supposed to be handling me.

I don't let the arm go. Carville just looks down at the spot my fingers are clutching, then looks back up.

"You lied to me," I say loudly, ignoring the now-silent strangers. "You creepy, mendacious NSC piece of shit. You looked me right straight in the eye and lied to me."

Carville looks at me for a second, jaw working, and then rips his arm suddenly out of my grip. He smooths his sleeve, shoots his cuffs, gets his composure back. Then he turns and gives the two 1963 NSC types a quick, knowing, apologetic look that says, *Chicks*.

[illegible]

[illegible]

[illegible]

[illegible]

[illegible]

[illegible]

[illegible]

[illegible]

[illegible]

[illegible]

[illegible]

[illegible]

[illegible]

[illegible]

The Year

1963

The Fourth Part:

ACQUIRING *yBC*

"We are wandering in the desert, men, just like the Israelites after they escaped from out of Egypt. We're free, but we're in exile, we got to wander. Outlaws, free but outlaws. We got no choice. This desert all around us tells you where we're at in this struggle of ours. The feds have all the rest of the country, everything [shouts]. They control everything. They've got the milk and honey that's the birthright of every free-born American. And the Fedman isn't ever gonna give it up. And so it's got to be taken [applause]. You know that, and I know it. All of us rallied here today under this killer sun, we all know it, as sure as we know we weren't meant to labor our whole lives long to pay taxes to support the system that's taking our way of life away. I'm gonna ask you to remember the Founding Fathers—not Jefferson and Washington and them, although God bless those boys. I'm talking about the other Founding Fathers, the second generation of men to get their backs up and fight for their country. I'm talking about people like Tim McVeigh [applause], who wore a T-shirt when he took down the Oklahoma federal building that read, and I fucking quote, From time to time the tree of liberty must be refreshed with the blood of patriots *[cheers, sustained applause]. Refreshed! You hear what I'm saying out there? And I'm talking about David Koresh—remember Koresh? Remember him [applause]? Branch Davidians? Waco, Texas? He was a man that wanted to have some religious freedom in another desert, thousands of miles from here, but he was another Freeman like you and me who found himself in the desert with the Fedman all around. Nothing to wet the desert down with except his own blood and the blood of his people. And that he did. That he did do.*

That's what I want you to remember, my friends. You want to know what will change this desert we find ourselves in? It's blood, my friends. The Fedman's blood, and maybe the blood of his family. Your blood, and maybe the blood of your family. No desert dry enough to hold that back. That's the only way, and it's the truth. Blood's the only thing'll do it."

—Unidentified speaker, "Blood on the Desert" speech, Freemen May Day Rally, Little Skull Mountain, Nevada, May 1, 2019; first documented usage of phrase "Founding Fathers" to include both T. McVeigh and D. Koresh (Library of Congress video archive)

23

STOCKHOLM SYNDROME, AND HOW TO GO WITH IT

The man I know only as James Carville is chattering in the driver's seat. It's July 22, 1963. These are two things for which I will never forgive the man I know only as James Carville.

"See, the big thing was," he blathers on, "would they take *direction*. Because even with the day codes and the nuclear codes—and the *abort* nuclear-sequence codes—we could never convince the NSC 1995 folks to accept our authority. We'd say to them, Look, here's the way the military works: if somebody's got the codes, you salute. But we got nowhere with 1995 NSC. Stubborn fucks. Bunch of conspiracy theorists. They'd write back and you could tell they really thought they were addressing a ring of Chinese Webcutters over in Taipei somewhere."

Outside the window, sand and road and scrub roll endlessly by. Occasionally a tumbleweed staggers across the road. The sun is up, and it is already monstrously hot. The big blue-and-white car is a flume ride, continually sluicing through the heat pooling over the desert.

Carville pokes his head out the open window to get a better look at a passing billboard. It features a line of pretty but slightly flabby-looking women in platform heels and show costumes. They are all smiling and speckled with dice: dice on their breasts, dice bracelets on their wrists.

On each of the women's heads is a hat-size die. Below them, the caption reads: THE STARDUST HOTEL, THE LARGEST HOTEL IN THE WORLD. 1,000 ROOMS!

AND THE GIRLS OF THE LIDO DE PARIS! STRAIGHT FROM FRANCE TO THE INTERSECTION OF THE STRIP AND TROPICANA AVENUE. WOW!

Carville takes it all in, then pulls his balding head back in the window. "Wow," he repeats, showing the canines, shaking his head. He lights a cigarette with the car's built-in lighter. He does this as though he's been riding around in automobiles all his life. The 1963 types have left a pack of Lucky Strikes on the front seat, as a gesture of friendship, and so here is Carville firing up a Lucky with the car's built-in lighter, making a point of pretending that this is all perfectly normal. He runs a hand slowly up the broad expanse of forehead.

"I mean, I don't blame them for that. I respect them. Stubborn fucks in 1995. They weren't going to take orders from an unknown source, no matter the extent of the information the unknown source could produce. Fortunately, the 1963 mind-set was still pretty rigid, pretty blindly hierarchical. Cold War mentality. And it worked to our advantage that in '63 they're still running all sorts of covert operations all over the globe, most of them with stand-alone command structures, *complete* insulation from other agencies, complete insulation within their *own* agencies.

"It was beautiful. So we never had to put over the knowledge of who we really were. As far as they know, we're 1963 guys too. It was ludicrous in a way. We touch down in a plane that's sixty or seventy years beyond their technology, easy. These guys don't bat an eye. They figure this plane is just another thing they haven't been cleared to see. That's the kind of blind faith they have in the covert principle. You gotta love that."

He baits me a little, catching my eye in the rearview. "You could learn a thing or two from those guys, Sal."

He thinks for a second, fingers drumming on the oversize blue steering wheel. Another, larger billboard swims through the heat waves: LIBERACE! PERFORMING IN THE STARLIGHT LOUNGE, AT THE STARDUST HOTEL. THE WORLD'S LARGEST HOTEL. 1,000 ROOMS! Beside the text is a picture of a youngish man wearing slacks and white bucks and a striped jacket. It looks like photos I've seen of Liberace, but minus the jowls and the capes and the furs and jewels, the extravagantly queenish look he brought into the seventies and eighties.

We are in 1963 now. Even Liberace acts straight.

* * *

The younger man I know as George Stephanopoulos is sitting in the passenger seat. Although he is taller than Carville, his head does not come near the roof of the Fairlane. This is a car built in and for expansive times. George's lanky frame has expanded to fill a good part of his end of it, all the same. He has an arm thrown out along the smooth leather crown of the front seat, and another arm is outside the window, curled up over the roof, fingertips drumming. Both he and Carville have shed their jackets and rolled their sleeves in the steadily creeping heat.

George has taken off his shoes, and he has the heel of one black silk-socked foot resting on the padded dash. His toe is absently stroking the windshield. I see now that George must have gotten a trim last night before we left the NATVAC complex. The unruly brown mass is thinned at the temples, reined in. He knew he was headed for the early sixties, all right.

I see something else as well. George Stephanopoulos is glad to be alive. He knew when he got on the plane last night that the Maopi installation had instructions to take us as we hovered over them in the jump jet. He knew that we were going to be converted into energy packets, and that these energy packets would then either resume being us—same place, different year—or cease to be us altogether. He knew that the packets might conceivably resume being parts of us scattered over a vast area of the desert, or disappear altogether, without even the dignity of carnage. Carville knew. Virginia knew. They all knew.

For Carville, the fact that we are here now seems to be just part of the plan. He is still rambling. "Of course, when you work it out logically, the 1963 NSC's got it absolutely right. We do have a kind of valid tactical seniority over them, in that we supersede them chronologically. The 1995 people, when you look at it that way, are insubordinate, although there's no way you'd ever convince them of that. Stubborn fucks in 1995." Carville is just calmly working out the new realities. He's pleased.

He can give orders to a hell of a lot more people than he once imagined.

But George is grateful to be alive, and George is enchanted. He has his eyes closed, as the hot wind roughs up his hair. He's grinning broadly. Occasionally he opens his eyes and lets his gaze fall on the features of the car carrying him forward. He looks with awe, with something approaching love at first sight, at these details. He fingers the small ventilation window beside the larger window set into his door. He opens the vent window, closes it. His index finger stretches out lazily and touches the little vanity mirror above his seat. At one point, he opens the glove box and pulls out the operator's manual and begins methodically to absorb the contents. But before he begins to read, he brings the little booklet up to his nose, opens it, and sucks the life from it.

Next to me in the backseat is Virginia, the Green Beret named for BC's deceased mother. Actually, last night she was named for BC's late mother. Today, she is named after a relatively healthy woman living in Hot Springs, Arkansas, a woman who smokes Pall Malls and gambles on the ponies and who dotes over her sixteen-year-old son, the golden boy she calls Bubba.

Our Virginia is still wearing her Beret uniform. She is the only one of us not wearing period costume, and I have to believe that there are at least two reasons for this. One, no doubt they wanted her in action gear in case the spooks from this time period met us with their guns drawn. And two, no doubt Virginia simply refused to go polyester. But that is soon to change.

At an actual Standard Oil gas station, Virginia disappears discreetly into the rest room with her Gidget overnight bag and reappears ten or fifteen minutes later dressed like Laura Petrie from *The Dick Van Dyke Show:* knee-length teal-colored shirtwaist dress, all-around pleats, very demure V-neck, cocktail-party pumps. The sleeves drop midway down her arms, camouflaging the softball-size biceps and deltoids. They're not ready for the fully buffed woman here in the early sixties.

Still, even with the conservative cut to the dress, she exits the bathroom with a new and unmistakable bombshell quality. Although her drab Beret uniform couldn't hide her sex appeal, it had helped to diminish it, to place it to one side. Now, clearly, she's been ordered to undiminish it. Her bust rides high and firm and unmistakable, the torpedoes-away look that the old Maidenform bras were designed to give you. She's wearing coral lipstick, and even in the housewife pumps she manages a smooth, sure shifting of hips that replaces Laura Petrie with Gina Lollabrigida for the duration of her walk to the car.

She's done something quick but drastic to her thick dark hair; it's been brushed to a shine, and it flows around either side of her face, then curls pertly just above her shoulders. The long legs, once rendered all but immaterial by dull green khaki, are now rendered decidedly material again.

She's wearing sunglasses, shades with a slight wraparound effect that set off the high bones of her cheeks, a craze the First Lady only recently ignited: Jackie glasses. Most of America won't be wearing the cheap knockoffs until fall. Not only is Virginia now blatantly and spectacularly female, she's a fashion plate.

But when she's folded herself into the backseat beside me, she takes a mirror out of her handbag and checks her face with what seems more like professionalism than vanity, and I get the sense that it's just another uniform to her. Then she turns and catches my once-over and gives me a quick look back that says: *Don't try breaking my balls about this.*

And me, of course, Sal. I'm also riding in the backseat of the Skyliner. When it became clear last night that I'd been the victim of a fairly elaborate temporal three-card monte game, I ran and hid in the desert, for no other reason than to break away from these lying, cheating military bastards. It wasn't a well-thought-out plan. In fact, it wasn't a plan at all. It was panic. I led them on a wild-goose chase for something like an hour, hiding in little hollows in the sand, sitting with my back to cacti, while they combed the desert with flashlights and yelled for me.

But finally, there was nowhere to go. Even if it were the desert of my time, there would have been nowhere to go. And so when I eventually returned to the car it was with every intention of holding a grudge as long as is humanly possible, of fucking up whatever intricately nuanced NSC plans were fuck-upable, of taking vengeance in any of the severely limited ways petite academics have available to them.

But it's dawn now, dawn of July 22, 1963, and none of that has come emotionally to pass. None of it. It doesn't make any sense, but it's very true.

Although a small part of me is crying traitor at the rest, I feel mostly buoyant, drunk with amazement, because the proof is all around me that this is real, Sam-Cooke-and-Lawrence-Welk-on-the-car-radio real. I'm a lot closer to George's enchantment than I am to the bitterness of last night, a lot closer. I've got 1963 sand in my shoes.

The Standard station where Virginia did her quick change had a cash register with mechanical buttons to ring in sales, and above it on the wall, small but unmistakable, was a paper notice that said, *We reserve the right to refuse service to anyone at any time.*

It was the sort of sign that started appearing in the early years of the civil-rights movement, a coded way of registering which way you fell out on segregation.

And there I was, looking through the station's dusty front window at it, the owner of the station looking back placidly, cigarette tucked in the corner of his mouth. He had the Vitalis-saturated crew cut and heavy black glasses that men affected, for no discernible reason, in the years before hairstyles went nuclear. He was wearing a Standard Oil uniform shirt that had the name *Neil* sewn in blue thread above the pocket. I wanted to go in and offer him ten dollars for the sign, fifty for the shirt; I had this mad desire to start collecting artifacts. I wanted to go in and ask him what he thought about the Civil Rights Act that President Kennedy and his pushy brother Bobby are currently forcing through Congress, or just what he thought about the Kennedys in general. Or, really, what he thought about *anything*—Perry Mason, interracial dating, Korea, the Russians, the Watusi.

But I realized after a minute that I was looking through the window at old Neil the closet racist like a gorilla in the zoo, and I was making him visibly uncomfortable, so I went back to the car.

Now we're thirty miles from Vegas, and Carville continues to blather.

"Our first order of business is to complete a set of verification procedures, thus the drive to Las Vegas, which has a fairly unmistakable growth pattern between the late forties and the early seventies, pretty much casino by casino by casino every three, four, five years. So that's quick and dirty—the Sands, the Riviera, the Fremont should all be there. Caesars Palace shouldn't be. They don't break ground on Caesars Palace until next year."

Carville waves amiably at a passing convertible full of young men in marine uniforms. They stare into our Ford, looking for females, exactly like the jarheads I'm used to in my own time frame.

"Too bad we won't make the Caesars grand opening. Supposedly they spent over a million on that—and that's a million at 1963 valuation. Prime rib, champagne, crab, lobster, real old-time Vegas swank. So that's a quick visual appraisal. Then tonight we have tickets for one of the most carefully documented events of the decade," Carville says grandly, then looks into the rearview and checks his smile for food particles or maybe the individual teeth for sharpness. "Title fight, Floyd Patterson versus Sonny Liston. The go-to refers to the fight as a cross-verifiable event, which essentially means we have multiple accounts, film, newspaper, radio, all of which agree on important particulars—time of the match, people in attendance, total number of seconds to the knockout—"

"Seconds?" Virginia repeats, not looking up from her nails. For the last thirty miles or so she has been giving them a stiff workout with the emery board, and she is now laying on a coat of thick red enamel from a tiny bottle in her purse. The fumes from it are all but making my eyes tear, even with all the windows open.

"Seconds. One hundred and thirty, to be precise. Liston was no average chin-banger. He knocked Patterson out twice, two fights, in the first round. Brutal."

"Where's the fight?" George inquires.

"Las Vegas Convention Center. That's brand-new too."

George looks interested. "Where's Patterson training?"

"Patterson and his people are at the Dunes. Even going in a loser this time, Patterson's still got some star power. Norman Mailer's holed up at the Dunes. Judy Garland. Those types."

"Liston?"

"Liston's camp's over at the Thunderbird. One of the original watering holes. Old mob hangout. He was supposed to work out at the Dunes, but Sonny's superstitious, and three other champs became ex-champs after training there. So no Dunes."

"Doesn't bother Floyd, though," George points out.

"And you see what end of the lollipop he's holding when the fight's over. Sonny's superstitious, but he's not stupid." Carville muses silently for a second. He steers the car with just two fingers flattened out over the skinny wheel. Then he reports, "When he works the heavy bag he has them crank up the R&B on the sound system. Animal on the heavy bag, Sonny Liston."

George nods, taking in the information. He's putting on his black wing tips now, getting ready for the Strip. "How about the Rat Pack? Where they hanging these days?"

"Sinatra, Dino, Jerry Lewis, Joey Bishop, and Peter Lawford. Nowhere but the Sands."

"Sammy Davis, Jr.?"

"Sands," Carville repeats, nodding knowingly, beginning the hunt for neon on the horizon. "Sammy's at the Sands. Bet your ass, baby."

"Why'd they call them the Rat Pack?" Virginia asks, blowing absently now on one completed hand. "What was that all about?"

Carville looks at me in the rearview. "Ask Sal. Twentieth-century guru there."

Virginia drops her glance from Carville to her nails, then raises it to me. I say nothing, leave my face a blank, and after a second Carville goes into a long-winded, apocryphal explanation. Ordinarily, this slice of conversation would almost make me gag—Carville, because he's privy to the actual orders we're under, the sacred go-to, knew what to read up on before we boarded the jump jet in the first place. So now suddenly he's Joe Vegas. George probably did his share of mission-specific prep too, which is why he, too, seems conversant with aging heavyweights from the mid-twentieth century.

But somehow it's not making me gag this morning. It's just amusing, ludicrous but comic and amusing. Because I'm happy, there's no way around it.

I'm happy.

My life wasn't extremely full or fulfilled where and when I was yesterday, even before the NSC snatched me. I can see that now; I wasn't happy with my life. Too much of it was spent in front of a Wide-eye, coming to scholarly terms with what other people had said and done. Way too little of it was saying and doing. I'd built myself a cocoon in Vermont and an air-conditioned cocoon in Little Rock, and then I killed whatever time I had left traveling by Bullet between them. There was no magic, no quickening of the blood. What little there was came from short romantic debacles with men I knew almost from the opening bell were really wrong for me.

And now, unless I'm still the object of some horrific, continuing scam, I'm doing what no historian has ever been able to do: go see for herself. I'm hanging my hand out the window of a 1959 Ford, feeling the wash of 1963 air. And I'm willing to admit that it's not a jump I could have made consciously, I'd never have been able to do it if they'd come to me and explained everything up front. I'd never have taken the risk. Never. They had to kidnap me. So that's where I'm at: full-blown Stockholm Syndrome. I'm *glad* they kidnapped me. I'm glad to be where I am right now.

The man I know only as James Carville will never know that, though. Never. Not if I can help it. Hence the silence. Hence the stone-face. Let the cocky bastard sweat.

George I don't have to tell. He's the kind that knows, feels your mood whether you keep your face a blank or not. Just before Las Vegas swims into view on the horizon—in that anticipatory instant before the desert divulges its tacky secret—George reaches his long arm back between the front seat and the door. The rest of his body doesn't move an inch, but his closed hand stops just in front of me. Carville notices nothing. Virginia sees the hand sticking out of a black sleeve but looks away discreetly.

I reach into the closed hand and feel something flat and metallic. As I move to take it, George closes his long hand on the tips of my fingers for a second. This touch is the last thing I expected; it's playful and somehow comforting and it's intimate, and then it's over. I don't have time to figure out what to do about it before he opens his hand and lets me take the object.

It's a stick of gum. He must have bought it from Neil at the Standard station.

I unwrap it and put it in my mouth, and the sharp, crazy taste of sour apples explodes over my palate.

24

LOST VEGAS

The Haydens are not given to keeping resolutions about silence, because we have very big mouths. This is true in general, but specifically this is true when someone as annoying as Carville begins lecturing authoritatively on things he knows next to nothing about. He's tossing out historical contingency scenarios as we motor the last few miles to Vegas, referring to some software bundle they put together at the NATVAC complex as though it were the Oracle at Delphi.

First he raps about how killing the Anti-Tobacco Accord would have zero effect on BC's reelection chances in 1996, and now he's arguing that preventing Timothy McVeigh from destroying the Murrah Federal Building would eliminate the Allied Freemen movement as elegantly as snuffing the pilot light on a stove.

"Great thing about McVeigh," Carville opines, stretching his back and both arms slowly and then dropping one hand back on the wheel, "is that for most of the 1990s he's a solitary bastard. Sure, he's dropping into nascent militia cells here and there but never really getting to know anybody. He affected other people's lives so little—I mean, before he took down the Murrah—that you'd hardly cause a historical murmur if you nailed his orange-jumpsuited little ass. What you'd lose is the media plume about the event itself. But the man McVeigh touches almost nobody. The macro model they put together at NATVAC said that."

George looks like he's going to say something, and then he turns in his seat and punts it to me. From his casual look, you'd never know he just held my hand for an eighth of a second. "Sal, what James doesn't like to point out is that we recruited you because NATVAC's software turned out to be right only about sixty-one percent of the time. And this particular bundle started life as a plankton simulator."

"It was a red-tide simulator," Carville shoots back, "and it worked just fine. Sixty-one percent is *smoking*, when you're talking about recalibrating a historical event and all the budded contingencies from that insertion point."

George snorts. "So smoking, in fact, that we were ordered to go take over a library to get someone who could actually do the job. Sal, do us a big favor, what's wrong with the McVeigh scenario?"

I don't have to think about it too hard. From Carville's ramblings, it's clear that they've been thinking in almost purely linear terms. They're thinking about people as pool balls and history as the table, angles and carom that a computer can tally. Which is dangerously stupid. So in spite of my vow, I begin to talk. "Look, Carville, I don't know much about the software you were using, but it sounds like it was a massive database of historical records, media input, that kind of stuff."

"*Buttload* of data," Carville says definitively, eyes on me in the rearview.

"And then you crunched the data to find out if removing one element, one name, produced unacceptably large changes in the records, or if removing that one name affected the lives of other people with enough historical standing to produce unacceptably large changes."

Carville nods, lips pursed. "That's a crude summary. But, yes."

Now I'm sitting up and leaning over the front seat. I can tell it's making Carville nervous, but I couldn't care less. "But there's more to an event like Oklahoma City than the number of stories it produces. Timothy McVeigh is more than just a guy who does or doesn't personally interact with other people. People don't write on the historical page, they stain it. History's seepage, capillary action.

"Just take BC, for example. BC never met McVeigh. But the Oklahoma City bombing was what really began BC's comeback in the polls, after, you know, his disastrous first year in office. That first year it was gays in the military, Travelgate, Hairgate, Nannygate, Nannygate II. If he even looked cross-eyed, the press and the Republicans slapped a *gate* on the end of it. He went from being a popular force for change in '92 to the government personified in '93, and it seemed like the people would never forgive him for it.

"Unless and until he began to fight something they found even more distasteful. That's where McVeigh came in. Oklahoma City allowed BC to finally come out and begin making the cut-and-dried moral distinctions that people were looking for. It allowed him to take on the whole talk-radio network that had been militating solidly for Republican candidates, most of them New Federalists, for four or five years.

"BC's addresses on that bombing were real watersheds, emotionally speaking, for the whole country. And it really began a process of tying the Republican Revolution's extreme rhetoric to extreme terrorist action, and that was what led to the disintegration of the voting coalition that overturned Democratic rule in the first place, in 1994."

Carville's listening, but it's hard to tell if he's just humoring me: he's struggling to drive and rip open a package of Mallo Cups he bought at the gas station. But Virginia's giving me a look like I'm making sense, so I run it out to the end.

"McVeigh was one of those accidents of history that lead—not directly, not proof positive, but arguably—to BC's second term and to the change back to Democratic dominance in the early years of this century. Go back to the macro model and run it without McVeigh, and ask it to tell you whether BC still gets his sudden upsurge in public opinion post-Murrah. And when it tells you no, then admit to yourself that BC is only one example of the indirect stuff you guys are paying absolutely no attention to. Only one of a potentially infinite number."

Carville ponders my theory for a second. Then he jams one entire Mallo Cup into his mouth, working his jaw vigorously. Almost immediately he screws up his face in disgust. "I thought these things had peanut butter in them."

Virginia pipes up from beside me. "The peanut butter ones were called Reese's Peanut Butter Cups."

"They call these *Mallo* Cups because they're full of *marshmallow,*" George explains slowly, leaning over and actually pointing to the word on the package before James crumples it and flings it out the open window.

If I had any lingering doubts about when I was, they vanish as the city of Las Vegas comes slowly into sight. I've been to Las Vegas twice for conferences, and the much older city I'm used to is a sprawling, spawning, Bosch-style orgy of neon and palm trees and erupting volcanoes and needlelike hundred-story resorts and an actual recycled space shuttle diving at regular intervals from one casino spire, all wound around with bows of concrete overpass and cloverleaf.

What we eventually approach looks more like a string of eight or nine medium-size rest stops set down haphazardly alongside a two-lane highway running through dry, ugly desert. Between each of these seeming rest stops is a lot of space, a lot of plain open sand. It looks like the light sprawl surrounding an exit on the *way* to Las Vegas, rather than Vegas itself. It's surprisingly disappointing. All four of us are just looking at it, silently. Everyone's trying not to look let down.

"There's more than there seems," Carville bluffs, sounding like a father with a carload of kids expecting a bigger payoff at the end of a drive. "Once you get down in it, you'll see. Plenty of glitz. And more stars than you'd ever see in the eighties, for instance. Vegas is seriously hip right now. All the big names are coming here to get married, not just divorced. Paul Newman and Joanne Woodward. The hotels have floating craps games so you don't have to leave the pool. That's the big gimmick."

I can't help but break my silence again. "Where are we staying, and what are we doing until fight time?"

Carville gestures toward the end of the Strip. "We're at the Riviera. European-style luxury. Right next to the convention center."

"But nobody hangs there. It's Nowheresville, man," George points out.

"Precisely. Less chance you spill a mai tai on Lauren Bacall." Carville lights another Lucky, which, having no filter, he drags gingerly, brushing tobacco from his lip after a second with evident disgust. "As for what we're doing, we're staying headquartered in our two adjoining suites. We're eating room service. We're not gambling, we're not catching the Folies Bergère at the Tropicana. We're under very explicit orders to stay low and out of the mix. I know I don't have to remind everyone that this is a military mission, governed in strict accordance with the Code of Military Conduct. Or that Virginia is along partly to help me enforce discipline, with whatever level of force is required. Up to and including field execution."

Virginia doesn't bat an eye when he says it. But she nods. It's a good time to remind myself that under the demure frock, she's completely ripped and steroid-enhanced and wouldn't have a problem taking any of the rest of us out if it ever came to hand-to-hand. She blows on her sassy-colored nails.

George leans over. "But it's completely nonsensical. We're in the mix *now*, we'll be in the mix all the way through the lobby. We're in the mix tonight at the fights. Nothing changes because we have a drink in the lounge while we wait."

Carville's got the Lucky between two fingers, and he points them at Stephanopoulos. "I've got one simple word for you, George. Fucking no."

There's another disappointed silence in the car. The mission has taken on all the nuance of a road trip to Disney Universe.

"Think of it as a Rose Garden strategy," Carville offers after another minute, initiating the long, curving exit from the little highway.

So it's 1963, city of Las Vegas, Riviera Hotel, but instead of shooting craps with Jerry Lewis and what passes currently for the beautiful people, I am in the drab fourth-floor room Virginia and I have been given to share, playing Loaves & Fishes with George. Virginia and James are holed up in the boys' suite next door, no doubt running over procedures for field execution.

George is lying on Virginia's bed, feet bicycling idly in the air. He's doing the major news cycles of the Roger Tamraz episode, a subsection of the Lincoln Bedroom/Camp David/donor-access scandal that peaked following BC's 1996 reelection. And he's doing them effortlessly. I realize too late the game is built for his strengths—retention, odd details, sequences—not judgment or big picture.

"Lebanese-American businessman," George says, puffing slightly, "wanted some backing for a Caspian Sea oil pipeline. Donated $177,000 to the DNC. Turned out BC duly listened to his tale of woe and put a guy to work looking into it for him. Looked for all the world like a smoking *quid pro quo*. Fortunately for BC, nobody cared before the election. Dole was going around blowing his stack, 'Where's the outrage, where's the outrage.' But when the election was over, boom, everybody's calling BC a panhandler."

"Counterspin," I call out from the little table beside our little window overlooking the cabanas. I call this out through a mouth of unexpectedly excellent room-service cheeseburger. Maybe the legends about the early Vegas are true.

"BC conveniently rips his tendon while playing golf—"

"Not playing golf. He was staying at the house of a golfer. Greg Norman. Minus five points for legend creep."

"Greg Norman, the Shark," George cuts back in. "Jesus, give me a chance to answer. Don't be so hasty. I was *going* to say he was playing golf at Norman's house, and he lost it coming out his front *door*. Could have made it around on crutches, but the White House put him in a wheelchair instead. It was like FDR redux, minor outpouring of sympathy and nostalgia. The pictures knocked the Tamraz story back to page twelve."

We've worked our way down through four or five levels of scandal, larger to smaller. Currently we're at the imbroglio stage, and George is almost rolling over me. Which I cannot allow, because, for one, this is my field of specialty and George is a rank amateur, even if he does have an eidetic memory. And for two, it's my game, I made it up, and I've never lost. So I take it suddenly down to the minor-flap level, hoping to rattle him.

"Okay, it's 1994. BC's speaking to a group of autoworkers in Shreveport, Louisiana, and he mentions this El Camino—"

"—pickup truck that he had when he was a young scamp in Hot Springs. Typical BC, trying to connect with the audience on whatever level, forget about appropriate. He tells them this story about how he used to have Astroturf in the back of his El Camino, makes it pretty clear it wasn't to play football on. Real locker-room stuff, and he got spanked in the press for a few days about it."

"Counterspin?"

"BC goes on a talk-radio show, one of the shock jocks who was popular back then, guy named Don Imus. And he makes the case that the Astroturf was not for shagging girls from the glee club but was really because—I love this so much—he carried his *luggage* back there." George stops pedaling to shake his head. "What a goof. Like he *had* any luggage at that point."

It's not looking good for the home team. In fact, as Carville would say, it's looking like shit for the home team.

"Counter-counterspin," I ask, to buy some time.

"Don Imus is the speaker at the gridiron media correspondents' dinner that year, and he makes some crude jokes about it in front of BC and his wife. White House tries to keep the tape off C-Span but no go. They run it three times."

I'm really sweating it now. I've got one more level down I can go. George doesn't even seem to be concentrating. So I hit him with a flurry of really minor Gates, in diminishing order of size, all the way down to the most ludicrous sub-sub-Gates. Try to max him out and then stun him.

"Troopergate."

"Please. Exert yourself a little. Accusations BC used Arkansas state troopers to procure women while governor."

"Hairgate."

"BC's first year. Has a stylist come aboard Air Force One, takes flak for holding up air traffic while getting the presidential coif. Turns out later no holdup, just effective Republican spin."

"Lampgate."

"Rumor from inside White House that BC's wife nailed him with said lamp."

"Piddlegate."

"Alternately known as Pissgate. BC's new dog, Buddy, pisses a rug, antique rug. Republicans cry historical desecration, children are loose in the White House. Counterspin points out JFK's dog messed *the exact same rug.* Turns piss stain into just one more eerie connection to Kennedy. Game, set, match."

I've got one more shot. That's it. After that, my mind's blank. I dip one of my few remaining fries in the pool of ketchup on my plate, suck my greasy fingers. Never let them see you sweat.

"Leogate."

"What?"

"You heard me."

George pauses, puts his legs down flat on the bed. His brow furrows. I don't say a word, just continue adding fat to my thighs. George rolls over on his side, facing me, hands pillowed underneath his face. It's an unusual face, both pretty and tough-looking. Pretty eyes, pretty cheekbones, tough mouth, tough chin.

And, not incidentally, a little on the baby-smooth side; he's not even out of his late twenties yet. I think about him taking my hand earlier. I'd bet twenty dollars he has no idea exactly why he did it, no idea whether he was saying something or nothing. Guys his age have limited emotional problem-solving skills, even guys who aren't government-reared sponges. "Thirty seconds," I tell him. "Leogate."

He starts to say something, then stops. I get the feeling he's reviewing mental photographs of all of the millions of pages on BC he's digested since Carville brought him into this assignment, since Carville tried to turn him into their me.

"Something to do with horoscopes," he ventures finally, with a straight face.

I don't say anything, letting him hang himself.

He makes it up on the fly, I'll give him that. "BC's at a state dinner with Sonia Gandhi of India, and he's caught on camera stroking her arm between courses and asking her her sign. She's a Leo, turns out. BC later invokes Nancy Reagan, claims he was a tool of the stars."

"I'm sorry, that's an outright fabrication. I'm going to have to disqualify you," I tell him.

He pouts his thin lips for a second, then looks toward the window, where we both know that crowds of paunchy Middle Americans are having all manner of tawdry, Las Vegas–style fun. Then he smiles, and his cat eyes very nearly turn into flat lines. "I gave it a shot. I'm ignorant. What was the deal with Leogate?"

"It's Earth Week, the year 2000, and the old American Broadcasting Company sends Leonardo DiCaprio—who at the time was this boy sensation fresh off a smash hit with the film *Titanic,* hadn't won the Oscar for *Trial of Harrison Savage* yet—to the White House to interview BC about the environment and stuff, what kind of weatherstripping they use in the residence, you know. Leo was the chair of the Earth Week committee or something. Anyway, he and BC do the interview, but almost immediately the big boys in the news division at ABC find out about it, and they start kicking up sand. So then BC claims the whole thing was ABC's idea, and ABC claims that BC just wanted to meet Leo and find out what all the fuss was about, that BC's, you know, a Leo *groupie*. So then BC's spokesman calls on ABC to come clean, admit the truth. BC needles ABC at a media dinner, saying when will you guys learn it's not the crime, it's the cover-up that gets you. It was really a pretty funny line."

I'm laughing while I'm telling it, because it's such classic BC—the desire to be a celebrity and mingle with other celebrities, balanced by the horror of seeming starstruck and galootish and unpresidential—and I don't even realize for a second that George is quietly examining me.

"What?" I say.

He just lies there quietly, getting me straight in his mind. Then he says, "This is really something of a sickness with you, isn't it?"

25

ONE HUNDRED AND THIRTY SECONDS IN JULY

It's later, just before sunset. Virginia's getting ready for the fights. She's wearing the same outfit, but she's gone from covert to overt bombshell, nothing much different, just bigger hair and another button undone, producing a respectable amount of cleavage, as these things are judged on Monday nights in early Vegas. I'm brushing my teeth, sitting on the toilet, as she works a set of oversize plastic hot curlers around in her hair. I can see from here that the prickly curlers are either vintage or clever copies—the idea, I have to assume, is that we carry nothing suspicious or history-revising in the event of arrest or accidental death. But Virginia is having no trouble with these Patty-Duke-era artifacts. She's disciplining her locks pretty effectively, putting major body in the sides and something like a modified bouffant at the crown. It's taken her about six minutes, start to spray finish. She's been practicing. They've all been rehearsing for this time, the bastards. I'm the only one stumbling around like an idiot. And I'm the expert.

"Looking forward to the fights?" I ask.

"Bet that. I used to box middleweight my first year out of basic." She mimes a kiss at the mirror. "If you can believe that. I still love a good fight."

"Were you any good?"

"If I was good, I'd be home now, signing royalty checks. I wasn't fast enough. Just a slow-moving middleweight body-puncher."

There's a little pause while we brush various parts of ourselves.

"So what's your job title?" I venture again, mouth full of the hotel's sweet toothpaste.

"What?" Virginia says absently.

"Job title." I spit, moving slightly aside as her hip shifts. Sharing a bathroom with Virginia is no simple affair; there's a Valkyrie quality to her stance that makes you give her measurably more personal space than you'd otherwise give, which results most of the time in you hugging the wall or the sink. "George is the sponge. James is the hard-ass. What's your job title? Are you my watchdog, or executioner, or what is it?"

She tests the spring in her bangs with the palm of her hand. She's not satisfied for some reason and puts a curler back in. "Sal," she says finally, "if I thought you'd understand my job title—what it meant—I'd tell you."

I stop brushing, then I pull the brush out and start to gesture with it. But I don't say anything finally because I can see she's not joking, and I'm not sure exactly how insulted to be.

"I don't mean you wouldn't understand the words," Virginia adds affably, "I mean the concept. You'd get hung up on a limited view of the concept and walk around thinking things about me that aren't true. But you can rest assured I have a job and I'm good at it. Does that do it for you?"

"What, because I'm a civilian?"

"You're not a civilian."

"Because I was a civilian?"

"Partly. Partly because you're a . . ." she hesitates, tactfully, and I think she's about to use an off-color term, ". . . a professor. Partly a lot of things."

I rinse my mouth out. Virginia's putting on lipstick now, but she's watching my reaction in the mirror. "Suppose," I answer, "I'm not as rigid and clueless as you think. Suppose I actually understood what you do. Don't you think that could be a good thing? If you want to put it in obsessively military terms, don't you think maybe that might help us implement the go-to that everyone but me has seen?"

She reaches down to tear off a swatch of toilet paper, and this time I resist the automatic extension of her personal space, staying exactly where I am on the bare white plastic toilet cover.

"Look, Virginia, you and I are the only two twenty-first-century women alive anymore. We should be allies in 1963, if not soul mates. We're all there is of who we are. If anyone is going to understand, out of the entire living population of the world, it's going to be me. Really. Think about it."

That seems to reach her in a way my sarcasm didn't. She's thinking about it. She blots her lips, purses them in the mirror, removes a coral crumb from the lower one with a pinky nail. "Okay, then." She turns to me. "I'm the bodyist."

"The bodyist?"

"That's right. That's how I'm listed in the go-to." She smiles, daring me to take it as literally as it sounds, and I guess I do, because how else do you take it?

And that's clearly all I'm going to get for now. She restores the curlers to their plastic tray, shoots it back in her Naugahyde bag. I realize that she's used all of her toiletries and put them back in the bag, along with the stockings she changed out of earlier. She's ready to scramble at any minute.

Then Virginia plants herself one last time before the mirror, both hands up to check her hair. The dress sleeves peel back for an instant and the big muscles of her arms surface and coalesce, then subside. She runs her hands down her flanks, smoothing the material of her dress, making sure she's finished. And she is. She's ready for the fights.

She's a knockout.

Carville thinks it will be fun to walk to the convention center, since it's within sight of our hotel, but it's not. The four of us trudge up the road, and before we've cleared the Riviera's circular drive we're all sweating, and it's painfully obvious that the walk is longer than it seems. The sun is still up, and the thermometer in the lobby of the hotel informed me that it is 106 degrees out here. It's Africa hot.

"You'd have thought, with global warming and everything, that we'd find it cool here," Carville remarks. None of the rest of us says anything.

But the convention center is what you might call aggressively air-conditioned. We enter, an overweight man at the turnstile takes our tickets, and I'm wishing for a sweater. People are swirling in all around us, though, thousands of them, and I have no doubt I'll be hot again before too long.

"Where'd you get the tickets?" I ask Carville as we move down a small carpeted ramp toward our section of seats.

"Same place we're getting the transport to take us to D.C. tomorrow—1963 NSC. I love those guys. I go, we need four tickets to the title bout. They go, what row?"

I knew that Vegas dress in the fifties and sixties was a lot swankier than I'm used to, especially at night. But given that it was a boxing match, I think we all thought we'd hit a good minimum. Again, we were wrong. We're underdressed by a good bit. Many of the men in the audience are wearing tuxedos, many of the women are in shiny gowns, some with elbow-length gloves. The closer you get to the ring, the classier the threads. I begin to get a little uncomfortable when we cross into the final section of twenty-five rows, because the people here are not only well-dressed, they radiate money and flash. Lots of slicked-back hair and bosomy cigar girls and bet-takers standing in front of fat men peeling bills from large, money-clipped wads. By comparison, the suits George and James are wearing make them look like vacationing exterminators from Newark.

Our seats are in the eleventh row, about as close as you can come to the ring without having your face show up in any of the fight photos. Here at least Carville seems to know what he's doing. Carville's seated on my left, George is on my right. Tension is crackling through the huge room.

Ahead of us a few rows, a man is standing holding a beer in a paper cup. I could swear I know him, and I have a moment of puzzlement: maybe other people from 2055 are hanging out in Vegas this weekend; maybe after we left, the Wars ended peacefully and it became a hip way to get away for the weekend. The man has short curly hair and very big ears, big forearms. He sits down and begins talking loudly to a man sitting next to him, waving the hand not holding the beer.

George sees me looking, and of course he never forgets a face. "Norman Mailer, the writer," he whispers, watching Mailer shift his burly body back and forth. Mailer's not in a suit, of course. He's got on what looks like a denim workshirt. "He always had a thing for watching big guys pummel one another."

The air here is a wild, rank mix of perfume and unfiltered tobacco smoke, Brylcreem and Lavoris over the first oozing suggestions of sweat. The preliminary bout—two big men who enter the ring with correspondingly big attitudes—is over in two minutes and twenty-three seconds. One of the big men opens up the other's defense, brings his guard clear of his face, and then pummels him.

Carville times it carefully, eyes on his vintage Timex. "See, part of the rationale behind our observing this particular event," he says in a low, conversational voice, once the roar of the crowd subsides and the unconscious man has been revived, hustled out, "is that the timing is really incredibly well-documented. Two twenty-three on the button. Of course, the go-to says nothing about what we would or should do if I timed it and it came out to two twenty-seven or even two fifty-two. I mean, I guess at that point we'd go about our business, you know. We'd keep on with the plan, but we'd have this nagging sense that the plan was fucked." He grins, and I can see he's relieved that the reported time checks out. "So far so good."

There is a short interval between fights, and the crowd noise swells noticeably. The blood of the first match has everyone's appetite sharp. A few rows ahead of us a tall young black man shouts toward the ring every few minutes or so. He's got his back to us. He's the only black man visible in the first ten rows, in fact, one of the few blacks I've seen in the entire crowd. But the fact clearly doesn't intimidate him. He's having a good time heckling the fighter we're here to see, Sonny Liston.

"Liston's a tramp!" he yells, getting to his feet, then dropping back into his seat. "Floyd's gonna lick him like a Popsicle!" The mass of white people sitting around him are openly staring at him.

But I don't have time to think about the weird, out-front uniformity of segregation here, because loud music begins to blare, and a spotlight picks out another black man in a silk robe coming down one of the aisles toward the ring. He's a tall man, lean-looking, his tight black curls shorn down to a single springy inch of hair. The crowd cheers, and it's a cheer that comes from the collective gut.

"Patterson," George yells in my ear. "He's got a wig and a bushy-beard disguise in his dressing room right now in case he loses. And he will. And he'll use the disguise. That's how ashamed he'll be. He's coming to win his title back, but he'll be humiliated again. It'll put out the lights for the rest of his life."

I look back to Floyd Patterson as he passes the end of our row. He's a good-looking man, with straight, heavy brows and an air of caution, almost suspicion. Once in the ring, he sheds the robe and stands in black trunks and red gloves. He doesn't look around but keeps his eyes on the hands his trainer is holding up for him to hit. Even to me, he looks apprehensive and downcast, which is to say scared, as these things are judged in Vegas of any time.

What's it like to be rapped unconscious and come to in a world where another man wears the god-size belt?

The spotlight suddenly picks out Liston coming toward the ring from the opposite direction, and the crowd boos loudly. Liston is bigger, broader, blunter. His expression is blanker. He is the champion, yet the crowd continues to boo him.

George goes on. "Used to be a robber, Liston. Twenty-fourth of twenty-five children, if you can imagine that. Hired to beat up strikers at one point. Started boxing in the penitentiary. Patterson knows Liston's something different. Their first fight taught him that. Patterson's manager tried to keep Sonny away from his boy for quite a while, after he got a look at Liston fighting one night. Now it's *so* too late. Now Liston's got a pinky ring and a swagger stick."

Liston's robe comes off. He's wearing white trunks and maroon gloves. His body looks meaty compared to Patterson's, heavy. His large muscles seem packed in shock-absorbing flesh. Now that the two are in the ring, Patterson looks smaller, nimbler, more vulnerable.

"Liston's the bad boy now. Boxing press loves to hate him, they call him King of Beasts. Patterson was the good boy after he became the champ, out at charity events, doing the softball interviews, taking the calls from the president."

And then, in the midst of the rising tension, "The Star Spangled Banner" begins to drift out of the overhead speakers. It rises in volume, and the booing dies immediately. I suppose I should have expected it, but it takes me absolutely by surprise. All of a sudden I think about my home, our wars, our dead, what the hell I'm doing here in the first place. I can feel my eyes get hot.

And then everyone stands, and the whole entire crowd does something I've only read about. They put their hands on their hearts.

It's over even more quickly than the first bout, one hundred thirty seconds by Carville's watch. And it's a horror to watch. Liston never seems to gear up, he simply locates Patterson against the ropes and immediately overpowers him.

The young black man in the fifth row is yelling up at Patterson, loud enough for me to hear over the crowd's roar: "Stick and move, Floyd. He ain't nothing. Stick him, move him, Floyd!"

There are two knockdowns, each followed by a mandatory eight-count. During each of the eight-second intervals, Patterson labors to his feet and nods desperately when questioned by the referee. He's struggling to make this a fight, but it's clear that it isn't, really.

To me, there's an inescapable aura of doom floating over Patterson, because I've heard Carville and George discuss the results all day. But even to the other spectators, this must exceed the parameters of mismatch and verge on the ordained.

Liston bores into him again, a left streaking up to the body, a crippling right to the head. Patterson falls, and his body flattens out completely against the canvas. There is a second of complete incapacitation. Then, at just over the two-minute mark, he tries awkwardly to bring things into focus, head rolling. By then it's over.

Patterson is finally led away by his corner man, head down, but somehow the two take the wrong turn, and after walking all the way down one aisle to the jeers of dissatisfied customers, Patterson and the corner man must retrace their steps and walk the length of another long aisle before they reach the dressing room, the wig, and the false beard.

And then, in the little tumult following the main event, with people surging to their feet, wondering where to spend the rest of their suddenly free evening, the young black man in the fifth row runs to ringside and hauls himself through the ropes.

I turn to tell George, but he's already watching. Like he's been waiting.

The black man turns and continues the yelling, the fulminating. He's got on a natty yellow check jacket and a skinny tie, black trousers. Now he's facing me, and although he's startlingly young, I'd know him anywhere. It's a handsome face, a movie star's face, with a smile like a searchlight, set rakishly down on what is clearly a lethal weapon of a body. There is no denying the truth of the matter. He is what you'd have to call pretty.

I grab George's arm, tight. "That's Muhammad Ali."

He corrects me. "Actually, that's Cassius Clay."

Carville leans over and adds, "The other reason why we're here."

Clay is all over the ring, moving in long sliding steps, what he'd later call dancing. He's mouthing off, performing, the bombast he learned from watching Gorgeous George wrestle on television. "Liston is the tramp! I'm the uncrowned champ! Liston is a bum. I got too much class for the boy. He's the *tramp*! He don't watch it, I'll lower the knockout round to five. I'll take him in five!"

A knot of Las Vegas marshals moves to pin Clay in one corner, and they manage to hold him there, bobbing and shouting over their pointed hats, for a minute or more. Then he breaks free, and he finds a convenient microphone that carries his rant to the house: "I want that big bum as soon as I can get him. I'm tired of talking. If I can't beat that big ugly bear—and he's *ugly*, that bear, he's a big ol' ugly bear of a bum—if I can't beat him, I'll leave the country!"

Insult banners unroll suddenly on the distant walls of the convention center: *Cassius Clay—the Desert Canary*. Liston's corner people were expecting him too. They come up with a huge mock-up of a newspaper's front page, big enough to read twenty rows back, reading, Clay has a big lip that Sonny will zip!!

Clay gets a look at the mock headline and charges the Liston corner, grabbing the poster board and ripping it into boxing-glove-size pieces. Then he dances backward several steps before stopping. And then his feet become a blur as his fists piston furiously. It's the shuffle. Clay is only a boy still, really, so it's not the masterpiece of show-trickery Ali will eventually make of it. But it is the shuffle.

Suddenly, I hear a loud shouting on the other side of George, and I look around him. It's Virginia. She's the only one I can hear actually yelling for Clay. Her face is jubilant, filled with something that looks like hero worship. Of course, she knew he'd be here too. And with those arms, and that jab, he couldn't help but be a role model for her, maybe for all the Berets.

He is beautiful, multiply magnetic. There is his voice, there is his physical power and grace, and there is the universal reaction to him, the crowd's admission that he is the center of the world, what they will talk about tomorrow. The people erupt into wails of delighted derision. Finally, someone who will entertain them.

Everything about Clay is played big, designed to reach the nosebleed seats. His expressions are wild and overdone; his voice rises like a street preacher, or a circus barker.

Clay's shouting out what to the crowd must seem like unadulterated baloney, the purest trash talk: "I am the uncrowned *champ*. You'll never get rid of me! Never! *Never!*" The marshals make another run at him, but he bobs aside, and it's like watching a man beset by pasty dwarves.

Then the man who will rename himself Muhammad Ali after humiliating Liston in another year or so suddenly calls out, "I will be the *best ever*, and you will never get rid of me!" He's jabbing a finger at his chest.

In four years, he will be stripped of his title when he refuses to go to Vietnam, insisting instead that his enemy is white America, not the Vietcong. And during those years of forced inactivity, he will lose the best, the most physically magical years of his youth. I know his life well, mostly because near the end it connected occasionally and importantly to BC's, but also because once you get a taste of it, you want to see more. He always had that effect.

I look at him clowning in the ring above me, and I remember the footage of Ali opening the 1996 Summer Olympics in Atlanta. BC himself walked Ali into the opening ceremonies; by that time, Ali's Parkinson's disease had made it nearly impossible for him to move unassisted. Ali looked terrible, ravaged, shuddering visibly, face wooden, voice silenced. It was BC doing what he did best: honoring others, supporting others, connecting. And maybe only BC could have led that particular man without seeming to lessen him or use him, because no one black or white can deny that if ever black America had a white president for a friend after Abraham Lincoln, it was BC himself.

Virginia is shouting even louder now, so loud that Carville leans around me to try to take her arm. She's not acting like the classy Jackie clone, and she's not even acting like Virginia. She's starstruck. "Kick his *ass,* Clay!" she yells, voice breaking. "You are the greatest, man! You are the *greatest*!" And then, in one of those slow-motion moments like dropping your car keys down a sewer grate, she adds what only seems natural and true and undeniable. "The greatest of all time!"

Carville visibly flinches.

Clay hears her, even in the roar. I swear he hears her. And he laughs, looking out at all the people, the people who will mock and despise him when he joins the Nation of Islam and who will eventually cheer the unknown and inarticulate Leon Spinks when he unexpectedly jolts Ali from his pedestal. He looks out at all of them, and he repeats it into the microphone clearly for all of them to understand.

"I'm the greatest! I'm the greatest! The greatest of *all* time!" he shouts in their faces, laughing, and not for the last time. "Of all time!"

26

THE THRILLA IN YOUR VANILLA

One afternoon I asked BC what event had caused him the greatest pain in public life. It was the sort of prying, marginally prurient question he most hated, and the sort I usually avoided for reasons having nothing to do with BC. It seemed to me more a talk-show host's question than a biographer's, and it still does.

But maybe it was payback: the first two hours of that day's interview had been more than a little much, with BC off on an unabashedly egocentric tear, making a case for himself as the Peacemaker President, the Economic Steward, the President of Racial Healing. He'd reminded me twice about winning the Charlemagne prize for contributing to peace in Europe. Maybe the question was my way of reminding him that I was an independent biographer, not a temp in the White House PR office.

In any event I asked it. His face clouded over slightly, his bushy brows drawing together. The wrinkled skin of his forehead drew taut. He got tight-lipped and for a second I thought he might have an outburst. He didn't have them often with me, but he had them, and often it was something unexpected that brought them on.

But BC bit his lip, and then he answered, the watery blue eyes linking up with mine. "You might think it'd be the whole scandal business, Sal—*businesses*, better call it, since so many people made a career out of it. Impeachment, all that." I could tell it took real effort for him to say the word *impeachment* out loud. He looked into the fireplace, brooding.

"And that was painful, ah'll tell you. Awful painful. Truly awful. But you know, when you look back, there's other things, more fundamental stuff, stuff you can't git your mind off of."

And then he just said it. "It was when the American people voted in George W. Bush for president in 2000. Voted in Junior. They didn't do it by much, God knows. Lost the popular vote. Something like six hundred votes in Florida was about all his mandate was, if you can call it that. But they did it, they put that zero in office. That hurt the worst. Because Bush wasn't qualified to be president—had five years in as governor of Texas, an' that was the state at the time with the weakest gubernatorial powers going. He was, they said it at the time, but he was nothin' but an empty suit, and I met him, talked to him. I know. But still the American people put him into the Oval Office." He laid a finger alongside the immense nose, absently stroking the bulb of it, thinking. Then he looked up, for support. "And that hurt."

At the time, I thought the answer was a bit of misdirection—move the biographer off the sore spot and onto a prolonged discussion of an election in which BC himself wasn't even a candidate. But I understand it now, I think. The 2000 election wasn't about qualifications or issues or character, or any of the other things normally thought to decide an election. It was about sending BC a message of displeasure, but a message of an amazing sort. It was about returning to a forked moment in history, and choosing the fork untraveled.

Here was George W. Bush, so much like a younger and more politically agile version of his father that he might have been genetically engineered, running against Al Gore, which is to say against the entire BC era. In the minds and the emotions of the voters it was Bush vs. BC, the 1992 election, all over again. And they chose Bush that time around, not by a landslide, not even by a clear plurality, but they chose him. It was like putting the whole BC era under a strange kind of erasure.

That was what galled BC, what ailed him decades later, that the voters had gone back in time and revoted the election that swept BC into the White House as the candidate of change. The 2000 election was about time travel, I realize.

I'm thinking about this as I go to sleep in my starchy Las Vegas bed. It's like learning an odd new word: suddenly, you hear it and read it everywhere. That's the way it is, now that I've actually experienced moving backward in time, as well as forward, which was the way I'd always done it before yesterday. I'm thinking, too, as I drift off, about Liston knocking Patterson out. To Patterson, it's time travel: he wakes and a referee informs him with waving hands that the future is a bleak place.

And then I think, what about Virginia's shouting at the match tonight? Carville chewed her out for the rest of the night about it, on and off, but I can't help but see it as benign intervention. It seems so clearly a case where she was giving Ali a phrase he was meant to have, which suggests that she gave it to him originally speaking, long before I was born. In which case, you'd have to guess that lots of other things are actually looped in time the same way, that this is a powerful organizing principle of the universe, a component of its construction, not its destruction.

Of course, if that's the only organizing principle for chronology, we're screwed, and this whole Hail Mary mission is doomed from the start.

And then I can't help but think: if we're here, it's lunacy to assume that we're the only ones here who cheated chronologically to get here, that it was a one-time-only thing. Technology as powerful as this doesn't get used like that.

Take Sammy Davis, Jr. Maybe Sammy Davis was a one-eyed Jewish black entertainer from 2061 whose act was too square for post-Cigarette-Wars Las Vegas. He's dying in the lounges, no one there likes the century-old retro thing he's got going. But maybe Future Sammy has a brother with top-shelf clearance working out at the Maopi facility, and Future Sammy's brother works the light-particle trick for him. *Just this once,* he tells Future Sammy sternly.

One minute Future Sammy's standing in a patch of moonlit desert scrub, the next he's hitchhiking into twentieth-century Vegas, a swinger comfortably ahead of his time. And to rechristen his temporally reshuffled self, he adds Junior to his stage name. A hipster is born, a man who could bearhug Nixon and make it look genuine.

You think about these things when you fall asleep fifty-three years before you were born. You think about them, and they don't seem all that strange, really.

I segue in and out of too-light sleep. The events of the day have my consciousness in a mental half nelson, and I can't push them away. My eyes come to rest finally on this strange little paperweight sitting on the desk beside our window. It's the sort of memorabilia that must strike inhabitants of this time frame as so much ticky-tacky trash, but I can't help but catch my breath when I see it, because it would be worth a mint in my day: entombed in the waters of the little dome is a small plastic replica of Red Skelton, the comic, face soured in one of his trademark bits of lunacy.

It's a promotional item put out by a photographic concern called Bernard of Hollywood. George and Carville have a snowbound Joan Crawford that George has promised to steal for me.

But in our room it's Skelton doing his famous Old Man routine, and the figurine's hunched posture and wrinkles and frantic, bony hands remind me immediately of BC, BC's likable decrepitude. The paperweight glows subtly, bathed in the neon and moonlight cast through the venetian blinds.

Help me, the BC-like thing inside it seems to be saying. *Sal, wait.*

And the next moment I'm swimming through the corridors of a sunken hotel, fingers and feet propelling me along in a loopy, weightless trajectory. Not a hotel, but a ship rather, a ship as large as a city, with wide corridors and mess chambers and endless riveted hatches. I realize that this ship is the USS *Reagan* only when the drowned, blue-skinned bodies of sailors begin to rise slowly through the water to bob all about me. Their eyes are empty, their bruised tongues swollen too large for their mouths. They gather around me, persistent but vacant, like a school of fish.

I am aware enough to know that this vision is the product of Carville's angry phrase from the jump jet yesterday, *thirteen hundred swabbies under the water,* and there is a moment when I believe that making this connection with reality will break the spell, restore full consciousness.

But it doesn't. It simply adds a layer of paralyzed frustration. I remain imprisoned in the ship's inner waters, followed not only by the imploring bodies but by the memory of the exact words that coaxed this nightmare into being.

The luminous dial on the clock beside my bed says it's a little after three o'clock in the morning. Even though the nightmare is gone, I can't sleep anymore. I want to go downstairs and sit at the bar and people-watch. Or go out on the street and sit on a bench and watch the traffic flow. I want to see *something* while I'm in this time period besides the Three NSC Stooges who brought me here.

The room is dark; Virginia pulled the heavy cotton curtains before she got in bed. I kabuki my way around the floor, finding the chair I laid my dress over, finding my shoes with my feet, and silently fumbling my way into them. I decide not to fasten the miniature buckles—I have problems with those even in daylight—and I'm walking to the door with the little leather straps tucked in between my toes when Virginia whispers from her bed.

"You know I can't let you out of the room, Sal. Carville was really specific about it. Brutally specific."

I don't turn around. "Just down to the bar for one drink. I had a really bad dream. I'll sit in a corner. No one will see me. One Cape Codder in the lounge isn't going to impact the tidal wave of history. Go back to sleep."

There's a pause. I can't see her face, but when her whisper sounds again, it's almost pained. "You can try to make a run for it, and you can probably make it to the hallway before I catch you. In the best case, I incapacitate you before you bring any unwanted attention. Worst case, security comes and we show them documents proving that we're transporting you from one psychiatric hospital to another, because you're delusional and violently paranoid. That way we have to sedate you heavily for much of the rest of the trip. You become luggage."

"And worse than worst case, you guys kill me," I finish for her.

I can't tell for sure, but I get the impression she's nodding. "Not us guys. George and Carville aren't cleared for that. Or capable, really. I'd kill you. We're taught to shoot for a window of three or four seconds once we have hands on the target. Conditions are about optimal here, so call it five or six seconds max."

She's being modest. No way she'd miss the Beret manual's low-end estimate. Not Virginia. No way.

So we compromise. It's now about a quarter to four, and we're eating room-service breakfasts: massive portions of huevos rancheros and big desert grapefruits and little side plates of silver-dollar pancakes. I've got my Cape Codder, and Virginia's got her hand wrapped around a can of Schlitz, the only beer they had in cans, something that went by the wayside around the time the Arab nations jumped into the Wars and maxed out the country's aluminum supply. Neither one of us had ever tried a can of beer. I didn't finish mine, because it had a strong metallic tang.

But Virginia takes to it instantly. When she finishes her first can, she slowly crushes it, watching with delight as the can buckles. "You can see why people liked to do that," she marvels.

And she has two empty shot glasses by her plate. Until about ten minutes ago, they contained real Russian vodka, the kind you can get six months in jail for trafficking in our time. It's probably the first time in her life she's been able to drink it without feeling guilty or paranoid about it. But who cares now? Now it's only a Cold War with Russia. No big whoop.

Virginia's in the middle of telling me how she became a Beret. Instead of T-shirts, what we would have been wearing to bed a week ago, we're both in actual nightgowns, pink and yellow, two of the three permissible sleepwear colors for women in the middle years of this century. So it's like a slumber party with your very best girlfriend in the world, with the added possibility that she may kill you and that under no circumstances can you leave the room.

Her Beret origin story has nothing to do with her family, to my surprise. I'd made a quick guess when I met her that she must be fourth-generation military or something like that. Turns out her father was a dentist in upstate New York, and her mother troubleshot software. But her first serious boyfriend, her fiancé, was a Beret.

"His name was Reynolds, and we went to high school together. We were both jocks, *maximum* jocks. I was captain of the soccer team; he wanted a football scholarship and had a bad senior year and didn't quite get it. He-Man and She-Ra, everybody called us.

"And so then he got his call-up, and he went in and eventually made his bid for Special Forces. We're still engaged now; I'm home in little Elmira, New York, and he's down at Fort Bragg, doing his Q course—Qualification course—which took about six months. And during that time, he writes letters on and off, some really long and mushy and then nothing for a month. Video calls half as often. And then, right before he goes to Nick Rowe—that's the training center—he comes home for a visit and tells me that he's got a little honey down in North Carolina."

Virginia narrows an eye, and she smacks her fist into her palm, hard. "And that's not the worst of it. No. The worst of it is that he starts to—really seriously—he starts to tell me how demanding and *grueling* the training is in Special Forces, and how Berets go into seclusion usually before a mission or before they start a new training sequence and when they end one. Like a meditation retreat sort of, in their bunkers. And he tells me that—"

I can't help it. "Don't tell me—his little commando unit just started retreating all the way into someone else's bunker, all on its own."

"Wait, it gets better! He tells me that he was trying to do his meditating and everything, but he couldn't get me out of his mind. Isn't that sweet?"

She shovels in a big spoonful of eggs and washes it down with Schlitz. "So in order to get me out of his mind, he started to see this woman who meant nothing to him, to clear his mind so he wouldn't get washed out." Virginia straightens up and pulls her hair away from her face, and her eyes get a look that even now you would have to call scrotum-withering. "And finally, he tells me the bottom line. If I knew how hard Special Forces was, I'd realize why most of them cheated on their wives. Because it made you part"—she starts cracking up, she can't hold it anymore—"part *animal* and everything. It made you this primitive fighting man."

She laughs for a second. It dies into chuckles, and she sits back in her chair, stomach pooched out, hair a mess, the beginnings of fatigue circles under her eyes. She looks less like the fighting machine she became and more like the pissed-off fiancée. She ticks off the consequences on her fingers:

"So no wedding; Reynolds goes back to Nick Rowe a free man. I figure I'm not doing anyone much good waiting around to be drafted and coaching Funster-league soccer; I enlist. Three years later Reynolds gets a medical discharge from the service. His LEAP gear—that's Lower Extremity Assistance for Parachutists, like, your powered leg and trunk brace—his gear seized up on him when he hit a rock dropping into Chechnya, and the gear itself cross-fractured his hip. Total freak occurrence. So all of a sudden he's managing a sporting-goods store."

Now she's smiling at me again. Now she's proud again, telling me how she got her get-back. "And three years later I'm in Special Forces training at Bragg. It was just a couple of years after they lifted the ban on women in extreme combat situations. Before that you could only be in intelligence, but I went through survival, powered armor, and weapons, hand-to-hand, everything. Got my beret."

She takes the orange wheel from her plate and tears the flesh off with her mouth, swallows it. The rind she launches toward the little wastebasket on the other side of the room in a quick sitting jumper. "And the weird thing is, Reynolds never really understood why I was so upset. He could just never track on that."

"It wasn't really the cheating that pissed you off," I say.

"Got that right."

"It was this bogus idea that he was doing something he *had* to do to get through the training when he cheated. It was this mystic macho bullshit he was hiding behind. What a skank."

But Virginia shakes her head. She can't believe I don't get it either.

"No, not *even*. What it really was was I couldn't believe all of a sudden he was trying to tell me, 'I can go here and you can't. If you could, we could talk, but since you can't, we can't.' All of a sudden he was treating me, you know—" She gestures absently with the Schlitz can, looking for the concept.

Now I get it.

"Like a girl," I suggest.

"Exactly," Virginia says, and then she gives an actual sigh of relief at being understood. She sits in her chair, in her modest big-and-tall-size pink nightgown, arms crossed over her chest, satisfied for a second.

"So let me ask you something," I say.

"Shoot it at me."

"You lost your mind at the fights tonight. I thought you were going to follow Ali into the ring. What was that all about?"

She takes a swig. "What was what all about?"

"All of a sudden you're a groupie, screaming, foam flecking your lips. Pissing off your commanding officer, because of this fighter. A fighter who made a point of not fighting in Vietnam, of avoiding the draft. Why was that? I'm curious."

Virginia assesses me again, giving it a second or two. I can tell she doesn't fully trust me, old-boyfriend sagas aside, and doesn't really fully understand who or what I am. "Look," she explains, "Ali was the greatest athlete of the twentieth century. And the greatest boxer ever. I used to work out at the Ali Gold Club where I lived in N.Y., and it was like a museum to the guy. And you may not get this, it may seem contradictory to you or whatever, but I respect the hell out of his not going to Vietnam. I do. That was a bullshit conflict. And Ali was man enough to say it and take his punishment."

"And you thought he was good-looking."

She nods slowly, smirking over the beer can. "That's putting it real mildly."

"The black Elvis."

"Black Elvis with a jab."

"Float over you like a butterfly."

"Sting you like a bee."

"The thrilla in your vanilla."

She cracks up, then comes back raunchier. "Nothing but the rope-a-dope, all night *long*. Nothing but that." Then she squints her eye, and I see she's almost serious, not just trash-talking. "If I thought I could have gotten his attention—and kept you on ice here somehow, and not had to answer to Carville—I'd have changed history, all right. I'd have ripped open a whole new parallel dimension with Muhammad Ali. Or young Cassius Clay. You better believe that."

We sit in silence for a second. And then she says, "He was pretty, wasn't he?"

"Is," I remind her.

The next morning we're back in the car, all four of us, seat belts buckled, windows down. But we can't see a thing, really, because the Ford itself is strapped down tight in the cargo bay of a huge military air transport.

We are on our way to a small military airstrip in Maryland, just outside Washington, D.C. We need to be at our motel in Alexandria, Virginia, by dinnertime, and since it takes about a week to drive it with the interstate system in its current condition, Carville has asked the 1963 NSC people to give us a lift. He's also asked them not to interact with us in any way, which doesn't, apparently, strike them as all that odd.

Once we were aboard, the car was secured with what looked like canvas straps, crisscrossing the windows and windshield, and I could hear a ratcheting noise somewhere beneath us, like a vise being screwed down on the axles. And then the flight crew vanished. And it was just us, in the car, in the cargo hold, in the plane, on the way to Alexandria, and from there to College Park, Maryland. Us sitting in a lot of plane noise and relative darkness. And a lot of heat, which slipped away finally as we hit the cloud layer.

"This is where our great expense and trouble in bringing you along on this trip begin to pay off, Sal," Carville tells me. He could smoke, but he is not smoking, which I take as a courtesy on his part. "The College Park segment of the go-to could be seen as the diciest, although hopefully we prep hard and execute easy. Later on, I'll show you some of the pages from that section, bring things a little more clearly into focus for you." He's being particularly nice today. We're approaching the moment where he'll need active cooperation.

And he's put me in the front seat, to facilitate this brief-back for the next segment of the mission, but maybe also because he doesn't want to seem to assume that the guys, or even the people with rank, should always sit in front.

"Maybe you could just quickly run over the high points for me," I suggest, "until I have a chance to study those pages."

"Could do that," Carville admits, though not very eagerly.

"What is it we're doing in College Park again? Basically?"

George leans forward from the backseat, interested to hear Carville's response. Carville takes in the movement with a glance at the rearview but keeps his eyes on where the road would be if he were in charge of the car's movement. "We're acquiring yBC."

George switches his gaze to me, to see how that goes over.

"Acquiring yBC?" I repeat. "I thought we were supposed to get a message to him. Now we're acquiring him?"

"That's job number one."

"We're talking about the actual young BC. BC when he was a boy."

"The same. yBC for short."

"And by acquiring you mean?"

"Bringing him in. Securing cooperation. Effecting transport."

I turn to face Carville in my seat. He hasn't shaved today, and there's a noticeable blue color to the stubble surfacing over the lower half of his face. I'm looking at his incipient blue beard and wondering why he didn't shave this morning, given that he seems to shave every morning as a matter of course, when it hits me. College Park is the home of the University of Maryland. BC stayed in a U of Maryland dorm when he came to the capital with Boys Nation as an overgrown sixteen-year-old in the summer of 1963.

He is, in fact, there right now, scheming to shake the hand of John F. Kennedy. I should have put it all together, but I've been so busy thinking about when and where I am, I haven't had time to think about where BC is right now, this week in July. And this is really the first they've tipped me off that one of the crazier suggestions in my own briefing book seems against all odds to have become the actual plan.

We're going to kidnap BC in College Park. Or young BC, at least.

"Job number one," Carville insists again.

And another thing hits me in quick succession, and I shoot Virginia a glance. Her name and her job title begin to make a certain repulsive sense.

She looks slightly hung-over, and she doesn't meet my gaze, staring instead out her window toward a distant blank wall of the plane.

"And let me guess," I say. "Virginia is tool number one."

Nobody says anything, and they don't have to. They've all read the go-to.

"That's sick," I tell Carville. "That is sick."

He keeps his eyes on the road. Never has the resemblance to H. R. Bob Haldeman been more pronounced. "We think it'll work," he says.

27

ONE GOES TO HOJO'S

Our plane touches down discreetly at an unassuming little military installation on the outskirts of Washington, D.C. For the thirty-odd minutes it takes for the Ford to be unratcheted, unstrapped, and finally birthed from the belly of the transport, none of the 1963 soldiers working outside the car looks inside the car. As in Nevada, it's hot. Unlike Nevada, it's also humid enough in D.C. to steam clams.

A small unmarked motorcycle leads us to the main gate, then veers off abruptly, without saluting, without so much as a look back in our direction. The GI at the main gate keeps his eyes on incoming traffic. No salute from him either.

Carville is in spook heaven. In our time frame, he was saluted but did not salute. Here he's ascended to even loftier heights. Here he is too potent even to salute, too powerfully black-op and deep-cover to gaze upon. He keeps a scowl on his face until we clear the gate, checks his rearview for signs of a tail, and when none appears, he breaks into a horrible grin.

"I *love* these guys," he says. He looks around at all the rest of us, then can't resist saying it again. "I really, really desperately love these guys."

But the love affair lasts only another five minutes or so, until Carville snaps on the radio and gets only static and faint, loopy electronic howls. He divides his attention between the traffic and the tuning dial for a second, then blurts, "Fucking low-tech piss-poor 1963 manufacturing." He snaps the radio off.

"I thought you desperately loved them," I needle him.

"Yeah, well, when you desperately love somebody, that's just exactly when they screw you with some piece-of-shit radio. Tell me I'm wrong."

"You have to trim it," George offers cryptically from the backseat.

There is a pause, a standard pause that I recognize by this time. George wants to be acknowledged for his freakish, spongy facts. Carville hates nothing more than having to *ask* George for the information George was *recruited* to provide. In this case, Carville seems to want music precisely as much as George wants to seem like a know-it-all, and the stalemate stretches out.

Finally, Virginia steps in. She still seems hung-over, and her voice has a thin, dry quality. "Trim what, George?"

"You gotta trim the signal," George begins, and I realize we're about to get a download from the driver's manual he consumed several days ago. "When you leave your local listening area—an area typically seventy-five to one hundred miles, or less in mountainous regions—you need to adjust the trimming knob for maximum reception. The knob's up under the dash on the side of the radio, Sal."

I find it with my fingers. "Check," I say.

"Now turn on the radio, keeping the volume just low enough to hear." I do so, and he continues, "Now adjust the trimming knob until the volume of the weakest signal rises to maximum volume."

"How do I know which is the weakest signal?"

"Just pick the one that sounds most like shit," George clarifies.

I find a weak signal, a man's voice trying to struggle up through the wash of static. It takes a second, but working between the tuning dial and the trimming knob I get the volume to climb noticeably. Then I use the tuning dial, and the spectrum of signals comes in sharp now. I settle on some light piano music, and George says, "Tasteful choice."

Something about the whole process—the universe of static stubbornly giving way to clarity—reminds me how uncertain all of us are about the physical rules that allow for us to be here in the first place. And how uncertain we are about what will make things in our time worse, as opposed to better. What if we need a trimming dial of some kind, and we don't even know we need it? What if nothing we can or will do matters, and the world is destined to return to static, to chaos?

But it feels good to have a sponge along, in any event, even though there's no manual to memorize in our case. "Thanks, George," I tell him.

Virginia seems as pleased as I am that there's something to listen to besides Carville. "Thanks, George," she says. "You have a killer brain."

There is another pause, as Carville decides whether or not to encourage George to withhold information he should voluntarily provide. But then he manages to say, "Good work, soldier," more or less splitting the difference.

Our motel in Alexandria is called the Towne Motel. The postcards in the top drawer of the little desk in our room advertise colonial design, another way of saying that the squat two-story brick structure is relieved on either end by a set of white shutters. Really, it's a brick box with twenty-five parking spaces beside it.

I'm fascinated by the line of sedans parked in a glistening line outside the door, an army of fins and chrome grilles and bombardier hood ornaments.

The postcard also promises Three Famous Restaurants across the street. One of these, I notice as I glance out our window, is a Howard Johnson's. We also have access to Free Ice, Room Telephone, Both Tub *and* Shower, Hot-water Heat, Wall-to-Wall Carpet, Deluxe Modern Furnishings, Fireproof Soundproof Brick Construction, Free Television, Muzak, and a Twenty-minute Car Ride to Lovely Mount Vernon.

I click the dial on the largish box beside the bed, and sure enough, what comes out is pretty wretched. I almost call out to Virginia, who's taking the first crack at the bathroom, to tell her it's actual Muzak that she's hearing. But then I remember that part of the reason she's here is to seduce a sixteen-year-old. And this sixteen-year-old is also, somehow, the one-hundred-and-nine-year-old man I know to be justifiably terrified of the sexual setup.

Although I'm not sure if it's motherly or daughterly in nature, I feel some kind of vague protective feelings for BC and any younger versions of him. And I remember that I'm not speaking to Virginia until I find out what, exactly, is what.

Carville seems to have read my mind. He knocks at the door, and when I open it he hands me a single page, folded down in thirds. I reach out to take it, but he holds it back momentarily. "Don't lose this piece of paper," he says, looking me in the eye. "I need to have it back when you're done with it. Read it, have a shower, brush your teeth, whatever you like, then we have brief-back in George's and my room in an hour." He lets go of the paper and goes back into the room next to ours and shuts the door.

I don't feel like reading this thing standing on the balcony, and I don't feel like going back into the room; Virginia knows I'm not speaking to her, and she's been giving me the silent treatment back. And no one seems to be watching me or too worried about me slipping custody.

So I go where one goes when one finds oneself in my particular situation. Stranger in a strange time. Temporal outcast. Looking for a semisolitary place to read eyes-only documents while maybe scoring some fried chicken and coleslaw.

One goes to HoJo's.

Howard Johnson's, in my time, is one of the cheap box motels located off the walkways radiating out from Bullet stations and skyports. It's where you go when you want a cheap roof over your head and basic imaging and Wide-eye capacity for less than eight hundred dollars per diem. One of the recent ad campaigns featured a young techie with a shaved head—the kind of aggressive, cost-cutting business whiz kid that all the hotels are targeting in the wartime economy—telling another techie what an ass he is for not staying at Howard Johnson's.

"Damn! Go HoJo, MoFo," the hip techie advises the stupid techie.

Howard Johnson's 1963 is a somewhat different affair.

Everything is still orange and turquoise, but the restaurant has a kind of cute, inviting look. There's a cupola on the top, with a weather vane. The sign says, 28 FLAVORS & GRILL. It looks neat and clean and right-angled. It looks like sanctuary.

I ask for a window seat, because I'm tired of not being able to see anything on this trip. My booth is clean and sparkling, and the tabletop is edged with ridged chrome. The waitress is a plump woman with permed hair, and she asks if I want to wait for my other parties. When I tell her I'm alone, she nods like she's seen my type before.

I wait until she's gone for my cherry Coke before I unfold the piece of paper.

There is no heading, no page numbers, no obsessive warnings to pay attention to page numbers. It begins in mid-sentence and then ends a quarter of the way down the page. I can only conclude that what Carville has given me is the final page of the go-to.

It's fairly disappointing.

is uncertain as to exact entry time; team will be deployed well in advance of early-end estimate.

PROTECTING TARGET (yBC)

Under no circumstances will target be injured or subjected to undue trauma. Target's physical well-being will be preserved at any and all costs. Team will bear in mind that, while this go-to provides for subject's acquisition, transportation, and return, subject enjoys a unique and unprecedented relationship to the office of Commander-in-Chief.

All attempts shall be made to accord subject the dignity and the loyalty associated with that office.

I read it through twice, but there isn't anything more there the second time. That's it. That's the superclassified information Carville has seen fit to pass on. They're under orders not to kill him, that's the revelation.

They still plan to kidnap him, but they'll do so with dignity, and loyalty even.

28

HOUSTON, WE HAVE A PROBLEM

"Here's how a brief-back *doesn't* work, Sal," Carville says in answer to my question about why he gave me only four and a half sentences of the go-to to review earlier. "A brief-back *doesn't* consist of you or George or Virginia asking me questions about how I implement the go-to. In fact, that's almost precisely what the brief-back is not. Almost precisely. The brief-back consists of me *communicating* to the three of you exactly how I see the four of us implementing the go-to. When I've communicated, you three question. Then I answer. And my answers then conclude that particular brief-back." His recent charm campaign seems to be over.

Carville is sitting in front of the little dressing mirror in his room, on a dainty white metal stool. For no apparent reason, since there is plenty of light from the lamps by the twin beds, he and George have the frosted bulbs around the makeup mirror lit. It gives a slightly silly air to this meeting, but in conjunction with the bald parts of Carville's head, the makeup mirror also makes it difficult to look Carville directly in the eye while he speaks.

I manage anyway.

He goes on: "In other words, this is not an academic symposium on our mission and various ways to complete it, with everyone delivering their two cents in the form of a twenty-minute paper and everyone critiquing everyone else's ideas and then all of us breaking for Danish and coffee in the hotel lobby, although I understand that that's the format you're used to. This is me stating manner of implementation and you three seeking clarity of what I have stated. It's a subtle distinction, but do you follow me?"

I feel my face redden, but before I can say anything, George clears his throat loudly. He's sitting in one of the Deluxe Modern furnishings, a chair that seems to be covered in patterned cloth but squeaks periodically like plastic.

"Lookit, James," George says, snapping his gum. He has one long leg jiggling up and down out of boredom or nervousness or both. The chair's deep enough and his legs are long enough that he has a kind of human grasshopper look. "I've been doing some thinking."

Carville's eyebrows go up in surprise, but he doesn't turn. "Glad to hear it, George. You're breaking some new ground, then."

"About this temporal-displacement idea, I mean, and how that relates to the whole chain-of-command idea."

Carville's head swivels around. The phrase *chain of command* has his nostrils winging out just slightly. "Oh, really?"

"Yeah. And how that relates to this whole drop-and-give-me-twenty attitude you hit us with periodically. Mostly hit Sal with, I should say, like that's going to get you anywhere with someone of her personality profile anyway."

Carville's not expecting this broadside from George, and his eyes go first to me, like he's been embarrassed in front of the person he was trying to rein in, and then they flick to Virginia, who's sitting at the head of the other bed, like he's checking to make sure he has backup.

George plows ahead. "Here's my thinking, in a nutshell. Your position with regard to the 1963 guys is that your authority supersedes theirs because you come from a later position on the timeline. By that logic, you have authority over anyone preceding you, back to and including Thomas Jefferson, George Washington, George Washington's dad, etc. In that sense, you could go back with the authority to alter the composition of the Constitution itself, which is really fucked up.

"Also under that logic, anyone empowered *after* you in the timeline has complete authority over you, which I don't think—knowing what sorts of things really chap your ass—you would go along with yourself. The problem with this whole way of thinking is it would mean the end of people electing their own representatives. You'd have people being ruled by whatever authority happened to come time-tripping back. Which could lead possibly to some sort of updated Boston Tea Party eventually, if you see what I mean."

Carville suddenly reaches out and flicks the switch on the side of the makeup mirror. The frosted bulbs fade quickly to black. He doesn't say so, but I'm guessing that the heat on the back of his head was starting to make him feel interrogated.

Then Carville says with elaborate calm, "I'm listening." He waves a hand pointedly toward Virginia, laying at least some of his cards on the table. "We're both listening."

Virginia has her back braced against the headboard, and she nods silently. She's wearing a man's military olive-drab T-shirt, which makes her arms and the musculature of her torso and back stand out starkly, especially given that the last I saw her she had on a frock with matching Gidget gear. Once I realize what she's wearing, I'm surprised; like me, I didn't think she was allowed to bring anything out of character for a 1963 woman.

No doubt Carville brought it in his own flight bag and then passed it to her in Vegas, feeding her bodybuilder's complex on the sly, buying her loyalty.

"So I tried thinking to myself how the Supreme Court might deal with this whole revision in physics and, you know, terms of office. And here's the best I could come up with. It seems to me that the Supreme Court would rule that the Constitution enforces the government of the particular time frame a person is inhabiting. Right now, for instance, 1963 people elected 1963 officials, who appointed other officials and created 1963 NSC. So they're the only authority here. Just like changing states or countries. When you change time frames, you step into the existing legal and political system. So our government and the people who voted it into being in our time frame, people who aren't even born yet, I think our government has absolutely no power here, no authority.

"And it gets better. For all we know, just our coming here in the first place has produced some kind of temporal-concussion wave that's knocked out everything we remember from back home. Our civilization lies in ruins, maybe. Or maybe the earth is just lying fallow, no people at all in the Americas, in the world. In that case, anyone looking at us from outside would find it pretty ludicrous to see us clinging to this weird military caste system that applies only in some defunct version of the distant future. It's too *Lord of the Flies*, if you see what I mean. I don't know if you've read that, but there are these little prep-school kids who crash on an island and some of them are, like, hall monitors or something—"

"I've *read* the goddamn book," Carville snaps.

"Calm down. You're well-read, okay? What I'm saying is, instead of this whole idea of an ironclad chain of command where you keep slapping everybody around when you have a mood swing, I was thinking of something more fundamentally cooperative."

Carville now looks as though he's bitten into a chocolate-covered cherry and found that someone in the factory replaced the cherry with a lawn grub. "Cooperative," he repeats.

George is sitting up now, both feet on the floor, and he wipes his bangs away from his eyes enthusiastically. "Cooperative command, if you want to call it that. You're in charge, but first among equals."

"*First among equals* is a phrase for people too afraid to look at reality."

"Not even, James. *First among equals* is one of those phrases for people who view reality as subject to improvement."

"You took an oath to honor the chain of command, Stephanopoulos. The oath stands, no matter what else might or might not come to pass."

"Don't kid yourself, James. An oath can also mean a swear word."

"That's the point. You swore."

"I said words."

"You stood before the flag and said the words."

"I repeated a bunch of words because I had to repeat them in order to get the job, just like I repeated a bunch of words at my Confirmation because I wanted thousand-dollar checks from all my aunts and uncles."

I haven't said a word to this point because my impulse to rush over and throw my arms around George has been so overpowering. But now I have to chime in. "I sure as hell didn't take any oath."

"Right, right," George says, nodding. "Sal's even less invested in the whole *Lord of the Flies* way of seeing the—"

"Shut up with the *Lord of the Flies* thing!" Carville says, a little more loudly than he seems to have intended, because he almost immediately lowers his voice and gives a good impression of meditative reflection. "It's interesting to me, this . . . uh"—he opts for neutral language—"well, call it a discussion. Because there were people in the original planning team who predicted this sort of thing—tension in the command chain after the time shift. They found the same thing in the early NASA days. Astronauts would get up a few miles above earth, and occasionally they'd start feeling like they were in a separate world, separate orbit. They'd get astronautitis. NASA called it *orbital insubordination*."

"The analogy doesn't work," George says, shaking his head. "Even if you're in orbit, everyday physics hasn't been suspended. You have radio contact, even visual. And even if you didn't, you'd know Houston was there somewhere underneath you. This is unprecedented. Nobody knows what's subject to change."

"Houston's there for us too, Stephanopoulos," Carville says deliberately, leaning over toward George. There's an unmistakably dangerous edge to the way he says George's name.

"I'm not saying it's not. I'm just saying we *may* live out our lives without ever seeing Houston again. There are a potentially infinite number of scenarios in which that happens. And I intend to live my life with some understanding of those scenarios."

"Well, another thing you should understand is that Virginia and I reject any attempt to weaken the command link between our NSC and this field unit. We will enforce compliance. I said that there was discussion of this problem earlier on, and it's not something that she and I are unprepared to deal with. This team will implement the go-to at hand."

"As you see fit to interpret it," I kick in.

"Exactly as I see fit to interpret it. The go-to stands."

"Total *Lord of the Flies*," George mutters.

"Houston's there, George!" Carville shoots back. "Deal with it, soldier."

And then Virginia speaks up. She's in somewhat better shape than earlier in the day. Her eyes are clearer and less shadowed, and her voice is no longer raspy. "Here's my thing," she says quietly. "I'm here to make sure that Carville's orders are followed. That's one thing I've got on my plate, implementing the go-to. I already explained to Sal last night what that entails. And I'm here to protect this kid we pick up tonight. Get him where he needs to get, get him back."

"Virginia's focused," Carville notes, sweeping his gaze back to George and me, the slackers. "You two could learn something by observing the attitude. It's called *professionalism*, people."

"But that doesn't mean George and Sal are wrong," Virginia goes on unhurriedly, buffing at her deltoid with the flat of her hand, almost polishing it. "At a certain point, it might become pretty obvious that we're screwed. That we're not getting back, or that the whole thing's a washout. Maybe we go to rendezvous with our jet and it never shows, presumed missing. Well, if that happens, and a year goes by, or two or three, I don't plan to stay mustered in. I get this big picture of us all living in Northern Virginia somewhere in a little gated community, in matching ranch houses, all of us turning sixty and you still expecting us to do your laundry, Carville. You know what I mean."

Carville doesn't say anything, but I can tell this is a gut shot. All of a sudden I find myself wondering about weapons. A guy like Carville doesn't go into the field with no weapons, and I wonder what he's got and where he packs it. Would he bring only early-sixties firepower or something a little more high-tech, something with a little more nuance than a forty-five?

"At that point," Virginia continues, "everybody's going to have to recalculate their options. But until then, like I say, I'm working the go-to all day, all night. I don't wear a beret because I like the color." She turns to face Carville. "And until then I don't see anything wrong with listening to what George and Sal are saying, which is don't treat them like grunts, like real military. You can see they're not anyway, and they take it personally."

She looks at me, and whether it has anything to do with our conversation last night or not, I sense she's not scamming her way back into my good graces. She's backing me up, incrementally, without cashing in her beret, but she's backing me up. "Run it a little more like an all-officers operation, ramp down the boot-camp approach. Ramp down the rhetoric, share out the intel a little more."

Carville is not a stupid man, and he sees that his ducks are no longer in a row. They're not scattered, but they're not in a straight line anymore either. He swallows the obvious resentment for the moment.

"We'll talk this over later, Virginia," he says, nodding slowly, eyes on the shirt cuffs he's turning back.

"No doubt," Virginia replies, arms crossed.

There's a short, uncomfortable silence.

Then George says, "Great brief-back."

"It's not over," Carville barks.

"I didn't say it was."

"Good. Don't. I'm willing to cooperate a little more, but I want a little more fucking cooperation while I do that." He stares at George for a beat, then swings around to me. "Can I get a little energy out of you, Sal, in the spirit of cooperation?"

I think about it. Then I say, "I'm prepared to trade cooperation for details and a say in what's going on."

There's another short silence. George breaks it again.

"Okay, group hug, everybody," he says, standing and stretching out his arms.

29

THE HIGH CONCEPT

No matter how much you know a subject, there's always something you don't know. There's always another shadow, another crevice, another cul-de-sac to the crevice. I know more about BC than anyone living—if we except maybe BC and, here in 1963, his mother and his grandmother—and that knowledge comes not only from deep, exhaustive research but through long, rambling personal interviews over a five-year period. Interviews with colleagues, school chums, enemies, teachers, secretaries, Arkansas state legislators. And interviews, of course, with BC himself. My interviews with BC would fill about ten thick volumes in their own right. I know, because BC asked me to consider publishing them after his death.

And of all the stories he spun for me, BC's sentimental favorite was his meeting with JFK. I can tell you details of it that no one else knows, like the fact that JFK's hand was heavily calloused, and the calluses were hard and raised up from the skin, so that if you gripped his hand with any force, it was like shaking hands with a carpenter or a steel worker, not a paper-pusher.

Yet the schematic of tonight's operation begins with a surprise.

"Where's young BC tonight, Sal?" Carville asks. George and Virginia are both watching our exchange silently.

"Tonight?"

"Yeah, tonight. Tuesday, July 23, 1963, say eleven P.M. Where is this kid, yBC? Locate this kid for us."

"He's at the Boys Nation summit. He's in his dorm at the University of Maryland."

"What's he doing there?"

"He's politicking. Boys Nation was a mock senate. They pass mock legislation. He's logrolling, trying to put together deals. They have lights out at ten. But some of the boys come out in the hall and sit there whispering in the dark."

"So yBC's a whisperer tonight."

"He's a whisperer. Sitting in that hallway, right in the thick of all these sixteen-, seventeen-year-old backslappers."

"Eating Moon Pies, working his dorm floor," Carville continues.

"Buttonholing kids from Wisconsin, Kansas, Connecticut; 'I'd sure appreciate your support.' That kind of thing."

Then Carville shakes his head slowly. "No, he's not."

"He's not."

"The kid is not. At approximately ten-thirty tonight, yBC will sneak out of his University of Maryland dorm. He'll bribe his roommate with the use of his car, a black four-door finned Buick. The roommate, a boy named Larry, has no car, see, so yBC offers to let him use the car when they get back to Arkansas if the roommate will keep his yap shut."

That part rings true. BC's always been able to figure out what to offer. But I can't believe BC never shared this part of the story with me. "So he sneaks out of Boys Nation?" I ask.

"The kid does. And he asks around for the wildest college-party spot in the area, and a guy running a hamburger wagon on campus points him to the Varsity Grill, a College Park watering hole. And after some trouble finding his way, he hits the Varsity, or the VG they call it now, and he attempts to put himself over as a college man. He is looking for a woman, surprise, but doesn't find one."

"And he told you this?"

"The old man did. It's never been something he let out before because he didn't want to, you know, tarnish the JFK story. But once he understood the thrust of what we were trying to do, he offered this information. You wouldn't believe how badly the guy wants to make sure that history treats him well."

"Do tell."

"Sorry. I take that back. You'd believe it."

"So what happens now that we're intervening? After he sneaks out and makes his way to the VG."

Carville doesn't answer immediately. I look at George and then Virginia. Both remain silent. They're not touching this part of the brief-back. Carville hunches over in his seat, face down over clasped hands for a dramatic second. This is the part he knows is the hardest sell.

Finally, he unclasps the hands and starts shaping a new part of BC's favorite story, a revision of the JFK handshake story. It's a pitch, more than anything.

"At the Varsity Grill, the kid meets a girl—a woman, really. The jukebox is playing, and even though there's no dance floor, maybe he and this woman get carried away and even dance a bit beside the pool table. And he falls in love, because this is the woman he's dreamed of his whole young life. And there is passion, like a live wire, like an amphetamine epidural. And it turns out that this woman needs his help. Desperately needs his help. She's actually ripped the fabric of time to get to him to ask for his help, and she needs the help because her world is crumbling, and in a way that he can just barely understand, the kid is the key to saving it all."

Now Carville's into it. He's a producer, a high-concept guy as much as an NSC thug. He really believes in the plotline. "And he makes a decision to help her and her people, with the understanding that when all is said and done, he'll be returned to his dorm, safe and sound, knowing that he answered the call, saved the future. And he'll always have the memory of this woman, this mission."

"And what if he doesn't buy it?"

"This kid will buy it. This kid already believes he was born to save the world."

"What if he balks at some point?"

"He won't balk."

"You're assuming that he's going to understand the Wars well enough to see why he should risk his skin to intervene. That he'll understand and make that judgment call."

Carville is still shaping with his hands, but now the gestures include me, the fingers start to draw me into the revision. "That's where the good-hearted older woman comes in, the maternal presence. Because of his particular history, BC's especially prone to trying to please the older women in his life." He sees the look on my face, and he hastens to add, "Not that you're old, but in our script . . . General role-playing. Virginia is his love. You're the woman he turns to for advice. You explain to him how the world came apart"—here he pauses for effect—"and how it can come together again."

"You're saying I'm the grandmother."

"All of a sudden you're insulted. Nobody said *grandmother*. Aunt. Teacher. Neighbor-lady. Giver of wisdom."

"All right, already," I say. At least what he's describing is voluntary. At least they've done some work trying to figure out how to recruit the kid, instead of chloroforming him. It's still sick, and I still can't bring myself to understand how Virginia takes on an assignment like this, but it's not as bad as it could be, I tell myself. I tell myself the kid is nearly seventeen, in any event. I tell myself that people back home are dying in agony, maybe, by the billions.

All of these rationalizations scroll through my mind, but I'm not kidding myself. I'd never stop this plan from going forward anyway, not in a million years. If there's one thing in 1963 that I must see, it's yBC. I'm a history junkie in general, but BC is my drug of choice. No matter what, I have to meet yBC.

Carville's watching my face. He knows this about me well enough.

But Carville's comment about BC responding well to older women sticks in my mind. I see now that the original storyboarding group must have gone beyond simple logistics and complex guesstimations about historical actions and reactions. They must have spent quite a while figuring story lines that would appeal to yBC's particular psychology and predispositions. They must have thought about creating a team that would feel familiar, in a queer way. I look over at Carville, who's watching me carefully to see if I'll accept this whole rose-tinted story line. Suddenly, I find myself seeing him as the sixteen-year-old yBC might see him. A man like a lot of the men who've drifted into his mother's life, and from there into her son's life. A big man with a big attitude who has a tough time taking no for an answer. A pushy man, with just a hint of the abuser at first, a hint that broadens as time passes. The sort of man from whom the boy has always had to save his mother.

Carville smiles and sits back finally, sensing that I won't try to derail the operation, that I'll go along quietly. And I wonder if the storyboarders picked a bully to lead this team on purpose.

* * *

George and I are the first ones to exit the brief-back. Virginia probably figures she may as well get her scolding over with as soon as possible. He and I come out onto the little balcony, into the wilting humidity, and Carville closes the door of the room quickly behind us.

I put my hand on George's shoulder, pull myself up on my toes, and kiss him on the cheek.

I mean it to be a peck, but he's so much taller that the act of jumping up for the kiss makes it stronger in the execution, gives it more contact. It becomes something of a solid smooch. I'm so intensely grateful is the thing, and that gives it additional thrust at the midpoint. It's the first time I've felt less than alone since I saw the Berets running up the lawn behind the Library.

And hey, Sal: you enjoy it. George is more than a little too young for you, and a sponge, and a spook, but he's got his charms. He looks amazed, but pleased amazed. His fingers drift to his cheek. The cat eyes crinkle.

"That's for being a human being," I tell him.

"Ah, come on. Guy was over the line. Guy didn't even know where the line was."

"But you did. You knew. That's my point."

He looks down at me and gives a little laugh. "Not always," he says, "but occasionally I know my ass from my elbow."

We grin at each other, and then all of a sudden he does it to me, leans down and kisses my cheek, and the side of his smooth face and his lips send a chill skittering down my bare arm, and in the heat it feels like a second's worth of snowfall. And then I nod and go to my room, and he stays out on the balcony to have a cigarette, his lanky frame bent over the wrought iron, skinny black tie dangling, and it's the first time in a long time that I wish I still smoked.

When it's finally time to dress, Virginia goes well beyond the chance Jackie elements I've spotted in her wardrobe to this point. Tonight she *is* Jackie Kennedy. Painstakingly, she recreates the sweet sensuality of Jackie's controlled bouffant. And when she's through with her hair, she assembles the other elements of the Look from her suitcase, and slowly she dons them.

The sleeveless and collarless two-piece dress, in a textured fabric the color of pulverized cranberries. A loose, tissue-thin sweater to obscure the anachronistic upper body. The alligator handbag. The cool cotton gloves. Two-strand pearl necklace. Slim black pumps.

And then Virginia removes the final element from a reinforced compartment in her bag. It is the pillbox hat, and it leaves its built-in hatbox the way a sword screams from the sheath: proudly, ruthlessly, without apology.

If I were rooming with an old-school assassin, I'd be continually watching him or her assemble, clean, and break down a sharpshooter's rifle. But rooming with a bodyist, to this point at least, means I spend a lot of my downtime watching Virginia accessorize.

She points to the dress when she has the hat situated. "Original Bloomingdale's," she confides. Her fingers work the length of the dress, smoothing wrinkles, removing invisible nubbins of material.

I'm in the tub for most of this, boiling myself like okra, trying to get rid of the hot sweaty feeling I've had since Maopi. I'm impressed. They've gone to great lengths to make sure that at least one of the images she's conjuring will hit yBC where he lives. These NSC people are nothing if not prepared. Even in terms of the target's potential sexual associations, there's an A plan, a B plan, a G plan. It's the buckshot approach to seduction.

I have to comment. "So you're Jackie tonight, I take it. The untouchable young Camelot queen."

"I guess maybe so."

"In addition to being his superfreak sex fantasy girl."

When it finally comes, her answer is mechanical. "Maybe so."

"And somehow also incorporating a hint of his mom. Just a touch of the forbidden. Very clever marketing."

She flicks me an annoyed glance, goes back to grooming the dress with her fingernails. I start to say something else, but she breaks in before I can. "Look, Sal, I know you're not going to understand this, but I need a little quiet right now," she tells me. "I'm trying to get my head into the zone."

"The zone? There's a *zone* for this?"

She doesn't answer me.

Since it's well after dark by the time we leave, Carville allows us to ride with the Ford's top down. The air smells vaguely of sea salt, and it's thick with moisture and heat. It feels like heavy hands pulling at me, patting me.

Just before we cross the Potomac on the way to College Park, Carville begins speaking aloud. He doesn't address anyone in particular. His voice is matter-of-fact, rising only when the Ford's tires coax a low, undulating moan from the iron bridge passing beneath us. It's the cover story, the party line, the actual, initial working ruse. Like everything else, it's been engineered with BC, or his naive teenage prototype, specifically in mind.

"At this moment, in Cambridge, Maryland, just across the Chesapeake Bay from where we are now, they're undergoing limited martial law. The Maryland National Guard is patrolling the streets, and black residents are forbidden to gather in groups of ten or more. This past weekend, troops gassed civil-rights protesters when they tried to enter the white section of the city. On Wednesday, Bobby Kennedy will announce a tentative agreement between the protesters and city officials. But until then Cambridge is a pressure cooker."

I had forgotten that martial law, and tear gas, came so soon in the decade. I forgot that major civil-rights legislation wasn't something Congress gave black Americans. It was something black Americans demanded.

"And that's why we've come to Maryland. We saw the images of all this, the horrifying images, back home in Vermont. We all four belong to the same Unitarian church in Burlington, and we decided to join the protests down here, to lend four white voices to the call for desegregation. It was a moral question for us, and it required a moral response. Vermont was the first state to outlaw slavery, and that civil-rights tradition played an important part in our thinking, in our commitment."

This scenario plays on all of the young BC's romantic idealism, his early, gut-level associations with the civil-rights movement. When he hears us say these things, he will feel like a child, playing senator in Boys Nation. He'll admire us for wading into the real fight. He'll feel a strong desire to convince us of his own convictions, his own willingness to risk for what's right.

Carville talks on. "We got in too late tonight to head over to Cambridge, but in the morning we plan to drive over the bay, drive into the city, drive right down Pine Street into the Negro section and join hands with the demonstrators. But it was a long drive down, and tonight we're out to have a little fun, let our hair down."

It's cynical, and mendacious, and liquid-nitrogen cold, this lie. But Carville's right: it'll work. Yes, indeedy. I no longer have even the slightest doubt in my mind that it'll work.

30

ENTER BUBBA

By 9:30 P.M., we're in position: Varsity Grill, College Park, Maryland. But the positions turn out to be anticlimactic at best. Virginia and I are poking through a game of eight ball on the VG's diminutive bar table. For all her time in military rec rooms, Virginia turns out to be almost entirely ignorant of the game, sending the cue ball over the cushion or missing it altogether. I'm amusing myself by playing only slightly over her abilities. Despite its bid for omniscience, the NSC seems to have no idea that my aunt Mary taught me to shoot pool before I could talk. And for the moment there doesn't seem to be any percentage in making it known. So I'm imagining misses in my mind and then trying to execute them, then saying oops a lot, along with Virginia, who really means it when she says it.

Not exactly what I call painting the town.

Carville is chatting amiably with the bartender, a lard-bellied, bearded man who seems pleased to have doubled his clientele with our entrance. Carville's being pretty free with his cash, buying us some good will should we need any at some later point. The other men sitting at the bar seem to assume that we four are two couples, but they stare intermittently at Virginia just the same.

George is hunched over the more intricate of the Grill's two pinball machines, eyes skittering crazily, long fingers stroking flippers, mumbling to himself. He's never seen a real pinball machine, one with an actual shiny mechanical ball, only the digital and holographic mutations that came with the next generation of amusements. A brilliant young man with reflexes honed manipulating multiple holographic objects and dimensions, George is clearly fascinated and pissed when he discovers that he really sucks at pinball.

It's been a while since I spent a Tuesday night out at the bars. I'd forgotten how god-awful boring it is.

In the briefing earlier, Carville said that yBC probably wouldn't enter the bar until eleven or so, but we'd need to be in place well before then. "You can't depend on the memory of a guy almost a hundred and ten years old," Carville said. "Truth is, I don't think BC could remember the names of all the *countries* he bombed, let alone what time of night he caught a beer when he was yBC."

So as a result, all four of us are now swiveling our heads to the door every four or five minutes, which, I begin to think, must seem really compulsive to the other people in the bar. I resolve not to look until 10:45. BC may be ancient, but he remembers the smallest details of his weekend with JFK.

His schmoozing complete, Carville wanders contentedly back to the pool table and stands, hands in his trouser pockets, watching Virginia and me play. He's fiddling with his change, a slight smirk coming and going from his face without ever quite registering. He winces once when Virginia shoots.

I look up from an easy shot on the six ball, which is hanging on the lip of the side pocket. "What?"

Carville purses his lips, shakes his head. "Nothing. Or well, yeah, I was thinking if you take that six ball, you leave yourself with no next shot. You gotta always be thinking next shot, positioning." He lifts a finger and points out the three ball I might have settled on if I weren't sandbagging. "That three's not so tough. You can make that. Then come back for your six." It's pretty obvious that the brief-back earlier wasn't quite the ego-booster he was expecting, so now all of a sudden he's Zenmaster Billiards.

I give him a snotty look, and then I poke deliberately at the six. The shot is strong enough to pocket the six, weak enough to leave the cue ball solidly snookered behind a knot of Virginia's stripes. It's exactly the shot I would make if I didn't know how to play pool and refused to take a hint from Carville.

He raises his eyebrows, unable to stifle the grin now. "So you got the six, Sal. Now where you going?"

I frown slightly. I pretend to see the impossibility of my leave for the first time. I make an attempt at a bank shot, screwing it up fairly dramatically.

"Good try," he says, nodding.

"Screw you, Carville," I say suddenly.

He laughs, hands on his chest. "What? I said good try. I didn't force you to box yourself in with nowhere to go. You didn't want advice."

"It wasn't advice, it was annoying—"

"You didn't want advice, and you left yourself clusterfucked."

My aunt Mary taught me a few things about hustling men on the felt. Number-one rule of thumb: no matter how many times they see it on television, men have difficulty imagining a woman who shoots excellent stick. They can't see it. It's a pig with wings. The difficulty is so great, in fact, that half the time you can't get a bet because the guy will think he has nothing to gain if he wins and everything to lose should he scratch on the eight ball.

Which leads directly to the number-two rule of thumb: a pool bet cannot be offered by a man to a woman, but it can be reluctantly accepted. Because a bet accepted by a man is not really a pool bet but an opportunity to settle the woman's hash—in fact, the hash of all women everywhere throughout the span of recorded and prerecorded history. And so it has to be presented as such. My aunt Mary was particularly good at that.

"You think because you're a man you rule the table."

"I think you don't know the game all that well. Don't take it as a criticism." He looks around automatically to check that no one is paying us undue attention.

"Well, let's play, then, champ. Virginia and I stick you and George."

"You don't have to get confrontational, Sal. If you want to play partners, just say, Hey, James, let's all shoot."

"It's not that I want to play partners especially," I say, beginning to gather up the balls from the failed game under way, "it's that I think you need a little lesson."

The word makes his head flinch, and he can't hold back the smile now. "Lesson," he says wonderingly. "Lesson about what exactly?"

"About testicular blindness."

"Whoa."

I've got the balls gathered, and I reach for the rack. I pause, eyebrows lifted.

I must have gotten the phrasing right. "George," he calls to Stephanopoulos, who's now hunched over the jukebox, scanning the forty-fives, "come on, my man. We got a game over here." Carville begins loosening his tie, his cuffs.

I drift over to Virginia. "Look," I whisper, "do you trust me?"

"No," she says. She locks eyes with a little guy at the bar who's appraising her wanly. He looks quickly back to the bar's black-and-white television.

"Doesn't matter," I tell her. "We can win this game if you do what I say. And if you go along with the bet I make him."

"So, what, you really are some great pool player?"

"I'm really pretty good."

"So you've been playing with my head for the last half an hour."

"Yeah."

She thinks about it, looks over at Carville. "Fine," she whispers, "but if we lose, and I do at some point wind up having to kill you, it's gonna take longer."

I take this for a yes, and I walk over to the other side of the table. Carville's rolling cues on the table, and I have to stop myself from gigging him about it. In almost any bar, all the cues are warped; only posers pretend there's much difference.

"Is that to see if they're warped?" I ask innocently. I can't resist.

Carville nods, squints down the length of his pick of the litter, then hefts it.

"Okay, here's the bet," I begin. The word *bet* brings him up from his first test shot. "We can't play for money, because you won't let me carry any kind of substantial cash. So it's got to be for privileges. That's all that's left."

George joins us, hooking a thumb at the record machine. "Sal, I found the perfect song for you. You'll know it when you hear it. What was that about privileges?"

"We're playing for privileges," I say, "men against the women, to the bitter end, no whining from the losers."

"Sal's got a death wish," Carville explains to George. Then he asks me, "What do you have in mind exactly?"

"I was thinking about the car. You always drive. And three-quarters of the time George rides shotgun. It's this tiny convertible patriarchy with wheels."

"The go-to indicates that I drive."

"No, it doesn't," Virginia interrupts. She's chalking her cue, and even though she can't play a lick, she's got a good game face. "It only says that Sal shouldn't drive."

Carville gives Virginia another narrow-eyed glance. "You don't know how to drive this model gas-burner."

"They mocked it up for me at NATVAC, same as you."

I figure it's time to seal the deal. "Look, if we win, I ride shotgun and Virginia drives tomorrow. End of story. That's what you got that we want."

"Right," Virginia says.

If Carville thought he could lose, he'd parse this out more, but rule of thumb number one makes this impossible. Still, he doesn't plan to give up the keys, no matter what, so he comes back both tough and sneaky. "George and I have no problem with that," he says. "And if you two lose, you address George and me as Sir and you don't speak until spoken to. Between lights on and lights out tomorrow."

"Please," George says to Carville, shaking his head, "I'm not playing for that. Like we need another reason for you to go into your goose-stepping mode."

Carville ignores him. "And you gotta call your shots. All your touches, all your pockets. Gotta make the shot you say you're gonna make. That's standard in any bar, and if you want to play for privvies you can't be claiming some kind of exemption because you're women."

"Done," I say.

"Done," says Virginia.

Carville looks at George, who says nothing. "Done deal, then," Carville finishes. He hands me the cue ball. "Sal, rather than lag for the break, I give it to you as a gesture of respect."

An orchestra heavy on the horns suddenly blasts from the guts of the jukebox. And then two women begin to sing, a cutesy little melody. It's only halfway through the chorus that I realize one of them has the characteristically awful but admittedly sexual voice of Marilyn Monroe:

We're just two little girls from Little Rock.
We came from the wrong side of the tracks.
But the gentlemen friends who used to call

they never did seem to mind at all
they came to the wrong side of the tracks.

I set the cue ball down in the old sweet spot, the place I've been breaking from for the last thirty-two years: off-center, maybe five inches from the back rail. I have two breaks, a high-voltage and a low-voltage, and I decide to go with the less dramatic. A steady controlled opening, one that could still conceivably fit into the notion of a lucky break, seems right. I run the cue along my curled thumb, the flared end of my own cockeyed, open-handed bridge.

It's a nice, understated break: eleven ball goes down, and the cue rolls clear of the pack, leaving me two possible long shots up the length of the little table. Carville doesn't look flustered; he's already thinking past whatever mess I manage to make of this next shot to his own potential shot combinations.

Unfortunately, this is where I need to give him the heads-up. I can't afford to make the next shot weakly just to keep up the amateur's facade. Plus, I'll need to carry the game through at least one of Virginia's shots, so we need a big fast lead. I lean out over the table and catch the fifteen ball precisely where it meets the cushion, taking it crisply down to the corner pocket. The leave isn't all that I'd hoped for, but the cue ball's in the clear, which is half the battle on a bar table.

"Very nice shot," says Carville courteously.

"Put them *all* in, Sal," Virginia adds.

I take the nine then with a sharp little cut, spinning the cue ball off into the bank and from there into the mass of barely broken balls at the foot of the table. The nine ball falls, but with this kind of shot that's almost irrelevant; you're really using it more as a remote launching platform, a place to recalibrate the cue ball. When it works, it's pretty: you suddenly create a little galaxy of shots out of nothing.

Of the three shots I've made thus far, only this last one is undeniably the work of a real player, a fact not lost on Carville. "She knows at least some tricks," he says to no one in particular, suddenly grinning at the balls. "She has played the game, ladies and gentlemen."

I'm just a little girl from Little Rock.
A horse used to be my closest pal.
Though I never did learn to read or write

I learned about love in the pale moonlight
and now I'm an educated gal.

I'm about to shoot again, but what I've just heard suddenly strikes me as so weird that I have to break off and ask George, "Did she just say that a horse was her closest pal?"

"Marilyn was a kinkster," George replies, nodding solemnly over his cue. "That's been documented."

The final rule of thumb, number three, comes into play now: once you reveal the fact that you understand which end of the cue is which, the man will feel cheated by you, although it was really his own determined ignorance that brought the whole scam off in the first place. At that point, the more you assume the role of a serious, no-nonsense player, the less chance he may get fired up with competitive spirit and play over his head. And, of course, the less excuse he'll have to turn ugly on you as the game wears on. And that happens.

This part my aunt Mary wasn't so hot at.

So after my exchange with George, I focus in again, ignoring Carville's little quips. I manage to sink two more stripes, but the shot on the second is fouled by a slight touch from one of Carville's balls.

"Our shot," Carville says quickly, although I'm already stepping away from the table. His eyes are darting over the table, working over the setup. He's down by five, and not altogether happy about it.

Virginia looks at me with some new respect. Not a lot of it, but it's new.

"Nice shooting," George tells me. "You got real finesse."

"Shit, George. Why don't you massage her shooting arm for her?" Carville says from his crouch. "God forbid you actually try to help me win this thing."

George and I watch Carville stalk the table, working first one end of it and then running the cue ball down to cherry-pick at the other end. He's the kind of guy who chalks his cue while he walks—either a good sign for us, or a very bad sign.

As Carville figures a relatively easy three-ball combination, George whispers down to me, "You know he's on a team."

I look up at him. "What kind of team?"

"What kind of team? Synchronized swimming. *Pool,* idiot. He's on a pool team in Virginia. I know because occasionally he cancels meetings when they advance to the finals, break into the nationals."

Carville's managed to drop three of their balls, primarily, I had been telling myself, because I broke out the field for him. Now I'm not so certain. Carville is still figuring angles, and I'm thinking, maybe he sees his way clear to the finish. Maybe he's just got one of those minds, and the stick to back it up.

"Sal," George says, interrupting my thinking again.

"What?"

"Did you believe that shit I just told you?"

"You skinny bastard." I smack him on the arm, and George lets out a delighted laugh, then begins doing a little dance where he stands, holding his draft clear. Out of all of us, he's the only one who fits in at a college bar. He could pass for twenty-one and stupid in a pinch.

Suddenly, the Marilyn Monroe song starts again, horns blaring. The bartender gives the jukebox, then George, a funny look. "I played it twice," George explains. "It really seemed karmic, so I went with it."

Just then, Carville holes the fourth solid but runs himself almost directly behind our thirteen ball. He closes his eye in disbelief but then makes the best of it, using the bank and a long soft shot to drop the cue ball as far away from our two remaining balls as possible.

"What should I do?" Virginia asks quietly at my other side.

"Will you be offended if I say don't try to make one?"

She doesn't think about it. "Taking offense isn't my thing. I like to win."

With me coaching Virginia on how to miss strategically, and Carville coaching George, who isn't half-bad himself, we wind up with two balls left on the table—the eight, and Carville and George's six ball. George has a near miss, and Carville gives him a withering look. Then it's my turn. I've got a relatively workaday cut to make, eight in the side pocket for the game.

Carville speaks up. "If I'd known what skill level Sal here could shoot, I'd have said let's play bank-the-eight."

"What's bank-the-eight?" Virginia asks suspiciously.

"Bank-the-eight means that when you get to the eight ball you can't just slam it straight in, you gotta calculate some angles and make a bank shot with it. Where I grew up that's how you won the game fair and square."

It's pretty ludicrous, but I can't help answering him. "Fair and square? What's not fair and square about my sinking this shot?"

"I'm just saying that people luck into their eight-ball shots. Makes it a game of chance. If you bank the eight you know the winner won by showing some class. Now, you were already leading us down the garden path about not knowing the game, so that probably won't matter to you. You're looking for the ugly win only."

"James," George begins, "lose with dignity. You got worked. Deal with it."

"And taking the easy shot is Sal's prerogative," Carville continues. "I'm just saying bank-the-eight is the way to know what's what. What's class and what's crass."

"Just put in the black one, Sal," Virginia says. "That backseat makes my legs stiff."

Actually, if Carville had suggested bank-the-eight at the beginning, I'd have jumped at it. It's a pretty good way of ensuring that the game goes to the person with more hours in practicing. But now it's just a way of giving James a second chance he hasn't earned.

I was young and determined
to be wined and dined and ermined
and I worked at it all around the clock.

"Sal, don't listen to this guy. He's scamming you," George offers.

"Shut up, Stephanopoulos. She's thinking through her game. Let her win the right way if she thinks she can win the right way."

Now one of these days in my fancy clothes
I'm agoin' back home and punch the nose
of the one who broke my heart
the one who broke my heart
in Little Rock, Little Rock.

The bank shot, if I take it, is a long but not an extremely difficult shot, as bank shots go: the classic table-length V, drawing the eight back up snug into the far corner pocket. It's not that I think taking the shot straight in would be unfair somehow; that's just Carville's desperate maneuvering. It's more the sense that making the bank would say something that the rest of the game hasn't quite said. Carville's right about that.

And in a way that I don't think Carville understands, he's picked the right way to get to me: on this mission, in this year, I need to say something about myself that's not getting said any other way. The random single men at the bar are looking our way now; they see I'm figuring the bank shot, and that's always worth a look.

And then I happen to glance to the far end of the bar, nearest the door, and there he is, paying for a draft. Him, yBC. Because they're watching me, none of the others has spotted him yet. It's a crazy instant, spotting him, watching him move. I've only ever seen this younger BC in static photos.

I don't let on. I can see why the bartender served him the beer—he's an even bigger kid than he seems in pictures, hair in a squared-off brush cut, and only the furtive, stiff way he stands and sips at his beer would tell you that he's underage. Khaki pants, white short-sleeve polo shirt. His face is not heavyset yet but exceedingly well-fed, an impression capped by the bulb of the nose. Bit of acne at the cheeks. He's looking the place over and working on holding a powerful grin beneath the surface. He can't believe he got served, can't believe he's here in the first place.

This glance before the others are aware is a strange gift, and without making it obvious I let it stretch out. I can almost see him feeling out the room, figuring out who can be approached, chatted up, and who can't. And before he's taken another sip he's moving slowly but undeniably toward the back of the Grill where I stand unable to close the door on this game. It makes sense—we're the liveliest energy in the room. He's drawn instinctively. He gets that from his mother.

And also he's noticed Virginia, that's clear, but he seems to be making a point of keeping his eyes off her. It's the way you approach a garage sale: you go first to the table of pointless knickknacks and look them over at length, studiously avoiding the Chippendale chair you spotted passing the house, so as not to drive up the price.

The others look up, catch sight of him. And then, when he senses that our little group have all spotted him standing, tacitly asking to join, he smiles a sort of gosh-golly smile. It's a wonderful smile, and with the oversize nose the effect is one of harmless good will, likable flawed beauty.

Because they've prepared so long and so hard to treat him normally, Virginia and Carville and Stephanopoulos manage not to overreact. They simply turn casually back to me.

And I decide that the moment can't really get any less magical no matter what I do or don't, and so I lean down and touch off the shot without any hesitation at all.

My aunt Mary used to say you get seven gifts in a lifetime, and never by asking for them. The finish to this game is one of my gifts. The shot turns out very pretty: the cue ball strikes the eight cleanly, and in turn the shiny black ball executes its elegant figure and then spins wildly up the bank and down into the hole. It not only goes down, it goes down with authority. Someone at the bar begins to clap loudly.

The kid, yBC, steps immediately forward before anyone can move. He takes my hand, softly but firmly, and he pumps it up and down excitedly.

"Gosh! Tha's a *great* shot," he says, shaking his head and smiling. The accent is an inch and a half thick. "I mean really fine. You're the best woman pool player I ever saw in ma' life. Man! Tha's jist *great*."

His impulse is to include the others, and still holding my hand he half-turns to Carville and says incredulously, "Can you believe she sank that one?"

"No, I really can't," Carville answers cheerfully, showing his teeth.

Feeling my hand clasped in the kid's hand, I can understand finally how the older BC can remember JFK's handshake so precisely after more than ninety years. I always thought he was making it up, but now I know he wasn't. I can tell already that the trick is to leave the memories dormant in your fingers and your wrist and the palm of your hand rather than moving them the long distance to your mind.

"My name's Bill," yBC says to me. "I'm from Hot Springs, Arkansas."

"Sal," I tell him. "Sal Hayden. Nice to make your acquaintance."

31

THE GIANT BLANKS OF HOPE

And then, before another second goes by, Virginia moves up by my side. "My gosh, you're from Arkansas? You're my lucky *angel.* You're really from Arkansas?" she asks incredulously, smiling, lipsticked lips parted, perfect teeth shining softly through.

She's moved up close to yBC, and as she asks this she reaches out and touches his forearm. Somehow—and believe me, if I knew how I'd tell you—somehow she's turned on her sex appeal like a set of Christmas-tree lights. An extensive set, the kind with elves hammering shoes. Her eyes are larger than they were a minute ago. There's a flush in her cheeks. Her hand goes smoothly to the wave of brunette hair poised just above her eyes, accenting it.

"Hot Springs, Arkansas," yBC repeats, "honest injun." He's turned now to face her, and his face is working with pleasure at the attention.

Virginia looks hesitant. "Do you know anything about Hope, Arkansas?"

"Know anything about it!" He turns to me again, letting me share in the foolishness of the question. "Man, ah's *born* there. Born *and* raised. We only moved to Hot Springs a few years back. I got all kinds of family in Hope."

"Well, come here, then, you," she says, taking him by the arm and pulling him to the booth and table behind us. yBC gives us a delighted, helpless look.

"That's Virginia, Bill," Carville kids him. "She's got a real mind of her own. You better watch yourself with her."

"That's my mother's name," yBC says wonderingly.

"You *are* my lucky angel—it was my mother's name too. And she always said miracles come in threes," Virginia answers. She fishes in her handbag and comes up with a little blue glossy-covered book, a game book I've seen her fiddling with on the road from time to time. Like everything else we're carrying, it's early 1960s vintage, full of acrostics, find-the-word, crossword, make-a-word: *Puzzles Across the USA,* the cover reads, *Fifty States, Five Hundred Games, One Million Laughs*. I have to admit that until now I've felt a twinge of disdain every time I've seen Virginia amusing herself with this bit of juvenilia. Actually, more than a twinge. Now I see she was just getting her props prepped.

And this prop is another particularly clever bit of strategy. The only thing that the young BC loved—loves—more than mango ice cream and banana-and-peanut-butter sandwiches is working puzzles.

Virginia flips to the front of the book, to Arkansas, and from where I'm standing I can see it's a half-completed crossword puzzle she's showing yBC. *"This snakes through the capital city,"* Virginia begins. "Eight blanks, then river."

"Ask me a hard one," BC says, delighted that he knows the answer, and he sits up straighter on the bench. "Arkansas River," and then he adds teasingly, "and that's an *s* on the end, not a *w*, for you Yankees."

"Thank you very much, Professor Smarty Pants."

Carville chuckles at this and then ambles casually back to the uncrowded bar. George takes my arm, adds a little pressure. "Come on, Sal. One-on-one death match, you and me."

It's time for all of us to leave and let Virginia work her bizarre Beret/escort/Jackie O/recruiter ploy, but my feet don't move. I nod, but I can't help but listen to what Virginia and the kid are saying. I'm afraid I'll miss something, something that could rework everything I know about BC, everything anyone knows. I feel like the biography I've been writing in my head for the last five years has become fully interactive. "Go ahead and rack," I tell George. "I'm right behind you." I stand off to one side of yBC and Virginia, listening over the unsteady blaring of the jukebox.

"The giant blanks of Hope, Arkansas," Virginia continues. "Eleven letters. If I can get this one, I think I can get most of the rest."

"That's the simplest question you could ask about Hope, Arkansas," yBC says proudly.

"Well," Virginia leans a little closer to him, "I'm not even going to *tell* you what Sal over there thought was the answer."

"Tell me."

"It was absolutely scandalous. That's why I won't tell you."

"Oh, come on, now you *gotta* tell me."

Virginia raises her voice to me. "Sal, you remember what you said was the answer to this one? *Giant blanks of Hope,* eleven letters?"

Since this exchange never actually took place, I can only answer that I don't remember it.

She leans close to yBC again, then stage-whispers it in a low voice. "Brassieres."

"Virginia!" I can't help but sputter.

"But I told her it only had ten letters!"

They're both laughing suddenly, and the kid is blushing. I'm blushing.

"Naw, it's *watermelons,*" he tells her quickly, and then they both burst into gales of embarrassed laughter again. It dies down after a second, and yBC gets his voice under control again. "No, really," he tries to say through his own giggling, trying to indicate that he's serious this time, "they grow the biggest melons in the world there. They're famous all over the world."

More laughter, even I'm laughing now. He struggles with it again, falls headlong into the joke again. "Really, they're huge, I mean, you don't know if you never seen 'em but they're about yea-big." He's holding both arms circled out in front of him, face scarlet, laughter shimmying over his lanky frame, looking to the rest of us in mock desperation. "Hey, come on, you all, you know I'm not talkin' 'bout *that*!"

"You're as bad as Sal," Virginia admonishes him.

"No, I am not," he banters back without thinking.

"Thanks a lot," I tell him.

He looks up at me. "Hey, Sal, I didn't mean that. I just meant I wasn't talking about, you know. I just—oh, you think you're *so smart* tricking me up like that," he says, turning back to Virginia and fixing her with a smile and a squint of his eye.

I'm struck, watching him, by how absolutely comfortable he seems, for all his blushing, underage in a bar, with strange men and women, talk suddenly turned bawdy. His body language is loose and relaxed. But I shouldn't be surprised. Hot Springs is a wide-open town, and his mother and stepfather have always run with the Hot Springs Guys and Dolls, small-time hustlers and their high-haired, afternoon-cocktail queens. His mother prefers the horse track to the Baptist church, and the Vapors casino to almost any other place in town. How many times has he visited her in those watering holes since he was a child, and how many times have the adults around him exploded into naughty, enveloping laughter?

"You're funny," Virginia tells him. "You really are. You make me laugh."

"That's okay, I'll be your clown. Just wind me up," yBC says playfully, shifting from earnest Boys Nation senator into honky-tonk mode, dropping his chin just a touch and letting his blue-blue eyes go momentarily soulful.

I'll tell you something about covert operations, or black ops, in Carville-ese: in my limited experience, they go fast. They've been planned and rehearsed and timed and then subjected to billions of dollars' worth of criticism and countercriticism, and then they've been rehearsed again. So when they actually happen, they *move*. George and I aren't even halfway through our best-of-three nine-ball series when I realize Virginia and yBC have disappeared.

I pause in the middle of my shot, suddenly craning my neck. George puts a finger to his lips and gives a nod to the booth in the far dark corner of the barroom. I can see the two heads in silhouette, matched in height, his early-sixties quasi-military, hers all soft bouffant, nearly resting against each other on the back of the booth. It's hard to see, but it looks as though they're kissing.

"Jesus Christ," I whisper to George. "Are they making out already?"

George watches the heads slowly bob and settle. "I would say canoodling, at this point."

"What? Is that NSC spook-speak?"

"Yiddish. They're nuzzling. I don't think they're doing body fluids yet."

"Jesus Christ, George."

"What? You asked. I answered."

"She's a little old for him."

"He didn't seem to think so. You sure you're not just ticked off about that comment Carville made earlier, about you being the woman he looks up to, etc.?"

"Please. If Virginia's going to go through with this sick little sting, and she doesn't feel like it degrades her, then that's her decision. But don't play me for jealous that I'm not getting used in the same way."

"I wasn't playing you for jealous. You just seem, like . . ." He's apprais-ing me. "I don't know."

"I just seem like what?"

"Like, peeved."

"Well, they just met forty-five minutes ago. I just think—you know, she's pushing it a little quickly. Don't you think?"

"Are you worried he's going to think she's easy, or vice versa? Whose virginity are you worried about? You gotta remember this is about making bombs not explode, aircraft carriers not sink. Sailors' lungs not fill with seawater. That kind of thing."

I chalk the cue absently, noting that Carville is keeping his own discreet tabs on the canoodlers from the front bar. "I'm not worried about anyone's virginity," I tell him. "I just think, you know, there's a decent pace to these things."

George laughs to himself for a second, then sends one of the balls shooting down the table, scattering the setup. The game itself doesn't mean much to him. Then he sits half his butt on the pool table, one foot on the floor, hands bouncing the rubber end of his cue against the tiles. I won-der if his parents ever considered medication for hyperactivity, and then I wonder if his restlessness and his sponge abilities are woven together somehow. "Sal," he says, "did you ever hear of Operation JUST CAUSE?"

"Military interventions aren't my specialty, but, yeah, sure. The U.S. in-tervention in Panama. Kidnapped Manuel Noriega."

"Exactly. But there was another big reason for the whole operation. There was a black op buried inside the op, maybe more than one but at least one. It was called ACID GAMBIT."

Something tumbles in my memory. "Some CIA guy, wasn't it?"

"Exactly. Noriega's people had captured this guy Muse, who was the CIA advance man in Panama. And so Noriega had this guy Muse in prison, around-the-clock guards, etc. Muse was his get-out-of-jail-free card in case the U.S. ever decided to launch a strike in Panama. ACID GAMBIT was really the driver for the whole conflict, and that little black op was basi-cally busting a guy out of a locked, guarded room. The Delta Force guys built a mock prison somewhere in Florida and practiced for months. They finally got the timing down to nine minutes. Nine minutes to land, blow a hole in the roof, stun the guards, grab the spook, hotfoot it back to the chopper, and night-vision the fuck out of there. And when they actually executed in Panama, in the dead of night, they beat their best practice time. Something like eight minutes, thirty-four seconds."

He stops me before I can butt in again. "So my *real* point is, that's what Special Forces do when the target desperately *doesn't* want the plan carried out. How long should it take to get into the target's pants when the target desperately wants his pants gotten into?"

"Jesus Christ, George."

"And besides," George goes on, eyes on the cue he's bouncing up and down on the grimy tiles, "the age difference between him and her is about the same as between you and me. And I know people might think it to look at us, but you don't seem too old for me."

It's sort of a compliment. "Why you silver-tongued devil."

"Hypothetically, I mean. Hypothetically." Then he goes further. He's actually putting himself out on the line a little now. "You seem like you'd be about right for me, in fact. I like maturity, complexity. Most women my age haven't got it. That gets extremely frustrating after a while." He bounces the cue again a few times. "And I'm especially turned on by women who have read a hell of a lot. That's just a personal sponge fetish." He stops and I expect him to smile and make that last bit a joke, but he doesn't and I get the sense that it isn't. Remembering the answer all the time must have gotten him his share of heartache as a kid. No wonder he wound up in an experimental school, and then an experimental military unit where no one knows his real name.

And what's it got to be like to date normal human beings who need to reexamine the menu every time you take them to their favorite restaurants?

"So I don't blame the kid for a second," George finishes up. "Or Virginia."

"Well, that's different. We're different," I say, without any idea what I mean.

He brings his head up, gives his bangs a swipe, and grins. "Right," he says softly, bouncing the cue. "We understand there's a decent pace to these things."

* * *

I excuse myself to go to the bathroom, because the last hour has maxed out my capacity for rational thought. Not only have I met BC at age sixteen-going-on-seventeen, but I'm watching him blunder into what will become the first of many traumatic and life-changing, potentially endless sexual mazes. I'm helping it along, for God's sake. And at the same time, my only real friend here is a twenty-seven-year-old—not exactly a kid, but not exactly my age either—who's now telling me I hit him right in his librarian fetish.

As I come down the narrow hallway toward the bathrooms, I look at the doors on either side: one bears the outline of a man in a bowler hat smoking a pipe, the other an outline of a woman with a high bust and a Barbie waist, wearing a flouncy skirt and heels. I'm about to opt for the latter when I realize that the heavy glass door at the end of the hall, between the bathroom doors, looks out onto a small courtyard stocked with dark picnic tables, an overflow area for hot, crowded nights. I wouldn't have focused on this rear door, I don't think, except for a small red dot of light hovering just above one of the picnic tables.

It's an LED, a ready-light. They're everywhere in my time frame, telling you that all the devices around you are in good working order. But this is the first of these I've seen in 1963. And this is because they haven't been invented yet.

Without thinking, I turn and press my forehead to the glass of the door. There's a man sitting on the picnic table, a heavy man, wearing a stiff-collared nylon shirt and Bermuda shorts. He's got on what look like dark socks and moccasins. His hair is a damp-looking, cream-colored swirl over a beefy head and neck.

In his hand is a small pen-shaped object, and he's pointing it through the door into the bar. That is, at me. It's a video wand, circa 2040, 2050. Auto-focus-and-track, auto-wave-search, auto-archive.

And I realize that no American of any century wears dark socks with shorts.

It's the Lurker from the Bullet crash, the Brit who was tailing me. A small Band-Aid cuts neatly across the upper tier of his forehead. He's here, now.

His hand comes up, and there's a second red glow that dies almost immediately: he's smoking a cigarette, and it's a smoke-miser, a technology the tobacco companies developed when lawsuits were still a threat, the sort that only heat the tobacco, and only heat it when dragged. The only people who smoke misers in my time are from the U.K. It's as good a symbol as any of their attempt to occupy some kind of middle-ground in the Wars, to hedge their bets.

He doesn't acknowledge me, but he doesn't move either. Just keeps smoking, just keeps filming. I push on the door, but it's locked. He must have gotten into the little courtyard from the outside.

And then he lifts his other hand and twiddles his fingers at me.

Give us a smile, Sal, the Lurker seems to be saying.

"Listen, he's not our guy," Carville is insisting—or yelling, really—into the wind stream above the open interior of the convertible. We're on our way back to the motel. Contrary to unit policy, we're doing well above the speed limit. The Ford's big engine is thundering away, and Carville is turning right on red at every light, in spite of the fact that this will be illegal for approximately another twenty-five years. At this speed and at this hour, the moist air over and around us is almost cool.

"If you calm down," he yells, "I'll tell you whose guy he's supposed to be."

"I'm calm. I'm just no longer confident. You people don't even seem to know who's who anymore."

yBC and Virginia were no longer in the Varsity Grill when I got back from going to the bathroom/spotting the Lurker. I'm not sure if it was a coincidence or if the go-to called for Virginia to wait until I needed to powder my nose and then make a break for it, but that's how it worked out. I came running back to the front room just in time to see Carville watching a boxy sixties cab pull away from the curb.

And of course the Lurker was nowhere to be found when the three of us trooped around the side of the bar to the picnic tables. Carville tried to convince me that I had imagined the whole episode—"You know how many fat, drunk guys in nylon shirts there are in this town waving at women on their way to the john?"—but I had the presence of mind to look for miser butts under the table. And, unbelievably, I found one: a stubby plastic tube, unburned but slightly melted and smeared with tarry residue. The tube bore the extremely stylized RM logo of Raleigh/Morris, Big Tobacco's U.K. subsidiary.

Now I'm in the backseat, leaned forward over the crown of the front seat, also yelling. "Okay, so whose guy is he if he's *not* your guy?" I'm even waving my hands around, a bad sign for the Hayden family. "How come he was your guy when he was slobbering around after me on the Bullet but he's not your guy here?"

"When you were traveling from Burlington to Little Rock," Carville answers, shouting more calmly now, "NSC asked a CIA type who happened to be in the Montreal area to pick up your primary surveillance for the length of that trip. It's a very common interservice favor to ask. That's the guy you call the Lurker. When your train got derailed and you parted ways with him, he gave us a heads-up that he was returning to his normal duty area. NSC picked up your normal surveillance from there. And that was it. He was never our guy. He was a loaner."

"You use him but he's not your guy."

"That's right. That's exactly right. You know how you can tell he's not ours? Look at how sloppy the guy is, walking around smoking anachronistic cigarettes, using anachronistic recording equipment. Total CIA ball-buster loose cannon."

George nods back at him. "I always think a completed CIA op looks like the sink when I'm done shaving. Hairs stuck everywhere. No attention to detail."

I make a mental note to begin at the crack of dawn enforcing the bet I won earlier. I'm getting tired of the back of the bus. I speak up again. "So what you're saying is that you and the NSC have complete deniability, whatever this guy may do. I don't buy it. Correct me if I'm wrong, but there's only one experimental light-particle accelerator or whatever, and there's only one go-to. So explain the Lurker."

Carville says nothing for a minute. George is turned in the front seat, his foot positioned in its normal wedge against the windshield, and he breaks the silence. "She's right in the overall sense, James."

"What a shock—you agree with Sal. If I had known you two were going to form your own voting bloc, I'd have brought another sponge on this trip. I feel like the car's the Security Council, and you two are Russia and China."

Stephanopoulos leans over and cups his hands, trying to light a cigarette. Finally he outpositions the wind, and an orange glow fills his hands. "Comrade Sal and I take exception to that remark," he says formally. Then he straightens up and drags the cigarette and starts ticking off assumptions on his fingers. "If you wouldn't remain so committed to the idea that Sal doesn't know anything of value, you might learn something. She's way ahead of you. Obviously this guy was set up to shadow us as we go through the go-to. If he's at the Varsity at the contact hour, then he's got the go-to. If he's got the go-to, he's effectively us, ipso facto."

"My point exactly," I say, turning back to Carville.

"Can we please stop pointing fingers?" Carville barks. "Let's just—can we just say there's a *guy*, okay? And he seems not entirely unrelated to us."

George ashes his cigarette above his head and the wind stream pulls it away. "So let's assume that the President and the Joint Chiefs weren't a hundred percent comfortable when they green-lighted us. Group Storyboard was one thing, but when it came down to turning an independent operations team loose in 1963 with no oversight, they got to worrying. So they jelly-legged finally and created an oversight team. A black-on-black-op."

Carville gestures angrily at George's last phrase. "I'm telling you no. There is no oversight team. Doing that would be taking me entirely out of the chain of command. And believe me, they would not do that to me. I know the Chiefs to a man. And you'd be doubling all the risks of unintended consequences."

"As a theory it fits all the facts."

"Except the fact that the Chiefs would never do that to me."

"That's not a fact. That's self-esteem management."

Carville stares mutely out the windshield for a moment, counting to ten or whatever he does the thirty percent of the time he manages to hold his temper. Then he says, "You don't sandbag a team in the field with unannounced activity. You run the risk that they think the unannounced elements are hostiles."

George is going to let it go, but then he adds, "You're thinking tactics in a single time frame, James. Nobody's ever fielded forces on multiple frames. There are new risks. I'm just saying my guess is they're trying new risk management."

I see where George is going. "So you're saying that there's a go-three."

"There's no fucking go-three!" Carville yells, and we overshoot the on-ramp for the bridge back to Alexandria.

32

GETTING TO YES

The Towne Motel is mostly dark and mostly quiet by the time we pull up beside it. Missing the bridge wound up turning into a half-hour search for the right expressway, and I have no idea if that unexpected delay is important or not. The lights are out in the room I share with Virginia, and I get a momentary sense of panic, that maybe yBC and Virginia were killed in an accident on their way back, that maybe my world has winked out of existence as a result.

But Carville seems satisfied. "She's got the blinds in a zigzag, see? One set closed up, one set closed down. Means they're back, plan proceeds at speed."

He turns around in his seat and hands me a room key. It belongs to Room 110, the room directly below the room yBC and Virginia are now occupying. "Some of your stuff has been moved into this room, but not all of it. Enough for you to change clothes and brush your teeth and do makeup or whatever. We had to leave the rest up there to make it seem like you two are really sharing the room. Virginia's told yBC that you're spending the night with George in his room."

I let that pass and take the key. "This whole plan smacks of college dormitory."

"Very astute, Sal. We're essentially working with a college kid here, so we keep some of the illusion at that level."

I grab my purse and put it on my lap, glance up at Room 210 again. "So, what, do we just wait for those two to finish? I mean, does Virginia have a certain number of times she's supposed to do it with him before the plan goes to the next phase, or what?"

Carville scratches idly at the short hair remaining at his temples. He's not going to let me annoy him into the equivalent of missing another on-ramp. "You seem very fixated on sexual intercourse, Sal. You keep coming back to that as if that were the only thing, or even the primary thing, happening tonight up there in that room. So if it will make you feel better—"

His tone is deliberately patronizing, and he expects me to interrupt, but I don't. I just let him go on with it.

"—if it will keep you from getting your teddy in a twist—"

I keep saying nothing.

"—then I'll put your mind at ease by explaining how the male of the species responds to courtship and sexual stimulation. In general, men respond to sexual flirtation and the first stages of sexual stimulation by thinking less clearly and taking greater and more frequent risks. Correct me if I'm wrong, George."

"I will," George promises.

"It's been documented that men will risk great wealth, security, power, and anything else they've spent a lifetime pursuing for the opportunity to consummate a particularly compelling flirtation. We don't need to look further than BC's second term to get a good sense for this sort of thing."

"You could even argue," George adds, "that the risk-taking fed the stimulation, as well as vice versa. Think foreplay during phone calls to legislators, for instance."

"Thank you, George," Carville says. "On the other hand, *following* sexual consummation, men become notoriously hesitant, risk-averse, and tired. They tend to want to return quickly to their burrows, if you follow me."

"Oh, I follow you," I say, still not taking the bait. "I've observed burrow-seeking firsthand. It's not a pretty picture."

"Good. Then you realize, if you take a second to think about it, that if we want this kid to do something almost inconceivably risky, at least from his everyday 1963 point of view, then this sort of thing has to be managed very carefully. That's why you bring a bodyist. Somebody who can bring some nuance and control to the process."

"I see."

"So you can put your mind at ease. Technically, if all things go according to plan, there's not going to be any real full-scale consummation effected tonight. So your moral criticisms, which keep being vented in the form of smart-ass commentary, are really somewhat misplaced."

Everyone considers this, and when no one says anything, Carville leans forward and touches a switch on the dash. The trunk slowly opens and the Skyliner's motorized top cranks smoothly out of its locked-down position. It slowly unfolds skyward, then curves out into a roof, clicking firmly into place with a final battery-powered spurt.

Carville turns and gives me another look and a nod, as though this process has proven his point. The three of us get out of the car, and we all begin speaking in whispers as we walk to the motel's staircase.

"Not that I want to get into any sort of extended debate with you about this, believe me," I tell him quietly, my heels sounding too loud on the blacktop, "but in my own limited experience, these things have a way of going beyond the point of no return pretty easily. A guy rounding the bases tends to build up momentum, especially a young guy. How exactly does she plan to go from lights-out, full-speed-ahead to time-out, I-need-you-to-come-to-the-future-and-save-the-world?"

"You're asking out of professional curiosity?"

"Call it what you want."

Carville pulls out his own room key and jiggles it slightly in his hand. He's really done a good job of contemporary disguise. From a car passing on the highway, he'd look for all the world like a middle manager for Sears or Dow Chemical in D.C. for a few days to drum up business. He's the picture of balding pre-Woodstock conformity.

"How does bursting into tears grab you?" he asks me.

Room 110 is an exact copy of 210, down to the pattern of the crinkly Dacron bedspreads and the two oversize oil paintings hanging on the walls. Both paintings depict tall-masted schooners struggling at sea, and both are screwed firmly into the wall. It's hard to imagine someone wanting to own one of these things, let alone wanting to steal one, but the motel owner no doubt knows a lot more about human behavior than I do.

Carville told me just before we split up that my part of this whole operation will begin sometime tonight. Once Virginia has finished doing whatever she does or doesn't, the plan calls for Carville to go to Room 210 and take over the job of persuading yBC to go along with a scheme that even to me still seems absurd on the face of it—traveling briefly to 1995 for a heart-to-heart with his older self before returning to his U of Maryland dorm just moments after leaving it.

Carville was silent on what his part of the persuasion phase involved, but when it's done he'll ring my room and then I'm supposed to walk the kid through the geopolitics of the next century or so, as well as act as some kind of reassuringly elderly female presence. *Be prepared for a call anytime, Sal,* Carville said cryptically. *Could be three, four, five, six in the morning,* he said.

Staying up isn't the problem. The scene at the Varsity Grill hit me like a thermos of espresso: I'm walking around the room bursting with questions and nerves, opening drawers, looking in the shower and the desk drawers, trying to find something to occupy my attention. And then I catch sight of the television set standing on its chrome legs in the corner of the room. I pull up a chair and switch it on, but nothing happens.

And then the picture wavers into life: a big man with very broad shoulders and hound-dog eyes wearing a killer suit, sitting casually on a desk, smoking a cigarette. It's Raymond Burr, and if this is 1963 he must be Perry Mason. Later, in the seventies, he'll play a paraplegic detective—Perry Mason but with a staff of neoradical young people instead of functional legs—named Ironside. I seem to have caught the last few minutes of the show, during which Mason apprehends the murderer and explains his train of reasoning to his adoring secretary.

I've seen clips of *Perry Mason* before, but now I'm struck by a couple things. One, there is almost no action; the show consists of Burr talking to various people in a blunt, no-nonsense way, followed by the surrender of the culprit. Two, Burr holds a lit cigarette during the entire ten minutes I watch.

The episode proper is followed by a commercial for Chesterfield cigarettes. This is followed by a commercial for the new Studebaker. Followed by a pitch for Lucky Strikes. In all, the idea seems to be that wearing a nice suit, strictly avoiding physical exertion, and smoking heavily will get you the girl and promotion to district attorney.

There is a knock at the door, and I jump in my chair. The knock comes again, softer. I go to the door and look through the peephole to see George standing with his hands in his pockets, coatless, tie undone and hanging loose around his neck.

I undo the chain and open the door. "What's the deal?"

"No deal," George says through the screen. "I didn't feel like sticking around. Carville's got eavesdropping capacity."

"You're kidding."

"Not kidding. At the moment, being in our room is pretty much like being in their room."

"Sick," I whisper.

"It would be sick enough just listening, without hearing Carville do the color commentary."

"Sick."

"Yeah. It's fairly gruesome. I thought I could wait down here with you. Play some Loaves and Fishes. I thought of a new variation."

Great. Now he's not only better at my game than me, he's improving on it. Pretty soon he'll be correcting me on the rules. "What's that?"

"The questioner can't use scandals involving sex, money, or influence-peddling."

I think about it as I unlock the screen door and he steps by me into the room. "What's left?" I ask him.

"Golf," answers George eagerly. "It's been the sport of choice for presidents since at least the fifties," he begins, then catches himself and adds, "and of course golf carts are the only vehicles presidents are allowed to drive themselves. Being chauffeured all the time eventually makes you look either snooty or not in control of events. So presidents like pictures of themselves at the wheel. And the media loves the golf course because it's such a great metaphor for politics and character. They pretend it matters, and so it does. It becomes subject to scandal, or fake scandal."

"Such as."

"Such as mulligan-taking. They treated it like securities fraud: BC taking *several* mulligans per eighteen holes, as opposed to one per eighteen holes. It used to crop up every year like clockwork. Call it a nano-flap. Duffergate."

George comes in and looks around, nodding his head at the familiar features of the room. He seems as keyed up as I am, and I'm fairly keyed up. I was before he came in, but now there's also the kind of self-consciousness that comes with knowing that someone is even marginally attracted to you and that you're attracted to them. In a way that I wasn't yesterday, I'm aware of how much or how little space there is between us.

"Got anything to drink?" he asks.

"Nope," I say.

"I do," George says, pulling a pint of scotch from his pocket. He probably picked it up at the liquor store down the street from the motel. "Want a snort?"

"Might be nice." I sit on the bed. It's like we're at the tail end of a date, like we've had dinner, seen a movie, and he's brought me back to his place, even though he's too young for me, and it's my place, and instead of a date we're about midway through a covert operation using an early version of a key U.S. president to rewrite history in our favor. But at that it's not as complicated as some dates I've had.

He unwraps the two glasses universal to all motel rooms of all time periods, fills each with two or three fingers of scotch. "Ice machine was broken," he apologizes, handing me the glass and clinking it with his own. "What were you watching?"

"*Perry Mason.* You could get lung cancer from a couple episodes of that."

"What was the guy's name in that?"

"Burr," I answer. "Raymond Burr. I think that's the first time you've ever asked me an informational question. I thought you had it all on tap."

"There are different kinds of sponges. I'm a text guy. I'll view video or film or whatever when I need tie-ins to whatever I'm reading up on. But mostly I'm just books and records. My mind doesn't bring up full-range image as perfectly as it does text. I tend to lose the backgrounds and just remember foregrounds. They gave me a test. Several hundred batteries of tests, actually."

He walks around the room a minute, then over to the doorless closet, sticks his head in, nods. "The early motel chains did these room-geography studies," he tells me, head still in the closet, as though to demonstrate the kinds of things his mind does bring up perfectly, "to try to understand how people used their rooms. Howard Johnson's and the rest. That's how the layout got finalized and standardized. They found out people wanted to drop their bags as soon as they opened the door, so they put the closet and luggage rack right exactly here."

He pulls his head out of the closet, wanders over to the other bed and sits down on it facing me, swirling his scotch. We sit there and he smiles slowly, and I smile back. This smile is one of those smiles that clears up a lot of confusion.

"And take floors, for instance."

"Take floors."

"The motel people went to real hotel owners and asked them about the floors. Hotel people said use wood floors, easier to clean. But the motel people went with carpeting. Thought carpeting was classier."

"Had hardwood beat all to hell."

"Yup. Same with the beds. Hotel people said, look, use *high* beds, because if you don't your guests will use them as seats, like we're doing now, and they'll screw up the beds a lot faster. But the motel people went with low beds anyway."

He gets up and comes over and sits down on the bed next to me. He touches my hair with his free hand, moving it away from my neck, then massages the base of my neck softly with his long fingers.

"How come?" I ask.

He's touching the tiny hairs on the back of my neck with the tips of his fingers. Touch, hover, touch, hover, hover. "How come what?"

I let him touch them for another few seconds before answering his question about my question. "How come they went with low beds?"

"Low beds give an impression of more space."

He moves next to me and very slowly circles my waist with his arms, slowly enough that I could object at any point. He leans closer and his lips press the lobe of my ear, then my neck just below it.

He's tall enough and his arms are long enough that it feels like he's enclosing me.

"They were right," I say softly. "I have this powerful sense of more space."

"Me too," he whispers in my ear.

My arms find their way around him and my hands travel over his back, stronger than it looks beneath the button-down shirt, more muscular, less rail-thin. Something similar is true of his lips: they look narrow but they feel soft and full. We kiss long and hard. I lean back in his arms a little, tilting my head back, and the lips go lower on my neck, and I feel his tongue suddenly brush my collarbone, feel his soft cheek rub against the tops of my breasts, his mess of brown hair stroking beneath my chin and across my chest.

"Motel people didn't listen much to hotel people."

"They knew they were dealing with a whole different ball of wax."

I hold his head in my hands, pressing it to me, working my fingers through all of that hair, and I feel rather than see his fingers open the next button on my shirt. His fingers slowly tug down on the cup of my bra, and his lips begin to search hotly over my breast. It's like I told Carville: when a guy starts rounding the bases, especially a young guy, he picks up momentum.

Whether it's because we're both less reckless than we'd like to believe, or because we realize that Carville could beat on the door at any minute, or because we each genuinely like the other and don't want to risk some kind of regret-recrimination-rejection scenario in the Ford tomorrow, George and I are each still wearing our pants when the call comes.

True, neither of us is wearing a shirt, and I'm additionally not wearing a bra, and we do have some undeniably Biblical knowledge of each other, but we're each wearing our lower garments and that's no small achievement. Because it's not accidental; it's taken a lot of shifting and unzipping and reaching around for things to move forward with those skirt and trouser bottom-halves of our outfits more or less in place. We're both obviously more comfortable or more excited somehow saving something for the sequel.

Still, even with this limited sexual agenda, it's fair to say that we're in the middle of it when the phone rings. The middle is putting it gingerly. We're thundering down the home stretch. Actually, I'm thundering. George is a couple of lengths back but staying with the field. I'm hugging George tightly, my teeth almost cutting into the freckled flesh of his shoulder, his bare arm running between my breasts and down the length of my body, long fingers urging. *Let it go,* I whisper fiercely, *he'll call back, let the fucking thing ring.* But George doesn't, he can't, and I know we shouldn't. He kisses my cheek and breaks off and I sit up, and then I jerk the phone off the hook.

"*What?*" I ask loudly.

"You're on," Carville's voice says.

Here's the scene when I open the door of Room 210:

Carville is straddling the little desk chair, facing the bed, arms folded over the straight back. He's wearing his coat, and his tie is still carefully knotted; where the coat hangs open, I can glimpse an old-school shoulder holster, something I've never seen him wear to this point. There's no way to tell what's weighing down the holster and the jacket covering it, but there's some kind of weapon tucked in there, and he wants it to be seen or at least suggested. In his left hand he's holding a large orange-and-turquoise Howard Johnson's take-out cup. He's pulling on a straw as I enter the room, and from the color of the straw when he pulls, I have to guess the cup is filled with strawberry milk shake. He lifts his eyebrows and smiles around the straw by way of greeting.

yBC sits in the center of the bed, size-thirteen feet still in sweat socks and hanging over the edge. His hair is a mess, the rear half of the brush cut lying down almost exhaustedly and the front fringe jumping straight up. His khakis are on and zipped but unbuttoned, as though he barely had time to raise them to full-mast before something or somebody burst into the room. He is shirtless, which makes a certain sense; the room is sultry in spite of the laboring air conditioner, which confirms my suspicion that Carville can only be comfortable in his jacket and tie because he has no pulse. Although it's four or five in the morning, yBC is wide, wide awake.

On the kid's face there is an expression that beggars description, equal parts astonishment and fear and exhilaration and horror and desire and wishful thinking and a creeping fear of insanity. Almost incidentally, yBC's holding a HoJo's to-go cup as well. The color of his straw indicates chocolate. I see another cup beside the bed, apparently empty. Carville, again, is no idiot. He's studied the briefing material well enough to know that yBC would want two.

Virginia is sitting behind yBC, with her bare legs flared out on either side of him. She is wearing yBC's long white polo shirt, and that could be it, for all I can see. Her dark hair is loose and tangled, and whatever lipstick she was wearing is long gone. She's got her hands on the kid's shoulders, massaging absently, providing a constant baseline contact.

She looks at me as though to say, *I am what I am.*

All of the things that Virginia and I had sitting on our little table by the window when we left—lotions, cigarettes, soda cans, books—have been swept to the floor at some point in the last few hours. It's impossible to tell whether this was an act of passion, pre-Carville, or an act of aggression, post. But the debris gives a chaotic feel to that part of the room.

I hadn't noticed it before, but next to yBC on the bed is a plain manila folder, plain except for the letters *yBC*. Stacked carefully on top of the folder are photographs, some black and white, some full color, and even from where I stand I recognize one of them: it's a 1958 photo of yBC standing beside the family sedan in rolled corduroys, hair in an early-Elvis pompadour. I can only guess that the rest of the photos are also photos of yBC, the color prints from some point later than now, from yBC's future. yBC has looked them over and set them aside. He'll want to examine them in more detail later. Much more detail.

The room, forgive me for pointing this out, smells like sex and milk shakes.

My only other initial impression is that it is very quiet when I enter, as though I've been announced prior to my arrival.

"This is Sal Hayden, Bill," Carville says then. "She's a professor and a historian of the Wars we've been telling you about, the Cigarette Wars. She's an expert on the geopolitical causes, the worldwide causes. She's also your biographer."

The word *biographer* seems to tip the intricate balance of reactions in the boy's mind. A slow smile breaks over his face, and then keeps breaking. It becomes an uncontrollable grin of delight, like the face he has in the famous Kennedy-handshake photo.

Suddenly the need for me on this mission becomes a little more self-evident; any of the others could easily have run down the causes of the Wars for the kid. The point of recruiting me, dragging me along, lies mostly in those three words: *She's your biographer.* Virginia was important to the plan as a lure, and as a continuing attraction, but she could never have convinced the boy to go along with any of this by herself. Only the credible promise of greatness could do it.

I hear Carville's voice, but I'm not really listening. I'm suddenly making sense of things from BC's life that never made sense to me before. Usually when you read a biography of a famous person, there are tiny indications in their personal history that they were destined for distinction: a teacher writes a note home predicting the kid will be president or a pop singer or a priest, etc. Some of these indications are created and enhanced by biographers themselves, as a way of creating foreshadowing for the central storyline.

But in BC's case there's always been something beyond this kind of storyteller's art. His letters, even from boyhood, routinely drift onto the subject of *famous men* or *great and famous men*. It becomes a tic, this phrasing. And in unguarded moments, the older BC will speak of his national political career as a fait accompli even when fresh out of law school, never having held elective office.

I've read and noticed these things for years, but I'd always come to the same conclusions reached by other biographers: that this effect is the product of a mother and a grandmother who whetted his appetite for adulation; that it came from being the oldest child, the savior, in a family riven by alcoholism; that it was the result of having visited the White House and shaken the hand of the President; that it was an uncommon but understandable result of superior ambition; that it was the fruit of genius, megalomania, careerism, or the inferiority complexes of a boy raised poor in Arkansas, a boy who'd outlived three fathers by the time he reached age thirty-five.

But now I know that none of these explanations is the real explanation. The truth is that from this moment forward, yBC knows. He will always know. He won't know the details, because Carville will prevent him from acquiring those. But he'll understand the main thrust, the general height and distance and brightness of his own star.

Carville clears his throat, prompting me.

I move closer to the bed, and the things I've prepared to say over the last few days are suddenly gone. My mind blanks.

How do you explain the evolution of the Cigarette Wars, a thirty-year-plus series of conflicts, to a sixteen-year-old kid from an era before AIDS and herpes 3plex, when America had yet to be bombed on its own soil, when dollars trumped yen and rubles, and when the only thing better than kicking Communist ass was smoking a Camel while you wound up and took aim? Even for a historian, even for a biographer with a specialty in this time period and in this boy here on this bed, it suddenly seems more or less impossible.

"Hey again, Bill," I say, pulling a chair a little awkwardly over to the bedside.

"Hey, Sal," answers yBC. My presence reactivates his modesty somehow, and he crosses his arms a little bashfully over his hairless chest.

And I begin. It's a tough job for a lot of reasons, not the least of which is that I have to refer to the kid himself—or the older version of the kid—in the past tense. It seems somehow impolite. I tell him everything I told you at the beginning of this story, about BC's use of Big Tobacco as a whipping boy in the 1996 elections, and the expansion of NATO, and the judgment of the World Court, and all the rest of it. About the Wars and about how America eventually learned that Korea and Vietnam were just small-scale simulations, Gameboys, handheld versions of war. How we learned that dishonor and humiliation—when they finally returned to America from the skies over mainland Asia, large and inescapable enough to blot out the sun—would be total, and forever.

And the whole time I'm talking, the kid's nodding and nodding, eager to gather the pieces, even desperate to gather the pieces, now that he understands there's a puzzle.

Much later, I make it back to my room, bursting with the need to talk to George, to put my arms around him and have his around me. But he's not waiting for me. And so after a half hour of trying vainly to go to sleep, I leave my room and tiptoe back up the stairs. I'm hesitant to knock on the door of the room he shares with Carville because, to put it bluntly, Carville might answer.

So I tell myself that with luck George is in yBC's room.

I stop in front of 210, and I bring my ear close to the door. The yellow bug lights illuminating the second story give off a faint hum, and insects whine. But below that I can hear a voice, Virginia's, speaking softly. I have my hand poised to knock, when I realize that she's speaking intimately to yBC. They must be in or on the bed near the door. I strain to pull words from the rise and fall of the voice.

You're legendary for that, I hear her say. *You make men switch parties and you make women melt from the inside out. They flirt shamelessly with you. Sometimes they pull off their clothes in public when you're near. Like some Greek god or something. You have this power, the power to excite people. Especially women. That's how you stay in power so long. Women never seem to stop wanting you, voting for you, believing you.* She goes on, over his delighted giggles and interjections, telling him exactly how magnetic and sexually unstoppable he's destined to become, the kind of man who can walk into a room and have any woman he desires. And each whispered word, of course, makes it increasingly impossible for the kid ever to become anything else.

33

EFFECTING TRANSPORT

It's only an hour or so later, with the car nearly loaded, with our bill paid, dawn soaking into the edges of the sky, and with Virginia holding his hand tightly and walking him across the Towne Motel's unremarkable parking lot toward the Ford, that yBC balks.

He is highly susceptible to flattery, and to notions of civic duty, and to sex, but finally all of this is too theoretical and substanceless. Instead of boarding a bus for the White House to meet John F. Kennedy, he is approaching an ordinary convertible with a group of people he met in a bar the night before who say they also want to take him to the White House, but circa 1995, and to meet himself, to shake his own older hand. I'm on the balcony, hauling the rest of my things from Room 210, when I look down and see the kid slow and finally stop. He is still hand in hand with Virginia, and she stops a step or two in front of him, their arms nearly taut.

And that's when Carville gets out of the car. He's been watching carefully, and he's not unprepared for this moment. My chest tightens because all of a sudden I have the sense that he's going to pull a gun or whatever it is he has in the show shoulder holster he's been wearing since yBC entered the picture. But he reaches back into the car and comes out with what looks like a bulky catalog. He walks purposefully to where the two of them are standing, and he thrusts the book at the kid, who drops Virginia's hand to take it.

The three of them stand there as yBC opens it, flips through it. Carville leans in and shows him something, finger tapping the book. After a minute, yBC stops flipping and begins fanning pages. From the look on his face, it seems to be the reverse of a catalog: it appears to contain everything he's never wanted.

It's too far away to see what's written or pictured there, but by the time George comes around the side of the building with the rest of the bags from his room, yBC has allowed Virginia to take his free hand again and, holding the catalog, he's reluctantly folded his oversize sixteen-year-old body into the Ford's backseat. Virginia climbs in beside him, and I see her take his face in her hands and kiss him slowly and passionately and gratefully. If I didn't know better I'd say she was deeply in love with him.

Carville takes the front seat, left arm dangling out the driver's-side window and rubbing the door possessively, bet or no bet.

Forty-five minutes later, when we prepare to abandon the Ford at the military installation and board a military aircraft for points west, Carville and Virginia and George all visibly relax, because yBC's chance to escape is past.

It's not until we're transferring all of our possessions out of the 1963 loaner that I spot the heavy green card stock of the catalog's cover. It's lying wedged under the driver's seat. yBC dropped it on the floor and then pushed it as far away from himself as he could. I open it where it lies, on the dusty rubber mat of the backseat.

It is a book of faces and names, and pictures of pieces of clothing and fragments of shoes and odd bits of jewelry, the remnants of mortar explosions or chopper accidents. It's a book of the dead, the U.S. military's most complete accounting of personnel lost in the thirty years of the Cigarette Wars.

The faces, when there are faces, are only as big as a fingernail. The names and biographical data, when there are names and biographical data, fill the space half the size of a Chiclet. It's like glimpsing a well-organized version of purgatory. The cover identifies this as Volume A through C.

I look up to see yBC staring at me through the open window. He's wearing a brand-new blue polo shirt, part of the limited baggage Carville packed for him. The shirt says *NSC* in gold block letters over the pocket. He looks sick, staring down at the faces, the burnt shoes and melted dog tags. He hasn't quite grown into his two large front teeth yet, and along with his freckles, the effect is just shy of bucktoothed innocence. "I hadn't never seen *anything* like that," he says softly, something like apology edging his voice.

"It's not your fault."

He looks like he doesn't know what to believe. "Well, not yet," he says.

"Not ever," I say, more forcefully than I intended.

He looks grateful, and I hand the catalog up to him.

And then he asks, "What kind of a man am I when you know me?"

It's a question full of so many oddities I have to think for a minute before answering. I pull myself up out of the car and close the door. And I try to be as honest as I can. "You're really, really nice. You like to talk."

"How old am I? When you meet me, I mean, meet me later on?"

This is exactly the sort of thing I'm not supposed to tell him, and he and I both know it. But I know he doesn't want specifics. He wants to know if he dies of a sudden stroke at fifty-three. Long or short, that's all he's really looking for, maybe all anyone would be looking for in his shoes.

"You're really, really, really old," I answer.

He looks relieved. "Gosh," he says.

Carville is personally strapping yBC into his seat, looking as though he wished the whole setup came with a padlock. But he's content for the most part, a little looser around the edges, having the kid now safely ensconced by military people and things. If he needed to, he could put the little airfield in lockdown mode with a word. Virginia is already strapped in beside yBC, and she gives me two quick eyebrow twitches, the equivalent of a thumbs-up. She's delighted, I have the sense, that this whole thing is coming off without her having had to go to physical extremes for her country.

I realize that I've lost track of George. I've been thinking of something for the last hour or so that I want to run by him, a corollary of my new theory that BC has always known he was destined for the presidency. I tap Carville on the shoulder. "Where's George?"

Carville doesn't look up from what he's doing. He asks the kid, "That feel like early-stage heart failure, real tight across the chest?"

The kid nods uncomfortably. "Yeah, it does feel kinda tight."

"Perfect," Carville says, smacking the straps lightly where they cross.

"Hey, James," I say again, "are you ignoring me or don't you know where George is?"

Finally, he straightens up and gives me his attention. "He's out in the car."

"What's he doing out in the car? You put him on cleaning detail?"

Carville can't resist making it sting a little bit. "He said he wanted to stick around and watch the plane take off."

George is sitting in the driver's seat of the Skyliner, smoking. It's the first time I've seen him behind the wheel, and as I walk toward the car I'm thinking to myself how much better it suits him than Carville. George can hang in a convertible.

I'm waxing slightly philosophical as I walk to the car, because I sense that he's not coming with us, and I sense that if he's not I'm going to feel like shit. I've known him only a few days, but I feel like he's one of the pillars holding up this disturbing but incredible new world of mine.

I'm not a child and I wouldn't say that I love him, but the groundwork's there in a way that it hasn't been there for a long time. And I'm reluctant to give up the groundwork. Because, even though admittedly I'm no expert, this really feels like some good groundwork.

I go to the passenger's side and lean in the open window. I beat him to the punch. "Let me guess. You're not coming."

He leans over a little, so I can see his face. It looks a little guilty and a little lonely. "Oh, yes, I am. I definitely am. I'm just traveling a lot more slowly."

The 1963 airport techs are hovering around the edges of our landing strip. They've been told not to interact with us, but they also have their preflight work to do, so they're all kind of milling around in a radius of fifty yards, smoking, pretending to fix machinery, pointedly not looking our way.

I open the door and climb into the car. We look at each other across the seat.

"Don't get smart," I tell him. "What do you mean?"

"I mean I'm staying in 1963. I've got a permanent assignment here."

"You *bastard.*"

He puts the cigarette out in the car's dainty chrome ashtray, then slides the assembly back into the dash. Smoke leaks from around the edges, and all of a sudden I hate cigarettes more than I've ever hated anything. If it weren't for cigarettes, the people in the book of the dead would be retired on half-pay from the army. If it weren't for cigarettes, I wouldn't be here, George wouldn't be *staying* here, to clean up Big Tobacco's mess.

"Give me your cigarettes."

He looks quizzical but hands them over. Pall Mall. BC's mother's brand, at least before she died of cancer. I crush the pack against my knee and throw them out on the tarmac. None of the ground-crew types appear to notice.

"I'm quitting anyway," says George.

Whenever you cross the romance line with someone, especially if it happens at night, there's this moment the next time you meet that has the potential to destroy everything or preserve the possibility that everything just might turn out perfect. Does he stop two feet away from you? Does he hit you with an intensely French kiss that says your body belongs to him now, regardless of your mood or how you see the half hour on the couch the night before? Anyway, George does what I have the impulse to do: he looks into my eyes and slides over on the seat, bows his head a little, and, regardless of who's watching or what the Military Code of Conduct says, he takes me in his arms. And that's where we begin the Conversation.

"I didn't find out for sure it could really be done until yesterday morning. I wanted to tell you last night but the fucking call came. And then, while you were giving the kid his history lesson, I was running the sound monitoring. And then," here he's a little more awkward, "you know, James and I thought it would be better to wait until we got here to tell you."

"You didn't want me to flip out and scare the kid."

"That was James's reasoning, you're right. I'm just a coward. I wanted to wait as long as I could. And I had stuff to do once the kid decided to go for it; there wasn't any time for me to find you and say it right. It was better here."

"You had time for a roll in the sack. You had time to sweet-talk me out of my clothes. You could have told me you were hitting the road."

"Your pants did not come off. I sweet-talked you out of upper-body support garments only. And part of the reason I didn't even try the rest is that I knew I wasn't going with you. I didn't want you to think—you know what I'm saying."

"You didn't want me to think you were the kind to fuck 'em, send 'em off into the future, and forget 'em."

"Exactly."

"Jesus Christ, George." I break out of his embrace and lean away. I can see Carville standing in the doorway of the plane now. He seems to be staring out at the horizon, in the general direction of the capital. He doesn't signal our way, but I've known him long enough to know that we've got about five more minutes.

"What kind of assignment is this you're taking?"

He's not sure how I'll take it, I can tell. And he genuinely seems to care if I take it well or not, so I make a silent promise to myself that I'll take it well.

"I'll give you a hint. I have to shave my head."

I'm thinking Marines and wondering how he'd ever let himself be talked into the Marines when he goes ahead and clears it up for me. "I'm staying here to become James Carville."

But I'm just more confused. I turn to the plane, pointing to the man leaning in the doorway. "You two are switching code names?"

He shakes his head. "No, that Carville remains the operative code-named James Carville. I become the real James Carville. I mean in real life."

"You lost me, George. Pretend I'm a five-year-old." I'm beginning to suspect something horrible. "You knock off the real Carville and assume his identity?"

He reaches out and takes my hand, holds it in both of his. "There is no James Carville right now, Sal. We've checked. And we had the 1963 types check too. In the state of Louisiana, at this moment, there is no individual named James Carville engaged in any of the things the young Carville is supposed to be engaged in. To us, that suggested a couple of possibilities. Strongest of which is the theory I argued for when they were fine-tuning the go-to. That there is no James Carville, literally, until we make one."

He takes both his long hands and runs them up under his bangs and covers his brown hair with them, letting me see how he'll look with no hair. To make it clearer, he squints his eyes a little and gives a slack-mouthed grin. And now I see it: he does look like a very young version of the man who'll dub himself the Ragin' Cajun, who'll put together the winning strategy for BC in 1992 and then fall from grace as BC moves further to the right in a bid for reelection. I never noticed it all this time, because of all that beautiful unruly chestnut-brown hair, that and the ample camouflage of the name Stephanopoulos itself.

He's still explaining, and I can tell it's the beauty of the logic that turns him on more than anything about it. "To me, it's clear that the military must have originally created the Carville identity. That's the only explanation for a full dossier in our time and nothing to speak of now. You'd only be able to retroactively create an identity if you did so from within the government itself. You begin with a short, failed stint in the military, the Marines in this case. From there, you've got a complete military record, and that's a viable human being, especially now, which is basically still a precomputerized society.

"And lest you think I'm talking out my butt, I should point out that this is more than a theory. James has already had 1963 NSC set the wheels in motion. I'm a few years older than Carville is supposed to be at this point, but that's nothing I can't fake. I'll have my documents by tonight. Then all I do is drift down to Louisiana and broaden my accent, pick up a little piss and vinegar, marinate in Cajun spices for ten or fifteen years. And the men in my family go prematurely bald anyway, so what the hell."

So he is going into the Marines, after all. "George, you act like this is a lark."

"That's my laugh-clown-laugh tendency. It kicks in."

"It's not a lark," I insist. "It's not something to do on a whim."

"Sal, be pissed, be disapproving, pop small blood vessels, knock yourself out. But don't think I haven't pieced this out for myself. I've been thinking about this for the better part of a year, reading up on it. I wasn't sure until a few days ago. I had the right to opt out if I wanted to. But I realized I didn't want to."

I look at him, and then I reach up and bring his face down low enough to kiss.

But the second the kiss is over, I have to ask the obvious. "Why in God's name do you want to be James Carville?"

"Look, somebody's got to do it." He's dead serious when he says it. "You're missing the point, Sal. I think I did this *originally*—I mean, I think in 1992 when BC gets into the primaries, I'm the guy who takes him through it. I think I am then, was, always will be, however you want to put it. I think I'm looped into history in a big way. And on the most practical end, it gives the NSC somebody on the inside through the 1990s, somebody with a fairly complete knowledge of period history, in case there turn out to be loose ends once you guys do what you do in 1995. I'm the ultimate mole. NSC almost squealed with delight when we proposed it. For one thing, it takes care of how we introduce yBC into the White House once you get him to 1995. This way I'm there to put you on the guest list."

He's got a look on his face not so different from the one I saw on yBC's face earlier this morning, like he's been chosen, preferred somehow, thrust to the surface by the river of time. "And I negotiated some things to make it a little more palatable, you know," he says. "Some minor changes."

"What sort of minor changes? You get to act like you have a mind?"

"Like I can stay in law school if I like before I pick up my first political gigs. I always wanted to give law school a real shot. With full sponge capacity, I always thought I could eat 'em up in law school. And that's not to mention just having the ability to be here, belong here, and . . . you know"—he's gesturing all around us with his hands, trying to put it across—"*live* it all. You know what I mean? Moon shot, Woodstock, Watergate, Reaganomics. Get to go watch Tiger Woods tee it up at Pebble Beach, get to play with the guy. I'm gonna be seriously connected after BC wins the big one. You know what I'm saying, Sal?"

"I think so." And I think I do. He's a sponge with no known saturation point, and he's been dropped into an endless sea of uncaptured knowledge. "I'm a historian. I feel some of that too," I admit, and it's true. A small part of me envies him this car, this bright, postwar–prewar version of America. But the other parts of me feel cheated. "You were the only thing I liked about this whole nightmarish setup. You were the only thing that seemed worth anything. Now I'm left with"—I look out at the plane, see Carville spinning a finger impatiently in the universal pick-up-the-pace sign—"those guys. The asshole, the bodyist, and the kid. And I never see you again."

George looks genuinely surprised. "Why not?"

"What do you mean why not?"

"I mean, we're going to the same place. You'll be there later today, God willing. I'll be there thirty years from now, God willing. I'll be a liver-spotted old bastard. But I'll be there."

I see what he means now. That's the thing about temporal displacement, about time itself: you keep missing the obvious because you keep mistaking it for space. You keep expecting it to respect itself, but it doesn't.

"You'll be married. To a Republican. With big hair and a big mouth."

George Stephanopoulos's face breaks into a fiendish grin, an ear-to-ear grin that can only be called vintage pre-Carville. "Glad you brought that up. I mentioned changes in minor trajectories. Now, here's a theory I have. I think James Carville and Mary Matalin were two very savvy self-promoters from opposite camps in 1992 who liked to sit around in pubs and swap insults and drink heavily. And I think they got a big reaction to their friendship—

big-time media play for themselves—and they made a deal to keep working the angle, eventually broadened it out into a sham marriage. Or at least that's how I intend to play it this time around. That woman's always given me the willies when I scroll through her old video."

I can't believe what I'm hearing. "Are you saying you'll wait for me, or something gallant like that?"

I said it as a joke, mostly, but I can tell it makes him think of what he's got ahead of him, the realities, the possibility that the future may have been inadvertently altered and he could die in a hang-gliding accident or eating a clam, the chance that he might woo one of the big-time actresses of the day, a Sharon Stone or a Meryl Streep, or that our jump jet might wind up as shiny chips scattered over the desert later this afternoon. So when he answers, he's offering me something, but with a potentially infinite number of conditions over which he has no control.

"What I'm saying is I'll meet your plane, if I'm able. And we'll see how you feel being seen with me when I'm no longer this hot young stud."

The propellers begin to turn loudly on the plane, and Carville—the man I'll always think of as Carville—starts a no-nonsense walk across the tarmac.

"You are a hot young stud," I whisper in George's ear.

I get out of the car, so as not to give the old Carville the satisfaction of telling me to get out of the car. I lean in once more through the open window. "I'll look for you when we get to the White House."

"I'll be the bald one telling filthy jokes," George reminds me, and that's all he has time to say before Carville takes my arm. He winks and makes a pistol out of his hand and shoots George good-naturedly in the face by way of parting.

As we walk back to the plane, Carville mops his high, broad forehead. "Fuck July in Washington, D.C.," he mutters. Then he looks over at me and, to his credit, tries to hit a high note. "Fortunately, where we're going, it's April."

The military aircraft we're hitching west is not outfitted for stealth, or near-stealth, and so it's possible to look out the windows. I manage to pick out the Ford leaving the base gate, looking smaller, more like a Matchbox car the higher we climb. I watch as George steers onto the main drag leading away from the base, and for a few seconds we're headed in the same direction, jet above, blue-and-white convertible below. I have this profound sense of déjà vu, a certainty that I've experienced all of this before, with the unsettling addition that the first time around I was a man watching a woman drive the convertible below.

And I wonder how much damage we've done to the way things are supposed to be, how far removed we may be right now from what we were before we started splashing around in the time stream.

But then I realize that what I'm thinking of isn't my life at all. I'm thinking of the end of an early George Lucas film, way before he did the whole *Star Wars* saga, this film I had to watch for a twentieth-century culture class one time a million years ago when I was a senior in high school, this nice, simple little picture called *American Graffiti*. It's about a lot of things, but as much as anything else it's about finding the person you've always dreamed of, almost by accident, and then watching them grow smaller and finally disappear as your plane takes you someplace you don't really want to go.

The Year
1995

The Fifth Part:

THE NEW COVENANT

In short, his youth, populated as it was by two mothers and a small Rolodex of fathers, inflected as it was by alcoholism's violence and ugly mood shifts, and abetted as it was by a small army of semipowerful family friends and well-wishing townspeople, produced a supremely adaptive young man. This more than anything else will astonish the student of his formative years: his ability to adapt instantly, to learn discriminately, to move forward confidently. His sense of self-confidence and self-worth seem always solid, almost preternaturally so.

——from *Inside BC: A Reevaluative Biography*, c. 2012, by Alan D. Bayh

The New York Times: *This next Monday marks the twentieth anniversary of your formal impeachment by the House of Representatives. Two decades is a long time for reflection. Can you tell us—if you were able to go back in time and do things differently, what might those things be?*

BC: Well, one can't, you know, one can never go back in time and—

NYT: *Hypothetically. For the sake of the question.*

BC: I don't mean to spoil your fun, even hypothetically, but I just don't like to go there, as the expression used to be. Because I believe, personally, that there's a weave of life, and it's in the hands of a maker beyond our powers as humans.

And if you try to change one set of errors, first of all you may lose the beauty of what's there, and second of all, you may just force new errors into the weave. Because it's something that's beyond our abilities. I believe that. It's not for nothing, I don't think, that God denied us the power to go back like that, and He did. Watching the road ahead of you is a full-time job. He knew we weren't strong enough to watch the road behind us at the same time. Which is why my mother always said, "Nothing like tomorrow to take the sting out of today."

——from an impeachment anniversary interview by the editorial board of *The New York Times, The New York Times Magazine*, 2019

34

THE FEMININE MYSTIQUE

yBC sits slumped on the left-hand side of the rear seat of our new ride, a 1995 Dodge Grand Caravan minivan, pretending to read a copy of *The Bridges of Madison County*. The slim paperback is the fruit of his request yesterday afternoon for some contemporary reading material to kill time during the drive cross-country. Carville obviously didn't want to give him anything too potentially revealing, historically speaking—*All the President's Men*, or, worse yet, any of the cheap attack paperbacks about BC himself—and yet had to find something acceptable within the limited stock of a Costco drugstore.

So yBC has had to settle for the wildly successful weeper about an unfulfilled farmer's wife and a sensual traveling photographer with hairy wrists, set in rural Iowa. People are still enamored of the book, at this point in time.

And yBC seemed to be enjoying it, until this morning. Or, put another way, he seemed to be enjoying it while Virginia sat reassuringly by his side. All day yesterday they shared the rear seat, sometimes hand in hand. They ate drive-through chimichangas and laughed at ludicrous 1990s things, like teenage girls tottering in eight-inch 1970s mock-retro platform sneakers, shoes that neither Virginia nor the kid had ever seen in their original context. Even though they were coming at 1995 from opposite directions, they seemed to meet in the middle, to find the same things worth pointing at out the tinted window.

Seemed is the operative word. This morning Virginia is sitting up front with Carville, in the bucket seat on the passenger's side, and she has reverted completely to type, fashion-wise: hair up under her beret, aviator shades, camouflage pants, and olive-drab muscle T-shirt, this last made possible by the fact that the 1990s shares with our decade a mania for fitness, although steroids and muscle-jackers like creatine will continue to be frowned upon for another twenty-five years or so.

Along with her outfit she has changed her attitude. Virginia is not ignoring yBC so much as ignoring everyone in the van. Through sheer aura, she has created the undeniable impression that she wants to be left very much alone. The impression has been enhanced by one-syllable responses to yBC's first attempts to joke this morning.

Now he stares at the book without reading, stares at the back of her head without comprehending, returns forlornly to the book, returns to watching her profile and wondering what has gone wrong since the sun came up on eastern New Mexico this morning.

I sit slumped on the right-hand side of the van. I'm not surprised by Virginia's invisible wall; I expected it at some point once we'd made the jump to 1995. It's not that she doesn't like the kid, because she clearly does, she feels all kinds of affection for him. But she doesn't love him by any stretch of the imagination, and pretending to it has been a strain. And his passion does have a doting, Labrador retriever quality to it. So this wall she's put up doesn't amaze me.

What does amaze me is yBC's ability to digest seemingly indigestible changes. Three changes in particular:

When our jump jet did not taxi from the Nevada installation but instead leapt straight up into the air, something the kid could only experience in the context of sci-fi pulp like *The Day the Earth Stood Still,* he looked over at me and said mildly, "Gets your stomach."

When we flew into the airspace over the Maopi reservation, catching the return wave of whatever light-particle effect caused us to coalesce in 1963 in the first place, yBC turned to Carville and asked, "Is this it?"

When Carville told him a little grimly that it was, and just before the plane began its three-second fall through time, yBC looked around soberly and gave the liturgy: "God bless everybody and keep us all safe."

And when we touched down at an all-but-abandoned Nevada airstrip and found the van parked in a locked hangar, with a note from a fifty-one-year-old George welcoming us to mid-April, 1995, the kid poked his head in the van door and remarked to Carville, "This guy on our street, Scully Street, he just got a VW wagon. That bus's got sixteen square feet of room in it, but this thing here's slick as a whistle. Brand-new-car smell too. Your friend George's taking care of us."

For all his talk the last two days to Virginia and to me, and to Carville, about the wonder of the near future and his own inability to comprehend the mystery and the magic of it all, the fact is that the kid acts like he's on a day trip to see second-cousins in Little Rock.

He's reached a kind of instant accommodation with this new reality, and he seems willing to go along with anything we lay out for him, on the condition that it lead ultimately to almost unlimited fame and power, that it lead to the White House. He doesn't care that we've come to him peddling time travel. He smells the truth of it. He smells the main chance.

All of that he's had relatively little problem handling. But now, this morning, he's completely flummoxed by Virginia's sudden chill. Science fiction come to life is one thing, women are another.

His brow is furrowed beneath the brush cut. There is an angry new red pimple on his chin this morning, and at some level I'm sure this figures into his worries about what's going on. I have to believe that given enough time, he'd find the right answer. This is the man who as president will memorize every dusty alleyway of Jerusalem in an attempt to find the solution to the riddle of Middle East peace. But like the Holy City, Virginia defies easy answers.

So yBC switches tacks, an old Camp David trick: if you're not making headway with Yasser Arafat, come at him laterally, by taking Barak out for a ride in the golf cart.

He puts *The Bridges of Madison County* down on the seat beside him, and he turns to me. He has a way of swiveling to face you and then staring at you with great intensity before introducing a fairly casual line of small talk. It's disconcerting in a sixteen-year-old. "Sal, you have one of the greatest jobs there is, I think. Being a professor. You get paid to sit and read. I'm always kind of in awe of people that are, you know, professional readers like that, because I think, even if they haven't read everything there is, they're a lot further down the road than I am. Professors and ministers and lawyers and such."

"Well," I'm modest before I have a chance to think, "you'd be surprised how little most professors really do read. Once they're comfortable in their jobs."

"Still, though," he keeps his gaze on me, "you folks deserve a lot of respect. And I envy you the time with the books. It keeps your mind moving all over the place. Like, what are you reading about now?"

"You. Your times. You know, that kind of thing."

"Oh, yeah," the kid says. "Right."

We ride in silence for another few seconds, and then he realizes he'll have to take a little more control of the conversation. He straightens against the wall of the van, excited about what he's worked around to discussing. "You ever read *The Feminine Mystique* by Betty Friedan? I been readin' that this past week or so."

When I don't answer immediately, yBC adds, "She's a feminist writer."

Carville's head jerks slightly in surprise at what he's hearing. Virginia doesn't flinch. I have this flutter of déjà vu: BC asking me in the hidey-hole if I've ever read *Gulliver's Travels*. I remind myself mentally for maybe the six thousandth time that the two men, this kid and that old man, are both BC.

And then I realize with a little panic that although I've read enough about the book in context to fake my way through a conversation, I've really never read the actual book. At the risk of losing face as the expert on the twentieth century, I go ahead and admit it. "I haven't. I mean, I know what she's about. But I never had the chance to sit down with the book."

"You oughta find the time," yBC advises me, making me wish instantly that I'd faked it. "That's a great book. *Great* book, really thought-provoking. This girl who lives next door to me got a copy from her aunt right when it came out couple months ago. Or, you know, couple months ago for me." He's talking loud enough to be heard in the front seat. "What her point is is that American women have been kind of locked inside their homes and locked inside their *roles* as housewives." He nods slowly, with all the wisdom of his dozen-and-a-third years. "She calls the American home a *thing-ridden place*, an unhealthy place, because women are denied careers and made to turn all their energies to buying things and consuming things, that and sex outside the marriage. Betty Friedan says that, that unfulfilled wives looking for a way out of what she calls the problem with no name will become sex-seekers. And their husbands feel unfulfilled too, and so over fifty percent of them, of husbands, are having affairs on their wives."

I'm not quite sure what to say after all of this, and I can tell Carville and Virginia are in the same boat. So I say, "A lot of those ideas are what lead to the women's movement in the 1970s. And it takes a while, but that has a huge impact on women's lives."

Carville seems pleased that I've kept this to vague generalities, or at least he doesn't seem displeased.

yBC nods eagerly, goes on with what he's saying. To him, I think, this discussion must still seem taboo. "I thought that would have to happen, because what she says, Betty Friedan's solution, makes so much sense. Basically, she says women need lifelong learning and useful work, paid work, not just charity work, although there's nothing wrong of course with charity work.

"And I understand that." He laughs in spite of himself. "Believe me, I understand it, because my mother is a career woman like you never saw. She's basically been running her own anesthesia business for the last ten years or so. If the ambulance goes by the house, she's up and out of bed because she knows the phone's gonna ring for her. She's technically a nurse, but she does a lot of a doctor's work, and I tell you, the doctors in Hot Springs treat her like a colleague.

"And my mom is a happy woman, you never seen a woman so at home in the world. And so that makes good sense to me. That's the way I'll want my wife to be someday. A working woman. Lot of men can't handle that, in my day anyway. Lot of men feel threatened by it, I guess. But I was raised that way."

His eyes swerve just momentarily to the back of Virginia's head, and that's where he sends the final few lines of his piece. "I don't know why someone wouldn't want a woman with a career, a strong woman. I can handle that just fine. That just seems natural to me."

The other shoe drops when we've stopped for lunch. It's a little combination ice-cream stand/hot-dog grill kind of place up in the higher elevations, set under a stand of fir trees, and for the first time since I left the Library in Little Rock, it's cool and shady. Except for a couple of big-rigs idling at the other end of the parking lot, we have the stand's four or five picnic tables to ourselves.

Which means that Virginia has taken her chili dog and Diet Coke to the table farthest into the fir trees, and again the aura suggests that she doesn't want company. Carville, now wearing a nineties suit jacket (double-breasted, wider lapels), with nineties slacks and the sixties shoes, chooses to eat his fried-clam roll standing up, next to the stand itself, as though he's most comfortable on his feet and on blacktop. So, as seems to be happening more and more, yBC and I take our food and eat where normal people would eat, the tables just under the fir trees.

After we've brushed the dry needles from the table and settled down, yBC takes a hamburger and folds the large, thin patty and bun over on itself. He pushes about a third of it into his mouth, as though it were a slice of pizza. For a second I think he's showing me some sort of party trick, but he's not. This is, of course, how he eats. Ketchup and relish show up on his cheek when the bite is complete; the condiment-spotted cheeks then work frantically at the bolus of burger, until the lump is dissected and each half drops visibly past the oversize Adam's apple. Almost immediately he pushes the folded burger in again, managing to smile as he does so.

I've read a good deal about BC's eating habits, none of it very appetizing, and so I'm prepared for this sort of thing. "What strikes you most about now?" I ask, feeling dainty as I eat my french fries with a plastic fork.

"Now, 1995?"

"Right. What you've seen of it so far."

To aid his thinking, he takes a long pull from his large orange soda. Having cleansed his palate, he takes a chorizo dog from the cardboard tray and pushes the end of it unceremoniously into his mouth, chews half of it at once. Then, when his windpipe is finally clear again, he says, "I guess it would have to be how little everything's changed, really. I mean, if I look all around me now, it could be my time, pretty near enough." He squints one eye, twisting his head slowly in a circle. "Okay, if you don't count those trucks, because I never seen windscreens like that before, and you don't count the highway itself, because this interstate is bigger than what we've got at home, and you skip over our van and that antenna on the top of the hot-dog stand—Mr. Carville said that was taking transmissions from satellites in space—then it could be up in the mountains in Arkansas pretty easy."

"The basics are the same."

"That's right. I bet when you get to the city, you know, it seems more like the future." The last half of the chorizo goes down. "I hope we go through some big cities on the way to Washington. Maybe we could run up through Chicago."

I figure I may as well forewarn him. "Actually, I think the point is to stay off the beaten path as much as possible. This time, really late twentieth century, is getting to be a fairly surveillance-heavy society, not just police but video—you know, cameras filming all the time. Like that gas station last night. Carville wanted you to stay in the car."

yBC looks pooky for the first time since he threw in his lot with us. "I hope he doesn't think I'm gonna stay in the car all the while we're traveling. I wanna see something of what's along the way. I mean, I'm doing him a big favor coming along on this trip, he can do me a little favor and let me sightsee a little bit."

"You're preaching to the choir," I say.

That's when Carville comes toward the table, brushing clam crumbs from the corners of his mouth. He smiles by way of greeting and sits down on the other end of the little picnic table. Not on the bench but on the table, his wing tips tapping softly on the bench. The shoulders of his nineties coat are unabashedly padded, and having seen him with no pads two days ago, I'm struck by the change. What he's got on now looks, comparatively speaking, like well-tailored athletic gear.

"How's your meal?" he asks yBC.

"It's good, for roadside food."

"Good. You feel like an ice cream? I might have an ice cream. They do chocolate dip here. I haven't had a dip since I was about ten years old."

The kid's taking small handfuls of french fries. "Maybe in a second," he says.

Carville nods and runs his hand around the back of his head, touching the fringe of dark hair there, his eyes taking in Virginia, now smoking a solitary cigarette back in the trees. "You have to be wondering what's the matter with Virginia," he says, clasping his hands over one knee.

yBC looks at me, but I'm staying out of this end of the pool.

Carville nods again knowingly. "We make our move to this time and suddenly—*bingo*—she's like a hermit crab. I would have told you before, but I wanted to give her time to sort it out for herself. I thought she deserved that. I've known Virginia for quite a while. I care about her."

For a second I think that Carville's going to lay everything on the table—the secret go-to, the way Virginia was designed to catch and hold this particular sixteen-year-old's heart, all of it—and give yBC the option of rejecting the entire project, that or signing on to it with a fuller understanding of its ends-justify-the-means ethics. I think he's going to open up, be honest.

"First you have to know that Virginia is married," Carville begins then, with a straight face, and any hope of the truth disappears like yBC's chorizo. "Her husband's name is Reynolds, and he's a Beret too. About a year ago, he was with a group trying to mine a railroad junction just south of Grozny in Chechnya. That's over in Russia, or the Soviet Union for you. And the Chechens took out their advance party with rocket-propelled grenades. Our soldiers found their three personnel carriers blown to bits. And Reynolds's body wasn't recovered, but let's just say there were a lot of parts lying around and nobody had time to clean them up and bring them home and so everyone just kind of assumed that part of those parts were, you see what I'm saying, were Reynolds's parts."

Carville gives me a particularly bland look, a way of conveying a particularly pointed threat if I contradict any of this.

"And so Virginia was informed that Reynolds was a casualty, and that was part of the reason she volunteered for this mission. She felt she didn't have much in our time to hold her there. You can see that, can't you? She was still grieving, but we thought the intensive training for this mission would be good for her. And it was. And I think by the time she met you, she was really almost ready to move on with her life. You know, make a clean start. And I know you're the first person she got close to since, well, since getting the letter about Reynolds.

"But to make a long, weird story short and to the point, when we got here—into 1995 airspace—and we hooked up with our people, they had some news for Virginia. Reynolds is alive."

Now I know he's making this up, because we have no official contact with the 1995 NSC; that's why we had to hide our jump jet and sneak across the country in a van left by our one influential contact here.

Carville lets this part of the story sink in to the kid, then he presses on. "He's alive, and right now, in our time, they're negotiating for his release. The Chechens have had him in a little stronghold up in the mountains there all this time. So you can understand how Virginia feels all of a sudden. Guilty as hell. For having forgotten about him, for almost moving on. For feeling things for someone else."

yBC looks down at his remaining bite of burger, the scattered remains of his fries. He's lost his appetite. Then he says, a little brokenly, "I keep forgetting you all are really at war, like a world war."

"That's okay," Carville consoles him, "you're helping more than any other single human being by going along with us to Washington." He drops a hand on the kid's shoulder. "And I know it's hard, with Virginia. But she needs space, and understanding." Carville's voice becomes softer, even more sincere. "More than anything she needs friends," he says kindly.

Uncontrollable projectile vomiting is something of which I have only a theoretical understanding. But I come a lot closer to firsthand knowledge with this last bit of baloney. I give Carville a poisonous look, but I turn my head away so yBC doesn't catch it. I understand the need for this, and in a way it's more respectful of the kid to give up the sex/romance hold they have over him. He'll be okay in a few days, probably, and Virginia will be able to return to being a normal, good-natured traveling companion.

But it still sickens me, the way the story's been written in advance to hook the kid in, boat him, and then unhook him but keep him wriggling in the boat as long as he's useful. I think that's what offends me more than anything, the way the story is always one step ahead, the way the story itself never breaks a sweat.

yBC is, of course, a young BC, and so once he finds out about Virginia's heartache he wants to comfort her. He insists on going over immediately to tell her that he's sorry to have put any kind of romantic pressure on her and that he understands completely that she's married and hopes that they can stay good friends. Carville and I sit silently as he approaches her table. We can't hear what he's saying, but it might as well be pantomime. The kid has his head hung a little low, as though he's ashamed of having inadvertently (almost) caused her to commit adultery on her heroic prisoner-of-war husband. He talks earnestly for a few moments, and then suddenly Virginia, apparently overcome with gratitude, overcome by his understanding of her tragic situation, leaps from her lonely picnic table and gives him a powerful (friendly) hug.

I turn to Carville. "What a bunch of really disgusting stupid asshole liars you people are. I've seen cats cough up stuff prettier than you people."

Carville, not surprisingly, is unrepentant. "I thought you'd be pleased. Sex is off the table as of now." He dusts off his hands. "We're going to get the kid to D.C. And you don't have to worry about anybody getting in anybody's pants."

"I don't have to worry? I don't care who he screws. Or she screws."

"Could have fooled me. You've been on your high horse ever since we hit D.C., treating Virginia like she's a whore, me like a pimp, and the kid like he's Little Lord Fauntleroy. Which we both know is not the case. And now all of a sudden you're mad because Virginia's *not* going to fuck him."

"I don't want her to fuck him."

"Well, at least now you're being honest."

"Look, Carville"—I start stacking the ketchup-soaked plates and white cardboard boats and cups that yBC has left behind—"my point is that you people fuck *everybody*. You lie whatever lies seem workable at the moment, and the fact that you're lying doesn't even register with you as a problem. You'd never lie to the president but you'll lie to the people who selected the president."

"I'd lie to the president," Carville says, after pondering it a second.

"My mistake."

Carville walks with me to the garbage can next to the stand, thinking intently as we walk. When I've dumped the trash, he gives me his answer, rocking back on his wing tips. "Okay, try this, Salswick."

"Don't call me that."

"I'm just gonna go ahead and concede that I don't care if I lie to an individual or a group of individuals. Because you're right. I really don't." A little laugh escapes him. "I do not care. In fact, I sometimes prefer to lie, because that way I can control a lot more accurately the impression I give whoever I'm lying to."

"This is my point. You think sentences like that last one are bold and ruthlessly honest. And they're not, James. They're sociopathic."

"You say tomato, I say tomato. Look at it this way. When I'm called in to manage a situation, by definition the situation is one where honesty and trustworthiness and freedom of information and everything you associate with good government in a democracy have taken a backseat to considerations of self-defense. We're going to get this kid to Washington, and he's going to get us the leverage we need with the current occupant of the White House. And our version of America will be defending itself by doing so. And lies are part of what will make that happen. Or call it fiction, if you want. I'm not the government's conscience—"

"Thanks for clearing that up."

"—and I'm not subject to the government's conscience. I'm the government's immune system, and when it's up against some kind of acute threat, I swim out into the bloodstream."

"Tell me you didn't just say you swim out into the bloodstream." I look up to see yBC and Virginia sitting on the picnic table together, looking like the best of friends. Both of them have looks of genuine relief on their faces. Again I wonder if I'm making something out of nothing. Then again, I wonder if prolonged contact with these NSC types is affecting my judgment. "Okay, Carville, let me give you a really clear case for what I'm talking about. You were not pleased at all, *at all,* when you realized there was a go-three."

He scowls briefly, then looks at the stand beside us and makes a point of lowering his voice. "There is no go-three. That's a paranoid fantasy constructed by you and George. What there is is a lone CIA type freelancing out there."

But I won't let him off the hook now that I've got him. I even step forward and punch a finger lightly into his chest. "You were pissed off because you know that the go-three is just a logical extension of your own go-to, just another set of antibodies out in the bloodstream, except their job is to watch *you* and to lie to *you* and to sneak around and observe and report on *you.* And you didn't like that at all. That's what I meant when I said that you people fuck everybody. You even fuck yourselves, and that's why you were pissed. You knew, all of a sudden, that it was you getting fucked, and you didn't like the feeling."

Carville draws himself up and puts his hands in his pockets. He starts to say something, then stops, jingles his keys and coins thoughtfully. Then he squints at me and asks, "You kiss your mother with that mouth?"

Like the split-level ranch, the mid-1990s Dodge Grand Caravan was designed with the peevishness and animosities of the American nuclear family very much in mind. I have no desire to interact with Carville or Virginia tonight, and no taste at the moment for the kid's combination of vulnerability and gullibility, and Dodge encourages me in these feelings. Dodge allows me to all but secede from the rest of the minivan. I have my own temperature controls, and I use them; I tilt my seat back so that my gaze rests on the natty maroon fabric of the roof; I use my personal earphones and stereo to escape the country-and-western music that Carville has gravitated toward over the last few days.

But even over the Brahms I have streaming into my headphones, I can hear Carville and yBC rehearsing geopolitics. While yBC is forbidden to know much of anything about the future drift of American political culture, or the central trajectories of his own life, he is free to learn as much about the Cigarette Wars as he can in a moving vehicle with no library and no sponge.

"Who got in next?" yBC prompts. He's leaning forward, almost hanging over Carville's captain's chair.

Carville negotiates his way around an eighteen-wheeler, and when he's clear, the trucker flicks the rig's lights, letting Carville know he can move back into the lane. Carville flicks the minivan's lights by way of thanks. He's showing off the little bit of twentieth-century road etiquette he's learned, and his voice is satisfied, expansive. "Next up was Kazakhstan. They got in and boom, boom, boom, fighting in three regions, north, south, west, before the ink was dry on their declaration of war."

"Kazakhstan, then boom, boom, boom." The kid's nodding.

"Right, conflict was immediate there. See, the EA and the U.S. had been circling forces around the old Soviet satellites for years."

"I thought Kazakhstan got in when Georgia and Latvia and them all got in. At the very beginning."

"Nope. You're thinking Kyrgyzstan. They got in with the original lawsuit, World v. Big U.S. Tobacco, 2016."

"Kazakhstan, Kyrgyzstan," yBC repeats softly, sorting through the sounds.

"Right. Except you got the order ass-backwards. Kazakhstan gets in near the end, or at least where our team left to come get you. Kazakhstan and Tajikistan, they get in together. And at the beginning, Kyrgyzstan and Turkmenistan and Uzbekistan, bunch of others, *buttload* of others, form the original EA, original in the sense of before the Arab states all jump in."

There is a long pause. Highway lights strobe the darkened cabin.

Then comes yBC's voice again, struggling to get it right, wanting to master it. It's almost as though if he recites these odd and almost indistinguishable new words in perfect sequence, a charm will be sealed, and all sorts of people will un-die. He seems that serious about it. "Kyrgyzstan, Turkmenistan, Uzbekistan, Latvia, Georgia, original EA. Then all of the Arab states get in." A short final pause. "Then Kazakhstan, Tajikmenistan."

"Just Tajikistan."

"Not Kazakhstan?"

"No, I mean the country's called just Tajikistan. Not Tajikmenistan. There's no *men* in there. Tajikistan. So, late in the game, it's Kazakhstan and just Tajikistan throw their hats in the ring."

"Tajikistan," yBC finishes, settling ruefully back into his seat.

"Gives you a splitting fucking headache, doesn't it?" Carville says and chuckles, kicks down his bright lights in response to an oncoming car. Even this he manages to do with a flourish. I offer a silent prayer of thanks that Carville's influence over this kid will last only a week or so, after which time he will be replaced by men like Senator Fulbright, men for whom the rest of the world represents slightly more than a splitting fucking headache.

"No, that was damn good, my man, that was damn good considering. Who needs Stephanopoulos?" Carville adds then, with a little deliberate cruelty, it seems to me.

But even though I know it's partly what Carville was after, I can't help hauling out my memories of George and my new little grief in leaving him behind. And finally I give in and pull out the note that fifty-one-year-old George left folded in the glove compartment of the minivan when he parked it in the abandoned hangar. There was no way to know if it would be us who actually found it, so the note is necessarily vague. It's signed only *JC*, because that's what George's initials are in April, 1995. I read it by the light of my own personal reading lamp.

> I'm anxious for you to come, counting days. No one here speaks my language, never have. It doesn't bother me a lot, but it bothers me a little at some point every day. These people all seem like me, but they finally just aren't. Their perspective on things is myopic. I feel like Methuselah, like I've been alive forever but I can never talk with anyone about it. That's just one of the reasons why I miss you.
>
> Somebody told me this joke today. This is what I mean, the guy thought he understood it. But he didn't, not really. You'll understand it:
>
> BC and the Pope die on the very same afternoon.
>
> But it's a busy day for death and judgment, and there's a bureaucratic snafu—somehow the Pope gets sent to hell, while BC ascends to heaven in his place. It takes a day or two to straighten out the records. But finally the Pope is called to heaven, and BC is informed that he'll be taking the Down Escalator.
>
> The two men meet briefly in the middle.
>
> "Afternoon, your Excellency," BC says politely. "You must be glad to be goin' up to heaven. I had just a great time. What you gon' do first thing when you get there?"

The pontiff thinks for a moment. "Actually, I'd quite like to meet the Virgin Mary."

BC looks suddenly nervous. "Um, what else would y' like to do?"

Every so often I pull it out of my pocket and read the message again. It's laser-printed on an otherwise plain white page. It wasn't addressed but I know it was meant for me, and Carville made no objection to my keeping it. He knew the *you* was me. It's not exactly a love letter, but there's something at least sort of strangely thoughtful in there someplace.

35

CHARISMA

For someone who's just been thrown over by the dark lady of his deepest and least probable fantasies, the kid's acting awfully cocky. We've spent the morning on Route 24, a tiny two-lane highway meandering through the northern third of Kansas and one of the least likely pickup spots, I would have to think, in the United States. We've seen more large wild mammals—two deer and a small family of possum—than sympathetic human females. But all morning yBC has been demonstrating his talent for scaring them up.

At every stop he begins by saying an elaborate hello to the oldest person on the premises, much bowing of the head and much shaking of hands. His voice is that of a sixteen-year-old, but spending so much time growing up with his mother and grandmother has rendered him fluent in the commonplaces of older Americans—flowers, weather, the price of gas and milk. The accent is thick, and his smile is shucksy and bright.

And so, in fairly quick succession this morning, I have watched him all but become an honorary grandson to an old woman in Colby, flirt openly with a middle-aged park ranger at the Webster Reservoir, and now on the banks of Lake Waconda, he's hit pay dirt, a mother-daughter team running the diner where we've stopped for brunch. The daughter, like the mother, is a little on the heavy side, with pretty butter-blond hair. yBC has chosen to eat his lunch up at the counter, in front of the window into the kitchen. As he eats, he's chatting effortlessly and loudly with the mother, who's cooking short-order. He switches his attention deftly to the young waitress each time as she loops back through her station.

Next to him, Carville sits silently, eating his own lunch of a Western egg sandwich and a side of cottage cheese. Occasionally, he glances at his watch, making sure we're running according to some unstated schedule. But he doesn't interfere or rein the kid in. All morning Carville has said nothing about yBC's fraternizing with the temporal locals. Instead, he's followed doggedly a few steps behind, like a Secret Service agent. Maybe it's the fact that in some bizarre but logical sense, yBC is a president-elect of sorts.

Watching the kid work the counter, I remember the sound of Virginia's voice back at the Towne Motel, the pillow talk about his powers of seduction. I try to catch her eye over the table in the back we're sharing.

"Hey," I say.

She brings her gaze back from out the window of the diner. "What?"

"We're not supposed to give the kid any information about his later life, if we can help it, right? Not supposed to telegraph later movements of his life."

She nods. "Right."

"Because that could make him overreact or underreact and then not get where he's supposed to be, historically speaking."

"Right." Virginia's not wearing her Beret casuals this morning. She's got on a pair of faded Levis and a pale blue T-shirt that she bought yesterday in Colorado. It's a Sierra Club T-shirt, with a picture of a low mountain and the legend *Hands Off My Butte*. That and a pair of beat-up period-style Reeboks. Her hair's up, but not dramatically or eye-catchingly up. It's up in such a way that her mane of remarkable hair disappears into normalcy. I feel the tug of envy, and then I just go ahead and envy her for a full second. She can be stunningly beautiful when she wants, and on days like today, when she wants, she can be as reassuringly plain as any other woman, as me, say. It's her choice.

But of course it's not, always. Sometimes she's ordered to be stunning, and I don't envy her that at all.

"So how come you gave him that long song and dance about how irresistible he is to women and how he's like a Greek god and all of that?"

Virginia looks full at me now. "Who told you that? George?"

"George didn't tell me anything."

"Carville?" Then she gets a knowing look, as though she's figured it out. "What, did he let you listen to the tapes from that night when we picked up the kid? At that motel? I'll kill him if he did."

I shake my head. "He didn't play me any tapes," I say. But I don't go on to explain how I know, because I don't really want to cop to listening at keyholes. And it's not such a bad thing if she believes I have my own ways of knowing things too.

Virginia crosses her arms over her chest. She's not really angry. But she's defiant. "I probably said some things like that to him that night. I probably did. What about it?"

"Why, though?"

"It was just kind of in the general idea of talking up the future. Making it seem magical and whatever, seductive. Making it seem like a place he'd want to visit. We still weren't sure at that point if he'd actually do it. I was just selling him the future."

"Where he's a god who can get whatever he wants from men or women."

She's not rattled. "Not a god. Somebody with magnetism. With charisma."

"But didn't you stop to think you might be creating behavior with that stuff?"

She's about to answer, but then something in the front of the diner catches her eye. yBC is sitting at the counter with the waitress, who has marked the fact that she's now on break by lighting a cigarette. The mother, not to be outdone, has come out from the kitchen and is hovering near the two from behind the counter. Carville is nowhere in sight.

"He didn't exactly die of a broken heart over our breakup," Virginia remarks, eyes still on the kid and the butter-blonde. She almost sounds offended. "Look at that. He's putting together some kind of greasy-spoon ménage à trois."

I turn and look, as discreetly as possible, then swivel back. "That's my point. Don't you think that stuff you fed him might have some really unhealthy effects on his ego?"

Virginia pauses for a bit, looking over her nails, which she cut back to the quick when we left 1963. You could tell she hated wearing them long, hated wearing them painted. She likes them like this, out of the way, action-ready, like her hair today. When she answers, it's with the air of someone who's given out two of her three reasons for doing something she regrets and is now about to offer the only explanation left.

"The Storyboard people thought that it was likely that telling the kid he was going to grow up to be president would have the effect of making him really cautious. Making him risk-averse. And if he became that way now, at sixteen, it would alter a whole universe of things later on. Like impeachment, to name one. So they didn't think it would be a bad thing to reinforce some kinds of"—she looks for a palatable phrase but there isn't one—"you know, risk-taking."

In a bizarre way she's right. A good part of the world's attention to the older BC is directed at his sexual misadventures. Changing his sexual habits would mean vast changes in his media wake. I can't let it go, though. "But didn't you stop to think that maybe—"

She stops me in mid-sentence by reaching over and covering my hand briefly with her own. She pats my hand, but the look on her face is hard. "Sal, let's try to remember who's who here, okay? I'm the Green Beret. You're the one who stops to think when you get an order." With that, she digs in her front pocket and comes up with a tangled mass of bills. "I gotta go talk some stuff over with Carville."

"I wasn't judging, Virginia," I say.

"Yeah, you were," she answers, but matter-of-factly, without rancor. "And the thing is, today's just not a good day for me to deal with it, that's all. It's really not." She extracts a wrinkled twenty and tosses it on the table, to cover both our lunches apparently, because she leaves without waiting for change.

I turn around and watch her go. When she gets to the counter, yBC introduces her to the waitress and her mother, and Virginia politely says hello then heads out to the minivan to join Carville. Mother and daughter head into the kitchen to take care of business.

So I am the only person left in the diner to see the look that yBC gives Virginia as the screen door slams shut behind her. It's a yearning look, and there is hurt there, that and a kind of smoldering desire. He still wants Virginia, I can see. These serial flirtations this morning are a kind of half-conscious attempt to shock her into choosing him over her (fictional) long-lost husband. He still wants her, and I have the sense that he always will: Virginia will become for him an icon of unfulfilled desire, the erotic White Rabbit who started him time-traveling to Wonderland.

And maybe it's the fact that Virginia mentioned impeachment, or maybe I've just been blind to it all this time, as I was with George, but I can see a dim resemblance suddenly between Virginia and the young woman who will one day nearly cost BC his chair in the Oval Office. The same luxurious black hair, the same big, dark, lemur eyes. I wish I had photographs to compare, but I don't and there won't be any for another two years or so, although when there are photographs, there will be quite a few. We seem to have done our part to be certain of that.

I cross the restaurant and sit down on the chrome-stemmed stool next to the kid, thinking to comfort him without letting on that I know he needs comforting. He turns as I do so, hides his little tumult of emotions with an easy smile. I have to keep remembering, this kid knows emotional tumult.

His brush cut is absolutely perfect, every hair standing in crisp formation, and I wonder how long he spent coaxing and fixing it into place this morning. So much of what's happening to him is entirely out of his control. But not the hair.

He sips his coffee, another habit he's picked up early from his mother and his mawmaw. And then he says smoothly, "You know, Sal, you never told me what's the biggest difference for you here." When I look confused, he adds, "Biggest difference between your time and now. What strikes you most powerfully."

I think about it, leafing through the sugar packets in the bowl before me. They're ducks, all different kinds of ducks, more different ducks than I ever knew existed. Ducks are big in this part of the country, I have to suspect.

"It's probably how—how *undeliberate* everything seems now, and in your time," I say, knowing as I do so that he has no idea how to interpret my phrasing. "I mean, in my day we've been at war for thirty years, two generations. When you're at war you give up a lot, a lot of freedoms, because there's this sense that everyone has to pull together and live with the unpleasant to make sure, you know, that everyone continues to live at all."

He nods, sipping the coffee. "Like rationing during World War II. Or like blackouts in London and stuff."

"Right, in a way," I continue, figuring out what I'm saying as I say it, "but what I'm talking about is the way that, over time, your country begins to reflect the rhythms and the tactics and the suspicions of the enemy. Here, right now, there's no one watching us, no cameras, no nothing. In 1995 there are only cameras in certain locations, and the functions are pretty limited. They're there in case a crime is committed. In my day, there are surveillance cameras and identification insert ports everywhere—city streets, public buildings, private buildings, parks, bathrooms, roads. And all of them are tied in to what we call FAB programs."

I realize from the blank look that for him a program is still a thirty-minute segment of television time. I unpack it. "FAB is short for facial and bodily recognition. Basically, there are huge machines working day and night, sifting all of the information that comes in through these cameras and registration ports—places where you check in with security of some sort, like airports or train stations or public stadiums. And these machines compare thousands of characteristics of your face or your body shape, even your gestures, with databases maintained by the government. Compare millions of images, billions, until they get a hit. And these machines never sleep."

"They record your gestures?" yBC asks incredulously.

"They do. People run their hands through their hair in signature ways, and at signature intervals, people crack their knuckles characteristically. People cough into a cupped hand if they're from one country, into the air if they're from another. People wink, people sigh. People do a million and one things that only their wives and husbands know they do, but in my day the government knows them too. So that's a big thing. Big, big thing. Here you're left the dignity of your own idiosyncrasies. They haven't been collected and distributed worldwide."

My little riff has taken his mind off Virginia, and I can tell that now he's thinking with all of his being again about saving the world. There's an intensity about him that's irresistible when he focuses it.

He slugs the rest of his coffee back. He wants more information. "How's this data port thing work? They check your fingerprints?"

I shake my head and smile a little. His naïveté isn't just his own at this point; it's America's ignorance of where it's headed and precisely why it's headed there. Then I lean close to him and widen my eye, bring it up real close to his, showing him the sensitive inner works, the humor, the capillaries, all the way into the tenderest secret, the retina that doubles as a license plate in my historical neck of the woods.

American road trips in 1995 are a lot like road trips in 1963. We spend five hours or so in the car, then stop for gas, at which point we ingest large amounts of meat, soft drinks, and fried potatoes, and then shoehorn ourselves back into the car. Fast-food restaurants are our only real hold on reality.

In Junction City, Kansas, just across the Oklahoma line this April afternoon, it's a McDonald's. Like all McDonald's in the nineties, this one is pushing itself as health food. Salads with strips of skinless chicken in clear plastic lunchboxes, pamphlets with caloric and other nutritional information.

"Jesus, imagine you're the guy who gets the assignment to sell this crap as good for you," Carville says, directing the comments at the other three of us. Occasionally he goes into his father-taking-his-family-cross-country mode, like now. He punches the kid lightly on the shoulder. "What do you think, y? Think you could pull that off, brilliant kid like you? Future big shot?"

Carville has taken to calling yBC just plain y, which the kid took to immediately. He knows that everyone but me on this trip is using a code name, and I think he sees it as a sign of acceptance that he's been given one now too. He's also agreed to wear a Kansas City Royals cap and a pair of sunglasses into the restaurant. This McDonald's does have a security camera, and Carville is touchy about it today.

"Aw, this isn't so bad, this stuff," the kid says, running his eye down the menu. "You got your four food groups in here somewhere at least."

It's things like this, when he occasionally pops them out, that help me remember how out of place this kid is at this point. To him, meat and fat are still a *necessary* part of every meal, breakfast, lunch, and dinner. Bacon for breakfast doesn't just taste good to him, it continues to register in his mind as good *for* him.

"What's a Big Mac?" he asks Virginia.

She doesn't miss a beat. "Two all-beef patties, special sauce, lettuce, cheese, pickles, onions, on a sesame-seed bun."

"Gosh! You should be on a quiz show. You got that off by heart."

"Your generation were the last kids who didn't," Virginia says modestly.

"What's special sauce?" yBC asks.

Carville fields that one over his shoulder. "It's the chemicals they put in the food to make you remember all the ingredients in the Big Mac."

"Oh, yeah, sure, right," the kid says, smiling broadly to show he's nobody's fool.

Then there's a little confusion because, if you can believe it, Carville has ordered a Happy Meal, and it turns out that Happy Meals come with a toy called a Beanie Baby. The girl behind the counter asks Carville which Beanie Baby he wants, pointing to a sign with pictures of four different bean-bag animals. Carville looks supremely uncomfortable. He points at random to one, a dog, but the girl says she's sorry but they're out of that particular Beanie Baby.

"Great," Carville says, looking at his watch again, "because I didn't want a Beanie Baby anyway." But when he says this, two women—one behind us in line and one in the line to our right—pipe up at roughly the same time and ask if they can have Carville's Beanie Baby. Which leads the girl at the counter to tell them that if they plan to order one of their own when they reach the counter, then they can't have Carville's, because there's a limit of one per customer per day. Which leads the two women to argue that they'll only actually be *buying* one per day, and then to argue over which of them was first to call dibs on Carville's unwanted baby. Which leads Carville to lean over the counter, into the startled girl's face, and say flatly, "Look, forget the Happy Meal. I'm no longer happy. Give me a fish sandwich, scrape off the tartar, and a Coke, and we'll call it the Disgruntled Meal, okay?"

Then something odd happens. Carville insists that we eat in the minivan, something we've yet to do thus far, mostly I think because Carville is the kind of guy who hates the lingering, rancid smell of french fries in his car. But this afternoon he's insistent, says it'll speed up the process and we need to pick up the pace a little.

So we eat in the van, at the back of the McDonald's lot, nose of the van facing the exit. It's a little before four in the afternoon, but it's a gloomy day, with the sun blocked by lowering clouds, and the almost-empty parking lot has something of an end of the world feel to it. Occasionally a car wheels in or out, and like a cop Carville gives each one the once-over, but in general we chew our food in silence.

But when we're nearly done—all of us but yBC, who has three different sandwiches to work through—the second odd thing happens. Virginia says she needs to go to the bathroom, and she makes some kind of laughing reference to cramps and her period. Carville chuckles and tells her to make it as fast as she can.

The second thing is odd because Virginia had the end of her period when we were in Las Vegas; I know because she went down to the gift shop for tampons and offered me some to keep in my bag when she got back. And it's odd because she's left her own handbag on the floor beside me. As she exits the car, Carville checks his watch again.

Somehow, for no really good reason, I'm suddenly convinced that Virginia has given Carville a line, that she's about to do something secretive, maybe even go AWOL. I remember her cryptic remark from this afternoon about today not being a good day to think through what she's doing. Something isn't right.

I reach for my door handle. And I slip the handle of Virginia's bag around my wrist.

"Where you going?" Carville asks.

"I've got my period too."

"Congratulations. I'll phone the networks. Just wait until Virginia gets back. Cool your jets. You can get whatever you need from her."

There's a Stop & Shop next door to the McDonald's. I reach for the handle again. "Look, Carville, I don't know how much you know about menstrual flow or how much you want to know, but Virginia uses tampons and today, since you want to make a big deal out of it, I need a maxipad. There's a store right over there."

Carville twists in his seat, bringing his arm around behind the passenger seat. For a second I think he's going to hold on to my leg. "I said wait for Virginia."

"The store's just over there," yBC says around a mouthful of McRib. His impulse is to defend me from the bullying. He's been doing it all his life.

I protest. "You know, I start feeling like a part of things, and then you do something like this that makes me feel like just a warm body along for the ride."

"Don't flatter yourself. You're not that warm."

"Hey," the kid says.

I take the insult as an opportunity to exit in a huff. "I'll be right back, James. *Jesus*," I say, and I let myself out. James looks like he wants to say something but he doesn't, and I walk across the parking lot toward the rear of the Stop & Shop.

"We'll pick you up over there," he yells out his window. He points precisely to a spot by the gas pumps. "Just wait right there for us."

I nod and keep walking. But when I come up to the side entrance of the convenience store, I don't go in. Instead, I walk quickly around the glass front of the store and from there to the front of the McDonald's. From this angle there's always a building between the back parking lot and me.

But when I get to the front doors of the McDonald's I have no idea really why I'm here. Probably Virginia is in the bathroom, dealing with late cramps. I look around, and then suddenly I spot her in the parking lot on the far side of the McDonald's from the minivan. She's walking quickly away from the restaurant. She's making a break for it, I think.

And before I realize what I'm doing I break into a half-run toward her. I don't know if I want to say good-bye or go with her, but I'm drawn to catch her.

Then I see that she's headed toward a tall, thin man in a windbreaker. The man's carrying a McDonald's bag to a car parked off by itself at the edge of the lot, under some trees. The gloomy sky makes it hard to see clearly. But Virginia's walking fast, as though trying to overtake him. I have the quick sense that she knows him, and I begin to suspect that she's had a larger escape plot in the works all the while, with this person waiting here for her. I've misjudged her.

The tall man with the bag is just folding himself into his car, and she has nearly come up behind him, when I decide to risk calling out her name.

But before I can yell her name, she calls out herself to the young man. Her voice is friendly, intimate. She says, "Hey there, handsome."

The young man looks out his window as Virginia approaches, a surprised smile coming to his face. She does know him, I think, there is something going on.

Virginia reaches the car, and in one smooth movement she brings something out of her pocket and points it in the window, at the man's chest. His face suddenly contorts, and he slumps over against the passenger seat, writhing. But although that's what I see, there's not a sound from the car, as though his vocal cords are frozen.

I take a few more steps forward, and then I stop. All I can do is watch.

Virginia leans into the window over the downed man, smoothly avoiding the jerks of his body, and she points whatever she has in her hand at the man's head. There's an odd, pneumatic sound, of air under force. A sound you might hear at a mechanic's shop.

Virginia hesitates another second, then pulls her arm back through the window. Without another look, she jogs quickly around the side of the car, back toward the minivan. She's not moving fast enough to excite attention. Anyone seeing her would think, from her clothes and her pace, that she was out for a quick five-mile run. I watch her go, her Reeboks casually slapping the blacktop.

And somehow, I have no idea why, I can't stop myself from moving toward the car. My mind is whirling, and I can feel my heart kicking. But I need to see.

With another few steps I'm close enough to see the head of the man, propped up at an unnatural angle against the corner formed by the seat back and the passenger door. The face is immediately familiar. It's a thin face with small, narrow eyes and thin lips, somehow like the face of a burrowing animal, a face you don't forget. A face I associate mostly with orange prison garb and manacles. I can tell without any doubt that the man is dead. I feel light-headed.

It's Timothy McVeigh. Now I understand. April 17th. He was here renting the truck to carry the bomb, his baby, to Oklahoma City. Now I remember that one of the government's exhibits at McVeigh's trial was footage from a video camera in a McDonald's in Kansas—Junction City, Kansas. Video with digital time and date signature at the bottom.

On one side of McVeigh's face, centered at his temple, a large wine-colored bruise has bloomed beneath the surface. No blood has escaped the body, not a drop, but beneath the skin is a deep, gathering pool of it. The windbreaker is stretched open, and I can see the Tree of Liberty pictured on his white T-shirt. But whatever Virginia used is designed to avoid actually spilling or splattering blood, and the Tree goes unrefreshed.

A woman with two small girls comes out of the McDonald's. The girls are both wearing paper crowns. For a second I'm terrified that the three of them will walk this way, but they don't.

I don't think about what to do then. I just do it. I run.

But not back toward the minivan. That's the last place I want to be.

I just run away.

36

RIDE OR SLIDE

I'm on a bus now, city bus. I don't know why, really. I don't know where it's going. All I know is that I ran flat-out for about three blocks before I realized that people on the street were staring at me. I was winded, and I was holding my ribs, and at one point Virginia's purse slipped out of my hand and showered gum and Kleenex and coins all over the sidewalk. In the litter was a thick wad of bills, which I jammed back in the bag and kept running. I probably looked like I just saw a murder.

Then there was this bus. It was idling beside a streaky plastic bus stop. On the bus stop itself there was a big poster with the basketball player Michael Jordan and, for no apparent reason, Bugs Bunny.

The last of a short line of people was boarding. I could just glimpse the driver through the open door—a muscular black man wearing reading glasses with heavy frames, the kind I associate with photographs of Malcolm X, and when I hesitated by the door he looked at me and said, "Ride or slide."

So I ride. Maybe it was a flashback to grade school, the two years I rode an actual bus before they replaced it with a whisper trolley, that comforting feeling of low-grade authority you got from the bus driver.

If you were on the bus, and the driver was the right kind of driver, not the drinking kind or the sadistic or the careless kind, then you knew you might get teased by the mean kids, but you'd never get hurt, really hurt. You knew that whatever happened, no matter how disheartening or ugly or bruising, the bus driver would put a stop to it, and then—by definition—he'd take you back home.

So I'm on this bus, sitting almost all the way in the back. I'm on the bus, and I'm not in a car with spooks with special guns that make murder look like a burst blood vessel, like natural causes. That's all that really matters.

Virginia told me in Las Vegas that she could take me or anybody out in three or four seconds. That was the window she was taught to shoot for, she said, and I thought it was trash talk. But that's what it took. She murdered him in the time it takes to yawn.

I'm thinking about all the things that will or won't happen now because a blood vessel in that particular young man's temple has been forced open, because his blood has been freed to flow into a relatively tidy, subcutaneous pool. There are forty or fifty things that come immediately to mind, enough to remind me that in reality the things that will or won't happen now approach the infinite. Like solitaire, I'm laying these things out in my mind. I know that this kind of rejection of what's around me, this focusing on mental minutiae, is denial. I know it, but my mind keeps listing them anyway. Which is the best thing about denial, really.

The food in McVeigh's take-out bag will have cooled by the time anyone spots him slumped in the front seat of his car. The police will trace the body to Room 25 at the Dreamland Motel on the edge of Junction City. They'll soon discover that Kling and McVeigh are only two of the names under which he travels. They'll tap into his military record, note the failed bid for Special Services, time in the Gulf. But chances are good they won't investigate long or hard enough to piece together what he was doing in Junction City, other than renting a large truck. Maybe they'll think he was planning an elaborate robbery, but there won't be much incentive to imagine. They won't make the connection to the anniversary of Waco. They will call his family, and his little sister will eventually delete the manifestos parked on her computer's hard drive.

One hundred and sixty-eight people will go on living. Many of those are infants, and those infants—barring other miscues, other maniacs—will have real childhoods, real adolescences and senescences. The Ryder truck's rear axle will not be blown, spinning end over end like a boomerang, through the windshield of a Ford Festiva in front of the Regency Towers across the street.

Timothy McVeigh will never be sentenced to death, because he has just been executed well in advance of having committed the actual crime. He'll never spend his years of appeals shooting the breeze in a maximum security lockup with Ted Kaczynski, the Unabomber. Kaczynski will need to find another kindred spirit.

I've never seen a man murdered. Especially not by someone I've grown to like, and mostly to respect. I remember the slump of the corpse, the sudden careless quality to the body. That could have been me. That could have been anyone. Anyone who got in the way of the new story they've been assigned to write.

Other things won't happen. In shock after the midterm elections of 1994—the watershed election in which not one Republican incumbent lost a seat and in which Republicans took control of the House, the Senate, and a majority of governors' mansions—BC will no longer have the late April tragedy to serve as a personal wake-up call. His poll numbers will not begin their sharp, steady climb. He will not promise swift, certain, and severe justice. Maybe, not certainly but maybe, this change in timing and in momentum will put a Republican in the White House in 1996. Dole, Gramm, Alexander, a rolling crapshoot of second-rate leaders and first-rate opportunists.

The image of Virginia pulling her head out of the driver's side window works its way through my mind again, and now I realize what that last flick of her head must have been: she was spitting on the body.

BC will never need to search out that confluence between president and preacher that allowed him to open his heart and deliver some of the simplest and strongest lines of his presidency: "The anger you feel is valid, but you must not allow yourselves to be consumed by it. The hurt you feel must not be allowed to turn into hate, but instead to the search for justice."

I know those lines by heart. I have for years. And when I make myself puzzle out why I ran away, why I'm still running now, those lines are the reason, I guess. It's because in their desperation to turn history to their advantage, Carville and Virginia and the arrogant freaks who direct them have allowed themselves to be consumed. They think the only thing that matters is that they murdered him first, but they have it wrong.

The only thing that matters is that they had a chance to rewrite the story so that it didn't include murder at all, and they didn't. That's why I'm on the bus.

The where I'm going turns out to be somewhat easier. Because the idea that you get on the bus to go home reminds me that this is 1995, and while my home doesn't exist because my aunt Mary hasn't willed it to me yet, that's only because she hasn't died.

She's alive, early thirties.

A young woman. Her lymph nodes haven't lost the fight for her system. They haven't even begun it. None of her cells has gone over to the other side yet. She's a nurse, probably plays pool in a league one night a week.

I've been so preoccupied with their story, and with the crackpot reality of everything that's happened since we reached 1963 and then leapt to 1995, that it's taken until now to dawn on me that my own story has roots here too. An incredible feeling of relief floods through me, relief and gratitude. I hadn't realized how cut off I've felt, especially since we left George behind to catch up with us the old-fashioned way. I have family here.

Virginia's bag turns out to be choked with cash. I don't want to make it obvious that I'm counting my money, but even a cursory look is enough: it's full of twenties and fifties and hundreds. It's all actual nineties currency. There's somewhere in excess of a couple thousand dollars, which, in April of 1995 anyway, is enough.

I go lurching forward and ask the bus driver the quickest way to get to the airport.

"*Quickest* way?" he repeats, never taking the Malcolm X frames off the road. "Quickest, not cheapest, am I right?"

"Right. Quickest."

"Quickest way is chopper. Rooftop chopper pad straight to baggage check. But that's impractical. So practical quickest is have your own car. Put it out on the highway, let it do what it does best." He nods to himself, big arms bracing the wheel.

I give him another few seconds, but he clearly feels he's answered the question. "Second quickest, then."

"*Second* quickest," he repeats loudly, for the benefit of the people riding just behind us, then points about a half block ahead. "You should have said that right off. You'd saved a minute right there. See that hotel, that yellow flag?" It's a Best Western, what I can only guess is the primo luxury stopping place for travelers to Junction City, Kansas. I've never seen one before except in movies. Their symbol is a big rising sun. Or setting, I guess, depending on your perspective.

"They got an airport shuttle van there for their people. Leaves every hour on the hour," the driver starts.

"I'm not a guest, though," I break in.

He raises his eyebrows over the frames, and I feel like Rebecca of Sunnybrook Farm.

"Not the issue. You got fifteen dollars?"

I nod.

"Then you're their people. Don't say nothing about *guest*. Screw *guest*. Just get on and come over with the fifteen dollars."

"I get it."

"Where you from, anyway?" the driver asks, giving me a sidelong glance.

"1963," I say after a second, because it sounds less naive than Vermont and more believable somehow than 2055.

With that the sidelong turns into a serious once-over. "Uh-huh, 1963. Must be sorta inspiring to see a black man up at the front of the bus, then." He slaps at a switch on the dash, and lights start to flash. "Get ready to de-bus, 1963," he warns me, aiming the flat nose of the vehicle toward the cars lining the street.

And then I slide.

If you've never been on a jet circa 1995, I can only say it's enough to make a lapsed Catholic claw for the rosary beads. You're packed tight, crushed-to-death-at-a-rock-concert tight, and then the thing lumbers down the runway and strains all the way into the air amid this completely deafening noise. The plane has no compensatory stabilization, and so every gust of wind causes it to pitch and roll, which in turn causes the pilot to illuminate a little sign confining passengers to their seats, and if you try to get up anyway the attendants all but take your head off.

And the experience goes on for hours and hours. I'm not kidding. Hours and hours.

Then, once you finally touch down in New York, they switch you to a little toy-size thing that holds fifteen people. And they smile and tell you to have a nice flight. It's genuine insanity. And for me, flying into Burlington, Vermont, in 1995 is a little like driving into 1963 Vegas. It's so different, so very much smaller, that I almost overlook it in my anxiousness to see it. This 1995 Burlington is a heartbreakingly beautiful small city. It sits quietly, modestly on the edge of Lake Champlain. Silicon Mountain, the hub of software and hardware and desperate innovation that dominates the twenty or thirty miles to the south of Burlington in my time, does not yet exist. I can't believe it as we pass over. No web of corporate parks and high-tech manufactories, no high-buck hotels and car dealerships and six-star restaurants to service the digirati. Silicon Mountain isn't even a counter-intuitive gleam in Silicon Valley's eye yet—the biggest computer names have yet to begin their reverse migration back East to the Snow Belt.

Now there's only IBM, what the locals call Big Blue, tucked discreetly back in the woods of Essex.

None of the Sprawl Cities that ring the Burlington I know—Williston, Greater Essex, Spear Center, Jericho Downs—really exists yet either. Now they're just small towns, with only the first splotchy signs of development and the first tier of bedroom communities. They're all still lost in the trees and the mountains as you fly in.

Route 7 is still a two-lane road ambling from the top of the state to the bottom. In about fifteen years it will be straightened and widened and converted into the Southern Connector, a six-lane superhighway that will claim most of the small roadside cider mills and maple-sugar stands and antique shops. And in twenty or twenty-five years the Southern Connector will itself be scrapped in favor of light- and Bullet rail and the whisper trollies.

They land my tiny plane out on the tarmac, and I and the other seven passengers have to pick up our bags from a pile under the wing and then hoof it into the terminal. Just like in my time it's called the Burlington International Airport, but here and now what they mean is that several times a day a small plane makes the twenty-minute flight to Dorval Airport outside Montreal.

The terminal has five gates in 1995, about 115 less than I'm used to. As far as the casual traveler can tell, there is no security. It's staggering how absolutely blasé and unconcerned the airport personnel seem. Sure, there's a pair of overweight older men joshing beside an X-ray machine at the entrance to my gate, but they're hardly glancing at the smudgy, ghostly images that float slowly across their monitor. No uniformed troops walk the terminal, no undercover cops seem to be hanging out in the lounges, no explosive-sniffing shepherds strain at short leashes, no FAB cameras anywhere. In my day my image and body shape and the particular way I swing my arms when I walk would have all been converted into digital bits, and those bits crunched remorselessly against other bits, and someone even now would be strapping on a sidearm and coming out to say hello, given that I am, after all, technically AWOL. But now I just go ahead and swing my arms, in that trademark Sal Hayden fashion, and nobody bats either an organic or a mechanical eye.

Another thing hits me as I drift through the terminal: there are stern warnings *everywhere* that one cannot smoke in the terminal, except for the occasional tiny, unattractive little quarantine zone. Where I'm from, thirty years into the Cigarette Wars, smoking in an airport is like wearing an American flag button on your lapel: it has its own little drawbacks, but it just might keep you from being separated from the herd and searched.

But one thing is exactly the same in 1995 Burlington. Even though no one's supposed to be meeting me, even though no one knows I'm here, even though hardly anyone I know in Burlington has even been *born* yet, I still enter the airport with that same pathetic half-hope that there'll be someone waiting at the gate, maybe even holding a sign with my name on it.

When there's not, I give myself a mental kick for being an idiot. But I remind myself that I'm not alone. I have family here.

The airport has no all-access terminals, but it's not completely primitive; this is the dawn of the information age, after all. So I have to go to a car-rental booth and pay cash, since I have no credit card, and even then they seem to hesitate over whatever it is that comes up on their monitor when they run the ID Carville gave me. In my time, I'd be the one at the terminal, but for now I have to smile and pretend that nothing's wrong. Whatever my card is saying to the Avis computer, it seems to be saying it with a heavy accent, because the Avis woman is concentrating and squinting.

In the time it takes to smile and look bored, I have several minutes to rethink the rental-car decision. I'm fairly sure that Carville doesn't have any sort of privileged access to data here—the 1995 NSC was pretty clear that it viewed Carville's messages as suspicious and potentially hostile. Carville and Virginia are in hiding here almost as much as I am. So chances are they won't be able to trace the rental car.

And I need both a car and most of the rest of the money I have. I haven't quite finished piecing it out, but some part of me is thinking Canada, maybe Montreal. Hole up in a little walk-up hotel on St. Denis and wait for Carville to finish his mission and retrace his steps out of this time frame, say another week. Give it a month to be safe.

That's where I am when the woman suddenly smiles and asks me if I want insurance.

I shake my head. Insurance is a little beside the point.

I'm also thinking about the worm embedded by now in one of my lymph nodes. I don't know much about them, but I know that in my time the army uses a battery of regional receptors to keep track of the signal information streaming from the bodies of American soldiers. There are no regional receptors now. Ipso facto, while Carville may have some sort of handheld device with short-wave radius, I doubt very much he can track me at a distance. I congratulate myself on slipping the leash, but I can't really get my heart into it. When all is said and done, I don't know enough about these various technologies to be even close to sure.

The residential information is here in the airport too, though it's the most laughably low-tech: I go to a phone booth and pick up a huge tattered White Pages directory and flip the pages manually. And there she is, under *Hayden, Mary*. The address is 353 Blodgett Street.

I know Blodgett Street, down near the lake in the Old North End. In my time it's a historic district, complete with antique light posts and benches. The entire section's been mostly reconstructed, gentrified. The young, rich hipsters own condos there. Not now. Now it's mostly people who rent and work too hard for not much money, like my aunt.

And then I start crying all of a sudden, sitting in the booth. Something about her name printed that way in the current phone book, all the perfect little letters.

Burlington even in my time is one of the prettiest cities I know. But now it's piercingly beautiful, leafy and green and dotted with brick buildings and the white spires of churches. April in central Vermont couldn't be more different from Little Rock or Washington. April here is 70 degrees, zero humidity, and a light breeze off the lake. As I crest the top of College Hill and begin the roller-coaster descent down Main Street, it's all spread out in front of me: the Adirondack Mountains across the lake, the waterfront, and the genial hustle of downtown. I'm not used to seeing the roads so clogged with cars, but even with that, everything seems quainter and more small-town than I remember.

More older homes, less apartment buildings and gated compounds. The university looks downright sleepy, still an agricultural college in its soul—they won't build the science and technology towers for another thirty years or so, when the Silicon Mountain types start making free with their donations.

Finally I cross into the Old North End, and the difference is staggering. It really is the poor side of town now, not the most overhyped and overpriced. I'm rolling down North Street, and I'm struck by all the wires strung everywhere—phone wires and electricity cables on huge poles, like a low-tech jungle canopy. People are out on their stoops, watching their kids weave their bikes through the streets, and I can't help thinking that all of these people or their children will be slowly but steadily forced out of the neighborhood in another ten or fifteen years by drastically rising prices.

At the bottom of the street, I see a little fish market housed in a tiny red brick building. RAY'S SEAFOOD, the sign says. In my day Ray's is the site of a digital art gallery. Across from Ray's I spy the tiny metal street sign: BLODGETT ST. I make a right, and I immediately begin searching the houses on my left for my deceased aunt, who's now not only alive but several years younger than I am.

Number 353 is a slightly wilted-looking two-story duplex. The dark gray paint is flaking, and the porch has a pronounced sag. On the other hand, the flower gardens and yard on the left side of the house are immaculate. The yard on the right side is a disaster area. I can tell immediately what's going on here—the landlord and the occupants of the other unit are pigs, and my aunt makes do as best she can. It's pure Mary. There's a psychic borderline drawn right down the center of the lawn.

I sit in the car for a second, trying to decide whether to come out and tell her who I am or not. What would I do if a woman stopped by my office in the Library and claimed to be my niece from the future? The problem is, I won't know until I look at her, look into her eyes, whether she'll believe what I tell her.

Finally, I decide to tell her the truth. I'm sure I know enough about her, about us, that I can make her believe me, if I stay calm and if I can stop looking the way I look in the rearview—sweaty and hunted and potentially insane.

I'm halfway up the walk when the screen door of the right-side unit opens suddenly. A large woman with watery blond hair comes down the stairs toward me, and I stop. This can't be my aunt, I'm thinking. She's about forty or so, wearing a baby-blue string top that does little to rein in the thick flesh of her arms and breasts. I have just enough time to see that she's distraught, when she comes up to me and takes my arm.

"Oh, Christ," she says in a horrified whisper. Her voice is high-pitched for someone with her heft. There's the thin smell of beer when she speaks. "It's my husband."

She tugs at my arm, and I hesitate. "What's the matter with your husband?"

"Please," the woman says, a terrible pain somewhere back in her voice, "please come help me with him. Mary's not home yet. She's the one who always helps, but she's still at the hospital. Please come help him."

I let myself be pulled forward, certain at least, and glad deep down, that this woman is not my young aunt. I should have guessed that, even though they do battle over mowing the lawn, Mary would still wind up being their private nurse. We mount the steps of the right-hand unit together, and she opens the screen door for me.

The interior of the house is cool and dark, and I step inside. In front of me is a dirty sofa with tacky brown-and-white checks. Seated on the sofa is a large man with thin yellow hair pasted carelessly down over his forehead. He's wearing a Chicago Bulls T-shirt and a pair of Bermuda shorts that reveal the twin white hams of his thighs. He's holding something small and recognizably pistol-like in his hand, and he has it pointed in my direction. It's the Lurker. I have just another half-second to try to make sense of what I'm seeing, but all I manage to pull together is another nonsense detail: on his lap, beside the weapon, sits a huge multicolored bag of some sort of snack food called *Doritos*.

37

GO-FOUR

The blonde's big hand shoves me unexpectedly through the door, and I strike the side of a ratty blue chair with my hip and fall over backward on the carpet, striking my head. I'm halfway through the act of tensing and springing back up and running or yelling or whatever there is to do, when the Lurker points the pistol-thing at me and I'm jerking and shivering, electrified.

I feel my head drum the floor, twice, three, four times, like an epileptic.

I'm blank for a second. And then I come to, with the feeling of fingers on the bare skin of my neck, and I try to wrench away. But I'm still paralyzed. The fingers keep pushing at my neck, almost kneading at the skin. Then they shift to the space between my shoulder blades, and suddenly they're pressing something metallic against the flesh there. The force of this last series of pushes is hard enough to force my face down against the braided rug, which smells like year-old cigarette smoke.

I feel my cheek rub and slowly burn against the carpet, and there's a detached quality to it: I can feel the burn developing micron by micron, and I can associate the rising pain with the lengthening abrasion, but somehow the pain isn't finding any hold. It's like the pain is orphaned somewhere in my body, howling to be heard.

The blond woman has closed the door, and I hear her shooting the chain into place. Then she closes the two-inch gap in the drapes covering the front window.

I hear the sound of heavy tape being ripped from a roll, the surgical snip of scissors. The tape is pressed tightly to my skin, smoothed once, twice.

And then all sensation below my neck drops away.

I'm suddenly quadriplegic. There's nothing where my body was, nothing. Not even ghost sensation.

The Lurker and his woman are watching me carefully, and they see the look on my face. I feel them take an arm each, and they haul me up and onto one corner of the sofa. My head rests in the hollow where the backrest of the sofa wings out.

The Lurker gives a huge sigh, pulls in a deep breath. The exertion was a strain; he's not exactly fit. "Not as bad as some I've done," the Lurker says in his fish-n-chips accent, "but not the easiest either." He grins at the woman and pats me on the knee, like a tuna he's finally boated. "I once rigged up a man while he was drunk, and he slept through the entire process. He even rolled to one side when I needed a little more working room. But what can you do when you're dealing with a teetotaler like our Sal here, eh?"

He pulls up the Chicago Bulls T-shirt to wipe his forehead, momentarily exposing his belly, which is the least attractive sight I've seen since being tricked into the room.

When he's repatted his damp lemon-meringue-colored hair into place, he reaches out and touches my neck with a big finger. "I just want you to know that I had several options. I could have killed you, and I didn't do that. And I could have hit you a few more times with the Taser I used as you came through the door. But in that case you'd have suffered actual nerve damage. Something like a stroke. It's anybody's guess at that point what would be affected. Right side, left side, speech center, bladder control."

He purses his thin lips in a show of tough love, and I realize with a start that this is BC's gesture. The Lurker's appropriated it either knowingly or unknowingly. Of course, he's been studying for this mission too.

"Or I could have Tasered you and then used manual restraints—duct tape, ropes, etc. But to my mind, those are always an offense to the dignity of the detainer, as well as the detainee. And what with squirming and straining, the whole mess weakens and is rather easily untied. I'm telling you this so that you appreciate your good fortune. What I have done is as follows. I've used a small, fairly benign neuromuscular device to interrupt signals between your head and your body. It's basically a neuromagnetic pulse. We use the same technology, on the grand scale, to shut down an enemy nation's communications grid before we carpet bomb. Think of your body as Kazakhstan, or Iraq. It is effective and has no harsh side effects. I have no idea what I may eventually need to do with you, but to the extent that I can, I shall always try to have your interests very much at heart."

The Lurker sits back on the couch, and he waves the blonde gallantly into what is apparently her chair, the one I fell over. "Tanya," he tells her, "you can relax. Take a load off your gentle feet. Sal understands that all we want to do is talk and that we won't be allowing her to leave for a bit. And that screaming won't be tolerated, for example, when her voice comes back."

I feel as though my voice may already be back, but I don't test it. Tanya takes a seat and gives me a look as she does so. The look is something like possessiveness, as though she's proud that this is her man and that he's so attentive to her needs.

The Lurker waves a hand toward the blue chair. "Sal, Tanya Jewkes. Tanya, Sal Hayden. And I'm Thomas, no last name necessary. You and I never exchanged names on the Bullet, of course. First there was no good opportunity, and then," he gives an embarrassed little chuckle, "you let me know in no uncertain terms that I was not your type."

Neither Tanya nor I say anything, but she gives me another so-there look. And then I've got it: the look says, *I stole your man*. Maybe she thinks I wish I'd grabbed him when I had a chance, or maybe it's just the fact that he and I are both from another time. But in either case, she's almost triumphant.

And then she does speak. "Your aunt's a really nice lady," she says, "really nice." She glances at Thomas, brushes her hair back from her face. She's trying for graciousness. "She got her own way of seeing things, and her and Tom get into it over the lawn and the skunk in the backyard, but she is a good neighbor. She brings over mail, you know, if it winds up over there by mistake."

Tanya was no doubt built like a brick shithouse when she was fourteen, but now, at early forties or so, she looks not fat so much as wildly overblown. Her arms, her breasts, her hips, all of her seems to be more than her top and jeans can contain, like a Bundt cake that surges out and curls down over the pan. She reminds me of someone from this time period, but I can't quite put my finger on it. She looks exactly like the sort of woman who would be easy pickings for a CIA agent with no conscience.

Then I've got it: she looks like Tonya Harding's older, bigger, dimmer sister.

She goes on: "And she did take a look at my heart when I got a heart flutter, that wasn't all bullshit. Took my blood pressure, and that turned out to be okay. It turned out just to be too much caffeine." There's a pause, as though she's waiting for me to ask about the caffeine. Then she seems to remember that I'm paralyzed and just goes ahead with the explanation. "I was drinking like a twelve-pack of Diet Pepsi every day. I just never thought about that as caffeine, you know, like coffee or something."

"I'd offer you a drink, speaking of which," Thomas says, turning to me and putting the conversation back on track, "but you can't hold the cup."

"Go fuck yourself," I manage. It's an effort, and it comes out thin and breathy because my lungs and my diaphragm won't really work. I have to force it using just my throat muscles.

He ignores me and reaches for the Doritos, says to the woman, "Tanya, would you mind getting me something to drink? And you might pour one for Sal also, and see if you have any straws in the kitchen. If not, could you be sweet and jog to the convenience store for some? She'll need to drink at some point, and I don't think either you or I want to spend the evening tipping the cup for her."

"Where's your wallet?" Tanya says, rising and moving toward the hall. As she turns I can see she has a small tag on the back of the jeans stretched across her butt: *No Excuses*.

"On the bedside table. Why don't you stop at the fish market also? I like the thought of scallops. Get a pound of sea scallops. But try to make sure that they're actually scallops and not trimmed flounder. Don't buy them if the edges look knife-trimmed. And we'll need a pint of heavy cream for the sauce."

From the bedroom, Tanya shouts, "All you got are four fifties!"

"Fine," Thomas shouts back, "take two of those for yourself." He turns to me and rolls his eyes, then raises his voice to add, "You know this is a fifty-fifty operation we have here, love."

A screen door smacks shut at the rear of the house, and Thomas turns to me, heaves a sigh of relief. He's got his puffy arm thrown out casually over the back of the couch. "Tanya is a wonderful woman, but she is long on loyalty and short on"—he brushes artificial nacho-flavor crystals from his fingers—"anything resembling acuity. She's not normally my type, I can assure you. But when I began surveilling your aunt's flat a month or two back, I noticed that Tanya lived alone on this side and seemed to be a good-hearted, think-with-her-gonads sort.

"And not unattractive. Her life before I came was mostly limited to drinking rum and Coke, cashing disability checks, and caring for her sister's two children. Sal," Thomas looks at me seriously, "you have no idea how many women in the world will swear undying loyalty to a man who takes them out faithfully for a prime-rib dinner every Sunday night, lets them pick their favorite dessert afterward. Take it from an unlovely man. They are legion."

Thomas lifts a hand to indicate the half of the duplex he occupies. "So this has become home, over the last seven or eight weeks. Not as bad as some. Mediocre food but plenty of it. A warm bed and a motivated partner. And really very easy surveillance of your aunt's flat. That's the heart of it—I'm shiftless. This situation offered itself like a warm pouch. And here I've waited, snug, like a little kangaroo, like a fat little joey."

"Take this thing off, for Christ's sake," I rasp. "I won't run away."

"I know you won't, because I plan to leave the thing on."

"Please," I hear myself softly pleading. My face is not altogether frozen, but it's numbed to the point where tears won't come. "Please," I say again.

"Pull yourself together, Sal. We have about another two hours before your aunt comes home from the hospital. And in that time you and I need to have a discussion about what exactly your team has on its agenda from here on out."

"You've got the go-to." The sentence finishes without sound, but he seems to understand me well enough.

"Of course, I certainly do. I have your team's operating plan, which has to this moment allowed me to carry out my own overriding set of instructions, mostly surveillance but some other interesting ancillary moves."

My words come out as a whisper. "The go-three."

Thomas chuckles in genuine appreciation, claps his hands. "Go-three, exactly. I quite like that. You are certainly the live wire. You must have livened things up considerably for your group—Mr. Stephanopoulos specifically, of course. You two seem to have formed a very intimate alliance. I wasn't surprised that he would take things in that direction—it was almost certainly part of his individual instructions—but I was surprised that you would"—he glances below my neck at the inert clothing-covered lump that used to be my body—"open yourself up to that sort of manipulation. I wouldn't have thought it."

He's trying to rattle me with the slur on George, and I'm mustering a response when he rolls on: "I know a lot more about your last several weeks than you may think. Mostly what I've been doing is shadowing your team and watching to be sure that none of you deviated significantly from your instructions. That's my central charge, and it comes from the President himself—the President in our day, of course. To oversee your team and watch for signs that you'd adopted your own personal agenda.

"And you haven't. With the major exception, of course, that you've now broken away and gone renegade, which gives me the right—at my discretion—to use lethal force against you. In fact, my instructions suggest that I do so as quickly as possible, to minimize unscripted revisions of the timeline. Obviously I'm stretching those rules.

"Both of our sets of instructions have at heart the same impulse, Sal—to preserve the historical status quo as much as possible, with the distinct exception of preventing the U.S. expansionism, both commercial and military, that touches off our wars early in the next century. For changing history, it's actually a very conservative agenda. To that end, you've been focusing on the young BC and using him as a lever to maneuver the current president. That and a little counterterrorism out Oklahoma way. Your bodyist was slated to pop that little pimple Timothy McVeigh, and I hope she did. He deserved it, richly deserved it."

His face clouds up at the memory of some wrong he's suffered. "Your team has had it easy, I can tell you that. You're dealing mostly with an unappetizing but unfailingly courteous sixteen-year-old with an overdeveloped libido. I, on the other hand, have been dealing with the unrivaled psychotic runt of the world, the humble Ross Perot."

Thomas grimaces, as though he can't get the taste out of his mouth. Even with a muscle-deadening disc on my back and an armed CIA assassin sitting on the couch beside me, Perot's name manages to get my attention. My eyebrows lift, and Thomas chortles and nods. "Yes, that's right. Mr. burr-headed Texan. Mr. I'm-Ross-and-you're-the-boss. Mr. I'm-not-gonna-slow-dance-with-ya." He enunciates the words *gonna* and *ya* with careful disdain. "Pie charts, vulgar phraseology, giant sucking sounds, and all the rest of his drivel. Patsy Cline wailing unsteadily over the PA system.

"Perot's run in 1992 was on target to steal the election from both the major parties, which, I might point out, speaks volumes about the dimwittedness of the American electorate. His pullout from and eventual return to the campaign eventually soured the public on him. They began calling him a coward and a yellow-belly. And you may remember that his stated reason for this erratic behavior was the intervention of some Republican dirty tricks squad. Some potboiled story about obscene lesbian photos of his daughter or some such."

Thomas waits for a response, and I nod slightly. I keep expecting my feet or my hands to tingle into awareness. But they don't. My body doesn't exist.

"Well, as the Storyboard group began looking into BC's career and the offshoot possibilities, they isolated the good Ross as the dark horse for changing the entire story line. He drew twenty percent of the popular vote, you'll remember."

"Nineteen," I whisper.

"Quite right. Ever the BC loyalist. The Storyboarders were uncomfortable with Perot's decision to drop out of the election. Even FBI deep documents could come up with no firm explanation, although an investigation was conducted following Perot's claim. They began to consider the idea of having their surveillance unit—me—move from 1963 to 1991, to keep a weather eye on—well, let's simply call him the runt.

"And this led them—inexorably, really—to the notion that their own surveillance man might well be the original provocateur who dissuaded the runt from running. So eventually they ordered it, and so it proved. It was a hellish year, traipsing all over the godforsaken state of Texas and pretending to be various sorts of individuals, but I succeeded. I came, I saw, the runt withdrew. And even his most loyal supporters called him a coward."

He looks plump and pleased for a moment, and then he taps my knee with the index finger. "Wait here," he says, without seeming to mean it as a sick joke, and then he disappears toward the bedroom. He reappears almost instantly, though, as if he's pulled something off a shelf in the hallway. It's a small plastic statuette, and when he's seated again, he brings it right up to my face so I can appreciate it. There's no mistaking that it's Ross Perot's face and glasses and Dumbo ears, but he's wearing a yellow gingham dress and yellow patent-leather shoes. The base reads *The Yellow Ross of Texas.*

Thomas looks down at it fondly. "The Yellow Ross of Texas. It was a brilliant bit of wordplay." He burnishes the toy's plastic head, picks at a bit of paint peeling from the glasses. "I picked it up in the parking lot of one of Perot's last fairly large rallies. By that time, even his rallies were full of people who thought he was a fruitcake. And while most of that was his own doing, the pullout from the race was mine. I had a great deal of compromising information that the FBI dug up after Perot's death.

"That was really all I had to do—confront him with the unseemly stuff of his own obituary. It was the high point of this whole odd mission. And then, you know, the last three years have been comfortable but fairly tedious."

Thomas looks around the duplex, at the sentimental paintings of unicorns and flower-filled fields, the cheap rattan furniture, the oddly extravagant wide-screen television. He bounces his fist lightly on the cushion next to him.

"Some things are good here, better than our time," he confides, a hint of kinship kindling in his voice, "like television. Television may not be surround-style or even high-definition now, but it's better, all the same. There's a fresh, mindless quality to it, an innocence. Television of our day is all run through the wringer of art; every producer's focusing somewhere in his mind on what the critics will say.

"Not now. Now it's just plugged directly into the medulla, pleasure, laughs, tears. Wonderful. I watch *Baywatch,* which is a show about gorgeous men and women patrolling a beach. I watch *NYPD Blue* and I'm wired to my seat. I have cried, several times, watching *The Simpsons,* a truly wonderful and acidic cartoon, but occasionally they play to the heart and catch you napping and," he titters again, helplessly, "you cry. You can't help but cry."

"But why are you here, living here?" I have a better handle on speaking now. I have to draw a slow, long breath and then use it to power each half-sentence. So I boil it down to what really matters. "Why my aunt?"

Thomas brushes his hair back, and he smiles just a bit before speaking. I have the same sense that I had originally on the Bullet, that he knows I'm repulsed by him but somehow for him that doesn't quite constitute rejection. He's still trying to be winning in spite of it all. "A fair question," he allows. "Burlington is nice, but it isn't exactly gay Paree."

He laces his fingers and puts on a look of serious contemplation. "Once Perot had dropped from the race, clearly I needed to disappear as quickly as possible. The 1992 FBI would be looking for me, and of course Ross would have three or four of his ubiquitous private dicks out on the hunt for me.

So I spent a while in Southern California in a little mobile-home park in Costa Mesa. Lovely place, really.

"End of last year, I was to slowly close out my life there and put myself in a position to pick your detail up in Junction City and shadow you on through to the White House and then your eventual exit from this timeline. But I did not do that. Oh, I did some monitoring, but on my own terms. I understood the composition of your team well enough to know that you were the only real renegade threat. And I also guessed, very accurately, that if you did drop out you would likely choose Canada, since you knew it, as one who grew up in northern Vermont. And you would also likely try to meet with your aunt preparatory to doing so. So you could argue that coming here the month before last was a good way to continue to do the job I'd been assigned.

"But the unvarnished truth is that the three years I spent out there on the beach in Costa Mesa gave me a great deal of time to think. The sort of thinking required, as Blake would put it, to see things as they truly are. That's what good weather three hundred twenty-five days of the year will do for you. It will allow you to string some very long thoughts together.

"And I decided that the revision of the timeline that you and I were assigned to effect was by definition a self-interested revision. Obviously the leaders of our day wished to preserve their own power and the history that led them to acquire it—what they wanted to change were the military facts-on-the-ground that suddenly threatened that power. And for this reason, they preferred a very narrow, very conservative plan for revision."

Suddenly I see where he's going with this. It's not so different from the brief-back we had in Virginia. *Orbital insubordination,* Carville called it then.

Thomas's voice continues thoughtfully. "Here I was with the knowledge of future history. Here I was with power over *anyone* in this time frame, by virtue of that knowledge. I drove a billionaire out of a winning race for the White House with a phone call and one oversize manila envelope. And here I was with power even over you four, the authority to terminate any of you as I saw fit.

"Some people handed that sort of unmeasurable power," he demonstrates with the dorky little Perot statuette, "hand it back. It wasn't mine to begin with, they think, as though *anything* is anyone's to begin with. Others take the power for themselves but can't do what's necessary to hold it. My time in my little mobile home by the beach convinced me that I am neither of these sorts of people." He wraps his fingers dramatically around Perot's head, thumb nestled in one giant ear.

"I am the sort of person who uses that power to make himself independent of small minds and smaller characters. You wouldn't believe, Sal, the genuinely stunted individuals I've reported to for years in the intelligence community, for *years*. Really appallingly dim-witted individuals. No more of that. No more living as a glorified nine-to-five employee. I will acquire enough influence and money to live very, very, very well, in higher style even than the dot-com robber barons at their peak, but also influence enough to make myself something . . . well, something historically significant. Do you know anything of George Soros, a financier in this time frame? Quite a brilliant man, really, just filthy rich and capable of accomplishing more than most governments, but limited of course by normal fluctuations in world markets and such. I'm not so limited. I'm Soros with next year's stock roundup in his hip pocket. And what I realized in my beach house is that I would simply like for the world to become, slowly but surely, a more Thomas-friendly environment. I'd like to have a much stronger hand in writing the rules.

"Once I understood that, the rest followed fairly logically." He starts ticking them off on his other hand, one by one, another gesture filched from BC. "One, your mission must be allowed to succeed—the Cigarette Wars must never start. I don't really care two figs for the U.S.—don't even care one fig for it—but it will be my home from here on out, and I'd prefer that it not be overrun by either Eastern Alliance or unwashed militia types. Two, I have to be certain that all of you exit this timeline. Three, I have to miss my own rendezvous for return, as well as the fallback rendezvous next week and the week following. Four, once I am the only one of us left in the here and now, I need to find a way to prevent other incursions from our timeline to this—to be certain that I single-author any further historical revisions."

Thomas pauses and tries to read the reaction on my face, which, since I can't move my neck, involves him leaning over and in toward my eyes. There isn't much there to see, but he goes on anyway. "Another reason I've immobilized you instead of executing you in a perfectly legal fashion is that I'm hoping you'll check my reasoning on all of this."

Of course, I think. *He wants me to check his story line.*

That's been my function through this whole rancid affair, ever since Carville came choppering into Little Rock with a swarm of Berets: script consultant. It turns out that that's what my life is valued at, ultimately. That's why I'm not dead already.

I pull in a long breath, slowly filling lungs I can't feel.

"Fuck you, you"—another long pull of air—"megalomaniacal lurking bastard, you."

Thomas smiles and then leans over to retrieve a pack of cigarettes from the far arm of the couch. The pack is brilliant red, and I don't need to see the lettering to know that it's a Marlboro package—for the years of the Wars, the classic Marlboro pack has taken on the iconic significance of Rosie the Riveter. Thomas no doubt tossed his Eastwoods as soon as he hit the nineties and could get his hands on the real thing.

He pulls out a childproofed miniature Bic lighter and fires one up. "Only in the nineties," he remarks, looking curiously at the lighter before returning it to the arm of the couch. "Make a lighter in the shape of a toy and then childproof it. The heyday of the mixed message."

Outside I can hear the sound of a car door shutting, and Thomas stiffens, then goes to the window to peer out. Satisfied, he returns to the couch. "I take it from your outburst that you'd rather not help me fine-tune my own set of revisions, then."

I give a slow nod.

"I thought you might rather not. And what can I do to you? Slice off your toes? In the state you're in, it would be as though you were watching television. The Sal Amputates Her Toes Show."

I'm hoping he's working himself up to letting me go. So I say nothing.

"I can't punish you very effectively. So I'll pay you."

"Let me go."

"Sal, you have a one-track mind."

"Let me go. And I'll help."

"We'll approach that question later. For now you're going nowhere. But I can offer you something. I can let you see your aunt. She'll be home at about four from the hospital."

"Talk to her. I have to talk."

"See, Sal. See only. She parks her car across the street, near yours, and then she goes inside. I'll let you have a good long look. Twenty minutes. That's the deal."

I'm silent. I can hear the sound of kids playing on Big Wheels in the street. It's funny how having your options reduced to nothing clarifies your thinking.

I'm thinking that maybe, if I watch her out the window long enough, she'll turn quickly and see my face, recognize me somehow. Call 911, or whatever you do in the nineties when you see something evil in the apartment next door.

"Thirty," I say.

Thomas drags deeply, shoots smoke from his nostrils. "Twenty. And this is not a negotiation, Sal. You're effectively paralyzed, but I can bring this cigarette up to the white of your eye, until the humor begins to boil, and get what I want that way too."

Twenty minutes it is, then. I nod.

His ruddy face looks pleased as punch. "So I'll run down my story line and you'll offer critiques based on your understanding of the potential historical disruptions. We understand each other."

I nod again.

"And this new story, this somewhat collaborative story, I will think of forever after," Thomas says, patting my knee and leaving his hand there a second or two longer than necessary, as though he's probably feeling it rather than just patting it, "as our go-four."

Thomas's go-four centers, it turns out, on Bob Dole. Robert Joseph Dole, currently Senate majority leader, and BC's grim opponent in next year's election. Bob Dole, once Nixon's Doberman pinscher. Darth Vader to Newt Gingrich's Evil Emperor. The man who has insisted loudly and at some length in every one of the many campaigns he's run that he will never talk about his war wounds to get votes. The Robert Dole whose hunger for the White House is so open and undisguised that in about three months he will stand in front of a Republican National Committee meeting in Philadelphia and say, "I understand the yearning for another Ronald Reagan, and if that's what you want, I'll be another Ronald Reagan."

That Robert Dole.

Thomas feels that Dole is underestimated as presidential timber. And that BC's second term will be a hopeless waste of time in any event. "What was it, really?" he says, his voice rising in amazement. "What was it but a series of legal defenses punctuated by hum jobs and budget agreements? Making the world safe from BC's second term is the strongest argument for what I'm designing. What was it but the spectacle of a weak man finally drowning in his own lies, a man dragged reluctantly to shore by voters too terrified of his enemies to let him die?"

"CHIP," I whisper.

"Chip what?"

"Children's Health Insurance Program." I pull in more air. "Biggest expansion of health care. Since LBJ."

"I'm not saying the four years were utter darkness."

"Conservation."

"Of course. You feel the need to defend him."

"Most land protected. Lower forty-eight states. Any president. Period."

"I'll have to insist that you shut up now." Thomas waves his hand to shush me. "The room is beginning to take on the sporty reek of soccer mom."

What Thomas has in mind specifically is a variation on one of the ideas the Storyboard people originally mocked up: using a huge campaign donation to buy access. In this case, however, Thomas is planning to use the side door rather than the front—his donation will be made to the Red Cross, the only thing Liddy Dole is president of in 1995. During one of their donor courtship meetings, he plans to hand her a small document. The document will contain an exact transcript of Dole's first debate with BC in 1996, both questions and answers.

Thomas will tell Dole's wife that she is holding advance knowledge of future events. She will not believe him, but he will be a six-figure donor and she will be polite about his eccentric behavior.

As Thomas figures it, she will keep the transcript and say nothing, until the first debate is over. And then, with her husband eternally twelve points down in the polls and with mid-October closing in, she will eventually call Thomas's Burlington number.

"You don't know these people," Thomas insists, waving his hands. "They're absolutely obsessed with the Oval Office. It's hard to know who's more compulsive about it, him with the withered arm and the survivor's fury, or her, the born-again debutante, all steel and no magnolia. Both of them have allowed themselves no life but the marathon of career politics. Now they've made it twenty-five and a half miles and they're only today sensing that they don't have it in them to finish. And I will happen by just as they're about to collapse in defeat and offer to drive them over the finish line."

From that point the go-four gets a little more fluid. Thomas has with him copies of period documents that he believes could force BC out of office, or at least put his poll numbers in a meltdown. He won't tell me exactly what they are, but he assures me they are kryptonite.

If Dole himself won't bite, or if he does and BC still somehow sneaks into a second term, Thomas plans to turn his attentions to Liddy. She is slated to become president herself as it is, but Thomas would set about making himself indispensable. Not for the first time on this trip I find myself wondering if Thomas's planned intervention is not a revision but simply the way things were the first time around. Like George becoming Carville, not a pretend Carville but the real person. Maybe Thomas is what has always allowed Liddy Dole to become the first female president of the United States.

But whomever he helps put in the White House will owe Thomas favors. And one of these will be to shutter the Maopi project recently begun in an out-of-the-way corner of Nevada, no questions asked.

What will Bob Dole care about shutting down an energy-research facility?

This is a man who would close down every emergency room in the lower forty-eight states if that's what he thought it would take to put himself on Air Force One.

I try my best to tell Thomas about the computer modeling that Carville and George did back at the military complex, how eliminating BC produced a tsunami of change large enough to wipe out the world of our time altogether. But Thomas doesn't seem deterred in the least. He doesn't plan to live there anymore anyway.

38

FINAL REVISIONS

I'm watching television now. The wide-screen in Thomas and Tanya's living room shows a woman in a nurse's uniform sitting on a couch in her own living room, watching her own television. Thomas is in the kitchen, apparently making scallops in some sort of cream sauce. Tanya is seated on the opposite end of the sofa, also watching the wide-screen.

This is my reward for cooperating on the go-four. The nurse on TV is my aunt. She got home from the hospital about fifteen minutes ago. That was when Thomas revealed that over the last month he's drilled six tiny holes in the walls and ceiling of my aunt Mary's apartment, and these six holes he's threaded with receptive fiber-optic filament. My million-to-one shot, that Mary would see me in the window, was never even a million-to-one. Thomas was never planning to let me near the window.

He's FAB'ed my aunt, basically, and there isn't the slightest thing I can do about it.

So far Tanya and I have watched Mary take her shoes off, check her phone messages, and watch *The Ricki Lake Show*. My protests that I didn't want to see her this way Thomas ignored. The sight of Mary alive, and young, is staggering. I can feel a horrible tearing feeling across my heart, with the longing to have her see me, hear me, the longing to run to her.

Tanya watches now without a trace of self-consciousness, sipping a microbrew that she brought back from the store earlier. She offered to pour me one and give me a long straw, but I declined. As she watches, she's eating cheese-covered popcorn and telling me about how she learned that Thomas was from the future.

"We were watching the Grammys. It was like one of our first real sort of dates. I mean, Thomas was just sleeping over then, not living here. And I said, let's bet a buck on who wins Best New Artist, and we both picked Sheryl Crow because she's a fuckin' goddess and she had that huge hit single. And then Thomas just keeps going. He's like, Bruce Springsteen, and Springsteen wins for Song of the Year. And then he's like, you know," she giggles and shivers a little at the memory, "picking Babyface and all the rest of them, bing bing bing. And he goes, I'm from the future, you know. Didn't you know I know everything that's goin' to happen? And I said I know you *think* you know everything. But inside I'm thinking, right, he must have some friend who works for the Grammys or somethin' like that, you know.

"Then, couple weeks later—and this was after we were moved in together—same thing, we're watching Academy Awards and Thomas says, If I predict all the winners will you believe I'm from the future and I'm here to make you queen of the world with me? And he's looking at me, like, *fuck!* I can't even explain it. He's looking at me just so serious.

"And so I go, yeah, I'll believe you. So he takes out paper and pencil and he writes down the ten big winners. And I look at the list, and he's got Nicolas Cage for *Leaving Las Vegas,* and I started cracking up because that movie was depressing, and, I mean, it's not like he's the great actor of the world. But so, sure enough, it turns out he wins and all the other ones too."

She's holding her bottle, and her eyes are shining. It's obvious that Thomas, good or evil, is something big, and she's never gotten a firm grip on anything big in her life. "And Thomas said we had a lot of work to do, and some of it was gonna be scary, or seem bad, like rigging up your aunt's place with the camera wires. But we needed to do it to get history where it needed to be.

"And it seems like every time I find myself thinking that I'm nuts to think this is all real, Thomas comes out to breakfast and tells me something huge that's gonna happen the next day, or next month. Couple of days ago he told me Superman's gonna get paralyzed next month, Christopher Reeve's gonna have a horse riding accident and break his spine. I started bawling, *big* time. I love Christopher Reeve. But Thomas was like, don't worry, he never walks again but he goes on and does work on getting a cure and keeps on acting and everybody in the world looks at him like this symbol of hope. That's the great thing. Thomas tells me something like that about what's gonna happen to Christopher Reeve and I get all freaked out and sad, and then he tells me how it comes out in the end. Being with Thomas is the first time I ever felt like I could really trust a man to tell me what was what."

She goes back to nibbling popcorn and washes it down with a sip of beer. My aunt gets up from her couch and walks out of frame. Tanya touches the remote control, and the screen picks Mary up in the kitchen, looking over cans of soup in the cupboard above her stove. We sit in silence. My aunt's life doesn't seem to be Tanya's favorite show, but she seems comfortable with it. The plot may be listless and the production values low, but at least she knows the characters.

I don't eat anything for dinner. Tanya comes out from the kitchen with a plate of spaghetti covered with thick cream-colored lumps. She offers to feed me, and I tell her, with much pulling in of breath, that instead she can kiss my ass. For a second she looks down on me like she's about to say something cruel or cuff me. But then she says in a low voice, "He's gonna cut you loose tomorrow. After he asks you some more questions. So don't get all bent out of shape."

She returns to the kitchen, and the two of them eat in silence, more or less. I can hear the kiss of bottles on glass occasionally, and I don't doubt that they're celebrating in their own way.

When they're done, they come into the living room and, like a little family home on a Thursday night, we watch a sitcom called *Seinfeld,* and then Thomas switches to the closed-circuit channel and we're watching not only my aunt but my father. He looks to be about eighteen or nineteen here, a baseball cap turned around backward with the brim bent around into a shape like a beak. He's wearing a baseball jersey, and I remember that he's a catcher now, for a minor league team in town.

My father, Ron, is arguing with Mary over something. There is no sound to the closed-circuit, thank God, but it's clear that Ron has pushed his luck with Mary again. He looks like a layabout, even viewed from above via fiber optics. When he takes off the cap, his hair is sweaty, mashed down close to his head. And as my aunt yells at him, he sips a beer, her beer, sitting on her couch. He seems to be clearly without even the faint traces of responsibility he'll show later in life, after his stint in prison. What my mother will see in him I don't know. My mother is about fifteen now, still living somewhere in central Texas. She won't move to Burlington for another four or five years, when her father relocates to work for IBM. Most likely my father will strike her as athletic and happy-go-lucky, someone to charm a carefree existence into being.

We switch around, from Ron and Mary to a medical drama called *Chicago Hope*, to CNN, and back around, in a lazy rondolet, to Mary and Ron. My father is now stealing scotch from a bottle my aunt apparently keeps hidden from him in her pantry. The last we see of him, he is seated on Mary's couch, drinking her scotch and smoking a cigarette.

When television time is over, Thomas and Tanya carry me down the narrow hallway, Thomas with his fat arms linked around my waist and Tanya carrying my legs.

They put me in a small room at the back of the apartment, what would be a guest bedroom if it weren't also filled with bags and boxes. Some of the bags are full of plastic recyclables, and some of the boxes are full of beer bottles. Thomas kicks a path to the single bed in the corner and they lay me on it.

Tanya takes off my shoes, and Thomas says, "I hope you sleep well, but if you don't you might give some more thought to the changes we talked about today. I'm hoping we can finish them by lunch tomorrow. Then we'll think about what's best for you, right?"

They go out, shutting the door. And Tanya cracks the door a bit, so that a thin shaft of hall light finds its way into the dark room. I want to cry from the weight on my chest, and my heart, but I still can't. I force myself to take long, deep breaths. I run my eyes over the darkened room, check my muscles again to find them still absent. With the lights out, it feels like I'm floating bodiless in deep space.

Something about Tanya's last gesture starts me thinking again of my parents, my little family. And what I'm thinking is that I'm destined, somehow, never to know them, not really. The first time around, my mother and my aunt died one after the other, and my father responded to his new responsibility by heading out for the islands. This second time around, things are no different: I'm separate from them all; nothing I do can bring me into real contact. My aunt and my father are alive now and sleeping somewhere about thirty-five feet away from me, and there is nothing I can do to bring any of us any closer.

I feel this certainty, deep inside, that if I were to work the light-particle trick again and show up five years from now, or ten, it would always be the same. Some people, and I'm one of them, aren't meant to know their parents or the little family they have. BC is one of them too, at least as regards his father, or fathers: just as soon as his mother would bring one into the family, the process of losing the man would begin.

I see now that my career focus on BC is only partly serendipity. It's also partly a feeling of deep, deep kinship. Both of us children of absent fathers, both of us sent scouring the world for people and projects big enough to fill the gap. In my case, biographies, the desperate gathering of facts and stories and documents that slowly begin to fill the absence, suggest a person; in BC's case, a bottomless desire for reassurance by the electorate, again to fill the absence. It's no accident that I grew up to write a biography of BC, and it's no accident that I am the only biographer of many he will choose to authorize. We recognized each other.

I wonder if that's part of the reason why BC and I wound up temporally tangled the way we are, multiple versions of me and multiple versions of him occupying mutually multiple versions of our interlocking histories. We make sense, if you're going to choose people to send looping back through the stuff of their own lives. Neither of us really sticks to what we touch.

There's a noise like a digital alarm clock, a soft but piercing chirp. *I'm late for work,* I think for no good reason, and then the door to the room bangs open and Thomas strides heavily through the darkness to my bedside. He snaps the bedside light on without saying anything, then pushes me onto my side and begins reaching under my shirt.

I can't scream, but adrenaline gives me the lung power to cry out.

"Oh, shut it. You're not being raped, you twit," Thomas whispers fiercely as his fingers find the edges of the tape he used to secure the pulse disc to my back. He pulls part of the tape back, then begins to work with barely controlled frustration on the metal works beneath it. "We need your body back, which should please you. The disc has to come off, and quickly, so just don't move a centimeter while I pull its teeth. Don't jog my hand or you could wind up in a wheelchair. And when your muscles come back, don't try to run or strike me. You'll be unable to do either with any effectiveness for an hour or so, and if you try anyway, I'll take your head in both hands and twist your neck until it breaks."

He works for another second, cursing. His breath is coming in short little snorts.

"What's going on?" I whisper.

"What's going *on*," Thomas repeats in a mocking voice. "Take one fucking guess. A couple of your friends are now in the greater Burlington area."

"How do you know?"

Suddenly the rough outline of my body, the tactile sense of where I am in space, jumps back into place. "Oh, thank Christ," I burst out without thinking. My eyes begin to tear. I'm still very numb and can't quite move, but when Thomas rips the rest of the tape from my back I can tell that it's my back it's been ripped from.

"I know," Thomas says, and I can see that what I took for frustration is almost boiling anger, "because the alarm that just went off tells me that two of their three worms just passed close enough for my system to begin tracking data streams. I would guess, as with you, that this means they are now circling to land at the airport. Which gives us about forty minutes before we might expect to see them crashing the party." He's still down on his haunches, and he takes my calf in one hand and squeezes hard. "Can you feel that?"

I can, and the sensation is so sudden that it's overpowering. It leaves my leg feeling twitchy, full of pins and needles. "For Christ's sake, let me—"

"Shut it. Can you feel my hand?"

"*Yes.* Yes, I can feel it."

He reaches under my back and heaves me to a sitting position, but I have no sense of balance and I still can't feel my torso or my back muscles, and I slip off to one side out of his arm. He pulls me back up roughly. Suddenly, he slaps me quickly across the face. Then he takes my hair and brings my head around to face him.

"Now, listen," he tells me in a whisper, and with it comes the sour, beery smell of his breath, "if you can't move in three minutes, you're no use to me. You understand that. We need to be on the interstate to Montreal by the time they find this house. We'll cross the border and find a place to stay for a bit. Once we've finished our planning sessions, I can let you loose north of the border. You take Canada, I'll take the U.S.A. Spheres of influence, as they used to say."

I know without needing to think about it that this is not true. None of the plans he's laid out for me involve anyone else from our time frame remaining alive in this time frame. He'll kill me there and then make his way back to the States. The mention of Carville and Virginia has started me praying for them, but I know they're too far away, and I can't hold things here long enough. But I try. "They'll stop us at the border," I say. My voice is coming back now.

Thomas is still leaning over me. "Why?"

"My name is the same as my aunt's, on our licenses. And in the early nineties she had a drunk-driving conviction."

"Drunk driving." This stops him. He knows how hysterical the nineties are about substance abuse.

"The Canadians won't let you over the border with that on your record; they detain you at the border. It's happened to me almost every time I've tried to cross, even in our time."

Thomas sits back on his haunches, gives me a long look. In the light from the bedside lamp, I can see the piggish folds of skin beneath his eyes and the vast tracery of broken blood vessels in his nose and cheeks. And then he smiles quickly. "You're a poolroom liar, Sal. Sal is for Salswick, which is a family name from your mother's side, as I remember. I find it hard to believe your aunt would be named after your future mother."

I can't say anything to that, and when I don't Thomas suddenly slaps me across the face again, and I fall back onto the bed. My head is ringing, blood pounding in my cheek, my temple.

He's looming over me. "Just try that again, Sal, just try playing me that way," he's saying, and then there's a noise in the hallway, and without warning the door bursts open, and standing in it is yBC.

I don't know why—the adrenaline, or maybe the deep effects of the paralysis—but this instant slows down and I see all of us from a drifting point of view above myself, above us all. I see it through some dizzy combination of memory and hyperawareness of the present instant, through what I can only call frame-by-frame déjà vu: Thomas rearing over me, paunchy and still half-drunk, meaty hand raised to yank me from the bed; me still nearly paralyzed, cheek throbbing, lying across the thin coverlet;

and yBC, having heard the fighting, now standing in the doorway, big for his age, face working with repulsion and fear and righteous anger. He's about to speak, about to halt this madness with his words, and again I realize I know the words before they leave his lips.

This is the scene—one of many scenes but the most important of all—that BC used to explain himself to the electorate in 1992. This is the story of how BC as a young boy burst into his parents' room and saved his mother from an abusive, alcoholic stepfather. The story of BC warning his stepfather never, ever to hit his mother again. The story that made BC the candidate seem morally far above and socially far below the average voter. The story that made it okay to love him. Somehow it's playing out again, and I'm in it. I'm the mother who wants desperately to leave but can't, who can't get away from the abuser.

yBC speaks and time surges forward again. "Get away from her, and don't you touch her again!"

Thomas looks stunned. He hadn't expected anyone so soon, but least of all yBC.

"You big coward, get away from her! You heard me, get away!"

Somehow Thomas now holds a weapon in his hand. It's not the Taser from yesterday; it's slimmer, deadlier looking. He must have had it in his pants pocket. But he seems hesitant to use it, stymied. And then I know: he has no idea what will die if he kills yBC.

"You wanna hit her again, you're gonna have to hit me first."

Then they come crashing together: yBC walks into the room and Thomas lunges at him. Although the kid is tall and fairly well-muscled for his age, it's not really a fight. They trade a few glancing blows, one catching Thomas in the neck, making him grunt and bull forward, arms pummeling. The pistol-thing is lost somewhere in this, but I don't see where it falls. The kid's bravado breaks and finally he throws his arms up to his face to protect himself. Thomas finally wraps his big arm around yBC's neck and then turns and flings the boy, like throwing the hammer, against the far wall of the room. He stands for a second, waiting for the kid to surge to his feet again, but the kid doesn't.

And that's when I land on him myself.

I've managed, not to walk, because I can't feel much below my waist, but to lock my right leg in place. And pushing myself forward as hard as I can with my arms, I use that leg like a pole to vault me forward, off the bed and onto Thomas's back. My hands and my arms are almost normal, and I lock them around his neck, digging my nails into the sagging flesh of his jowls.

I can hear myself screaming: "Leave him alone! Leave him alone!"

Thomas howls in pain and twists around, reaching frantically for me, pawing for me, but I'm powered by almost a day of wanting desperately to do just this, to have the muscles to do just this, and I hold on like an insane woman, beating him, tearing at him.

He swings back wildly the other way, and I feel my torso pivot and my lower body swing with his move. That part of me is still just dead weight, but it doesn't matter; the momentum doesn't break my hold. Here, being a small woman works in my favor. He swings me like a rag doll, and my hand works its way slowly around the side of his head to his face, and my fingers find his eye, I stab with my nail, and now the howl of pain is a roar.

Finally, he digs his fingers in between my wrist and his neck and he quickly unwinds my arm, sending me crashing onto the floor.

But most of the fall doesn't affect me. My lower body can't really feel it except as dull force, and I grab for his ankle with both hands and pull, sending him heaving to the floor.

It's the end of what I can do. On the floor I can't maneuver the dead weight of my lower body, and Thomas scrambles up, and when he does he brings his shoe crashing down on my right hand. I feel and hear the bones break at the same instant. The pain washes through me, almost making me black out.

I'm just barely aware that he's found the pistol-thing and is standing over me, when a hair-thin ray of sapphire-colored light shoots through the window over the bed and strikes Thomas's forehead just below the meringue line of his hair. As the light strikes him, there is a sound like the spit of escaping steam, and a tiny dark cloud jets from the back of his head. It's not like gunfire. It's more like laser surgery. The cloud, I realize, is blood and brain, atomized like perfume.

For a moment Thomas is clearly dead but still nearly unmarked. There's only a pinprick of red on the bland expanse of his forehead.

And then time and gravity reassert themselves. Thomas's body collapses against the far wall. The fineness of the entry and exit wounds has the blood under pressure, and it begins to spray rather than well. It's weird: watching his blood escape softly into the air is like watching the credits of a really, really god-awful movie. You sit through them to the very end not because you care in any way about the information but to assure yourself, once and for all, that there isn't any more of this horrible thing.

There's a tapping at the window, and I look up. It's dark out there, but in the light cast by the bedside lamp I can see a bald man in what looks like a white T-shirt. He's got high cheekbones and narrow cat's eyes.

It's a face I've seen before, thousands of times. My first thought is that it's the real James Carville. My second is that it's my George Stephanopoulos. The third thought is that it's really both.

39

GHOSTS IN THE STREAM

Within a half hour, all of us are gathered in the living room, all of us: the man I know as James Carville, George/Carville, Virginia, yBC, who seems bruised but otherwise all right, and myself. Virginia's given me some sort of battlefield painkillers and wrapped my hand around a tennis ball to hold it steady.

I'm literally feeling no pain.

The two bedrooms each hold a dead person. It turns out that Thomas killed Tanya with an injection in her sleep sometime before he woke me. Unexpectedly, a pang goes through me when I hear this. Tanya didn't want anything but to be Queen of the World, and she was worth ten of Thomas.

It also turns out, according to Virginia, that Thomas had wired the gas furnace in the basement of the duplex to ignite about the time our car was reaching the Canadian border. It was a textbook CIA job, Virginia says, one that would be virtually indistinguishable from an accidental breach-and-ignition scenario. In this way, the duplex, Tanya, my father, and my aunt would all be eliminated at once.

Carville picks up on this last point. "Now, this is really fascinating. He clearly decided to expunge you from the time stream by taking out your father. Yet he needs you, that's why he's got you along in the car to Montreal. I mean, for all he knows, the duplex goes up, your father buys the farm, and you pop out of existence. Then where is he? But clearly, see, he had a theory, that you'd continue on in your current form as a kind of residual embodiment. Kind of a ghost in the time stream, until the you sitting here now died somehow, when there would no longer be any Sal of any kind anywhere. See what I mean? I mean, that's fascinating to me."

George is sitting on the sofa beside yBC. Although he looks exactly like the pictures I've seen all my life of the real James Carville—although he now actually is the real James Carville—I can't help but refer to him in my mind as George. George is now in his late fifties, of course, and his accent is pure Louisiana bayou. "Goddammit, James," George says, "these people've been through a goddamn trauma here. They don't need some kind of half-assed philosophy lesson."

"You all think there's any food in the kitchen?" yBC asks sheepishly. "We haven't eaten anything really since Kansas. I mean, we had that snack on the plane, but that wa'nt like a meal or anything. You think I could look?"

"Sure," Carville snaps, "why don't you go ask the dead guy and his woman if they'd like a chicken leg too, while you're at it."

Virginia leans forward and makes it a non-issue. She's in her favorite cargo pants and camouflage T-shirt. She has the air of somebody with an entire Thanksgiving dinner to cook. "Look, we've got two dead people and a future president in this apartment. That's not good. Everybody needs to be out of here in five minutes or less, except for me."

I look over at her and watch as she pulls surgical gloves from a pouch down the leg of the pants. "You're staying by yourself?" I ask her.

"I'll make my own way back to D.C. later today."

"She's the bodyist, Sal," Carville reminds me. "It's called professionalism."

"Shut up, Carville," Virginia says, pointedly not looking at Carville. "What it's called is you guys have no idea what's involved with sterilizing the site and dumping the corpses. You'd be lumbering around the house spraying DNA markers over everything. And what it's also called is once we get back from this trip I retire on full pay, plus bennies, plus a little less than a century of back combat pay. And then somebody can attend to my body for a while."

She stands and punches a gloved fist into her hand, then reverses the process, seating the gloves. "All I need before you guys take off is for somebody to make sure both those people's eyes are closed, because I *totally* hate that shit."

As we're all standing, it hits me. I haven't seen my aunt. Or my father for that matter, but seeing Mary is the important part. "I have to go see my aunt before we leave."

Carville shakes his head. "Don't even think it. You're AWOL right at this minute. We didn't come all the way to godforsaken Vermont to allow you to make unscripted contact with near relatives who might be adversely affected by the contact. We came here to contain you."

"Look," I say, searching all of their faces, "my aunt *dies,* okay? Of breast cancer. When I'm just a young girl. And it fucked up my entire—my entire life. I have to see her. I'm not leaving until I see her."

"You try to go into that apartment and alert those people to our presence, and we will terminate you. I don't give a shit if we just prevented your termination. We will do it."

"I'm staying. I'm speaking with her."

"Sal, there's two corpses here. Don't make Virginia lug a third. I don't have time for this. I got a pubescent president I have to deliver to D.C. Then I have to smuggle him into the White House so he can help convince his older self not to launch World Wars Three, Four, and Five. Then I have to get him back to 1963, so he can press the flesh with JFK. Don't complicate my life unnecessarily."

It lasts five or ten minutes, the argument, but it's finally George who makes the argument that allows me to let it go. "Sal," he says, pulling me to one side, "do you want your aunt to remember you as you were—as you're gonna be, I mean—little girl to grown girl, or do you want your aunt to remember you as a woman in trouble with the law and involved with some really shady things like her neighbor's disappearance?

"Think about it. If you go see her now, every single time she ever looks at you you're gonna be a girl in trouble and she's gonna want to prevent that with every fiber of her being and she's gonna know she can't. It'll mean you and she'll never have a carefree moment together, not one."

It draws me up short; I can't think of anything to say, except how much I still want to do it. But I don't. I get the first inkling that I'll fly away now without seeing her, and that there's no way to change that, not for the better, anyway.

"Pretty goddamn persuasive," I manage after a minute.

George gives me a little grin. "You try writing attack ads twenty-four/seven for a couple years and you better believe you're gonna be a whole lot of persuasive 'fore you're done."

But I still can't quite let it go. I make one last try. I turn to Carville. "I can ring the doorbell and say my car's broken down and I need to use the phone. I won't tell her who I am. Can I do that?"

"No," Carville says.

We're on our way to the airport in Carville's glossy-black rented Lincoln Town Car. When I point out that my rented Taurus is still parked at the curb, Carville gives a dismissive snort. "Don't second-guess the bodyist," he says.

I've got George on one side, and yBC on the other, and they're telling me about how they got to the duplex first. George's voice is authentic Cajun as far as I can tell; he's done a miracle of remaking himself, losing his Massachusetts accent over these last thirty years. Listening to him is almost like listening to someone do an imitation of the real James Carville, but, then, the real James Carville's voice always had an unbelievable quality to it. "See, the four of us started trackin' you almost as soon as you went AWOL in Kansas. Carville called me in D.C. and I met the three of them in Montreal. Idea was to drive down into Burlington rather than fly. See, Virginia and Carville had worms seated because they were regular Army, but I never had one because I'm a floater, black op to black op." He jerks a thumb at the kid. "And yBC never had one neither. So we took two cars, me and the kid out in front by an hour or so."

The kid breaks into his sheepish grin again. "I don't even know what a worm even *is*, really. They keep saying it but I never seen one or anything." He giggles; it's obvious he's higher than a kite over his heroic stand. He stood up to Evil, and Evil was vanquished. I can't help but think how odd it must have been for him, to open the door on the same scene he confronted when he was fourteen, two years younger than he is now.

But then I think of something even odder. Maybe the scene with his abused mother never really happened. Maybe what happened today is the story he'll tell when he's older, after making his mother promise to relate it as family truth. Maybe rather than reenacting BC's coming-of-age story we actually wrote it. Maybe this glee that he's feeling now over Thomas's death is what moves him to support the death penalty later, even as a Democrat. Maybe a thousand things.

George goes on, touching my thigh to get my attention back. "Carville figured that this CIA guy Thomas would be waiting for you at your aunt's house. Guy wasn't an idiot, for whatever else he was. And Carville knew this guy was gonna have a worm-tracker. So the idea was, the kid and I come into town first and reconnoiter. We wasn't supposed to do anything but look. Unless something didn't look good, you were in danger or some shit."

yBC leans over and picks it up eagerly. His accent complements Carville's nicely. "And I was supposed to stay in the car while he reconnoitered, but it got to be fifteen minutes and then a half an hour, and I'm waiting there in the dark, and I thought I'm goin' for this."

George leans over and slaps the kid's brush cut carefully. "You did exactly what I told you not to do."

"No more'n you did," yBC shoots back, mouth still open in a slack grin.

"Anyway, it was takin' me a long while because I could see through the windows that it was a hostage-style situation. I couldn't see you had a disc on your back, but I knew he had you in there one way or the other. I almost tried that window of yours, but for sure he'd wired his perimeter. Turned out the bathroom wasn't wired, but that's twenty-twenty hindsight. So I went around the other way and I was trying to get a bead on how many people, where were the weapons, because I know damn well when Carville and Virginia come into town behind us they're gonna wake his ass up, set off his alarms. And that's what happened. I guess that's when he gave that woman in bed with him the needle. And then I seen him headin' into the room you were in. So then—"

"So then I jumped out of the car," yBC cuts in, miming the way he slipped down the dark street, "and I come over to the side of the house."

Carville can't resist turning in the driver's seat and bellowing, "And you *jeopardized* everyone's future when you did so. You disobeyed a direct order, direct order of the highest priority. It was a stupid-ass move. Glory-hog move, kind that gets people killed."

"Show some respect," George puts in. "This kid's your boss right this point in time, if you think about it for a second."

yBC looks abashed for a second, but when Carville turns back around in his seat, he giggles softly and continues. "And I saw that guy hit you, and I said that's not happening again." He's telling it for effect now, now that it's over and he's in control of the events. He's tweaking the story, I can tell. "That is *not* happening again," he says, squinting one eye, and it's just like watching the older BC convey determination for CNN. "And so I went around to the bathroom and went in through that little window. And then I came right in the bedroom door."

George taps my good hand again for attention, and I can tell suddenly that he's trying to make physical contact somehow, as well as get my attention. It's been thirty years, but I still feel, in a weird way, that I know the man inside this bald head. Even with the shift in age and the new accent, he still feels like the closest thing to a friend I've got. And I figure we can sort out later what feelings we still have or don't have for each other. So I just go ahead and slip my hand into his as he finishes the rest of his story.

He closes his fingers around mine. "So then the kid busts in and I'm thinking, last thing in this world that I need to do is blow the head off the president who's currently signing my paychecks, if you see what I mean. So I had to wait outside the window for a good shot. And when the kid went down, I thought, here we go. And then you jumped on his back. Couple of fuckin' heroes, the two of ya. Then when you got dumped, I'm like, here we go again. And then you knocked him on his ass and I lost my shot and he got his sidearm back. Well, mama mia, I thought that was the finish. But then he had to stomp your hand like a sadistic bastard and that gimme the clear second or two I needed to line him up and shut him down."

In the front seat Carville's shaking his head.

"What?" George yells up to him, still holding my hand.

"That phony accent," Carville says, eyes on the rearview. "Please."

George runs a hand over his bald head, slits his eyes, and gives the killer grin I remember. "Ain't nothin' fake *about it,* boy. All us swamp Catholics talk like this here."

It's funny hearing George call Carville *boy,* but not the funniest thing I've seen today. I nudge George, and he turns. "Can you still sound like the George Stephanopoulos I remember?"

He purses his thin lips, starts to make a joke but thinks better of it, and finally says, "I probably might can. In private. Give me a little time to practice."

And then I haul it out into the open, what I've been thinking about since we made the jump from 1963. "But if memory serves me right, you're married these days. To a Republican attack animal."

"Mary's a good woman, but she and I went our separate ways last year. I know, that's not supposed to be how it worked out, historically speaking. You'd be surprised how many things're different from what you and me learned before we left on this trip. I don't know if we changed things, or if the reports we learned from were wrong, or what. But some small things are different, and one of the small things is, Mary is now having a supposedly secret affair that everybody knows about with a fat piece of shit named Rush Limbaugh. And I am a free man. No hair to speak of and a liver marinated in bourbon, but I am a free man."

He looks over at yBC, and I know that for George now the kid is not simply a figure from the past come to life. The kid is also the younger version of the man George has spent the last five years or so putting into the White House, the younger version of an actual friend.

And then I feel a sweeping sense of longing to see the house I own in our time, and I sit up and tap Carville on the shoulder. "Carville, could you take College Street to the airport? I'd really love to just get a quick look at my house the way it is now. Can we do that?"

"No," Carville says, and he takes Main.

40

THE SUMMIT OF SELVES

You know, you can go insane trying to make this time-travel stuff surrender to logic. Because it won't, even I can tell you that much. There are too many unknowns, too many x-factors, and just when you feel you've got it perfectly sussed out, you find yourself making out in one of the rearmost rows of a Boeing 727 with a bald Cajun in his early fifties who was only in his late twenties the week before. And it makes no intellectual sense.

But the touch of the man and the touch of the boy are the same, and your body makes no arguments. It feels right, feels fated.

And finally that's how I start judging everything that's happening as this story draws to its end, as the Storyboarders' script reaches fruition. Instead of worrying about budded contingencies and unintended consequences and impossibilities, I feel myself moving slowly but surely to trust in my feelings, because they seem to be sending me the kind of messages that can't be ignored. Maybe I've gone nuts, or gone native, in the time-twisting sense, or maybe I've just started listening now because that's all I can do.

But I'll give you an example: once George has gotten us into the White House and we're making our way down the long portico toward the Rose Garden, where BC has agreed to wait for us, I feel this overwhelming sense of rightness. George is talking a blue streak about BC, and I can sense how proud he is of his friendship with the man, how proud he is that he can give the rest of us the open sesame to the world's single most powerful leader.

Carville and Virginia are walking behind us, and they seem content. They've pulled off a miracle, or several really, and there's a certain rightness in their contentment.

And up ahead of the four of us is yBC. He's wearing the same outfit he will wear when he meets JFK: khakis just pressed by a White House valet in George's confidence and the Boys Nation polo shirt. Beneath the brush cut, his face is wild with excitement. He's walking faster than we are, his long legs flashing ahead of me. Occasionally he looks back, mouth split in a grin.

We come around a bend in the portico, and through the pretty white latticework, I catch sight of BC, standing alone in a beautifully tailored blue suit, reading from what looks like a briefing book.

The sun is out, and it could be a shot staged and spun by the White House press office: the President in a reflective moment, the lion thoughtful and at rest.

And in his eagerness the kid rounds the loop of portico and strides into the unmarked but palpable zone of contact around the President, and a man in a dark suit and dark glasses moves immediately out from the shadow of the White House to cut him off.

But BC draws himself up and waves the Secret Service agent away. He drops the briefing book on the grass behind him, and he walks slowly toward yBC. The BC I know is a wizened apple core of a man, but the man approaching is BC in all his glory, tall, broad-shouldered, silver-haired, powerful in a way that only an emperor or a single-superpower president could be powerful. The sight of him is arresting.

I can finally understand how he stayed in the White House even during the worst of his troubles: for all his flaws, people—men, women, young and old—simply loved him too much to let him go. Call it charisma, call it sex appeal, call it the dream of the Democratic savior, but even at this distance I can feel it and I can appreciate it for what it is. And the fact that it was unfashionable for most of BC's two terms to admit to such feelings only reaffirms the underlying power of them for voters.

BC was always something of a guilty pleasure for America, and watching him advance I can understand that too.

George looks down at me, one eye squinting. "Good-lookin' fella," he says.

"Not so you'd notice," I answer, squinting back.

There was a walk that BC developed in his later years in the White House, a steady, chin-high processional walk that encapsulated executive power every bit as much as the bullet-proof limo or the Seal of the Office of the President of the United States of America. This is the walk that BC uses as he approaches the kid, almost as though this is a diplomatic meeting of some sort, a summit of selves.

Closing the last several feet, yBC seems suddenly abashed, and he stops, uncertain.

And there on the grass, on a spot that can only be inches from the spot where the kid will shake the hand of another young president, the two come together.

There's a sharp sense of almost mathematical precision, as though an emotional equation were reducing itself to felt certainty: the boy we began calling yBC, and finally came to know as y, reaching his hand out toward the figure the entire world knows as BC, in a scene imagined and abetted by their ancient counterpart, the one-hundred-and-nine-year-old I can only think of now as the x president.

At the last second, BC ignores the kid's outstretched hand and opens his arms in an embrace. It's pure BC, the hug where only the hug will do.

And it feels right, watching it as I do from the shade of the portico, fingers laced with George's fifty-something-year-old fingers. It's fitting, in some way I'll never be able to explain to you or make you feel, that BC should himself become the father he never had.

EPILOGUE

DON'T STOP THINKING ABOUT TOMORROW

Thirteen days have passed since my single, brief visit to the White House. I have been debriefed at exhaustive length by the current NSC people. It seems that 1995 BC has prevailed upon them to make nice and share information and authority with Carville. No doubt each of the parties, and BC himself, has a different reason for promoting the collaboration.

And 1995 BC seems firmly convinced of the need to avoid the global train wreck produced by NATO expansion and the government's support of Big Tobacco's invasion of the Third World. With great reluctance—like a small boy surrendering a train set the morning after Christmas—he has agreed to forgo the signing of the flawed Anti-Tobacco Accord. Even as I write, this decision of his is unweaving the bloody historical tapestry that smothers my own era; even as I write, napalmed landscapes are greening, and generations of young soldiers, men and women, are blissfully civilian.

Or at least we hope. There is no way to know for certain.

For his part, BC is willing to believe that he's saved the world. Clearly, though, he'd be a great deal happier if he could tell the world that it's been saved. He is now frantically searching for a substitute quality-of-life issue for the 1996 elections, maybe arthritis, one of his advisers suggested to me, maybe childhood obesity and the collusion of the fast-food industry. BC was a heavy kid himself, and he's used this material to good effect earlier in his career, so who knows where the issue will take him.

Carville and yBC and Virginia left last week by jump jet for 1963, with—hopefully—continuing service to 2055. Largely thanks to George's aggressive support, I've been allowed to remain behind to make my case for staying in this time period. I thought the NSC types would reject the idea out of hand, but they didn't. They seem genuinely to be musing on it. I have until the jump jet's second and final rendezvous to convince them that I won't be a loose cannon, won't try to contact family members, won't remove my worm and vanish suddenly into the population.

I've been trying to make a case that I can be helpful here, because I realized a long while back—I realized in the desert outside of Vegas—that I have no real reason to go home. My elaborately researched biography would be a farce now; I understand now that what seemed like biographical cause-and-effect was just the shadow of my own ignorance. Lecia has probably taken over my floor of my house by now. And the Library will never feel the same to me, never feel safe somehow. This is where I feel I belong. I'm the reverse-Dorothy, because it turns out that for me there's no place like Oz.

We have a final hearing in the morning, during which they'll tell me whether I can remain here, under an assumed identity of my own. I've spent the day trying to think of some final argument to lay out to them. But all I can think of to say is this: Don't send me back to the place where I'm dead. Everything that's ever made me feel alive is happening around me now, here.

Specifically, tonight, I'm holed up on the top floor of a yellow-brick town house in Georgetown, lying naked on a king-size bed made up with Watergate sheets—clean white cotton sheets spotted with tasteful silhouettes of Dick and Spiro and Elliot and John and Martha. They are George's sheets. He says what he likes mostly about them is how good it feels to throw them the hell off you in the morning. We've been drinking wine, but now the wine is gone. A group called the Gipsy Kings are stomping and lamenting softly from the old-school compact-disc player on the ground floor.

On my stomach is a good-size bald head. I'm resting my hand on this head, touching it absently. George's head. I've grown to like it more and more these last two weeks. The NSC people didn't bat an eye when we told them we'd be rooming together. As far as they were concerned, it was one less residence to lock down and surveille.

It's funny, the first few days after George and I rekindled our dormant romance, I kept suddenly catching sight of him out of the corner of my eye, as he exited the shower or talked on the phone, and I'd draw in my breath like when you bolt up out of a horrific nightmare, thinking the unthinkable: *I just slept with James Carville!* But in the next instant I'd remember that I hadn't, not really, not in any way that counts after you die and answer for your sins in heaven.

I pat the head again.

"Feels like a pig's ass, don't it," George mutters.

I'm surprised to hear his voice. I thought he was sleeping. I give the head another exploratory series of touches. "It only looks like a pig's ass. It feels like horse."

"Like stud horse, you mean."

"I think I said what I meant."

Although he's facing away from me on my stomach, I can tell he's smiling. I look at his long, lean body splayed out at right angles to mine. He's kept himself fit. Twenty-four-hour rapid political response will do that for you, I guess.

There is another long pause, and again I think he's nodded off. But then he says, "Let's play some Tag Loaves."

Tag Loaves is another variation on my old Loaves & Fishes game, one that George developed at some point during the thirty-odd years of our separation. It grew out of the realization that all of BC's best scandals depend on tag names, like morality plays or bad eighteenth-century novels. Unlike my version, where you try to stump the other player, in George's version you ask questions that are obvious enough not to need answers.

It's all very George, because there's no way I can pretend to compete with him at my own version of the BC scandal game now—he's lived it all, sponged it all up. So he's invented a version where we can both show off, one in which we're still equals.

George mumbles his opener into my belly.

"What? Talk human."

He kisses my stomach and swivels his head a bit. "Five-letter surname for a lawman brought in to clean up the Dodge City of the White House."

The digital clock on the bedside table reads 2:31 A.M. Where else could I find a man who both can and will play my kind of games until 2:31 A.M. on a Tuesday night?

"That's weak."

"Why's that weak, now?"

"Weak, you heard me. Too self-evident. Both weak and excessively self-evident."

His hand snakes up and pats the pad of my butt. Then he makes a slight hefting motion. "Speaking about self-evident here, Sal—"

I take a bit of the skin at the nape of his neck between my fingernails.

"Ah, shit. Careful. I'm old now. You're young, you don't think nothing of stripping me down and then beating up on me between the sheets. Working me over repeatedly. You got to remember I'm aged."

"I remember. You're the one who forgets."

"Your turn, girl. You gonna take a whack?"

I give him the nails again. "Say it like George."

"Shit. Okay." His voice loses almost all of the Cajun spices. "Sal, I believe it is now your turn, if you'd still care to play." It's not exactly George's voice, or what I remember of George's voice. Maybe that's because he's much older now, or maybe he actually doesn't remember how to talk like the twenty-seven-year-old I almost slept with last week.

"Best four-letter word for a billionaire fugitive pardoned by a president dogged by scandals involving wealthy donors."

He nods. "That was stylish. Comin' back at you. Five letters, large woman over whom the whole BC administration stumbles just at the beginning of term number two."

As he says it, George starts chuckling softly to himself, and he turns fully onto his back to allow himself to laugh it out. Looking down at his profile, I realize that for as little as I know this man, I know a few things about him no other woman has ever known about him, or known in advance about any man. I know I was attracted to him when he was a young man, and I know I'm attracted to him in middle age. And I know he makes me feel upbeat and excited and young and content, at either end of the life spectrum.

Every other woman in the world has to make an educated guess and leap off a cliff and fall into the future with her young man and hope that when they hit their late fifties she's right. But I know, I know it right now.

And every other woman in the world just has to hope that somewhere inside her trash-talking Carville, way down deep, like nested Russian dolls, lies an inner Stephanopoulos. But I know.

He catches my look and turns his face on my belly to look back. It's a serious look for ten full seconds, taking in the enormity of everything, the absurdity of us here together now as we are. And then he grins and stretches, and the eyes flatten out to mere slits.

But I can still see him in there if I look hard enough. Carville-coated Stephanopoulos.

"What?" he whispers finally.

"Nothing," I say.

The Gipsy Kings also fall quiet. The only sound is the sound of the NSC guard walking slowly back and forth on the pavement in front of the town house, a sound like a wing-tip metronome.

And then the CD player's random function brings up a song that cannot be a random selection. It's the theme song from BC's 1992 campaign, a bouncy little tune that became the music of generational change itself. Fleetwood Mac, the group called themselves. I suspect George of playing this particular song at this particular moment, but his hand is nowhere near the remote.

As I listen, I'm thinking about George's backup plan in case the NSC decides against my staying in this time frame. George has been covertly working his media sources all week, playing up the story of his break with Mary and Mary's tryst with Rush Limbaugh. He's been staying on deep background, priming all the various outlets for the possibility that he may have a major public announcement later in the week.

Throwing chum in the water, George calls it.

"This way here," he told me earlier tonight, "if the NSC boys say you can't stay, I call in the press, and let me tell you it'll be a madhouse. You got one of your loudest right-wing mouths all of a sudden cast as a homewrecker and a turncoat on Family Values. Me and Rush are the Ali and Foreman of partisan media politics, it's the cable-news wet dream. Need be, I'll let drop the possibility that Mary was feeding her big boy notes on BC's budget strategy she stole from my files while I was sleepin'. That way we tie it in to the White House, and that puts a first-class booster rocket on the whole scandal.

"And I'll have you next to me on the podium, and I'll introduce you as Sal, my true love, just Sal. The press'll beg, but we won't give 'em anything but your first name." He'd obviously worked it out elegantly in his mind. "All of a sudden you'll be like Cher or Sting or Madonna. Just Sal. Drive the media apeshit.

"And that'll put the NSC in a position where they'll have the global media investigating one of their temporally displaced operatives. We layer you into the media the way I'm layered in. Deep exposure. And in that case, I think they'll field a decent, usable identity for you quick enough. They got no conscience, but they ain't stupid. They're gonna find out we won't let 'em send you back."

I'm thinking about this plan, and I'm imagining this press conference. It would have seemed absurd a month ago, farcical, but now I can see it with preternatural clarity. The concentric rings of microphones and lenses, the barking anchormen and the clawing anchorwomen, the cicada din of two thousand cameras advancing. I see George giving them exactly what they want, riffing pugnacious on Limbaugh, squinting an eye and cocking his fists, looking straight into the cameras and telling Mary, wherever she is, *Just remember, girl, once you go fat, you can't never come back.*

And when the anchorpeople ask how serious we are, George takes it over the top, getting down on one knee and clasping his hands over his heart. He looks up at me with a sweet smile, and I rest my hand on his bald head, the way you palm a bowling ball.

That, of course, is the shot that all the dailies splash across their covers the following morning; that is the shot the networks mock up behind their anchors when they turn to the scandal night after night.

And it is the image that fills the screen when you visit BC's library sixty years from now and sit down at one of the interactive archive terminals and scroll through the endless menus and submenus of scandal. The footage has been painstakingly three-sixtied, so clicking on the image renders it fully interactive, and you stand at the back of the hall and listen as George and I finish our first press conference with a big kiss and the applause and whistles and catcalls explode around us.

My biography will never make it into BC's library, but I will. For the first time in almost longer than I can remember, for better or for worse, I will be one of the answers to my own questions.

PHILIP BARUTH is an award-winning commentator for Vermont Public Radio. He teaches at the University of Vermont, in Burlington. *The X President* is his third novel.